DEMON·QUEEN wants to *Paint*

AMBER ATLAS

DEMON QUEEN WANTS TO PAINT
BOOK 1

Copyright © 2025 Amber Atlas

ISBN (print): 979-8-88993-084-6
ISBN (e-book): 979-8-88993-085-3

Cover Illustration and Design by FuyuDust
Interior Design by Tancgu LLC

Published 2025 by MoonQuill®
Arlington, VA
www.moonquill.com

TABLE OF CONTENTS

Chapter 1: A Broken Dream 1

Chapter 2: Demon's Daughter 9

Chapter 3: Saving an Elf 16

Chapter 4: Unexpected Visitor 24

Chapter 5: Family Dinner 32

Chapter 6: Blending into Shadows 40

Chapter 7: The Underworld 48

Chapter 8: World of Doppelta 56

Chapter 9: Baby Learning Magic 64

Chapter 10: First Birthday 72

Chapter 11: King's Present 80

Chapter 12: Aftermath 88

Chapter 13: Evening with the King 98

Chapter 14: Basics of Magic 107

Chapter 15: (Re)Introduction to Art 116

Chapter 16: Birth of a Dragon 124

Chapter 17: The Announcement 132

Chapter 18: Goodbye 140

Chapter 19: Sunshine, Lollipops, and Deziara 147

Chapter 20: Dinner with Lady Lily 155

Chapter 21: Window to the Past 164

Chapter 22: The Exposed Secret 172

Chapter 23: Suspicion 180

Chapter 24: Becoming Azrael 189

Chapter 25: In a Demon City 198

Chapter 26: Demon in Distress................................208

Chapter 27: Phantom and Lightning................................216

Chapter 28: Writing Lessons................................224

Chapter 29: Library Raid................................232

Chapter 30: Elf's Apology 240

Chapter 31: To the Royal Treasury 248

Chapter 32: Demon Castle Dungeon 256

Chapter 33: First Flight................................264

Chapter 34: Return of the King 273

Chapter 35: Through the Dark of the Underworld 281

Chapter 36: Chasing a Princess 288

Chapter 37: Back Home 296

Chapter 38: Second Chance................................304

Chapter 39: Meeting Mother................................313

Chapter 40: Birth of Morrigan 322

Epilogue................................330

CHAPTER 1

A BROKEN DREAM

"Why does this always happen to me?" Rosa grumbled as dark storm clouds gathered on the horizon and rolled in from across the sea. She was about halfway across the pier, heading towards the lighthouse with a large easel and canvas strapped to her back, weighing down her petite frame. People on the beach gathered their belongings and quickly headed towards the wooden pathways which led back into the city.

Rosa sighed and adjusted the uncomfortable straps that ate into her shoulders.

"I knew I should have checked the weather forecast..."

She exhaled and turned to follow the crowd back into the city when the phone in her shorts pocket vibrated. Curious, she pulled it out to check the notification. When she read "E-mail from Studio Goblin," the phone nearly slipped out of her hand.

Her heart began thundering in her chest, and her palms clammed up uncomfortably. She tried unlocking the phone with her fingerprint, but the device wouldn't recognize it through all the sweat. After wiping her hand on her white shirt, she tried again. This time, it was successfully unlocked, and she opened the email app right away.

However, as she attempted to read the email, her trembling finger accidentally tapped an advert sitting right above it. Cursing a few times at the beautiful model in the shampoo ad, she hurriedly closed it and returned to the email app. But instead of opening the message, her finger hovered above it.

"It's okay, it's okay," Rosa chanted to herself, looking over the perfectly calm sea as dark clouds crept further and further over the sky. She took a deep breath, held it for a few seconds, and then slowly exhaled. With a shaky finger, she finally tapped the message.

Hello, Rosa. After carefully reviewing your portfolio and considering the answers you gave during the interview, we would like to inform you that you've been accepted as an intern at Studio Goblin.

Rosa jumped and squealed in delight, earning a few odd glances from people who were hurrying off the pier. Her easel painfully hit her back, but she paid no mind to it, instead removing the heavy weight from her shoulder and setting it down against the ledge.

"I did it! I actually did it!"

A wide grin spread on her face as she felt an urge to shout to the whole world about her big achievement. Then her face hardened, and she looked back down at her phone, her heart thumping in her chest.

"But first things first…"

She opened her *contacts* page. Shifting her weight nervously from one leg to another, Rosa scrolled through the short list to find the name *Mother*. She hesitated, her heart pounding. Dialing her might have been more challenging than getting this internship, but she shook her head and resolutely pressed the call button.

Her hands trembled as she waited through the dial beeps. One. Two. Three. Four. At the fifth, her hand faltered and lowered, but the call finally connected.

"Yes?" replied a cold, familiar voice.

"H-Hello, Mother," Rosa said nervously, twirling a lock of her hair in her free hand.

The sky had been completely taken over by the dark clouds, and an eerie quiet hung in the surrounding area. Most of the beachgoers were already gone, and the few remaining stragglers were on their way out.

"What do you want?" her mother spat.

Rosa could imagine her mom's face scrunched up in disgust and disappointment. In fact, that was the only expression she could ever imagine her wearing.

"I'm just c-calling to tell you that I got a job at Studio Goblin," Rosa said resolutely, straightening her back and puffing out her chest proudly.

There was a pause on the other end of the line, and the world around Rosa seemed to still and quieten as if the sea were taking a measured breath.

"So?"

A cold raindrop struck Rosa's forehead, making her flinch.

"It proves that you can make a living by doing a-art. That you were wrong about me not being able to achieve anything," she said as calmly as she could, but her voice cracked multiple times.

A sharp, mocking scoff crackled through the phone. "You've just proved that we made the right decision by throwing you out as soon as you turned eighteen. Studio Goblin? What kind of company even is that? No respectable person would ever call a business that!" Rosa's mother mocked.

More and more heavy raindrops began falling from the sky, mercilessly pelting her with their growing intensity.

"If you had begged and apologized for your horrible behavior, I might have considered accepting you back into the family. If you could have achieved even one-fourth of your younger sister's achievements, then I would have thought about meeting with you again. I had hoped that forcing you to be independent would have taught you a valuable lesson, but you're still the same ungrateful, lazy brat leeching off the hard work of others. If only…"

Mother continued ranting, but Rosa couldn't hear her anymore as the hand she held her phone with slumped to her side. The rain was coming down hard, soaking Rosa from head to toe.

"I only wanted you to be proud of me just once…" Rosa whispered, lifting the phone just enough to end the call. But before she could push the button, she heard her mother snarl.

"Never call us again. You're no daughter of mine!"

And the call disconnected.

This was supposed to be a day of celebration… I had hoped that maybe, just maybe, my efforts would be recognized if I joined a large company. But I should have seen this coming.

The cold rain had already soaked her clothes, making her body shiver in a desperate attempt to retain the quickly escaping heat.

"What was even the point?" Rosa complained to the sea, which threw its waves with increasing intensity as if trying to reach her and pull her into its depths. She sat down on the rocky, wet edge that separated the pier from the raging sea and watched the waves crashing against the stones that made up its base.

"All that work and I couldn't get even a single word of acknowledgment…"

The sea roiled, and a bright flash appeared near the horizon. Hot tears began to stream down her face, but they remained unseen under the heavy raindrops.

"I wish… I wish I had been born to parents who loved me no matter what I chose to do," she whispered to the sea, her words drowned out by the loud crashes of the deluge. The fury of the storm emboldened her—it had no fear, nothing holding it back.

Why was I trying to prove anything to the one person who never cared?

"Being a monster's daughter would have been better!" she yelled into the sea, letting her frustration out. A low rumble of thunder resounded through the area. The anger inside Rosa boiled over as she stood up on the ledge and shouted.

"Even a demon would care more!"

The wind tugged at her clothes and whipped through her hair, but she stood tall and strong against its force.

I will not be taken down by this storm. I'll get through it just as I have gotten through all the other difficulties in life.

Feeling a bit better after screaming her feelings out, Rosa was about to descend from the ledge when a strong gust of wind threatened to throw her into the sea. She wobbled unsteadily, arms flailing to keep her balance. She managed to find her footing and breathed a sigh of relief—until a strong blast of water suddenly swept underneath her, and her knees buckled under the massive force.

Dumbstruck, she fell backwards, crashing into the dark waters. Rosa thrashed about, trying to swim to the surface, but the sea tossed her around mercilessly, not giving her a chance to reach the pier. Panic set in as her lungs became starved of oxygen.

I can't die like this!

Her limbs flailed desperately, but the harder she fought, the deeper the sea pulled her into its embrace. Then her vision began to blur. Darkness overcame her senses and cold filled her limbs, weighing them down like lead.

* * *

Rosa woke up with a jolt as if struck by a strong electric current. Her lungs felt like they were seized, and she was unable to breathe.

Another strong jolt and her eyes opened for a brief moment, but not long enough to register her surroundings.

Why can't I breathe?

Before she could properly begin to panic, there was another jolt, and she was finally able to take in a lungful of air. She coughed violently, tears rolling down her cheeks.

A soothing male voice spoke in a language Rosa did not understand. As her coughing fit slowly subsided, she finally opened her eyes.

As Rosa's eyes adjusted to the light, she saw a giant man towering over her. His skin was ash gray, not a color that could be attributed to a living person. He had long, blood-red hair and eyes as dark as night. But what stood out the most were the two black horns attached to his head.

Rosa froze, unable to fathom what exactly she was seeing. She was in a small room with dark wallpaper and no windows, lying in what appeared to be a crib.

The man froze as well, staring at her with unblinking eyes. She opened her mouth to scream, but the sound that escaped was not what she expected. It sounded like the cry of a... baby? She stopped, and the man looked at her intensely, waiting for her reaction. But for a moment, she shelved her worries about the giant man and instead tried to lift her arm.

It was incredibly difficult to do so—it felt like she had no strength in her arms whatsoever. But once she managed to move, she saw a tiny hand with stubby, little fingers.

No, this can't be right.

She mustered her strength and lifted her other hand. It was just as small and had the same kind of stubby fingers. She tried to lift her head to look down at her body, but it was too heavy.

She squirmed, trying to move her body upright, but her attempts were futile. Rosa didn't have enough strength. As she moved about, she felt something wriggle between her legs.

No, that couldn't... Could it? Please tell me it's not what I think it is!

Rosa lost it completely and started screeching at the top of her little lungs. She had, without a doubt, been turned into a baby. And a baby *boy*, no less.

No, this can't be happening! It must be a nightmare.

Worried, the man bent down to pick Rosa up, not bothering to cover her. His hands were huge and strong, and it felt like they could squish her like a blueberry. Rosa screeched hysterically.

This has to be a nightmare. This can't be real! I have to wake up.

But the man rocked her in his arms in a soothing motion that managed to calm her down—her hysteric cries turning to mild sobs. He said something, but she couldn't understand a word. The giant horns on his head scared her, as did his rough features, which made his attempts at a calm expression look forced and awkward.

Who is he? Is he a demon? Did he do this to me somehow?

As Rosa pondered these questions, she felt that weird squirming in between her legs again.

Wait... male parts aren't supposed to move around on their own, are they?

She tried to wiggle it and felt how the appendage moved at her will. After more writhing, she understood that it was actually a tail. However, she wasn't sure whether that was better or worse.

Wait. If I have a tail, does that mean... Oh God!

Rosa struggled, and with the last bit of her baby strength, she managed to touch the top of her head. It was so difficult—her arms felt so tiny and utterly useless, while her head felt bulbous and large. Nevertheless, she found what she had hoped not to find—two tiny stumps atop of her nearly hairless head.

The man spoke again, his expression more confident now. She looked at the large hands holding her and saw how his skin tone nearly matched her own. He seemed to take her curiosity as a good sign and continued speaking. Though the language was foreign to her, his intonation made it clear that he was excited.

He walked up to a large body-sized mirror in the corner of the dark room and pointed towards it with his chin while he continued to speak to her. With some effort, she turned her head and saw that the baby in the mirror had the same blood-red tuft of hair as the man. Now, she was sure without a doubt—this man was her new father. Rosa began wailing at the top of her lungs again.

CHAPTER 2

DEMON'S DAUGHTER

Rosa didn't know how long she had cried, but she eventually got so tired that she fell asleep. She only woke up when horrible hunger pangs gnawed at her stomach, growling with a furious intensity.

Is this really how babies feel hunger? It's so intense that it's actually painful. No wonder babies cry so loudly when they're hungry.

Despite mentally being an adult, Rosa barely managed to hold back screams of discomfort. But before she could begin to worry about it in earnest, a man with a bushy, brown beard appeared, saying something in a calm voice.

His voice didn't suit his appearance at all—it was soft, like a woman's. Rosa thought she saw a smile behind the bushy beard, but it was hard to tell. The man apparently took the fact that she hadn't begun crying as a good sign and picked her up while carefully cradling her head.

That's when Rosa realized she had been dressed in a soft and warm cotton onesie. Or at least it felt like cotton. As the man held her close, she also understood that she was mistaken. This was not a man, but most definitely a woman, as she could feel the soft breasts on the woman's chest.

But how can a woman have such a magnificent beard? A woman having a beard isn't impossible, of course. There are illnesses and hormonal imbalances that can cause that, but I've never actually seen it in person.

Much to Rosa's delight, the bearded woman did not have any horns or tail. She murmured something to Rosa and then produced a glass baby bottle with a nipple for the cork.

I'm not supposed to drink that, am I? Just suck on the bottle like a baby? Well, I am a baby now, and I am hungry, but there's no way I'm going to accept it so easily!

As the woman brought the bottle closer to Rosa's mouth, she considered knocking it away. However, the sweet smell of milk reminded her of how hungry she actually was, and she didn't exactly have teeth to chew real food, nor a voice to demand it either. Begrudgingly, Rosa latched on to the bottle and drank. It was thicker, creamier, and more filling than cow's milk. She quite liked it. The bearded woman nodded in satisfaction as she suckled, her lips curling happily behind the beard.

Rosa was almost finished with the bottle when the door suddenly burst open with a loud clang, and the same demon from before entered—that's what Rosa decided to call him. What else was he supposed to be? He was no doubt at the core of her misfortune, pulling her away from her world for his own nefarious plans.

With her stomach full, Rosa began to worry about how she'd return to Earth.

Did I die? If so, what happened to my body? Will I even be able to go back if I am dead? Maybe someone found me, and I'm in a coma in a hospital, attached to machines and tubes, and...

Overwhelmed by the swirling thoughts, she began crying again. The bearded woman grumbled something to Demon Man, who awkwardly scratched his head. Rosa wanted to shout at him to send her back to her world, but her baby tongue and lack of teeth made her completely unable to speak.

The bearded woman began rocking her in a futile attempt to console her, and after a few minutes, Demon Man gently took Rosa from the woman's arms. She then realized how much taller he was than the bearded woman.If she were to break her down proportionally for a drawing, then she would be five heads high. Normally, humans were about seven or eight heads high. This woman was a dwarf.

Good God! I was pulled into some world filled with weird, inhuman races. Do humans even exist here? And what about technology—phones, computers, cars, and other daily conveniences? What about movies? What if they don't even exist in this world?

Rosa frantically looked around, searching for any sign of modern technology. The room was decorated like a Goth nursery—dark walls, a black crib with tacky frills, monster plushies piled in one corner, and a dark changing table that no doubt contained everything a baby needed, all dimly lit by a lamp hanging from the ceiling.

At first, she was relieved, thinking it was an electric lamp, but upon looking more carefully, she noticed it was different. There seemed to be a movement within, but she couldn't tell from afar.

The dwarf woman noticed her interest and clapped her hands twice. The light turned off, plunging the room into darkness. Then she clapped once more, and the light returned. Rosa outstretched her hands towards it, hoping that Demon Man would bring her closer so she could inspect it properly.

He asked the dwarf woman something, and she nodded. He then raised Rosa closer to the object. It was still rather high above her, but she was able to see that there were no light bulbs inside of it. Instead, tiny glass balls containing an odd liquid moved inside—like a lava lamp but much smaller.

What is that? How does it even work? If it is some sort of technology, it certainly isn't anything you would find on Earth. Then again, everything looks so archaic; it's unlikely there's anything like computers or movies here, which also means...

Goblin Studios popped into her mind, and tears formed in Rosa's eyes. The thought of losing her new job left a gaping hole in her heart, and her expression darkened. In a pitiful attempt to get her to smile, Demon Man wiggled his finger above her, no doubt hoping that she would grab it.

This is all your fault! You pulled me into this world, didn't you? I might not have any proof, but I just know it! I won't let you get away with this!

Rosa took a deep breath and then began hollering for no other reason than to annoy him. Being a baby, this was the only thing she could do. But as she let her petite voice carry loudly through the room, forcing Demon Man to wince in displeasure, she swore an oath to herself.

One day, I'll find a way back home. No matter how long it takes, I'll keep getting stronger and keep searching. Then I'll become the artist that I've always dreamed of becoming, even if it takes me a hundred years!

* * *

Rosa stared at the demon, and the demon stared back. Neither of them said anything or did anything. She because she couldn't, and he... well, she didn't know why he was silently staring at her. His expression was incomprehensible, but there was something there. Curiosity, perhaps? Or maybe something exclusive to demons.

How long are you going to keep staring?

The dwarf woman said something, a question, judging by her tone. The demon blinked and finally turned away from Rosa, responding to the dwarf woman. She nodded, and a small smile peeked from behind her beard, and she left the room in a hurry.

Hey, don't leave me alone with him!

Their awkward staring contest resumed, and Rosa began counting the seconds until the woman's return. After exactly three minutes, the demon lifted his arm and Rosa flinched, fearing what he might do. Seeing her reaction, he slowly lowered it, his gaze unbreaking.

Thankfully, it didn't take long for the woman to return with a baby basin in tow. It was made of metal or something akin to it and seemed too large and heavy for someone of her stature to carry. Much to Rosa's surprise, she put it down with one hand as if it weighed nothing at all.

The demon nodded at her and then pulled the bath closer to Rosa's crib.

Are they going to wash me? I suppose a bath doesn't sound too bad.

The dwarf woman approached the basin, holding a large marble ball in her hand. Before Rosa could even begin to ponder its purpose, water poured out of the ball as if from a tap.

Is that magic?

Noticing Rosa's interest, the demon leaned closer to her and spoke.

I can't understand you. And even if I could, I can't answer you.

The demon waved his hand above Rosa, and a ball of water formed in his palm. Rosa marveled as he moved the water above her head, making it flex and turn, inflate, and deflate.

That's amazing! He just created water out of thin air. It has to be magic. I wonder if there are rules he must follow in order to do that.

Much to her surprise, the demon chuckled. A tall demon with black horns and horrifying black eyes who no doubt killed puppies for sport just chuckled! Not in a creepy, maniacal kind of way, but like a normal human who found something amusing.

It must be a ploy to make me forgive him for kidnapping me. Not today, you evil fiend. I will not fall victim to Stockholm syndrome!

Attempting to glare at the demon, Rosa hardened her expression, but he was already discussing something with the bearded woman. The bath was now full, with a towel and a bar of soap sitting on a tray beside the basin.

The man approached her and began unbuttoning her onesie.

Do you intend to bathe me? No way am I letting a demon wash me!

Rosa opened her mouth to cry, and the demon instantly stopped, wincing in anticipation. When the sound didn't come, he resumed his task, and Rosa opened her mouth once more. He paused again but didn't remove his hand entirely. However, as soon as he tried to undo another button, she let out a glass-shattering screech, and the demon backed away with an annoyed huff.

The dwarf woman spoke soothingly, then came over to Rosa to finish the task. Ideally, Rosa preferred the man leave instead of gawking at her naked body, but she had a feeling he would stay right there no matter how much she screamed.

Once undressed, the dwarf gently lifted her while supporting her head and then deposited her into the tub. The warmth of the water was pleasant, and her body floated helplessly inside of it.

Unfortunately, the calming experience soon morphed into panic as the memory of the violent sea waves dragging her underwater flashed through her mind.

No... I don't want to go into the water!

Rosa flailed and shrieked as much as her miniature body allowed. In the struggle, she slipped out of the woman's grip, and her head plunged under the water. But before she even realized what had happened, strong arms pulled her out. She coughed up the minuscule amount of water she had managed to swallow as the demon cradled her close to his chest and angrily shouted at the dwarf.

The woman lifted her arms defensively and muttered something while shaking her head. The demon made a commanding gesture towards the bath, and the dwarf bowed profusely then hurried to draw the excess water out by magically sucking it back into the marble ball.

That was the first time Rosa felt gratitude towards the demon.

Chapter 3

Saving an Elf

Rosa found it difficult to keep track of the months that followed as they were some of the most boring days in her existence—stuffing an adult mind into a baby's body was proving to be a great torture device.

There were so many things Rosa wanted to do, like explore the surrounding area, find out more about her new world, and maybe even discover if art held any significance there. Walking would be nice, too.

With the lack of windows in the nursery, she had no idea whether it was daytime or nighttime. The only difference was that during the night, the lights were turned off. Or so she had assumed.

Whenever Rosa wasn't eating or sleeping, the only thing she could do was stare at the gray ceiling, following the swirling patterns from one side of the wall to the next. Resentment of her gloomy surroundings slowly worked their way into her brain. Nothing but hues of gray and black taunted her with their dullness. Sometimes she wondered whether she had just died and this was her personal hell.

But there was one thing that convinced her otherwise—her dwarf nanny. Whenever the bearded woman came, she would chat with Rosa in a cheerful tone and play some silly baby games. It sounded stupid for an adult to enjoy such things, but after spending day after day staring at the ceiling, even something as mundane as peekaboo became a great source of entertainment.

Of course, what she *truly* appreciated about their interactions was her developing ability to understand the language. For example, Rosa understood that her name in this world was Morrigan—a dreadful name in her opinion—from how both the nanny and Demon Man addressed her.

The nanny's name was Gunna, while Demon Man was called Alphegor. Quite honestly, she expected him to have some stereotypical name like *Lucifer* or *Azazel*, but this was another world, so earthly clichés didn't apply. Nonetheless, Rosa still decided to refer to him as Demon Man because calling him by his name would be like acknowledging that he was a person and not a monster.

And I'll never acknowledge him as a person, much less as my father, especially not when he's changing me.

The nappy-changing times were by far the most embarrassing for Rosa. Oddly enough Gunna never showed any disgust, instead chuckling from behind her bushy beard.

But this day turned out to be different from others. Sometime after lunch, Alphegor stepped into the nursery, followed by a scrawny, bespectacled man with long, greasy hair.

This is new. He's never brought anybody but Gunna to this room.

Rosa felt excited, seeing someone who looked human. But after carefully assessing the man, her excitement quickly faded.

He had horrible red marks around his wrists as if he had been painfully bound. His scrawniness wasn't something natural, but rather it looked like the result of malnutrition. There was also a dark bruise under his eye. But the most unusual thing about him was the extremely long ears.

An elf? But why is he in such a horrible state?

Demon Man pushed the elf towards Rosa, glaring at him in the process. The man glanced fearfully at Demon Man then came towards her crib with shaky steps. She saw that he was holding what appeared to be a slab of some sort of stone. He glanced at the demon again, who glared at him so hard that Rosa thought the poor elf would just drop dead on the floor.

With trembling hands, he brought the slab towards her.

Is he giving this as a gift? Surely not.

As he held it out to her, he stared with a pleading look in his eyes as if trying to send her an unspoken message.

What do you want me to do? I'm just a baby.

The only thing she could do was touch the stone with her tiny hand. And so she did just that, though mostly out of curiosity. It felt like any other rock, cold and smooth.

Relief washed over the elf's face, and he muttered something. The slab began glowing with a bright, red light. Demon Man let out a loud cheer, making Rosa flinch away from the stone while the elf and Gunna looked thoroughly shaken. They regarded her with fear in their eyes. Rosa was not surprised that the elf feared her—after all, she was the biological offspring of a demon—but she felt somewhat hurt at the fact that Gunna had the same fear in her eyes.

Demon Man boasted loudly, laughing like a maniac. She didn't understand what he was saying, but she heard her name woven into the gibberish. Then he turned towards the elf, and Rosa saw a red glint in his dark eyes. Her whole body shivered as she felt murderous intent emanating from him.

He's going to kill the elf. No, no, no!

Rosa began to wriggle frantically, trying to think of a way to prevent a murder from happening right in front of her eyes. The elf was still looking at her and didn't notice that the demon had lifted his hand.

What can I do? What can I do?! I must stop him!

She reached towards the elf, hoping to grab him, but he was too far. Demon Man tensed, ready to lunge at the elf, and Rosa instinctively tried to scream, "Don't!" but with her toothless mouth and uncooperative baby tongue, all that escaped was a sad little "Do."

Everyone froze, their wide eyes snapping to her in shock. Rosa wasn't sure why they looked so surprised, but at least she had their attention. Determined, she repeated the sound, mumbling, "Do, do, do," while stretching her hand towards the elf.

The elf looked flabbergasted, terrified, and astounded all at the same time. Rosa was worried that the mixture of emotions was going to make the man faint. Demon Man disregarded the elf completely and ran up to Rosa's crib, lifting her high up in the air with a wide grin on his face.

How can you be so happy after almost murdering somebody? Damned demon!

Rosa regarded him with the same look she would give to a fly sitting on a pile of poo. But Demon Man clearly had no understanding as to the meaning of her expression and proceeded to lift her up and down while happily muttering something.

He then looked at her with an expectant gaze and said something. She didn't understand his words but had a feeling he probably wanted her to "talk" again. But she wouldn't do that just because he wanted it, so Rosa scrunched her nose instead and glared at him.

Gunna suppressed a laugh, hiding it behind her beard. She then said something in a calm voice and pointed towards the elf. The elf lifted his arms in defense, and Demon Man glowered at him.

After a moment of consideration, he handed Rosa to the elf. The man took her with shaky hands, but his hold was gentle, and he made sure to support Rosa's head. She didn't need the support anymore, but she appreciated his efforts nonetheless.

Then, just to spite Demon Man, she smiled at the elf and repeated the *"do, do, do,"* while sending a mental message to the villain.

Don't you dare kill this elf! Or any other person for that matter.

The elf's lips quirked up slightly while Demon Man left the nursery with a huff, pouting like a little child.

Serves him right for trying to kill somebody!

The elf looked unsure of what to do with her, but Gunna took Rosa from him and said something in an encouraging, albeit slightly sad tone. The elf nodded absentmindedly in response, but the whole time, his eyes were locked on Rosa as if trying to understand the inner workings of her mind.

* * *

After a few days of trying to count every single raven's feather displayed on the wallpaper, something interesting happened. Along with Gunna, the elf from before came to Rosa's nursery. He was carrying a bag and looked much healthier. Instead of dirty rags he wore a nice, scholarly tunic and pants which matched his brown eyes with their earthy tones. Now that his hair was washed clean, Rosa could see it was a deep, dark brown. Previously, it seemed black from all the grime and dirt. Most importantly, the bruises on his wrists and face were gone, as if healed by magic.

The elf approached Rosa's crib cautiously, and she saw a nervous bead of sweat rolling down his temples. He asked Gunna something, but it was too quiet for Rosa to hear. With a gentle expression, the nanny gave him a reassuring pat on the back.

"It's alright!" She motioned for him to approach Rosa. Rosa just looked curiously at the nervous man and wondered what he would do. He began rummaging through his bag and then pulled a book out of it. He displayed it before Rosa, so she could see it. The book was thick, with a leather spine and dark blue letters on the cover. She could not read what it said, but whatever those letters were, they were nothing she'd seen on Earth before. There was some resemblance to Celtic runes, but it was very distant.

The elf pointed at the letters and spoke a few words, which Rosa assumed was the title of the book.

I know you have the best intentions, but you can't really expect a three-month-old baby to understand you.

Rosa scrunched her nose in displeasure, and the man flinched. Gunna walked up to him and pulled the book aside. She pointed towards Rosa and said something about telling her his name, and then something else. It was still difficult to understand anything that didn't involve the most basic words, but the elf seemed to understand the nanny and nodded. He then pointed to himself.

"My name is Faenor," he said, slowly enunciating each syllable. This Rosa understood without issue. She smiled at him in response, and the elf visibly relaxed. Then he turned towards Gunna and retrieved the book from her. It looked like he would begin reading, but the nanny interjected again.

Their conversation was too fast for Rosa to understand, but after a bit of back and forth, Gunna lifted her out of the crib and offered her over to Faenor. He shook his head vigorously while rapidly muttering something. Rosa puffed out her cheeks.

How rude! He doesn't want to hold me.

He noticed the change in her expression and visibly paled. Perhaps he thought that she was about to cry. Faenor then extended trembling arms towards Rosa and finally took her. His hold felt bony.

He was much leaner than Gunna and didn't have the large muscles that Demon Man did. But Rosa wouldn't complain about something so petty, so she just looked at the book he held in his other arm and waited.

Seeing that Rosa wasn't going to cry, Faenor released a relieved sigh and settled into one of the gloomy chairs. Gunna nodded with satisfaction and began cleaning around the nursery. The elf pointed at the cover again and slowly enunciated the title of the book. Rosa still didn't understand what it said, but she heard every sound clearly. When someone spoke too quickly, she couldn't make out a single word—it all sounded like a jumbled mess.

Faenor looked down at Rosa, and upon seeing as she was still staring at the book, he opened it. The first page showed a picture of a red dragon, but the art style was rather cartoony. Rosa almost squealed with delight.

A picture book? Finally, something that isn't just black and white.

The elf flipped to the next page, and there was an egg lying in a pile of gold. Faenor slowly read the text above the picture, and Rosa tried to listen to his pronunciation and commit it to memory. She heard most of it but got a little bit distracted by the pretty artwork.

Finally, I get to see more colors than just black and gray. How I missed all these beautiful shades of red and gold.

Faenor flipped to the next page, and there was a picture of a little red dragon emerging from the shell while spewing dramatic blue flames. Rosa watched and listened carefully, trying to understand the story being told but without much luck.

When the first book was finished, Faenor put it aside and pulled another from his case. Rosa was excited to see the art within. Unfortunately, as the elf was about to begin reading the title, Demon Man burst into the room without as much as a knock.

Rosa glared at him in annoyance, mentally willing him to go away. But instead, he just stomped over and took the book from Faenor's hand. The elf began shivering in fear, and he clutched her baby form tighter as if she was the only thing that protected him from the demon. Demon Man looked through the pages of the book and scoffed.

He then said something with a disdainful expression and tossed the book on the ground.

How dare you?! I wanted to see that book. I won't let you get away with this.

She waited for Demon Man to take her from the elf and then screamed at him. He tried to rock her, shush her, reason with her in a soft voice, and she was pretty sure he threatened her a little bit as well. But she did not relent in her screams until Gunna finally took her away.

If you insist on ruining the best time I've had since coming to this damned world, then I'll be sure to make your ears bleed!

Demon Man left looking like a puppy that had been kicked by its owner. But Rosa did not feel sorry for him. In fact, she felt proud for teaching him a lesson in humility. Unfortunately, Rosa would later find out that it would take way more than just screaming to keep Demon Man away.

CHAPTER 4

UNEXPECTED VISITOR

The next morning, Rosa barely managed to open her eyes when Demon Man rushed into the nursery with a slightly concerned Gunna coming in after him. He barked something at her with a slurry of impatient gestures, and she just nodded obediently in response, still trying to catch her breath.

Gunna produced Rosa's usual bottle of morning milk and then gingerly picked Rosa up to feed her. Rosa was already sick of drinking nothing but milk every day, but unfortunately, she still couldn't eat anything else. Her little baby body wouldn't be able to handle anything more serious. Not to mention the lack of usable teeth. So begrudgingly, she latched on to the bottle and began drinking while keeping an eye on Demon Man.

He tapped his foot impatiently between pacing from one side of the room to the next. She watched him, her annoyance growing with each of his steps.

What do you want first thing in the morning that is so damn urgent?

She noticed that he was holding something. It was some kind of case, but Rosa wasn't sure what exactly it was for. She had a strong suspicion that she'd find out soon enough and she also suspected that she would not be too thrilled about it.

Her bottle was soon empty, and the moment Gunna was done

changing Rosa's cloth diapers, which Demon Man observed, much to her chagrin, he grabbed Rosa. She considered screaming at him again, but then he opened the large case and pulled out a book.

So that's what this is about! You got jealous of Faenor. Petty Demon!

Demon Man smiled at Rosa enthusiastically and read the title while Gunna nervously observed the situation as she changed the sheets in Rosa's crib. Rosa just stared at him with a vacant expression. His eyebrow twitched at her lackluster response, but he managed to maintain his cheerful demeanor and opened the book. It had no pictures in it whatsoever—just black and white text. Rosa puffed out her cheeks in displeasure.

Demon Man's eyebrow twitched again, but nonetheless, he began to read. She understood maybe three words from it, the rest sounding like absolute gibberish. It's not like Demon Man was reading slowly; he was speeding through the story as if this was a speed-reading contest. Once he was done, he plastered a wide grin on his face and looked expectantly at Rosa.

She just stared right back at him, her cheeks puffed out and nose scrunched. This was nothing like her enjoyable reading time with Faenor the day before.

What are you even trying to accomplish? I'm not going to like you just because you attempted to read a book for me once. A book I couldn't even understand.

She imagined that the demon was only skilled with violence, or something where he could belittle people all day, like a lazy CEO of a large company where workers barely had enough to eat while their glorious leader had his own private island.

Demon Man groaned dramatically. His previous smile was completely gone. He looked straight into Rosa's eyes and slowly dragged out each word as he said, "What do you want, Morrigan?"

Oh, I actually understood that!

Rosa was so pleased that her knowledge was slowly improving that she inadvertently smiled a little. Perhaps she could understand their words better if they all spoke much slower. But how could she convey that? Rosa tried to move her little tongue and produce some sort of coherent sound.

"Sow, sow," was all that she managed to draw out, instead of "slower," which was what she really wanted to say.

Curse this infuriating baby tongue! How the hell is it moving in every way that I don't want it to?

But despite her failed attempt at speaking, Demon Man's eyes were sparkling with delight. He stood up from the chair and laughed in triumph. He said something to Gunna while mentioning Rosa's demon name, "Morrigan," and the nanny just laughed awkwardly at him. Then he handed Rosa back to the dwarf woman and stormed out of the room while loudly congratulating himself.

Why do I have to deal with this lunatic?

* * *

Several months passed with a simple but far more enjoyable routine than before. Demon Man came to read his indecipherable stories in the morning, from which Rosa understood a maximum of ten words, and that was on a good day. She never shied away from showing her displeasure to Demon Man, who, despite her best menacing glares, still came to read each morning.

Thankfully, Faenor came every afternoon with children's storybooks to offset the useless reading done by Demon Man. Rosa learned a great deal from him, so she had no doubt that he must be a scholar or teacher of some sort. Thanks to his efforts and patience, she could understand most conversations without much issue.

Gunna started feeding her solid food. Well, calling it solid was a crime against actual food, but it was food other than milk—fruit and vegetable purées, as well as some simple porridges. Their flavor wasn't the best in the world since they had no sugar, salt, or spices in them, but at least it was something different than milk. Rosa liked the fruit purées since their natural sweetness made for a wonderful treat.

Her body was also getting stronger—she could sit up now and was slowly working towards standing. Her legs, however, remained weak and wobbly. One might assume demon babies would grow faster than human babies, but no. They developed at pretty much the same rate.

Demon Man and Gunna were delighted the first time they saw her sitting in her crib. Demon Man called her a "genius baby," and Gunna agreed with much fervor. Faenor was more reserved with praise, generally only complimenting her when she did something that was actually impressive. That didn't happen very often since there weren't many impressive things a baby could do.

This day, Gunna decided to put on a puppet show using the toys in Rosa's nursery. Had it been Demon Man doing this, Rosa would have put up her best annoyed face with an icy glare on top, but since it was Gunna she did her best to pretend to be interested.

It's alright, Gunna. Stop and go rest. I'll be fine on my own. Just… please stop this…

The door to the nursery burst open, abruptly ending the puppet show, much to Rosa's relief. She was about to give a small smile to Demon Man for saving her, but it was someone else who entered. It was a small demon girl. She was no older than six, had black hair tied into two ponytails, and a purple Gothic-Lolita-style dress. But what stood out the most were her black eyes. Those eyes instantly reminded Rosa of Demon Man.

The demon girl scrunched her nose at Rosa as if she had just spotted a cockroach crawling on the floor. Some shouting came from the hallway, and the girl quietly closed the door behind herself.

"Don't you dare to say anything about me being here, slave!" the little brat ordered Gunna, tilting her nose so high that Rosa thought her neck would break.

Slave? That's a rude way to address somebody. Do all demons think themselves better than other races?

But thinking about it carefully, it was certainly odd that a demon would have a dwarf as a nanny. At least, none of the fantasy stories Rosa had read ever had a dwarf willingly work for a demon. They were usually enemies—their interactions were limited to those on the opposite sides of the battlefield. Not to mention that Gunna always appeared skittish around Demon Man.

"I wouldn't dream of going against your wishes, Lady Deziara!" the nanny said in a humble voice and inclined her head towards the girl. The girl produced a "*hmph*" as if to indicate that Gunna's answer was subpar but would suffice for the time being. Rosa, however, had no intention of upkeeping manners and gave Deziara her best piercing glare.

"Why are you staring at me like that, you stupid baby? Don't you know who I am?" the girl hissed, pointing her finger at Rosa.

I've never met you before in my life. How am I supposed to know who you are?

"Please, calm down, Lady Deziara. She's just a baby; she cannot understand what you're saying," Gunna pleaded, attempting to pacify the brat.

"Don't talk back to me, slave! I'll have my father cut off your head!" she screeched, making the nanny flinch at her words.

Is Gunna afraid of this rude little brat? I think she has overstayed her welcome.

Rosa took a deep breath and then began wailing at the top of her lungs. She planned to attract the attention of whoever it was that the brat was trying to hide from.

This will teach her not to burst into other people's rooms and start ordering them around.

"W-What?! Shhh! Stop crying, stupid baby!" The brat shook her fists angrily at Rosa and stomped her feet, but she just continued screaming. A few moments later, the door swung open again, and a demon woman with the largest breasts Rosa had ever seen in her life entered the room.

Good God! Those can't be real! Do they have breast implants in this world? Or breast enlargement magic?

"Lady Deziara, there you are! We must get back to your lesson at once!" the demon woman said without so much as sparing a glance in Rosa and Gunna's direction, then quickly whisked the girl away.

"There, there, Lady Morrigan! It's over now," Gunna said, trying to pacify Rosa, although the dwarf woman was much more shaken up herself.

Is that little brat the daughter of someone important? Whatever! Good riddance!

* * *

Time passed, and Rosa finally grew strong enough to stand on her own. She could even manage a few steps before her little legs gave out from exhaustion. It felt very odd walking with a body that had such a disproportionately large head. It constantly weighed her down, making stability a constant challenge. Not to mention that her legs felt more like jelly than actual legs and were incredibly unstable.

But despite her clumsy walking posture, Demon Man couldn't have looked any prouder. He came to the nursery more often and stayed there for longer periods. His new hobby included coercing Rosa to walk towards him. Much to his dismay, she made a point to always walk away from him.

Sometimes, it would turn into a sort of game of "Avoid the demon," where Demon Man would run in the direction Rosa was walking, and Rosa would abruptly turn away from him. Usually, it ended with her getting exhausted and almost falling face-first onto the floor, except that Demon Man would always catch her.

You may not be the worst demon father in the world, but I still don't like you, Rosa thought after Demon Man caught her yet another time and held her close.

"Most excellent! Now that you can walk, we'll be able to introduce you to the rest of the family," Demon Man said with a satisfied nod, and Rosa noticed how Gunna, who was quietly observing from the other side of the room, paled.

"Don't you think it is a bit early, Master Alphegor?" the nanny asked with a shaky voice. Rosa noticed a slight tremor in her beard.

Why is Gunna worried? Isn't it good that I am finally meeting my family? But wait... Why am I meeting them only now?

Rosa, of course, had wondered where her biological—most likely demon—mother was. She was already seven months old, and only Demon Man, Gunna, and Faenor came to the nursery. The only other person she had ever seen in here was that bratty girl, but that was an accident.

Many scenarios crossed her mind, starting with her demon mother being divorced from Demon Man—if demons even got married—and ending with her just being dead. But she had no idea.

Nobody ever spoke of her mother, and she wasn't yet able to form any coherent words to ask.

"No, she is ready! Morrigan is exceptionally strong and talented for her age. It'll be a good opportunity to introduce her as my heir," Demon Man exclaimed confidently, and Gunna had no other choice but to nod in agreement.

Heir? I am his heir? He must have a high social standing to need one. But who would need to declare a baby as their heir? This is very odd.

CHAPTER 5

FAMILY DINNER

A few days later, Rosa's room was invaded by a horde of demon maids. Despite Gunna's protests, they swarmed around Rosa and began tugging at her from all sides. Rosa was so startled by the sudden onslaught that she couldn't manage more than to just gape in shock as she was quickly undressed and redressed in a small, black-and-red, Goth-style dress with her short hair tied into two twin-tails with large black hairbands. When they were finished, they set Rosa in front of the mirror to admire their handiwork.

The demon maids looked very proud of themselves, but Rosa just grimaced at her reflection. She looked like some demonic Goth doll that people set out on their porches during Halloween.

This is not how you dress up a small child! What is wrong with demons and their sense of style?

Of course, she could not voice her complaints aloud, so she glared at the maids with distaste while they fawned over her, saying how cute and adorable she was. Before they could smother Rosa too much, Demon Man entered the room, forcing them to scatter and scurry away like mice.

"Excellent! You look like a proper princess now!" Demon Man said with a self-satisfied smile and picked Rosa up.

So, you're the one responsible for these horrid clothes! I should have known.

He was wearing a grand black-and-red suit, and quite honestly, he looked like the perfect villain of every fantasy story. Rosa could only sigh in resignation as he took her outside the nursery for the first time since her arrival.

There were bulky demon guards stationed by the door who gave a curt nod to Demon Man. They tried to appear stoic and disinterested, but Rosa saw how they occasionally stole glances at her. No doubt they were interested to find out who exactly they had been guarding this whole time. Though until now, Rosa hadn't even known that she *was* being guarded.

Demon Man must be pretty high up on the food chain to have slaves, servants, and even guards. I wonder if he's like a demon noble or something akin to that.

Rosa took in everything with keen interest. The interior of the hallways was similar to her nursery—dark and gloomy. There was an occasional painting or a sculpture of a monster, but mostly it was just walls and doors that all looked much the same. After a few minutes of Demon Man turning this way and that, Rosa felt completely lost. She'd always had trouble with directions, usually relying on the GPS.

Demon Man stopped in front of one of the large doors at the end of the hallway and looked down at Rosa.

"Keep your head high, and don't show any weakness!" he said sternly. Rosa shifted uncomfortably in his arms, and a bad feeling rose in the pit of her stomach.

What? Why would you say that to a baby? A baby is nothing but a bundle of weakness.

He swung the door open and strode in with his back straight and head held high. The sight that greeted Rosa was probably the last thing she imagined. This was supposed to be her first meeting with her family, which she assumed to be a gathering of demons at various ages—grannies, grandpas, aunts, uncles, cousins, and little demon babies like her running about.

Instead, she, or to be precise Demon Man, was greeted by what could only be described as a harem. Demon women of all possible hair and eye colors, wearing colorful dresses that barely covered anything, all sitting around a ginormous dinner table, each with a little miniature version of themselves sitting beside them.

Please, don't tell me that all of those demon girls are my sisters?!

As Demon Man entered, the women and girls rose to their feet, offering him deep bows and curtsies. Rosa was surprised that their dresses actually managed to hold their breasts in place.

It must be done by magic because there's no way that little amount of fabric could contain all of... that.

"Greetings to the Dark King of the Underworld!" they said with sickeningly sweet smiles as they batted their eyelashes at Demon Man. Each woman tried to pucker their lips and show off their cleavage as much as possible.

He is the Demon King? I knew he must be pretty high up in demon society, but the king himself? Does that make me a princess? Oh, no. This might be even more troublesome than I initially thought.

Rosa barely contained a disgusted grimace. If it weren't for the many eyes looking at her right now, she wouldn't have bothered to hold back.

But with these concubines—or whatever similar title they held—Rosa knew she had to be careful. Unlike Demon Man, they had no reason to like her; they undoubtedly would prefer to have her out of the picture so he could focus on them and their daughters. She'd seen enough historical dramas to know that. Only one of them, namely Rosa's biological mother, would be her ally.

Which one is my mother? I don't really feel... a connection to any of them.

"Greetings to everyone in my flower garden! I am pleased you could all attend this special occasion," Demon Man said in a deep, commanding voice that exuded a strength and authority Rosa hadn't heard from him before. While he could be quite pushy, he never really struck her as an authoritative figure. But here, he appeared and spoke like a true king.

But you're calling them your flower garden? Really? I'm yet to see any flowers in this dingy place.

"We wouldn't dream of missing it, Your Majesty," said a voluptuous demoness with wavy, purple hair that stretched all the way down to her knees. Her starry, dark blue dress left very little to the imagination, and quite honestly, Rosa would classify it as lingerie rather than a dress meant for a formal occasion.

The girl beside her appeared to be the oldest child in the room, about fifteen or sixteen. She was already developing shapely curves and was clearly making an effort to present herself as more mature than the other girls in the room.

Why do all demon women have such huge breasts? Or is it just some weird benchmark to enter the king's harem?

Demon Man nodded and lifted Rosa forwards for everyone to see.

"I am proud to introduce my youngest daughter, my last gift from the late Queen Eirwen, and the Crown Princess of the Underworld—Morrigan Nachtstern!" he announced in a voice that reverberated throughout the room and sent a shiver through Rosa.

All of the women looked straight at Rosa, and she felt like a lamb that was about to be thrown into an enclosure full of crocodiles. Although they wore smiles on their faces, their eyes were filled with malice and hatred, and their tails flicked like cats preparing to pounce on their prey. Rosa's breath hitched, her heart began beating faster, and she felt her hands turn clammy.

Every single one of them wants to kill me...

Rosa cursed her luck for being dragged into another world and becoming the daughter of a powerful man. There could be nothing worse than this! She'd no doubt be the target of many assassins and political ploys. They'd try to stab her, poison her, marry her off to some fat, old, graying demon with a bunch of money.

Well, maybe not that last one.

Rosa's little hands began to tremble while thinking of all the horrifying scenarios she'd have to live through. But just as she thought she'd completely lost her nerve, Demon Man pulled her back and put her in his lap.

"Now, let's enjoy the feast to honor the Crown Princess. Let her grow strong and prosper!" Demon Man took a cup that looked to be filled with wine and downed it in a single swig. His close proximity to her seemed to repel the grudging looks of the concubines, so Rosa took the opportunity to scuttle even closer, hiding herself behind his arms.

"Morrigan looks so much like you, Your Majesty. She's absolutely beautiful!" said the concubine sitting on the king's right. She had unusually pale skin for a demon that contrasted with her bright pink hair, styled into two high ponytails. Unlike most women in the room, who went for a sexy look, this one was clearly pushing towards being cute—although her clothes were no less revealing.

"You shall address her as 'Her Highness' or 'Princess Morrigan,'"

Demon Man growled in response, and the concubine quickly dropped her gaze.

"O-Of course, Your Majesty," she muttered through a forced smile.

"Your Majesty, how old is Princess Morrigan?" asked a demoness with a long, black braid and alluring glasses. Rosa noticed that Deziara, the tantrum-throwing brat from before, was sitting next to her, biting her lip in frustration and glaring daggers in Rosa's direction. No doubt, she had recognized the baby who had sold her out.

"She is seven months old," Demon Man replied coldly and took a bite of meat that was served on his plate. Then he snapped his fingers, and a maid with a trolley came up to him with some sort of porridge on it. She set the bowl in front of Rosa and Demon Man. He took the small spoon that the maid had set next to the bowl, scooped a bit of the porridge, and offered it for Rosa to eat. All the eyes in the room once again turned to her, judging her every tiny movement.

"What's wrong, Morrigan? Are you not hungry?" Demon Man asked and moved the spoon closer to her lips.

Of course, I'm hungry, but I can't eat with all of these women glaring at me! I thought that being a baby meant I would be safe and doted on. Instead, it turns out I am a princess with a father who has a harem full of concubines who hate me.

Nonetheless, Rosa opened her mouth, and Demon Man fed her the porridge. It was delicious, sweet, and reminded her vaguely of plums.

"You never fed Viana like this, Your Majesty," the purple-haired demoness closest to Demon Man noted with a tinge of bitterness. She quickly collected her expression and put on a smile, but her daughter looked like she was about to burst from jealousy, her cheeks puffed out. It was kind of cute, in a way, seeing an almost-adult demon revealing her childish side.

"I am the king, not a nanny," Demon Man stated, and the woman flinched back.

He sure is harsh towards women he supposedly takes to bed. I didn't expect such a heavy atmosphere in a harem.

Demon Man continued to feed her the porridge while occasionally taking a bite from his own dinner.

"Your Majesty, has Her Highness manifested any powers yet?" the purple-haired demoness asked, trying to divert Demon Man's attention. But that was clearly not the right question to ask, as he abruptly stopped feeding her to glare at the demoness. Then he stood up from his seat while holding Rosa close.

He's about to snap!

"Morrigan has more magical potential than any demon born in the last ten thousand years. She'll become the most powerful demon queen and raise the Demon Kingdom to heights it has never seen before! And you will all support her as her loyal subjects and sisters," Demon Man boomed, his voice reverberating throughout the room and filling the air with a heavy, oppressive weight. The women bent their heads low as the smaller girls clutched their mothers in fear.

S-Stop! There's no need to go this far!

Rosa tugged at his coat in an attempt to pacify him. Demon Man's icy gaze broke, and he looked down at her. The women in the room gasped for air.

Demon Man regarded them with annoyance before turning on his heel and leaving the room. Rosa couldn't understand how he could be so cold and cruel towards them. She could somewhat understand his overbearing stance towards concubines—they'd slit Rosa's throat at the first opportunity. But what about the girls?

Aren't they your daughters, just like me? Why don't you show any affection towards them? Is it really all about power?

Then Rosa recalled how Demon Man had said she possessed more magical potential than any demon born in the last ten thousand years. Her stomach churned, and she felt her head spin. She didn't want any magical power or unmatched strength! All Rosa wanted was to return home and paint in peace.

Chapter 6

Blending into Shadows

After the disastrous dinner, Rosa spent a long time thinking over her situation. Previously, she had always swept all these unpleasant topics to the side since a small, irrationally stupid part of her hoped that this whole situation was nothing more than a dream. But it was time to face this new, unpleasant reality and figure out what it was that she needed to do.

First, I should compile all the things I know about this world.

Rosa wished she had a pen and paper to write it all down, but obviously, her nursery had none of those things. So instead, she decided to organize the information she knew in her head.

One, I am the youngest daughter of the Demon King and his designated heir.

Two, my mother, the demon queen, is dead.

Three, I have magical potential that hasn't been seen in ten thousand years. Apparently.

Four, elves and dwarves are treated like slaves by the demons.

Rosa tried hard to think of anything else that might be important, but she realized this was all that she knew for certain. The rest was nothing more than her own guesses or assumptions. She didn't even have a clue whether there were humans in this world.

There must be, but I haven't heard anyone talk about them yet. Even the books that Faenor and Demon Man read never mentioned anything about humans. Though, I can't take anything written in these books at face value, since I don't know what's fiction and what isn't.

Rosa's conclusion was simple—she knew far too little about this world. She needed to learn more. But to do that, she had to acquire two of the most important skills—talking and reading. The thought of trying to understand the weird writing of this world made Rosa cringe. Their letters were complex, and even after all the books she'd seen, she still hadn't picked up on a single character. Rosa guessed that, most likely, the writing worked much like Japanese or Chinese, where a letter could actually represent a whole word.

She probably wouldn't be able to easily learn the writing on her own, so her best course of action would be to start talking.

"M-Me neim is L-L—" she stuttered in her crib, trying to force her unruly tongue to cooperate. Rosa wasn't sure whether it was just her undeveloped baby body that made it difficult to speak or the new language.

"I a-am Rosa," she said in human language. It turned out better than expected, albeit it sounded foreign with her new voice.

So, Rosa continued her talking practice late into the night. Mostly, she spoke in English because whenever she spoke the Demon language, she often stuttered and pronounced words incorrectly. It frustrated her to no end, so after a few failed attempts, she called it a night and went to sleep.

* * *

Rosa diligently continued her talking practice for the next month, doing it whenever she was sure that nobody was around. It didn't take long for her to master the unruly baby tongue and form coherent English words. But the Demon language... Well, let's just say that her pronunciation was not the best.

Why is this language so hard? It's like they mixed German with French and Chinese. My tongue is going to twist in on itself.

It was going so badly that Rosa considered abandoning her efforts altogether.

Who am I going to talk to? Demon Man? The only thing I would tell him is probably a slurry of curses. Talking to Gunna and Faenor could be more productive... I'm sure they wouldn't mind answering some of the questions I have...

Rosa sighed and continued practicing. She had to find a way out of this. Ideally, she'd like to return to Earth, but if that wasn't an option, then she'd at least like to lead a peaceful life as an artist in some human city. Or at least an elf city. Or at least a place where her own supposed family members wouldn't glare at her.

She also worried that not sketching anything for an extended period of time would cause her skills degrade. If she couldn't find a way to draw soon, it was possible all of her skills would be lost by the time she got out of this mess.

Perhaps I could ask Gunna to bring me some pencils, paints, or crayons—or whatever it is they have in this world. All the more reason to hurry with my practice.

"Me neim is L-L-Roza," she kept repeating at the swirly patterned ceiling above her. It was already late into the night, but despite the many attempts, the words sounded wrong. They weren't as smooth as when others spoke, instead reminding her of a jagged, rough stone wall.

I should call it a night since I'm not improving anyway. Tomorrow, I'll try repeating the words Gunna and Faenor say throughout the day.

With this thought, Rosa's eyelids slowly closed, exhaustion beckoning her into dreamland. Her breath became steady, her heartbeat... slow. A vague dream of the seaside began to form in her mind when she heard the light sounds of the nursery door opening and closing.

Who is coming in this late? Gunna? Or Demon Man? He probably decided to watch me sleep or something creepy like that.

Rosa opened one eye to get a look at her late visitor. Her breath hitched as she saw a figure covered in black from head to toe. Only their murderous eyes were visible through tiny slits. Their hand raised high, clutching a dagger that glinted in the sparsely available light.

They're going to kill me!

Rosa grabbed the crib's railing and pulled herself out of the knife's path. It dug deep into the bedding, and Morrigan used all of her baby strength to pull herself over the edge while the assailant was busy untangling his weapon. She hit the floor with a thud, and a pained grunt escaped her lips.

"You actually avoided me?" they snarled in a barely audible voice. "Impressive for a baby, but I guess I should have expected no less from the Demon King's daughter." It was unclear whether it was male or female; the voice was too gurgled.

The assailant slowly circled the crib, dagger primed in their hand. Rosa scrambled away on all fours, trying her best to get as far away as possible.

This can't be happening! I don't want to die! I don't want to die! Somebody help me!

"Hahaha! There's nowhere to run and nowhere to hide! Even your daddy won't be able to save you, since you'll be long dead before he even realizes what is happening," the figure gloated with disgusting glee. They clearly didn't care about the consequences as long as they completed their mission.

Rosa crawled into the corner and looked straight at her assailant. Death. It was like she was staring death in the eyes. Soft, muffled laughter came from underneath the mask.

No, I don't want to die! I want to live! Please, just let me melt into the shadows and disappear!

The dagger glinted as it swung down at Rosa. She braced herself for the pain, but instead of cutting her flesh, the dagger dug into the wooden floorboards with a dull *thunk*.

"Whaa? Where did you go?" The intruder frantically looked around the room, searching for her left and right.

What just happened?

She still felt herself pressed against the same corner, yet the dagger hadn't touched her. Something wasn't right. Her vision seemed... different. More perfect. She could see everything in the room—even areas she shouldn't have been able to see from her position. And her body felt incredibly light—as if floating in the air, except in a more solid way.

The attacker then stopped and focused on the corner, staring right at Rosa but not seeing her. Then he laughed hysterically. It echoed through the quiet of the night like thunder on a clear day.

"To think that a baby less than a year old would be able to turn into a shadow. It's almost a shame to kill you." They cackled in pleasure. "But kill you I shall. After all, nobody has ever escaped my blade before!"

A purple, misty substance erupted from the hilt of the blade, surrounding it as it became translucent—ethereal, like a shadow.

I have to run.

Rosa willed her body to move. She couldn't feel her body in the usual sense, but she felt herself gliding along the nursery wall. The sensation was nauseating, but she pushed herself forward.

If I don't move, I'll be killed!

This desperate thought propelled her forward as the assassin began stabbing at the wall, following closely behind her.

Faster! Faster!

Rosa made it to the door, but without a physical form, she couldn't open it. However, she noticed a small crack underneath. She didn't understand how, but her instinct told her she could slip through it. So, she forced herself under, and slid into the hallway outside, the intruder stabbing into the door right as she slipped out.

Two corpses—the guards who had given her curious glances the previous day—lay in a puddle of their own blood. Rosa would have screamed if she had a mouth to scream with. But the intruder smashed through the door, launching themselves straight at her.

She frantically moved through the dark shadows of the wall, going as fast as her form allowed her. There was no time to think or try to understand what she was doing, as every few seconds, the dagger collided with the wall where she was less than a second ago.

Rosa propelled herself forward with all of her might. She could feel her core shake from exhaustion as she was slowly nearing her limit.

If I stop, I die! RUN!

She turned a corner and melded into shadows below the staircase, moving down at a speed that her assailant couldn't match. She slid underneath the first door that she saw. Light footsteps continued chasing after her, keeping close no matter how much she twisted and turned.

I can't do this for much longer... But if I stop, I die. I mustn't give up.

Rosa felt her being almost slipping apart from the exertion, but no matter how much it protested, she held on to the power with an iron grip.

"Dammit! This has dragged on too long. I need to end this now," the figure snarled from behind her, and Rosa felt the room instantly turn cold. The change was so sudden that her momentum faltered for only a moment, but it was enough. The dagger flew straight at her, and she saw a delightful glee in the murderer's eyes.

I'm going to die!

Desperately, she tried to move away from the weapon, but this time she was too slow. The dagger hit the wall, but not before passing through her shoulder. She let out an agonized scream as she materialized out of the shadows, tears of pain streaming down her little cheeks.

"Amazing! You dodged a death blow. To think that my most spectacular prey would be a baby. It is horrifying to think what you would be able to do as an adult." The assassin heavily stepped forward.

Somebody, please...

Death and cold were spreading from Rosa's wound and slowly taking over her body.

"HELP!" she forced herself to scream as loud as her little lungs could manage. The murderer froze, perhaps shocked by her sudden cry, but then went very still. A bloody blade burst through their chest—exactly where their heart would be.

They choked, an ooze of crimson seeping through the mask and staining their clothes and the floor in thick, dark streaks.

"This quick death is too merciful for you," said the loud and clear voice of Alphegor. He pulled his sword free from the corpse and threw it to the side like it was nothing more than a bag of trash. Then he ran to Rosa's side.

"Get a healer! Immediately! I'll kill you all if they're not here within three minutes!" his voice boomed menacingly, but his face was distraught with worry and fear as he looked over Rosa's injury.

"I... I..." Tears streamed down her face as she reached her arm towards him.

Alphegor grabbed her without hesitation and cradled her close.

"You'll be fine! You'll be fine! We'll get you healed in no time!" He muttered it like a mantra, but his face was panicked. Alphegor moved her clothes aside gently to look at her wound. His hand began to tremble as he seemed unsure of whether to remove the dagger or not.

"We're going to get this fixed," he said, a slight tremble in his voice as his grip on her tightened.

Rosa's vision blurred; she was unable to endure the pain any longer. But before her consciousness faded, she saw a single tear roll down Alphegor's face.

So, demons do have feelings...

CHAPTER 7

THE UNDERWORLD

Rosa woke to a sharp pang of pain in her shoulder, which slowly subsided into a gentle ache. When she finally mustered the strength to open her eyes, she found herself cradled in Alphegor's embrace.

"You're awake," he exclaimed, relief washing over his face. His features seemed strained—a furrow in his brow, lips pursed into a bare smile, and his nose and forehead scrunched with worry. "Thank the Darkness that you're alright..."

Alphegor brought Rosa close and held her gently so as not to strain her injured shoulder. It felt warm, comforting, and *safe*.

He saved me as soon as I called for help. Did he hear me, or did he notice the ruckus caused by the intruder?

As she remembered their murderous eyes, she instinctively clung to Alphegor's clothes. She smelled a light stench of blood coming from him and almost recoiled.

No, he protected me. I am safe with him.

"Rest, child. I shall not leave your side," Alphegor said, and Rosa relaxed. She was so physically and mentally exhausted that his comforting warmth and closeness lulled her back to sleep.

When Rosa woke up again, she was surprised to find herself in a completely unfamiliar room. She sat up to get a better look at her surroundings. Alphegor was sleeping right next to her on the left, while on the right there was a net installed by the bedposts. Without a doubt, it was there to prevent her from rolling out.

Beyond it she saw a huge room—at least four of her nurseries could easily fit inside it. The bed alone was so large it probably wouldn't even fit inside Rosa's apartment back on Earth. The bed sheets were made of black silk with tasteful golden and red accents, while the dark blue curtains were tied to the engraved wooden bed posts.

Two wooden dividers, one with a dark dragon motif on it and one with a mountain landscape, separated the bed from the rest of the room. The art style on them was rather simplistic but tasteful, choosing to remain more as a background element rather than something that caught your attention.

Beyond the dividers, Rosa could see that one side of the room appeared more like a study, complete with a desk, bookshelves, and a weird, round apparatus in the corner. The other side of the room was more obscured; she could only make out part of a coffee table and what she thought might be a couch.

This must be Alphegor's private room. Why has he suddenly brought me here? Was it because of the attack?

Rosa observed the sleeping Demon. His face was contorted in a scowl, and his body seemed tense. Much to her discomfort, his upper torso was completely naked, showing well-defined muscles and perfectly smooth ashen skin.

Even if this is your room, couldn't you wear pajamas or something?

Still, she knew she had little right to complain. Some of his genes, no doubt, had passed to her, so that meant she should be at least somewhat attractive. Or at least more attractive than she had been before.

The silence in the room stretched on, and Rosa's mind flashed back to the horrid eyes of the murderer. His laugh echoed in her ears as she moved her hand to touch where the dagger had struck her shoulder. A small bit of pain came from it when she pressed down, but no more than from a regular bruise. She pushed her shirt to the side and saw that her skin had a reddish line with a faint bluish tint around it.

I must have been healed with magic. I couldn't have healed so quickly on my own unless demons have some super regenerative power. But judging how Alphegor called for a healer, I would assume not.

Rosa shook her head, trying to forget the unpleasant incident. She didn't want to get involved in all this demon business, but at the same time, it was not like she could get up and leave. First, it was necessary to find out more about this world as a whole. Second, figure out what exactly happened to her and what she could do to improve her life—whether that involved becoming stronger or finding a safer living place.

Why did I have to become the Demon King's daughter? If I were to be reborn in another world, couldn't I just be a simple farmer's daughter? Or better yet—an artist's daughter.

Rosa sighed, and her body began trembling despite the room being warm. She didn't want to accept the unpleasant reality she was living in. She did not want assassins preying on her life or the envious gazes of her half-sisters and demon concubines. She just wanted to go back home—to the little apartment where she kept her painting supplies.

Suddenly, Alphegor stirred next to Rosa, making her flinch in surprise. His eyes fluttered open, and his scowl softened.

"You woke up before me, Morrigan? How are you feeling?" he asked as he sat up. Moving Rosa's shirt aside, just like she had earlier, he examined her injury and grimaced when he saw the ugly mark.

"Those healers didn't do a good enough job. I should cut off their heads."

"No!" Rosa protested before she even realized what she was doing. The demon looked at her in shock while she stared back at him wide-eyed.

Keep calm, keep calm! It's not like you said any difficult words. While an eight-month-old baby's talking is certainly not normal, a simple word like 'no' shouldn't get you into trouble.

"Was that a real word I heard?" A wide grin appeared on Alphegor's face, and he lifted Rosa up. "Say that again."

Rosa pondered for a second whether she should, cold sweat forming on her body.

"No..." she said with much less confidence, hoping that repeating the same word wouldn't make her seem too advanced for her age.

How would he react if he figured out that I'm actually human? I'd rather not put it to the test—not until I understand my situation a little better.

"Amazing! Despite being so small, you're already saying your first words. Not a single one of your twenty-three sisters could do that," Alphegor said, his proud smile revealing long, unnatural canines.

I have twenty-three sisters? I didn't see that many girls at that "family gathering."

Rosa grimaced, unable to hide her disappointment. It seemed like demon men were much like some human men—unable to keep their hands to themselves.

"Why do you suddenly look so disappointed?"

"No," Rosa babbled in response and turned her head to the side.

"Heh, cheeky little one, aren't you?" He chuckled and then moved out of the bed with Rosa in his arms.

Alphegor walked past the large divider, and Rosa finally got a proper look at the room. The right side was indeed a resting area with a couch, coffee table and a small wine cabinet. What she hadn't noticed before was that next to the large, round apparatus on the left side of the room, there was a large window. It was the first window she had seen since coming to this world.

Rosa outstretched her hands towards it, fidgeting, trying to indicate that she wanted to look outside.

"Want to take a look outside? I suppose there were no windows in your room. I hoped that it would keep assassins at bay, but it seems like it was naive to believe that a mere lack of windows could achieve that." His expression turned cold enough to send a shiver down Rosa's spine, and she felt an urge to move closer to him. Then she realized that he was still mostly naked and abandoned the idea.

Alphegor went up to the window, which was currently covered with curtains, and slowly pulled them apart. Rosa was eager to finally see the sun for the first time in eight months, but when the King opened the curtains, all she felt was disappointment.

"Take a good look, Morrigan. This is the Demon Kingdom of the Underworld—the strongest kingdom in the whole world. None other can match our might!" he announced proudly as he pointed towards the dark, dreary scenery outside.

There was no sky; there was no sun... There were no lush forests, green fields of grass, or bright, blue seas. There was stone, darkness, deep, endless ravines, and fields of lava and fire. Instead of a vibrant garden with bright flowers, there was a murky garden with gray foliage and the occasional thorny bush. Shimmering river water was replaced with a river of lava that destroyed everything in its path. The endless sky was absent, and the dark cave ceiling trapped everything underneath it like a cage. Rosa felt like a part of her had just been crushed.

"It must be a lot to take in at once, but I'm sure you'll learn more about your kingdom as you grow older. For now, you need to focus on healing," Alphegor said, but Rosa could barely hear him.

I truly am in hell. There is no sunlight, no life, not even a gust of wind. It is only darkness, death and suffering.

* * *

Since that day, all of Rosa's baby things except for her crib were moved to Alphegor's room. Much to her chagrin, Rosa had to sleep next to Alphegor every night and she was constantly watched by somebody. Most of the time, it was Alphegor himself keeping a close eye on her.

The demon was reluctant to ever leave Rosa alone, even under Gunna's watchful eye, and quite honestly, she herself felt nervous whenever he was not around. While Rosa liked Gunna and enjoyed it when Faenor read books to her, she was constantly haunted by visions of the murderous intruder. She couldn't help glancing at every dark corner, constantly watching out for any moving shadows or strangers.

"It's alright, Lady Morrigan. You are safe," Gunna soothed her during mealtime. But Rosa kept glancing behind the nanny to make sure nobody unknown was lurking behind her.

"To think that somebody would try to murder a child," Faenor said with clear disgust in his voice. He was waiting on the couch as the nanny fed Rosa. "It must be something only demons are able to do."

"Shush, Faenor! You'll get us into trouble."

"His *Majesty*," Faenor spat out the word as if it were poison, "is currently away from the castle, and the guards don't really care what slaves talk about as long as we don't confront them directly."

"Still, Lady Morrigan can hear you." The nanny glanced at Rosa nervously, but she just cocked her head to the side and poked the floor, feigning interest in its wooden pattern.

"Lady Morrigan is a baby. A smart baby, but a baby nonetheless," Faenor said and pulled out a colorful book with a rainbow on the front cover.

You expect me to smile at that, don't you?

Although currently, Rosa was in no mood for stories, she forced herself to smile. It was better that she acted like nothing had happened. After all, a real baby certainly wouldn't have understood anything.

If I were an actual baby, I'd already be dead. Rosa shuddered as she tried not to show her nervousness.

"See! She's just as eager for story time as always," Faenor said and picked Rosa up, setting her down on his knee as he always did.

"It would be nice if Lady Morrigan weren't affected. It'd be a horrid memory for a child to have. But even so, there will be more attempts on her life."

"Barbaric. If she'd been born an elf princess, nobody would ever even dare to *think* of killing her. Or any child for that matter."

"If she were a dwarf princess, then dwarves from all over the world would come to the capital to pay homage to her. And anyone lucky enough to see her would be blessed for life."

But I was born a demon princess, so instead of praise and worship, I get contempt, malice, and countless assassination attempts.

Faenor began reading the colorful picture book, but Rosa couldn't find it in herself to find any enjoyment in it. The children's books had fulfilled their purpose at that point—to teach Rosa the Demon language. Her baby body was developing: she could walk, she could talk to an extent, and she could even blend into shadows in case of an emergency.

In all honesty, Rosa still had no idea how she managed to step into the shadows and become a part of them. The whole experience was so jarring and unpleasant that she preferred not to think about it at all. But whether she liked it or not, without this power, she would almost certainly be dead.

CHAPTER 8

WORLD OF DOPPELTA

Three months passed—by far the slowest since Rosa's first arrival in this new world. She wanted to learn to read, write, and, most importantly, find a way to escape from this world. But she also realized she couldn't just get up one morning and ask Alphegor, "Would you please teach me how to write? And while we're at it, why don't you explain how I, a human, became a demon?" In an especially bold daydream, she demanded he send her back home.

Naturally, that one was quickly dismissed. She could just imagine Alphegor's outrage if he found out that his most precious heir used to be a human from another world. Who knew what he would do? Perhaps he hated humans so much that he would just spear her head on a pike himself. After all, the most dangerous beings in the Underworld weren't the secret assassins or the mothers of Rosa's many half-sisters—it was the Demon King himself.

And so, Rosa decided that the best course of action for the time being was to slowly ease everyone into the fact that she could talk. Of course, she had no patience to wait until she was three years old when most children started speaking coherently. Instead, she steadily increased her spoken words day by day. Initially it was one word a day, then two, then three.

Alphegor's reaction was much as she expected—he grinned like a fool, praised her as an absolute genius, and urged her to speak more new words. His lack of suspicion allowed her to add some extra spoken words to her vocabulary. Gunna was also delighted by her progress, gently correcting her if she pronounced something wrong—Demon language was hard. Faenor, on the other hand, regarded her suspiciously once her vocabulary clearly expanded beyond what a normal baby could do.

In fact, whenever she would talk while Faenor was around, he would observe her carefully, making Rosa wonder whether she had been too impatient.

But I can't wait for long. I'll be killed if I just sit and do nothing. There might already be assassins trying to find a way to get to me.

"It's time to read again, Lady Morrigan," Faenor said and motioned Rosa closer. She approached him as always, but he regarded her somewhat differently today. She was about to turn to Gunna, to plead to the nanny to play with her instead, but the dwarf had already left Alphegor's room.

Rosa turned back to Faenor, and for a fleeting moment, the memory of her attacker's dark eyes flashed in her mind, causing her to instinctively take a step back.

Seeing her reluctance, Faenor's expression softened, and he made a beckoning gesture to invite her forward less demandingly.

"It's time for your story, Princess Morrigan," the elf said with more eloquence than she was used to hearing.

It's alright. It's just Faenor. Why are you being so paranoid all of a sudden?

Rosa waddled over to him, and he put her in his lap just as he usually did. His book choice for the day, however, was far from the usual. Instead of a colorful picture book, he held a thick, heavy tome—its numbered spine hinting at something far more serious.

"I thought it would be useful for you to start learning more about this world, so I've picked out a more serious story," Faenor explained as he opened the book. The letters inside were still large, like in a children's book, and there were plenty of drawings, but this was clearly something meant for older children rather than babies who could barely talk.

"Today, let's start with some knowledge of our world. It is called Doppelta, the name stemming from the fact that it is actually two worlds in one." The elf pointed at the picture, which depicted two planets: one blue and green with continents different from the ones Rosa was familiar with, and one black and red, which looked completely foreign.

Two worlds in one? How is that possible?

She looked over the two planets, carefully trying to find some correlation between them, but then she realized that Faenor was observing her with alarming intensity.

"Ball!" Rosa pointed at the blue-and-green planet and forced herself to smile widely at the elf.

Don't get nervous. It's alright. Why would anybody suspect you not being a baby?

"Yes, a ball," Faenor said, disappointment clear in his voice. Nonetheless, he continued. "First, we have the Overworld—the surface, or just the *top*. This is the world under the sun. It is bountiful and full of plants, animals, and life. There are vast oceans, tall mountains, and fertile fields."

I must act like I understand nothing.

"Sun?" Rosa cocked her head to the side.

"It's a... giant ball of light in the sky," Faenor explained, his shoulders slumping lower.

"Sky?"

"It's like a never-ending blue ceiling."

"Wow!" Rosa deliberately over-exaggerated her reaction, making the elf slump his shoulders even further down.

"The other world is the Underworld—the world below the surface, or just the underground. This is the world of darkness where the sun never shines. It is without light, so the plants here are sparse, and even those that grow here never gain the green luster of their surface cousins. It is a place of monsters, fire, and death."

Great, and I'm the princess here. What does that say about me?

"Princess Morrigan, are you perhaps—"

"Lady Morrigan!" Gunna swung the door open, carrying a large tray in her hands. "His Majesty has sent you some of the new fruit harvest to try. It was just picked this morning."

"You can hardly call that fruit," Faenor grumbled, his already sullen mood dropping even further.

"Oh, hush! Don't be such a wet sock," the nanny reprimanded and began peeling the dark-blue skin of something that vaguely resembled an orange. Rosa barely restrained a laugh, instead trying to appear excited about the fruit. "See, Lady Morrigan loves her fruit."

"That's only because she doesn't know that better things exist," Faenor replied, his voice dripping with pity.

Hey, this weird blue citrus might not be the sweetest thing out there, but it isn't bad. It is certainly better than no fruit at all.

The nanny picked Rosa up and began feeding her neatly cleaned pieces of the fruit. The dark blue color wasn't very appetizing, and the flavor was something between a blueberry and an orange. It was an odd but not entirely unpleasant flavor once she got used to it.

"You're in an awfully bad mood today. Did something happen?" the nanny asked as she continued cleaning the fruit. Faenor snapped the book shut and put it down on the coffee table.

"No, I just had hoped…" The elf's eyes lingered on Rosa, but she deliberately stared at the blue wedge in front of her, admiring the glossy surface as if it were the most interesting thing in the world.

"Hoped for what?" the nanny asked with a raised eyebrow.

"Nothing. It's not important. I just got impatient. I'll go down to the library to switch the book. I accidentally took the wrong one." The elf showed the heavy volume to the dwarf woman.

No, don't take it away! I wanted to learn more about this world.

Rosa did her best not to let her thoughts show.

Be calm. Nobody can know that you're actually a human from another world. If God forbid this information somehow gets to Alphegor, I am undoubtedly done for.

"Oh, *Guide to the World of Doppelta*. They had that in the library? I thought demons would surely denounce anything created by humans," Gunna said, reaching for the book. Faenor handed it to her without any resistance.

So, humans do exist in this world! Finally, some confirmation. But it appears that the demons really hate them, just as I had suspected.

"Yes, I was surprised as well. I guess it is just too good to be cast aside."

"Indeed. I still remember how much I loved to study from it as a child." Gunna flipped through the pages, but her gaze became distant—lingering in old, bittersweet memories. "You read this to Lady Morrigan?"

"Yes, but I don't think she is old enough to understand it," Faenor said with a disappointed sigh.

What's with the dramatic reaction? Did you seriously expect a baby that's not even a year old to understand it? Well, I do understand, I just can't show it.

"It's not like she's old enough to understand everything that's written in the story books either. It's the reading process itself that is important. Why don't you continue reading it?"

Faenor looked a bit surprised at first but then his expression softened.

"Yes, you're right. Even if she doesn't understand it yet, she might still grow to love this book."

Gunna nodded in agreement as she handed the volume back to Faenor.

"Our little lady is very smart; I'm sure it won't take long for her to understand." Gunna patted Rosa's head, then began cleaning more fruit.

* * *

"Begin Morrigan's lessons?" Alphegor asked Gunna, after she had suggested that Rosa would need proper lessons to further improve.

"Yes, Your Majesty! Lady Morrigan is so advanced that I am sure it would not be too early to begin."

The Demon King looked down at Rosa, who was sitting in his lap. She tried to appear unaffected by the conversation, instead pretending to be interested in one of his coat buttons.

Act natural! Act natural! Why did Gunna have to bring it up? I know she has the best intentions, but I don't want Alphegor to get suspicious.

"Hmm... I suppose if it's Morrigan, then it wouldn't be a problem. She is extremely intelligent after all—just like her father," Alphegor said with a proud smile. Then his expression turned to that of contemplation. "Perhaps it is also time for her to start practicing magic."

"Isn't it a bit early for magic?" Gunna asked nervously.

Learning magic? That sounds exciting, but wouldn't it be weird for a baby to learn magic? I'd think that babies wouldn't be able to do magic, except by accident.

"No. She already took a shadow form once. In fact, it would be more dangerous if she did it again by accident and got stuck," Alphegor explained. A chill ran down Rosa's spine at the thought.

So, I could have gotten stuck in the shadows? That's a scary thought.

"It... doesn't seem like Lady Morrigan is ready to learn magic..." Gunna said in a somber tone as she regarded Rosa with pity-filled eyes. Alphegor remained silent, his expression thoughtful as he mulled over her words.

"How about this, Morrigan? I'll have a teacher check on you, and then we'll decide whether it's too early or not for you to learn?" Alphegor finally said and gently stroked Rosa's hair. The motion was surprisingly soothing, not something she expected to feel from a demon.

Meeting the teacher wouldn't be the end of the world. I could pretend to not understand the teacher and maybe begin practicing magic in secret. That sounds kind of exciting. I wonder if I can use magic for painting.

"Okay," Rosa conceded.

"Excellent! I'll inform Azrael of his new duties this evening," Alphegor announced with a wide grin. Rosa thought nothing of it until she saw her nanny's expression. Gunna's face had gone pale, her eyes wide, and even her beard trembled slightly.

"Azrael?" Rosa repeated the name in hopes that somebody would elaborate more on this character.

"Don't worry, little one! He's the best mage in the Underworld. After your father, of course, but I'm not very good at teaching," Alphegor said with a dismissive wave while Gunna raised her finger slightly.

"I-Is Lord Azrael a w-wise choice? He doesn't strike me as being suited for dealing with children yet."

"He's still a child himself. I'm sure he'll find a way to relate to Morrigan."

"A child? Isn't he over two hundred years old?"

Two hundred years old? How long do demons even live?

"Yes, two hundred and eight if I remember right. Such a small age gap between him and Morrigan. I'm sure they'll be on equal footing in a century or two."

A century or two? Rosa struggled to keep her expression neutral, while Gunna didn't bother to hide her shock. Alphegor looked quizzically at the nanny, and then realization dawned on him.

"Oh, that's right. Dwarves don't have very long lifespans. Merely eight hundred years, if I'm not wrong."

"Yes, that's right, Master Alphegor," Gunna confirmed with a bow.

Eight hundred years is not very long? Then exactly how long do demons live?

CHAPTER 9

BABY LEARNING MAGIC

The next morning, after breakfast, Alphegor wasted no time and ordered Gunna to dress the Princess in clothes appropriate for training. Well, to be exact, she found baby clothes that had the fewest frills and laces so Rosa wouldn't trip over them. It was refreshing to wear somewhat normal clothes for once, even if Alphegor scrunched up his nose in distaste.

Once dressed, Alphegor picked Rosa up and began weaving through the castle corridors. It had been a while since he'd taken her outside of his room—not since the incident. The demons they met on the way instantly bowed at Alphegor's approach while curiously eyeing Rosa. She did her best to ignore the stares and instead focused on memorizing the maze that was the demon castle.

But after a few swift turns and going down ornate staircases which ended in open halls that led in every possible direction, Rosa began to feel like all the corridors melted together, and she completely lost track of where she was.

This must be a tactic to confuse intruders. Who the hell could find anything in this place without a map? Everything looks gray or black, with some occasional blood-red thrown in for good measure.

As Rosa grumbled at her inability to remember the layout, Alphegor entered a large, empty room with weapon racks and training dummies for decoration. It was completely different from the rest of the castle, as it was more like a large cavern rather than an actual room. The walls were rugged stone with occasional scorch marks here and there, as well as a few shallow cavities that looked as though something had been slammed into them.

In the middle of the dimly lit area stood a tall, proud demon man. His skin was dark gray, much darker than Alphegor's and Rosa's ashy tone. His white hair was cut short, while his vivid purple eyes starkly contrasted the rest of him. As Alphegor approached, the demon gave a small, respectful bow.

"Good morning, Your Majesty! It is surprising to see you at the training grounds," Azrael greeted the Demon King with a tiny, mischievous smile. He didn't spare Rosa so much as a glance.

This guy doesn't bring me much confidence. He disregarded me completely.

"Naturally. There's no way I'd entrust you to remain alone with my daughter. I must ensure you'll show her the respect that she's due," Alphegor said in his kingly voice, his eyes as cold as ice.

"Oh! I didn't think that the genius you were talking about was your daughter. From what I recall, none of them showed any special magical aptitude." Azrael scratched his chin thoughtfully. Alphegor's eyebrow twitched briefly before he composed himself, smiling with a polished air of pride.

"You haven't met my youngest yet—Morrigan," he stated proudly and put Rosa down on the floor as if she were the centerpiece of an art gallery.

Azrael looked down at her in disbelief. He looked up at Alphegor, then back down to Rosa with his mouth agape. He then laughed hysterically, the noise echoing through the room and bouncing from wall to wall, making it all the more annoying.

"Hahaha! I get it, Your Majesty. You're just trying to get back at me for accidentally killing that dragon. I'm really sorry about that. I'll make sure to hold my power back properly next time," Azrael said through his laughter while wiping a tear from the corner of his eye.

I know that I'm a baby, but even so, this is just...

"Rude," Rosa stated flatly, giving Azrael her best impression of Alphegor's cold glare. He gaped at her while Alphegor sneered in satisfaction.

"She talks? How old is she? Six months?"

"Eleven," Rosa replied with a huff. Azrael's jaw opened even wider.

"E-Eleven months? Not even a year old? And she can talk?" The demon gaped, then squatted down and eyed Rosa suspiciously. "Are you sure she isn't possessed by something? Like a thousand-year-old elven spy sent here to learn our secrets?"

Rosa took a step back, supporting herself against Alphegor's legs. The Demon King just shook his head and picked her up again.

"You know that demons can't be possessed."

"Maybe she was exchanged at birth!" Azrael straightened but kept his gaze locked on to Rosa.

"I was present during her birth! Azrael, enough of this. We're here for you to train her to use magic, not to make up conspiracy theories," the King said firmly, but the other demon just furrowed his eyebrows.

"Your Majesty, let's say that your daughter here is a genius. After all, most babies her age just babble without saying proper words. I'll concede that it is an amazing feat. But magic is a completely different matter. Even I, the most amazing magical prodigy, manifested my innate ability only at age three."

Quite a narcissist, this one, isn't he?

"Clearly you're no prodigy, then. Go on, Morrigan. Show him."

The Demon King sneered as he set Rosa in a darker corner of the room. She stared up at him.

You don't expect me to become a shadow again, do you? I'm not sure if I can even do it on demand.

But judging from his expression, it was exactly what he wanted.

"Your Majesty, really. Enough joking around. There's no way she could do it." Azrael shook his head. His scornful attitude reminded Rosa of her mother, who always belittled her, saying that she'd never accomplish anything.

I'll show him.

Rosa moved closer to the shadowy wall, as far away from light as possible. She tried to recall how it felt to become a shadow while ignoring the unpleasant memories of the attack.

"Aww, that's cute! She's actually trying." Azrael chuckled as he walked up to Rosa and crouched down near her, talking in a condescending voice. "Come on, just imagine melding into shadows."

I am a shadow, I am a shadow, I am a shadow!

When Rosa opened her eyes again, her vision had expanded. Everything was clearer, and the heaviness of her body disappeared. She glanced around and saw Azrael crouched in front of her, his jaw so wide she feared it might just fall off.

"I told you!" Alphegor cheered with such a beaming look of pride that Rosa would have blushed from embarrassment if she could.

"H-H-How?! She's a baby! Did you somehow do it, Your Majesty?" Azrael jumped up and waved his hands around frantically.

"You have no faith in your abilities anymore, Azrael? Wouldn't you have felt it if I had done something?"

"I certainly would have, but..." Azrael ruffled his hair, then stared at the spot on the wall where Rosa was hidden. "She's a baby."

"Imagine what she'll be able to do once she's an adult…" the Demon King purred with delight, a wide smile spreading across his face. Azrael gasped, and Rosa could see the cogs in his mind beginning to turn.

The tone of Alphegor's voice scared Morrigan as it felt almost bloodthirsty. She scrambled out of the shadow to gain a physical form again. Both demons gasped.

"She got out so easily…"

"I honestly hadn't expected that. I thought she would have trouble getting out on her own." Alphegor looked surprised, but then he hummed in satisfaction. "She's my daughter through and through."

"Your Majesty," Azrael said, bowing low, all traces of his earlier mockery gone. "May I request that you leave the magical training of your daughter to me?"

"You may. But remember this, Azrael—you must also protect her with your life, whether she's with you or not. Many will try to hurt her or take her power for themselves."

Azrael suddenly straightened and drew a large circle in the air with his hand. To Rosa's surprise, blue, glowing lines formed in the air where his fingers had been. He continued drawing an odd pattern in the air—like one of those ominous demon-summoning circles in anime.

"I, Azrael Ultimagi, swear an unbreakable oath—from this day forth, I shall protect Morrigan Nachtstern. I shall never do her harm and shall do everything in my power to help her develop her abilities."

The circle shrank down and floated towards Azrael. It went straight to his chest and then disappeared. The demon opened his shirt and revealed that the circle was now etched on the right side of his chest.

"Very well. Then I have nothing to worry about. I leave Morrigan in your care," Alphegor said, appearing satisfied, but Rosa noticed a mischievous glint in his eyes.

Did he plan this?

"Thank you, Your Majesty. I'll make her into the most powerful demon this world has ever seen."

Alphegor nodded and then left the room without another word. Rosa and Azrael watched him leave until the door slammed shut. Then they looked at each other awkwardly.

"So, I said... but even if you can use magic, you're still just a baby. How do I teach you anything?" Azrael muttered seemingly more to himself rather than to Rosa. "Hey, can you understand what I'm saying?"

Rosa nodded slightly. She didn't want to give him the impression that she was too competent, so she decided not to talk.

"Okay. Normally with my pupils, I push them to their absolute limit the first time to see what they are capable of." Azrael stroked his chin, then looked down at Rosa and grinned awkwardly. "But I don't think I can do that with you."

Rosa shook her head vigorously in response.

"Yeah, thought so. But I do need to know your limits somehow..." Azrael looked down at her, then shook his own head. "Nah, His Majesty will put my head on a pike if I make you feel even slightly uncomfortable."

A moment of silence stretched through the room as Azrael thought. Then he snapped his fingers, making Rosa flinch from the sudden noise.

"I got it. Show me how you became a shadow again," he said.

Shewas a little nervous about doing it again so soon, but nonetheless, Rosa waddled over to the wall, touched it, and imagined herself becoming a shadow. A second later, she once again became one with the darkness.

"Wonderful! Good job. Now, could you try moving to... let's say here." Azrael went further down the wall and slapped a spot a few meters away from Rosa.

I wonder what he's trying to accomplish.

She willed herself to move closer to him. The feeling was peculiar—it was as if she was sliding and gliding, yet at the same time, she had no weight, no gravity to pull her down and keep her grounded. Rosa reached Azrael much faster than she thought possible and had to force herself to a stop. The movement caused her to feel nauseated, and she unwittingly materialized out of the wall.

Rosa apparently had moved up the wall while in shadow form, and now gravity was mercilessly pulling her down into its embrace. She braced for impact, but Azrael swiftly caught her.

"Couldn't maintain the shadow form any longer?" he asked. Rosa shook her head and pressed her hands to her mouth, nausea still lingering.

"Oh! You're nauseous. I completely forgot about that. It's normal to feel that the first few times when you move as a shadow. It'll disappear the more you practice," Azrael assured her with a smile, but it did little to make her feel better.

I didn't feel like this when running from that assassin. Then again, that was a do-or-die kind of situation. Oh, dear, it's getting worse... I can't...

Rosa squirmed furiously, trying to break free from Azrael, but the demon held her tight.

"Hey, stop squirming! What's wrong with you suddenly?"

"Let... go..." Rosa uttered, but it was too late. The queasiness overtook her, and she emptied the contents of her stomach onto Azrael's shirt. The poor demon was so mortified that he just stood there stiff as a rock, holding Rosa at arm's length. His face looked like it was frozen in time—forever displaying his disgust and horror.

"Sorry..." Rosa muttered, unsure of how to save the situation. She had tried to get away from him, but he stubbornly held on. In a way, it was his own fault.

"Ghhhhhh..." was the only sound that came out of Azrael, and his eyes seemed to roll back into his skull.

"Sorry," Rosa said again, a bit louder.

If he hadn't sworn that oath not to do me harm, then I'm pretty sure I'd already be dead by now.

Azrael stretched out his arms, moving Rosa as far from him as possible, practically carrying her with his fingertips as he began walking. His movements were slow and stiff; it was clear he did not want any of the... *mess* to spread or drip. Slowly, step by step, they moved forward out of the training grounds and through the many castle corridors.

The servants they encountered stared in horror and scattered out of the way. The walk was long and embarrassing, and Rosa wished she had never tried to become a shadow again.

Great—first day with my magic teacher and I barfed on him. Now I'm sure he'll start searching for loopholes in his oath, if only so he won't risk being barfed on again.

<h1 style="text-align:center">Chapter 10</h1>

<h2 style="text-align:center">First Birthday</h2>

"No, no, no!" Rosa squirmed with all of her one-year-old might, desperately resisting Gunna's attempts to force her into the frilliest black-and-pink dress Rosa had ever seen in her life.

It was the day when Rosa had officially lived in this demonic kindgom for a whole year. Or in other words, her *second* first birthday.

"Lady Morrigan, please stay still. I understand that you're nervous, but we have to prepare for the party," the bearded nanny huffed after her twelfth attempt at putting on the dress was swatted away.

I'm sorry, Gunna. Normally, I wouldn't cause you trouble, but today is different. I have to avoid that party at any cost. All of those concubines are coming as well as some other important demons. I don't want one of them throwing a dagger in my face or slipping some poison in my food.

"No, no, no!" She flailed her tiny arms, continuing her tantrum.

"Is Morrigan ready?" Alphegor suddenly stormed into the room, wearing the most extravagant black, red, and golden suit Rosa had ever seen in her life. It solidified the fact that he was indeed a king.

"I'm sorry, Master Alphegor. Morrigan must be awfully nervous. She just doesn't want to get dressed." Gunna fumbled through her words, her hands trembling at the sight of the Demon King.

"That's unusual. Morrigan usually isn't one to cause trouble."

Alphegor squinted at the dwarven woman, then turned to Rosa, who puffed out her cheeks double the usual size.

"Come, let's get dressed and head to your party. I have invited the whole Demon Kingdom to celebrate!"

And that's exactly the problem! I don't want the whole Demon Kingdom to see me. I already have assassins sent by my gracious family trying to kill me. I don't need more people joining the list.

"No, no, no!" Rosa shook her head violently, having no intention of complying. Gunna looked absolutely helpless, just holding the unwanted dress in the air.

Alphegor chuckled, taking the dress from the nanny. "It'll be fine, little one. I'll be with you the whole time," he assured her.

Rosa paused, hesitating for a moment as she stared back at him. But Alphegor took this chance to swiftly pull the dress over her head.

"No!" Rosa gasped with indignation as she fixed a cold glare on him. Alphegor just chuckled in response and picked her up.

"Now we just need to do something about your hair. Stay still for a bit while I comb it," he said and grabbed the comb from the nearby dresser.

Rosa winced as the comb neared her hair, certain that the demon would pull out a good chunk of it in the process. But to her surprise, he started at the tips and then slowly moved his way up. Even Gunna seemed surprised by his gentleness.

"I never thought you'd be good at this sort of thing, Master Alphegor," the nanny said, voicing Rosa's thoughts.

"You forget that I have twenty-three daughters. Did you really think that I had never combed any of their hair?" he replied, but there was none of the usual sharpness in his voice.

"I—I'm honestly not sure..." Gunna stammered awkwardly and then handed Alphegor the hair ribbons that matched the horrid dress.

For a moment, Rosa considered making another scene, but curiosity got the better of her. She had to know—Could the Demon King actually tie ribbons in a girl's hair?

She felt him parting her hair into two sections, then gently pulling up half into a neat tail. After some fiddling, the ribbon was tied, and he moved on to the other side. Once that was done too, he moved towards the mirror to show his handiwork—two perfectly tied tiny twin-tails.

"Wow!" Rosa clapped, genuinely impressed. Many fathers fumbled with making girls' hair, and yet the big, bad Demon King himself did it flawlessly. Alphegor looked at her with a somewhat disgruntled expression, but it soon became more relaxed.

"Well, you're ready now. Let's go to your party!"

"No," Rosa whined quietly, praying that some unseen force might still rescue her.

* * *

What the hell is all of this?

Rosa stared in disbelief at the sight before her. For the first time since her birth in this world, Alphegor had brought her outside of the castle. It was still within the castle walls, of course, but she could see just how strange the Underworld's outside truly was. Endless sky was replaced with darkness. No stars, no moon, no light. The only light sources were the magical lamps set out within regular intervals throughout the yard, some larger to illuminate a wider area and some smaller for individual tables.

There were thousands of demons gathered outside, waiting for them to emerge from the castle. The moment the doors opened, a deafening wave of cheers erupted from the crowd. It was so loud Rosa nearly covered her ears.

The front yard—well, "yard" wasn't quite the right word—was a ginormous space spanning at least two football fields. It was filled with tables of various sizes, some smaller and intimate, others large enough to host entire groups. In the distance, Rosa noticed what seemed to be attraction areas, though they were too far away to make out clearly. There was no shortage of food or drinks, dishes piled almost on top of one another. But even with the seemingly never-ending number of tables, it still wasn't enough—leaving many demons milling about.

Much to Rosa's horror, she discovered that not all demons were as humanoid as Alphegor's concubines or Rosa's half-sisters. Further in the back, she could spot demons with bright red skin, large wings, disproportionately large limbs, and other odd features. Some even had more animalistic features like fluffy tails, ears, or animallike muzzles.

"I welcome all of my subjects to the grand celebration of my youngest daughter Morrigan's first birthday!" Alphegor's voice boomed through the yard, amplified by some magic, no doubt, and the crowd once again erupted into cheers. Rosa held on to his coat with trembling hands. She never had been able to handle crowds, and usually avoided any large gatherings. Yet, here she was—the center of attention of a massive crowd. A feeling of nausea began to creep into her stomach.

"Feast to your heart's content, my dear subjects, but remember that it's all possible thanks to the little demoness I hold in my arms." A cold warning slipped into the Demon King's voice, but the crowd still reacted with a loud cheer. Satisfied, Alphegor nodded and began descending down the castle stairs. When he reached the party area, dozens of concubines began swarming around him like wasps around rotten fruit.

"Your Majesty, let me congratulate the Princess on her birthday!"

"I've brought a special present for Her Highness, if you'd allow me..."

"No, Your Majesty, my present is far superior! I am sure the Princess would..."

"Silence," Alphegor commanded in a quiet but stern voice, and the buzzing ceased. Rosa still clung to him, wishing to all the holy beings she knew to be anywhere but here. "Morrigan will decide on her own which presents she will accept."

The concubines turned their gazes to Rosa, smiling sweetly while their eyes bore into her like poisonous needles.

Why me?

Rosa turned to Alphegor, hoping that he'd at least have the courtesy to listen to her request.

"Hungry..." she managed to squeak out. Her voice sounded unsteady, but she was only a baby so she could probably get away with that.

"Then we shall go eat!" Alphegor announced loudly, and the swarm of concubines parted, allowing the King to go to his designated table. Rosa could see their glares as they retreated and wondered how many of them planned to assassinate her. She shook her head at the unpleasant thought and instead focused on the food.

The Demon King's table obviously was the grandest table out of them all. It was surrounded by a dark hedge, effectively hiding them from the other guests. Alabaster statues stood in each corner of the hedge, and the table itself was filled with the best-looking foods, drinks, and desserts she had ever seen. In fact, it looked so good that Rosa could barely stop herself from salivating.

As they approached the table, she saw that there were already demons sitting by it. Four were concubines Rosa had met in the family gathering, accompanied by their daughters and Deziara included among them. Then there was Azrael and another older-looking male Demon. It was the first time Rosa had met a demon who did not look young. She didn't quite think of him as "old" since he had no gray hair like humans would get, but his skin wasn't as pristine and smooth, and there were small wrinkles at the corners of his eyes.

Rosa looked at Azrael guiltily after Alphegor sat down with her in his lap, but the demon just smiled at her without a hint of malice in his eyes. The four concubines made no effort to hide their disdain for Azrael but Rosa was just glad their malice wasn't directed at her.

I guess they can't glare at me since Alphegor is here.

"Happy birthday, Princess Morrigan. Here's my gift for you." Azrael pulled an ornate black-and-gold box from under the table and put it in front of Rosa. "You just have to pull the ribbon for it to open."

"How rude! His Majesty has barely sat down, and you've already opened your mouth without even greeting him first. As a matter of fact, by what merit are you even allowed to sit at this table?" the concubine with wavy, purple hair said incredulously while waving her black fan as if moving it faster could make Azrael disappear.

"Peace, Vivian. Azrael has sworn an oath to Morrigan so as her first subject, magic teacher and guard, he is allowed a spot at her birthday table," Alphegor explained, seemingly in too good a mood to reprimand the concubine in earnest.

"An oath?" all of the concubines echoed as one, their glares growing in intensity.

"That's right!" Azrael said as he nudged the gift closer. "So go ahead and open your present, Princess." Unsure of a better course of action, she reached out and pulled on the golden ribbon. The box opened with a soft pop, revealing a golden necklace with a bright red gem in its core. Another wave of gasps came from the concubines.

"A protection talisman?" Alphegor mused, lifting the talisman by its chain and watching as light reflected on its golden surface.

"Yup, one of the best ones I've ever made, Your Majesty. No physical attacks can harm the Princess if she's wearing it. It doesn't matter if it's arrows, fists, swords, or hammers. Heck, you could probably drop a mountain on her head, and she'd still be fine." Azrael chattered excitedly as he shot a knowing smirk at the concubines.

"Thank you..." Rosa muttered as Alphegor placed the talisman around her neck. It felt large and heavy at first, but then it shrank in size as if to fit Rosa specifically. She touched it in awe.

"It also adjusts its size to the wearer. I figured that might be useful since the Princess still has a lot of growing to do," Azrael announced proudly.

"That is an unusually considerate gift coming from you," said the older Demon. "I didn't think you were capable of that much fore-sight."

"You underestimate me, old Lucius. I can be very thoughtful when I want to be." There was a mischievous spark in Azrael's eyes, but Lucius just waved it away.

"Young Princess, allow me to introduce myself properly. I am Lucius Dammerung, His Majesty's right-hand man, and also the Prime Minister of the Underworld." Lucius stood up from his seat and bowed respectfully at Rosa.

Finally, somebody actually introduced themselves to me.

"Hello..." Rosa replied nervously.

"My, so the rumors are true—you're already capable of talking. It is most encouraging to have such a capable young Princess," Lucius said with a hint of amusement playing on his lips and then produced a box from his coat pocket. "I have also prepared a gift for you."

Alphegor took the little box and opened it in Rosa's stead, quickly breaking the ribbon. Inside was a small bluish-green gem.

"An alexandrite?" Alphegor asked. His pleased expression signaled that this was another good gift.

But what use does a baby have for jewels? Or even if I wasn't a baby, what would I do with them? It's not like collecting expensive trinkets will help me in any way. Although I suppose a bit of wealth wouldn't hurt.

"Yes, Your Majesty. Of the highest quality. Her Highness should be able to learn shapeshifting magic from it," Lucius explained proudly, and Rosa could hear Azrael scoff.

Learn magic from a gem? How does that work?

Rosa peered curiously at the crystal, but to her it looked like any normal gem.

"It might be too early for the Princess to learn new magic," Azrael protested somewhat meekly.

"With Morrigan's capabilities, I'm sure it won't take long. You'll make sure of that, won't you Azrael?" Alphegor smiled at the white-haired Demon, who swallowed hard, his previous nonchalance gone.

"Of course, Your Majesty. We'll be training hard," Azrael replied and shot Rosa a piteous look.

We're both in trouble, aren't we?

CHAPTER 11

KING'S PRESENT

"Your Majesty. We have also prepared gifts for Her Highness," the overly cute, pink concubine said sweetly while her daughter, dressed in equally pink attire, nervously held a pink satchel tied with bright gold ribbon.

That has to be poisoned, right? Or cursed?

Rosa eyed the satchel suspiciously while imagining what could be hiding within it. She got a feeling it wasn't chocolate chip cookies.

"Put your gifts on the gift table along with the others," Alphegor said dismissively, and Rosa sighed with relief.

"But, Your Majesty, we all worked so hard to pick the perfect present..." the concubine objected, but Alphegor silenced her with a bored wave of his hand.

"As did every other guest here. Your gifts will be opened later."

The pink demon girl gritted her teeth, and Rosa thought she would fling the satchel across the table. However, the girl managed to compose herself and instead exited the hedge-enclosed area, likely to probably deposit the gift along with the others—or throw it in the trash. Two other demon girls followed her, not including Deziara, who fidgeted from side to side, holding something behind her back.

She spoke up and slowly edged closer to them. "Father! I wish to g-give a gift to my s-sister now!" Alphegor appeared a bit annoyed but didn't outright dismiss the child.

"And why is that? I thought I made it clear that any gifts will be opened later." The question clearly caught the girl by surprise, and she looked down at her shoes, trembling slightly under Alphegor's scrutinous gaze.

"I l-left a bad impression on my sister when we first met. I wanted to remedy that, Father," she stammered. Rosa had a suspicion that her mother was the one who put her up to this, but on the other hand, she was just a child. It was sad to watch her tremble in fear in front of her own father. There was no need for Rosa to make matters more difficult, so she decided to act as an adult.

"I want to s-see my sister's gift," Rosa said, and Deziara's mother lit up with a victorious smile while the other concubines glared at her. Deziara also smiled and walked up to Rosa, revealing a teddy bear from behind her back. It was a gentle sandy color with a giant pink ribbon around its neck and round button eyes.

"Cute," Rosa said before she could stop herself and reached out towards the teddy. This place severely lacked cute things, so the plushie appeared out of place. But it also felt like such a normal, human gift. It reminded her of Earth.

"Well... as long as Morrigan likes it." Alphegor sighed, clearly not agreeing with her sentiment. Deziara, on the other hand, blushed from the compliment and quickly retreated back to her mother.

"Thank you," Rosa said, and Deziara nodded.

I know you're probably only trying to get into Alphegor's good graces, but I still appreciate the gift.

"Alright. With gifts out of the way, let's begin the feast!" Alphegor announced, and all the adults around the table picked up their wine glasses while the girls picked up their juice glasses. "May Morrigan live long and grow strong!"

Alphegor's voice was once again loud and booming, reverberating throughout the area. Cheers erupted from behind the hedge, and Alphegor finished the drink in one swift swig. The concubines and girls each took a small sip of their drinks, while Azrael and Lucius also finished their drinks, albeit with less gusto than the King.

"Now, tell me, Princess. What would you like to eat?" Azrael moved his chair closer and bent forward to be as close to Rosa as possible. His smile was radiant, almost blinding.

Gosh, haven't you ever heard of such a thing as personal space?

Rosa tried not to admire his handsome features.

And why do all demons have to be so good-looking?

"Back off, Azrael. I'll be the one to feed my daughter!" Alphegor growled and began piling dish after dish on Rosa's tiny plate. Rosa helplessly stared as the pile grew larger and larger.

"Your Majesty," Lucius interjected before the pile could topple over. "I don't think the Princess will be able to eat so much."

"I'm just making sure she has plenty of options to choose from," Alphegor interjected, pushing the towering plate closer to Rosa. "Go on, choose whatever you desire."

Rosa took the small fork placed in front of her and then just stabbed it into the thing closest to her. She couldn't quite focus on what she had picked up as all four women at the table were glaring daggers at her. But before the food made it to her mouth, she recoiled—liver.

Out of all things, why does it have to be liver? I hate liver!

"It seems His Majesty doesn't know the Princess' tastes too well," Azrael laughed. Alphegor glared at him, and Rosa wondered if she should eat the liver just to avoid the Demon King's rage. It wouldn't be directed at her, but she still didn't want anyone to suffer on her behalf.

She glanced at the liver again, hoping it might at least look more appetizing than she remembered. While it had some fancy glaze and was cut in a more pleasant round shape, at its core, it was still liver.

"I am sure the Princess was just surprised by its great flavor. Just give her a moment, and I'm sure she'll eat the leviathan liver without any issues," said the blonde concubine with a short bob, and she smiled pleasantly at Rosa.

Leviathan liver? This came from a monster!?

Rosa resisted the urge to gag and throw it into the bush.

"I am sure that is the case," Alphegor agreed and watched her with hopeful eyes. Now her back was truly against a metaphorical wall. She gulped and stared at the unappetizing piece on her fork.

I don't want to eat this...

She slowly brought the liver closer to her lips, trying to imagine that it was just a tough piece of pork.

"What are you two talking about? It's her birthday! She should be eating desserts, not liver," Azrael exclaimed, putting a dark chocolate cupcake in front of her.

Yes, my savior! I owe you one.

Rosa grabbed the cupcake without any hesitation, abandoning the sad piece of liver, and took a bite before anybody could object. The flavor was rich but not overly sweet—a perfect chocolate dessert.

"I suppose you're right in that regard," Alphegor begrudgingly admitted and then snapped his fingers. A servant materialized right next to him the very next second, making Rosa flinch from their sudden entrance.

"Yes, Your Majesty?" the demon servant asked solemnly.

"Bring the birthday cake!" he ordered with a self-satisfied smirk.

Somehow, I have a bad feeling about this.

The servant disappeared after a curt nod. For a moment, everything seemed peaceful, but then she heard some low rumbling, like a heavy vehicle driving on a road.

"Let's go and see it," Alphegor said, picking Rosa up. The others around the table followed, eyes full of curiosity. As they exited the hedged space, Rosa's jaw dropped open. On a giant platform with wheels, there stood a cake the size of a small house. Each layer was at least three times larger than Rosa and decorated with utmost care. Everyone gaped at the giant marvel, unable to comprehend the absurdity of its size.

How do you even bake something this big? There's no oven to fit this thing into. Did they just combine a bunch of smaller cakes into a huge one? Or perhaps only part of it is edible?

"Your Majesty, this cake..." Lucius pointed at it while desperately trying to keep his expression under control. But Rosa saw how his eyelid twitched.

"Magnificent, isn't it?" Alphegor laughed proudly. "Big enough so every citizen of the Demon Kingdom can have a slice."

Rosa saw how the Prime Minister was doing mathematics in his head as he examined the cake from top to bottom, his expression hardening.

"I'm sorry to say this, Your Majesty, but even with a cake of this size, there still wouldn't be enough to provide a slice to every citizen of the Demon Kingdom."

That much was obvious—no cake, not even this monstrosity, could feed an entire kingdom. Rosa had no idea how large the Demon Kingdom was but assumed it had to be at least as large as the country where she had come from.

"But it should be more than enough to provide for all the guests, no?" Alphegor retorted and waved towards the crowds of demons packed into the castle yard. They cheered in response, equally horrified and awestruck by the giant birthday cake.

"Now, then, Morrigan. Why don't you do the honor of cutting the first slice?" The Demon King looked down at her, and at the same moment, a servant appeared with a dull-looking knife in hand. Alphegor took it and then held the handle towards Rosa.

She nervously reached out to the knife, fully expecting to drop it to the ground, but Alphegor kept his hold on it and guided it towards the cake alongside Rosa. There was a warm feeling in her gut as they cut the cake together. It slid smoothly down the soft, spongy dessert, and they ended up with a small, neat square piece of rich-looking red velvet cake.

The crowd erupted into cheers again, and Rosa couldn't help but flush. All this fuss because of her birthday.

Nobody on Earth ever cared much for my birthdays. Sure, my parents would set up a celebration when I was younger, and they'd buy me cake, but it was more out of obligation rather than actual care for me. And once I started showing interest in art, those celebrations ended.

Rosa shook her head—there was no guarantee that these parties would continue when she got older. Currently, she was just a novelty, an oddly clever baby with vast magical potential. Once Alphegor realized that she would not become his perfect demon heir, he would undoubtedly be just as disappointed as Rosa's mother.

"Hey, what's that?" Alphegor suddenly pointed towards the spot they had just sliced into, breaking Rosa out of her thoughts. Something red glinted deeper inside the cake, but it didn't match the rest. The color was smoother and shinier. It reminded her of scales.

Rosa looked quizzically up at Alphegor, and saw a mischievous glint in his eyes, his lips curling up in a restrained smile.

Oh, he must have hidden his gift inside the cake. I wonder what it is.

"Present?" Rosa asked him, and the crowd cheered at her guess.

"Young Princess is so smart!"

"She can already speak, it's amazing!"

"Truly the daughter of our majestic king!"

The crowd kept praising her, and Alphegor hummed with satisfaction.

"Yes, a present from me to my dearest daughter!" Alphegor announced in his booming voice for everyone to hear. Multiple servants scurried over and began methodically cutting the cake and placing the slices onto plates, thus slowly digging out the present underneath.

Rosa watched with bated breath as more and more of... something was revealed, but she couldn't understand what it was exactly. It was just red, shimmering, and scaly.

Perhaps it was just a container for the present. He probably wouldn't have wanted to ruin it with cream and icing.

Slowly, more of the present emerged until, finally, two servants grabbed hold of a giant red egg and put it in front of Rosa and Alphegor.

"Egg?" Rosa asked.

Certainly, an unusual choice of container for a present, but it is pretty.

"Not just any egg! This is the egg of a fire dragon," Alphegor announced proudly. A stunned silence swept over the crowd until Azrael began clapping, rousing the crowd from their stupor. Slowly, they began to cheer, although it felt much more forced than before.

"Your Majesty, don't you think a dragon egg is a bit much?" Lucius whispered as he leaned closer to the king. "Couldn't it cause some repercussions from the dragons?"

"Hahaha! There's nothing to worry about. I'll make sure that no dragon dares to step foot into the Demon Kingdom." Alphegor laughed like a madman while Rosa stared at the egg, pale as a sheet.

She didn't know much about dragons, but between the stories she read before coming to Doppelta and the ones Faenor read to her, she knew they weren't exactly friendly. They were usually described as vicious beasts guarding hordes of gold, stealing princesses, and burning down cities as if it were as natural as breathing.

He just wants that dragon to eat me as soon as it hatches!

"Is this the offspring of that dragon I killed?" Azrael mused loudly as he bent down to inspect the egg closely.

"Indeed, it is. And it'll be your task to make sure that the hatchling obeys Morrigan," Alphegor announced with sly satisfaction. Now, Azrael looked just as pale as Rosa despite his dark skin color.

"Wait... me?"

"Yes, you. You're the one who killed the dragon, so it only makes sense that you clean up after your own mess."

How did Azrael's punishment become my birthday gift?

Rosa glared at the white-haired Demon, who just sighed in exasperation.

"I knew you wouldn't just let that go. I just hoped that swearing an oath to the princess would have been enough to appease you."

"Clearly, you don't know me very well then, Azrael," Alphegor replied with a smirk and then retreated back to the celebration table. Rosa just prayed that she wouldn't have to open any more presents.

CHAPTER 12

AFTERMATH

You have to be kidding me...

Rosa stared at the giant mountain of gifts with a mixture of awe and fear. Gunna and Faenor wore matching looks of astonishment.Azrael, on the other hand, looked utterly bored and uninterested, instead prodding at his nails.

The grand birthday party was over, and all the gifts and presents that had been received were brought to an empty room near Alphegor's bed chambers after passing a thorough inspection by the castle staff. Although only the most obviously dangerous gifts had been disposed of, there could still be some nasty surprises inside.

"Do we have to look through all of them?" Faenor asked as his face drained of color.

"His Majesty said that we're to inspect every gift that Lady Morrigan wishes to open," the nanny said, and both looked down at her.

"Alright, let me do the check so I can leave and do actually important things," Azrael grumbled, walking up to the giant pile of gifts and waving his hand. Five boxes floated out of the pile. Their wrappings burned away, revealing five creepy-looking objects—a dagger emanating a dark aura, a black rose, a bracelet made from teeth, a necklace with a tiny vial that seemed to contain blood, and a rattle made out of tiny bones.

What are those creepy-looking things? I never thought an object could be evil but those definitely do feel evil.

"Are those—" Gunna gasped, and made an odd gesture with her hands, something similar to a cross.

"Yeah, totally cursed," he said nonchalantly, and the items burst into flames. Initially, the flames were normal, but then they turned to a sinister black color until the creepy things burned away without leaving even so much as a speck of ash behind.

"W-What would have happened if Lady Morrigan had opened them?" Gunna asked with a trembling voice.

"Hard to say. Probably nothing too horrible since she is the Demon King's daughter. But it might have been... unpleasant."

I bet it would have been more than unpleasant. No, I am done with this. I do not want to open another present in my lifetime.

Rosa shook her head and turned around to leave the room. Much to her dismay, Gunna instantly panicked and blocked her way.

"Lady Morrigan, how about we look at a few of the gifts? Now that Master Azrael has made sure that there is nothing dangerous inside, we can open them without worry," the dwarf woman said with a smile, although her voice sounded shaky.

Could it be that Gunna was ordered to open the present by Alphegor? I imagine if none of the presents get opened then Gunna and Faenor would get into trouble. I'll pray that the oath Azrael made is enough to protect me.

"Yeah, do that. Wake me up when you're finished," Azrael said and with a snap of his fingers, a couch appeared in the corner of the room. He laid down on it and closed his eyes with not a care in the world.

With a sigh, Rosa waddled back into the room and inspected the giant pile. Normally, she'd be happy to receive gifts for her birthday, and on Earth, she treasured every gift that she had received even if she wasn't close to the gifter anymore. But with this many, they had completely lost their appeal, even if she disregarded the possibly that cursed items could still be hidden somewhere in the pile.

A gift wrapped in dark green paper and an aquamarine band around it caught Rosa's attention. She approached it and saw Gunna's smile grow wider.

"From Gunna?" Rosa asked and pointed at the gift.

"Yes, that one is from me. How did you know? Lady Morrigan is indeed very smart," the nanny praised and went to open the ribbon tied to the package. It wasn't difficult to deduce that it was from her. After all, it was the only gift with a gentle color scheme. Well, this one and another, which Rosa assumed to be from Faenor.

Once the ribbon was undone, Gunna handed the present to Rosa, who swiftly tore the paper off. Inside was a long scarf in a beautiful verdant green. The color looked so odd in this mostly dark place, but it was so refreshing and vibrant that Rosa instantly hugged the scarf close to her chest.

"Thank you, Gunna," Rosa said, trying not to sniffle.

"Aww, it was just something I made in my spare time. I—I never expected you'd like it so much, L-Lady Morrigan," the nanny said and began crying. This broke Rosa, and she too began crying. Gunna hurriedly picked her up, and both of them wailed momentarily.

"You two are being a bit dramatic." Faenor sighed, but gave them a few minutes to calm down.

"You're just impatient because you want Lady Morrigan to open your present too," Gunna teased him as she wiped away the tears.

"N-No! I am perfectly capable of waiting!" the elf retorted, crossing his arms over his chest.

But you never denied that you wanted me to open the gift.

Rosa waddled over to the other colorful gift, which was in a pale lilac package with a bright violet ribbon.

Rosa tugged at the ribbon, which slipped off effortlessly, as did the wrapping. Underneath was an unusual, somewhat shabby-looking book.

"Faenor, what kind of a gift is that? Certainly, you could have done better!" Gunna pressed her arms against her hips and looked at Faenor incredulously.

"For your information, this book is extremely rare and extremely valuable. I've had quite a hard time finding it," Faenor replied with a puff. "It contains information about all of the known magical stones in our world."

Magical stones? Like the alexandrite gifted by Lucius? I wonder what exactly they can do.

Rosa reached up to touch the stone embedded in the protection talisman hanging around her neck. She wondered if it was also magical.

"We can look through it during our next story time," Faenor promised, and Rosa nodded enthusiastically.

"Thank you!" Rosa held the book close, wondering what could be written inside it.

The nanny sighed and conceded. "As long as you like it, Lady Morrigan. Now which gift shall we open next?"

Oh, right... There were other gifts...

* * *

A few hours of intensive gift opening later, Rosa, Gunna, and Faenor had barely made a dent in the giant mountain of wrapped boxes. They had unpacked clothes, both adult-sized and child-sized, a plethora of plushies that depicted one monster or another, shoes of every size and shape imaginable, books of all genres, and fabrics of every color. There was even a live bird in one of the presents which had flown away as soon as the box was opened. Rosa was just grateful that the poor little creature had survived.

Azrael snoozed away happily the whole time, not a care in the world. It made Rosa annoyed that the one person who could probably unpack all these gifts in a few minutes was sleeping.

"Too many..." Rosa muttered, her little hands tired from unwrapping and ripping all of the paper and packaging.

"We'll never get through all of them on our own..." Faenor agreed as he grimaced at the remaining gifts with unhidden disgust.

"Yes, I thought we could make decent progress today, but there are far too many," the nanny agreed with a grim nod.

Why do I even need to open all of these gifts on my own? I know that they're meant for me, but it's not like the people, or demons, who gifted them actually know me. They only gave me these for Alphegor's sake.

"No more presents," Rosa grumbled to her caretakers and waddled towards the door. Gunna caught up to her and picked her up.

"Yes, that's enough for one day."

As everyone was about to turn and leave the gifts alone for the day, Morrigan heard some odd noise come from the pile. She stopped and listened.

"What is it, Lady Morrigan?" the nanny asked, noticing Rosa's odd reaction.

"Some noise," she said and pointed at the presents. The dwarf and elf both stopped and listened carefully. A quiet chirp came from one of the boxes and all three of them looked at each other with horror.

"Somebody has stuffed a bird inside one of these!" Faenor gasped, his face contorted in shock and anger. Rosa also felt a furious bubble rise within her. Who in their right mind would put a live creature inside a box?

demons, that's who. Why am I even surprised?

She followed the chirping sound, and then deduced it came from a rather small box wrapped in dark blue paper. Rosa tore it off without a second thought and opened it. Inside, a distressed golden bird fluttered anxiously. The moment it saw the lid open, it took flight and darted through an open window before anybody could react.

Will it be alright out there? I don't think the Underworld is the right place for a bird to live.

"What if somebody has put another live creature in their gift box?" Faenor suddenly said with a pained expression. Rosa's heart clenched. It was so sad seeing the poor bird trapped in that box. She had wanted to feed it and give it something to drink, but the poor thing was already gone, and there was no way of getting it back.

"But we can't just sit here opening gifts all day. Lady Morrigan is already tired," Gunna objected, but her eyes were downcast, showing that she didn't want to abandon whatever poor animal may or may not be trapped within the many boxes. Rosa thought for a second, her gaze wandering to the white-haired demon sleeping on the couch.

It's about time this guy did some work.

"Azrael," Rosa said, startling both of her caretakers out of their glum thoughts.

Azrael didn't react, instead just continuing his nap. Rosa went up to him and poked him mercilessly in his stomach. The demon woke up with a sputter and glared at her.

"What?" he said, voice filled with annoyance at the interruption.

Rosa glared at him, then pointed towards the remaining mountain of gifts.

"Help open." She kept her speech simplistic so as not to arouse any suspicion of her intelligence. The demon laughed.

"No way! I'm a magic teacher and a guard, not a servant. Besides, I already got rid of all the cursed items. What else do you want?" Azrael said, rejecting her request with a smug grin on his face. Gunna's lip quivered, and it appeared she wanted to say something but couldn't find the courage to do so.

"Open," Rosa persisted and pointed towards the gifts again.

"Sorry, Princess. I am not obliged to comply with your requests," he teased, with a wide grin. He was waiting for Rosa to start crying and throw a tantrum. If she were an actual baby, she would have no doubt done just that.

"I tell Father," Rosa stated flatly, and the temperature in the room got noticeably colder.

"Nice try, kid. But I won't be intimidated by a baby," Azrael sneered, but Rosa noticed that there was a bead of sweat forming on his forehead.

So, despite his nonchalant attitude, he is afraid of the king. That will work in my favor.

"Lady Morrigan, perhaps we could just continue unpacking another day?" Gunna finally cut in, finding the courage to speak.

"Help, or I call Father," Rosa repeated and adopted the icy expression she'd seen the Demon King use.

"Alright then, call your daddy!" Azrael waved his hand dismissively. He undoubtedly thought that the demon king wouldn't just come at the beck and call of his one-year-old daughter. Honestly, Rosa didn't think he would come either and hoped that Azrael would have been more cooperative.

Oh, well. It's worth a shot...

"Father!" she shouted, her voice coming out so loud it surprised even herself as it projected throughout the hallways of the castle.

How did I do that? It seems similar to the way Alphegor speaks when addressing a large crowd.

Before she could ponder the question any further, a large, dark shadow appeared before her, and out of it rose the Demon King himself.

He really did come.

Alphegor emerged with the biggest, goofiest grin on his face. He instantly bent down and grabbed Rosa into a bear hug.

"My darling daughter called me 'Father' for the first time. I am overjoyed! What do you need, little one?"

Silence stretched for an awkwardly long time as everyone stared at the Demon King in utter disbelief.

M-My darling?

"Your Majesty, are you quite alright?" Azrael asked, breaking the silence. His face pinched into a somewhat awkward grin as he slowly, step by step, neared the exit.

"Azrael no help," Rosa said before the demon could run away. Alphegor's expression instantly grew as cold as ice, and the temperature in the room dropped even further. Only this time, it wasn't metaphorical—Rosa could see Azrael's breath forming in the frigid air, while Gunna and Faenor began to shiver.

"Really now?" Alphegor said in a sweet tone that didn't match his icy glare.

"I—I just said I couldn't do it now since I have to..." Azrael trailed off as ice crystals began forming around his feet. "What I mean to say i-is that I'll be glad to help!"

"Excellent!" The king's expression turned pleasantly warm, and the cold instantly disappeared from the room. "See that it's done as Morrigan demands. I'll be finding out all the details later."

"Of course, Your Majesty," Azrael said with a forced smile as he shook off the thick layer of frost that had formed on his feet.

Alphegor patted Rosa on her head once, then handed her to Gunna and disappeared back into the shadows.

"You little brat..." Azrael muttered quietly. Rosa decided to just take the win and ignore his comment.

"So, which should we start with?" Azrael grumbled and skulked over to the mountain, grabbing a random gift and throwing it up and down in the air.

"Find animal," Rosa commanded.

"Animal? Why would there be animals here?" Azrael scoffed, but Faenor stepped forward, gathering his courage to speak.

"We previously found a bird inside one of the presents. The Princess is afraid there might be more animals trapped inside."

Azrael regarded the elf like a mosquito that had dared to bite him, then turned his focus on Rosa and sighed.

"I suppose it wouldn't be nice if they died and their corpses began stinking up the place." His purple eyes lit up, and he carefully looked over the pile of gifts. He then waved his hands, and some of the presents began floating around the room and rearranging themselves.

After a minute or two of sorting, one smaller box floated to Azrael's hands.

"This is the only live creature I could find," he said in a cold voice, and then the box burst into flames.

"Wha—" Rosa gasped in horror. The creature inside shrieked in pain as it was burned alive in a matter of seconds.

"I'm sorry, Princess, but this creature is not friendly. It is without a doubt that somebody sent this in an attempt to harm you."

"What creature was that?" Faenor dared to ask.

"A soul worm," Azrael said coldly.

What the hell is a soul worm? On second thought, I'd rather not know. It sounds more sinister than those cursed objects.

Rosa shivered and decided that she wasn't going to open any more of the birthday presents anytime soon.

CHAPTER 13

EVENING WITH THE KING

"Today was a busy day, wasn't it Lady Morrigan?" Gunna chimed as she gently scrubbed Rosa's arms with a sponge.

"Mhm," Rosa muttered, absentmindedly bursting a soap bubble with her tail. She was becoming better at controlling it but still found no practical use for it. The tail was too weak to hold things and was not very attractive either, like a rat's tail with a pointy end.

Her mood was somewhat gloomy since Azrael had found all those cursed objects and the soul worm among her presents. She still didn't quite understand what exactly the soul worm did, but from the whispering and muttering among Faenor and Gunna, she had gathered that it could cripple one's cognitive ability beyond repair. To think she had almost come in contact with such a horrifying creature.

The bathroom door swung open, and Alphegor strode in, wearing his usual evening garb—a simple black shirt and gray pants. Despite their simplicity, the Demon King still managed to look regal and dignified.

"Good evening, Master Alphegor," Gunna greeted him with a bow, and he acknowledged her presence with a curt nod.

"You may go for today."

"But what about Lady Morrigan's bath?" the nanny asked nervously.

"I'll finish it myself."

His gaze left no room for questions, so Gunna bowed and quickly excused herself. Rosa watched Alphegor quizzically, wondering why he was here. He hadn't overseen the bathing process in some time— not since Gunna had corrected her initial mishap of overfilling the bath and nearly drowning her.

Alphegor walked over to the baby bath that was set down next to the larger tub and got down on his knees.

"Is the water warm, Morrigan?" he asked with a somewhat bittersweet smile and dipped his hand inside the soapy water.

"Warm," Rosa confirmed and carefully studied his expression. She couldn't tell what he was thinking, but it seemed like there was a lot on his mind.

Even the Demon King has some worries.

Alphegor absentmindedly grabbed the sponge and began wiping Rosa's back. He was surprisingly gentle, not daring to press too hard. His eyes seemed to be filled with sadness, and she began feeling sorry for him.

I wonder what happened to make him feel so down. Maybe I should lighten the mood a bit.

She thought that but she wasn't exactly sure how to cheer a demon up. Without any good ideas in mind, she flicked her tail and sprayed a mixture of soap, suds, and water on Alphegor's face. The Demon King froze, but before he could properly process what had happened, she sprayed him again.

Now, that's something not many people can get away with.

"You little rascal," Alphegor growled and mercilessly covered Rosa with the bubbles from head to toe. She flailed in protest, trying to shake the suds off, but there were too many. Before she could begin to panic, the king unceremoniously dumped warm water over her head, washing the suds away.

"Bully..." Rosa muttered in her human tongue, not knowing the word in the Demon language. The Demon King just laughed and then pulled her out of the water, wrapping her up in a soft towel.

"Time for you to go to bed," Alphegor said, and carried her to the bedroom still wrapped in a towel.

"No sleep," Rosa protested. Ever since she had started sleeping in Alphegor's room, her bedtime had also become much earlier since she couldn't just pretend to be asleep until Gunna left. Alphegor was always in his room in the evenings and never left no matter how long she pretended to be asleep. Mostly, he would just do some paperwork by his desk until he decided to go to sleep.

"Yes, sleep," he objected sternly and put her on the bed. With smooth, gentle motions, he began drying her hair which she didn't resist.

"Not sleepy."

"Today was a long day. You should rest." The sad note returned to his voice, although his expression remained unreadable as he dressed Rosa in pajamas. "Need to potty first?"

Rosa shook her head furiously. Thankfully, diapers were a thing of the past, but she was still uncomfortable that somebody always insisted on being around when she went to do her business. She understood why they did it, of course, but that didn't mean she liked it.

"I went!"

"Good girl." Alphegor ruffled her hair and then grabbed a brush to untangle the mess he just made. Rosa observed as the demon carefully brushed her hair. His face was a cold, stoic mask—almost unreadable. Upon closer inspection, she noticed that the corners of his lips were slightly downcast, his eyes squinted ever so slightly and his fingers tense around the brush.

"Something wrong?" she ventured to ask, and Alphegor flinched slightly. After a moment, he chuckled.

"You're a sharp little one. You know that, Morrigan? Sometimes it feels like you're an adult already."

Rosa's heart skipped a beat.

He doesn't know, does he? Did I give it away by talking too much? I shouldn't have been so impatient!

"And yet, you are so fragile. Somebody could have seriously injured you today..." The Demon King sighed, sat down, and put Rosa into his lap. She looked up at him as he wrapped his large hand around hers. Both of her tiny arms completely disappeared within his grasp.

"You are still so small. So weak. So fragile." He spoke somewhat absentmindedly.

No, it doesn't seem like it. I'm just being paranoid. He was just worried about those cursed items.

"I'm strong!" she objected and puffed out her cheeks, trying to appear braver than she actually was.

Alphegor laughed loudly, then fell onto his back and lifted Rosa high above him. It was odd looking down on this powerful, tall Demon.

"Of course, you're strong! And one day, you'll be the strongest demon alive," he announced loudly, then put Rosa onto his chest and bopped her nose with his finger. "And I'll make sure nobody hurts you until that day comes."

Rosa watched Alphegor as he lay there. For a moment, he looked vulnerable—almost human. Despite the horns on his head, and the long tail that lay limp on the bed, he seemed like a...

"Father?"

"What is it, little one?" Alphegor lifted his head and looked at her, his gaze soft and gentle. Something warm and fuzzy swelled in Rosa's chest, but she couldn't understand what it was. She had never felt anything like this before.

"Let's sleep," she murmured softly.

"Good girl!" He ruffled her hair again, albeit more gently, and pulled the silky covers over them. After a few minutes, they were both sound asleep in complete peace and silence.

* * *

When Rosa opened her eyes the next morning, Alphegor was already gone, and Gunna was dutifully sitting in a chair next to the bed, waiting for Rosa to wake.

"Good morning, Lady Morrigan," the nanny chimed, a bright smile sticking out from behind her beard.

"Morning," Rosa half-mumbled, half-yawned in response.

"Let's get you ready for the day." Thus began their morning ritual—wash face and hands, dress up, comb hair, eat some porridge with odd but tasty fruit, and play. Rosa could have done without the last bit, but she indulged the nanny to keep up her baby appearance.

After an hour, there was a knock on the door, and Gunna visibly flinched at the noise.

"It is time for your magic lesson..." the nanny said awkwardly as she picked Rosa up. Another impatient knock resounded on the door, so Gunna quickened her stride to open it.

"G-Good morning, Master Azrael."

"You're too slow, slave!" Azrael's eyes looked like dark, angry thunderclouds.

All because Gunna didn't answer the door the moment you knocked?

"Childish," Rosa muttered at the demon whose gaze snapped to her. It instantly lost some of its ferocity, and instead, he appeared mildly annoyed.

"What's childish?" he demanded.

"You," Rosa retorted, crossing her tiny arms over her chest. Azrael narrowed his eyes.

"Slaves need to respond instantly."

"Gunna nanny, not a slave."

"She may be your nanny, but she is also a slave."

"You slave." This childish response forced Azrael to take a step back.

"I'm not a slave. I'm the second strongest demon in the Underworld!" He puffed out his chest and struck a pose as if posing for a portrait.

"Gunna, what is 'second?'" Rosa asked innocently and saw how Azrael's face turned bright red from anger.

It's a good thing he's sworn an oath not to do me harm. Otherwise, I might not get away with this.

"Oh, well..." the nanny stammered, unsure of how to respond.

"Let's just go to your lesson," Azrael snarled and snatched Rosa from Gunna's grasp. His hold was firm, but not tight enough to hurt her. He stomped furiously towards the training room while Rosa delighted in his sour mood.

"Smile while you can, brat. We'll see how you'll manage to keep your breakfast in while walking as a shadow," Azrael snickered.

Is this supposed to be an adult demon? He acts no better than a pompous seven-year-old.

Rosa had no intention of complying with Azrael on that day. In fact, she wanted to get the whole magic training out of the way as quickly as possible then spend some time reading the book Faenor had found for her. It could help her understand magic better because she didn't have much hope that this demon would begin by explaining the basics of magic.

"Alright, squirt. Let's begin your training. Turn into a shadow," Azrael commanded as soon as they stepped inside the training grounds, putting Rosa unceremoniously down on her bum. But she wasn't dismayed and instead put her plan into motion.

Instead of complying with his demands, she cocked her head to the side and pretended not to understand him. "Play?"

"What? Where did you get that from? No, we are training. Turn into a shadow," Azrael said impatiently, pointing at the wall. Rosa just blinked at him, pretending not to understand a word.

"You know... like you did the last time? Shadow? Wall? Turn into a shadow!" he insisted, gesturing towards the wall as if he were playing some sort of a guessing game. He looked so funny in his desperate attempts that Rosa barely contained a laugh.

"Shadow? What is a shadow?"

Azrael groaned and hit his head with his palm, sliding it down his face dramatically.

Pretending to be a fool is more fun than I expected. I should have done this the first time around.

"Alright, alright. I'll show you. You—repeat!" Azrael went up to the wall and then disappeared into the darkness. After a moment, he reemerged.

"You saw that, right? Now you do it."

"What's that?" Rosa pointed at the dummies on the other side of the room and began waddling over in their direction. Azrael grabbed her before she could get too far.

"No, we aren't playing with the dummies. You need to train your magic. Turn into a shadow." His eyelid twitched as he barely managed to keep himself under control. Or perhaps the oath was doing its work already.

"Magic? Show magic!" Rosa cheered, throwing her hands up in fake excitement. Azrael groaned, placed Rosa on the floor, and then crouched down while clutching his head in his hands.

That's what you get for bullying Gunna. Nobody will call her a slave under my watch!

The door to the training grounds swung open, and Alphegor strode in, followed by a few male demon servants who carried some books and documents in their hands.

"How's the training today?" the king asked, addressing Azrael, who straightened the second the door opened.

"Not good, I'm afraid, Your Majesty. Princess Morrigan is just too young to understand what she's supposed to do," Azrael explained calmly.

"What exactly did she not understand?"

"I asked her to become a shadow again, but she wouldn't do it no matter how many times I repeated the request. Instead, she thought we were playing."

"Really? Morrigan, would you mind becoming a shadow again?" Alphegor asked with a sort of satisfied smirk. It was like he knew that Rosa would do as he requested. Normally, she wouldn't agree so readily, but she felt like bullying Azrael a little bit.

She went up to the wall, took a deep breath, and thought about becoming darkness, about her vision expanding and the heaviness of her body disappearing. The next moment, she was part of the dark wall. The servants next to Alphegor gasped in shock and awe.

"Young Princess is already able to turn into a shadow? That is most amazing, Your Majesty!"

"Of course!" Alphegor said with his chest puffed out proudly as he walked up to the wall. Rosa materialized right into his arms while shooting a knowing smirk at Azrael, who was turning red from anger.

"You little... You did understand me!" Azrael pointed angrily at Rosa.

"Azrael rude," Rosa stated simply.

"What? Is this still about that slave?"

"What slave?" Alphegor asked.

"The dwarf woman. Who even cares about some slaves?"

"Morrigan does. Gunna is her nanny, so obviously, she wouldn't want her to be belittled." Alphegor paused and then sighed. "I might have overestimated your abilities. Although your magical knowledge is on par with the greatest of demons, your manners haven't evolved past those of a twelve-year-old."

Alphegor turned on his heel and began walking out of the training grounds.

"But the lesson..." Azrael called out helplessly from behind.

"I think you need lessons in manners first before you teach my daughter," Alphegor replied, and Rosa stuck out her tongue at Azrael.

That'll teach you.

CHAPTER 14

BASICS OF MAGIC

Having successfully ditched Azrael's magic lessons, Rosa was now comfortably situated next to Faenor in the far corner of the castle's library. As was proper for every library within a castle, it was grand, spanning three floors and a space large enough to contain hundreds of thousands of books. All the bookshelves were neatly lined and dusted by demon maids on a regular basis. Meanwhile, the many librarians cared that no book would ever be out of place, diligently returning them back to their rightful place when not in use.

When they first entered, the librarians regarded Faenor with looks of disdain, but upon noticing Rosa in his hands, their gazes completely switched to her. They continued sneaking curious glances at her. They were trying to be subtle, but Morrigan still felt herself being watched at every step.

It should be fine. These are just librarians and maids. They are curious about the Demon King's youngest daughter. That's it.

Rosa tried to keep calm. She knew that Alphegor would come the moment she shouted for him, but the fact that so many eyes were on her again made her uncomfortable.

The people who sent me those cursed items couldn't be among them, right? No, I'm just being paranoid. These people are just simple workers and stand to gain nothing from hurting me.

"Lady Morrigan?" Faenor broke her out of her thoughts.

"Huh?" She blinked at him.

"I said we don't have to worry about being noisy here. The barriers in the library are completely soundproof. Unless somebody crosses the barrier, you can be as loud as you want," the elf explained and pointed towards the gentle gray lines stretching around the little reading area Faenor had picked out.

I'm so glad that Faenor always takes the time to explain things to me. Without him, I wouldn't know half the things I now know about this world.

"Wow!" Rosa clapped her hands, intentionally making loud noises.

"Yes. That way, nobody needs to worry about bothering other library guests." Faenor smiled, then continued after a pause. "I wasn't sure that there would be sound barriers here in the Demon Kingdom, but I'm glad to see that demons have the bare minimum sense of courtesy."

Faenor doesn't like demons very much. He doesn't bother hiding his thoughts when nobody else is around. Then again, I can't blame him. Alphegor almost killed him, and he has been forced to babysit me against his will.

"Let's take a look at the book." Faenor pulled the old book from his bag and set it on the table. He then put Rosa in his lap and opened the first page.

"*Encyclopedia of Magic Gems,*" he read aloud, then flipped the page again. Rosa eagerly scanned the slightly faded letters, excited by the prospect of learning something so fascinating. Although the book was old and had been read many times before, it appeared to be handled with great care.

"This is a compendium of magical gems, both rare and common,"

Faenor began. "It is by no means a full record of all magical gems, and I am sure many remain hidden. However, I hope that even the little bit of knowledge I was able to collect will help you gain insight into various forms of magic that appear in our world. Arbane Inavaris."

I wonder if this Inavaris guy is a known scholar or one of those researchers everybody denies.

"Doctor Inavaris is well known, but not exactly in a positive way. He was known as an eccentric obsessed with other worlds and researched gems only to find proof that other worlds existed," Faenor explained as if he could read Rosa's thoughts and then looked her in the eyes. An uncomfortable knot formed at the bottom of her stomach.

Other worlds? Why did he look at me when he read that?

"There are many ways to classify gems but by far the most common way is by their magical potential. The scale goes from 1 to 10 with 1 including gems that can do simple magic like changing the color of hair and 10 including gems that can shape the very world around us. Very little is known about these more powerful gems, however, it is without a doubt that they exist," Faenor read, and Rosa took note of how he observed her through the corner of his eye.

"Huh?" Rosa tilted her head, pretending not to have understood him.

"Is it still too difficult for you? That's alright. We can at least look at the drawings." Faenor's expression brightened as he turned the book a few pages ahead. There was a drawing of a white rock there. It looked rather brittle and not very impressive.

I'm not a geologist, so I have no idea what this is. It looks kind of like chalk.

"First entries probably won't be too interesting to look at, so why don't we skip ahead a little? How about we take a look at the gem that was gifted to you?" The elf flipped ahead before Rosa could understand what he was doing, and he stopped on a page where there was a perfectly drawn replica of Rosa's birthday present. One picture depicted it as mostly bluish green; in another, it appeared purple, but in the largest one, it was shown transitioning between the two colors.

"My gift?" Rosa pointed at it.

"Yes. It is called an alexandrite. It is rated at a level 8.5—a really powerful gem. Alexandrites contain the ability to change shape."

"Change shape?"

"Yes. With it, you could become anything—an elf, a dwarf, a bird, even a human," Faenor said solemnly, and Rosa paused in surprise.

Humans! I can't believe somebody is finally talking about them. I've barely heard anyone mention them before. I'm just glad they exist in this world as well.

"What's a h-hooman?" she stuttered, trying to appear wholly ignorant.

"Humans are the most numerous race on the surface. They have very short lives—they can't see in the dark or hear very well, they can't fly, and their bodies are incredibly weak and susceptible to various illnesses. But despite all that, they are extremely adaptable and troublesome to deal with."

"Huh?" Rosa cocked her head, pretending to be perplexed by his description.

"Yes, I am sure this race must sound very strange to you. But they look much like you and me, only with round ears and soft skin. They are really quite unremarkable to look at," Faenor said with a smile.

We're not that bad. Besides, humans are very innovative. If only you could see all the technology we have created on Earth.

"I'm sure in time, you'll learn to use your gem," Faenor said and closed the book. "But let's stop for today. I think I've read something more difficult than I'm supposed to."

"Pretty," she forced herself to say in a cheery voice, but a nagging feeling told her that Faenor may have seen through her ruse.

Maybe I'm just being paranoid. Granted, I don't always act like a normal baby, but would he really suspect something as absurd as that so easily? Does it have something to do with the author of this book and his research about other worlds? Maybe I'm just overthinking it. Everything seems suspicious in this world.

"Yes, we'll study this book more seriously once you're ready," the elf said, and Rosa couldn't help but notice that he didn't say, "once you're older."

* * *

As they exited the library, Rosa saw a familiar face approaching—Deziara, accompanied by the same strict-looking, large-breasted demoness from their first encounter. Upon seeing Rosa, the girl furrowed her brow, and her expression turned to that of disgust once she looked at Faenor.

"Why are you always together with slaves?" the seven-year-old girl grumbled and pointed an accusatory finger at the elf. "If you're my sister, you should have proper servants!"

"Princess Deziara, that is not for you to decide. It is the king's decision to make," the demoness reprimanded her, gently nudging the girl towards the library. But she stomped her foot angrily on the ground.

"No! Nobody seems to care that there is only one slave with her! What if somebody attacks her?"

Well, there are actually two guards following me at all times, but they like to stay hidden. And I can't just explain that—it'd make me seem really suspicious.

"We must go to my father at once!" Deziara announced loudly

and began purposefully striding forward.

"Princess! We must get to your lesson," the demoness protested, running after the girl.

"No! This is more important than the lesson. I have lessons every day, but this issue has been unresolved for the longest time!" Deziara looked at Faenor, then clicked her tongue in annoyance. "Follow, slave!"

With a resigned sigh, the demoness followed Deziara and waved her hand at Faenor, indicating him to follow. Left with no other choice, the elf, with Rosa in his arms, followed after the demon child.

Deziara purposefully held her head high in imitation of her royal father, and Rosa had to admit that she looked cute.

I bet you just wanted to escape your lessons, but that's alright. Maybe you'll be less resentful of me if I can serve as your excuse to get away. It's not like I had anything better to do anyway.

After winding through the corridors in a pattern unfamiliar to Rosa, they arrived at a set of double doors guarded by two bulky-looking demons. Their stern gazes grew to that of confusion once they saw the demon child marching towards them.

"Let me through. I have urgent business with my father!" Deziara announced to them, waving her little hand as if trying to will them aside.

"Nobody is to disturb His Majesty while he works," one of the guards replied but made no attempt to physically block the little princess.

"This is of utmost importance."

"Nobody is allowed inside."

The guard and Deziara stared at each other, neither one daring to blink, but the guard became increasingly uncomfortable, his fingers flexing and relaxing their hold on his spear.

"What's this ruckus outside?" Alphegor's familiar voice resounded from behind the door.

"It's nothing, Your Majesty!" the guard replied, but Deziara stomped her foot and puffed out her cheeks.

"It is very important!" the girl called in a loud voice, no doubt hoping that Alphegor would hear her. Her efforts were rewarded as the door swung open and the king emerged, his expression dark with annoyance.

"What's going on?"

Everybody but Rosa froze on the spot, and Faenor's hand began to tremble. Alphegor looked sternly over the scene, but his gaze softened once his eyes met with hers.

"Morrigan? What are you doing here?"

"F-Father, I have something important to discuss," Deziara spoke up, but her voice had lost all of its previous confidence.

"Oh, do tell," the king said, not removing his gaze from Rosa.

"Y-You see! My little sister is always together with s-slaves. Shouldn't she have proper guards and servants?"

Alphegor rubbed his chin, then looked at Rosa, a small grin playing on his lips.

"You seem to be quite interested in your little sister, Deziara. Why is that?"

"W-Well... I th-thought maybe we could get along. I—I don't get to play with my other sisters."

She doesn't? But we have twenty-two sisters. Surely, at least one of them would be willing to play with her.

Alphegor's expression hardened as he seemed to consider something deeply. Then he approached Deziara, looking down at the little girl with a scrutinizing gaze.

"Your mother didn't put you up to this, did she?"

"W-Wha? No! Mother d-doesn't know I am here," Deziara stumbled over her words, looking like she was about to cry.

There is no need to intimidate your child so much. She's about to burst into tears...

"Sister, no cry," Rosa protested, instantly drawing Alphegor's attention to herself.

"Do you like your sister, Morrigan?"

Rosa restrained a frown. It was not like she liked Deziara. In fact, she was fully convinced that she was a spoiled brat. But the way Alphegor treated his other daughters was rather harsh.

"Yes," she said with as much conviction as she could muster. A wide smile appeared on Deziara's face while her teacher visibly frowned.

"Most excellent. Lady Asdeus, I trust you wouldn't mind teaching Morrigan together with Deziara?"

"Wha?! Teach Princess Morrigan?" The demoness looked at Rosa with confusion, her black curls falling over her shoulder.

"Yes, I would be most grateful if you began her studies early," Alphegor said, turning his charm up to ten. The teacher almost melted into a puddle under his gaze.

So that's how he has twenty thr—twenty-four daughters. Skirt chaser!

"I—Of course, Your Majesty! It is no trouble at all."

"Wonderful!" Alphegor's expression turned back to normal as he addressed Faenor. "You can entrust Morrigan to Lady Asdeus now. Dismissed."

Faenor didn't look too pleased with this decision but nodded and handed Rosa over to Lady Asdeus. She took her somewhat awkwardly, her large chest squishing Rosa from both sides.

How did it end up like this? I'll get smothered to death at this rate.

"I trust you'll do everything to keep Morrigan and Deziara safe while they're under your watch," the king said with a sharp edge to his voice.

Lady Asdeus flinched, then forced a smile. "Yes, of course, Your Majesty! You have nothing to worry about."

Alphegor nodded and walked over to the woman, leaning close. The demoness blushed and wriggled nervously under his gaze.

I swear if you kiss her, I will fart on your face while you sleep.

Instead, Alphegor gently rustled Rosa's hair and then turned away. He was almost back at his office when a quiet cough resounded through the hall. Deziara was fidgeting on the spot, her cheeks bright pink, not daring to look him directly in the eyes. He chuckled and then went over to rustle her hair as well.

"Behave, girls," he said and disappeared behind the heavy doors.

It was difficult to describe the expression that came over Deziara's face. Her eyes were wide as saucers and sparkling in delight. Her lips were twisted in a goofy grin, and she held her cheeks with her hands, barely containing a delighted squeal.

"Did you see that, Lady Asdeus? Father patted me! He actually patted me!" The girl jumped up and down, joyfully waving her hands.

Was Alphegor really so cold towards his other daughters that a simple pat on the head would warrant such a reaction? Maybe I should push him to pay at least a little more attention to them. They are just children, after all.

Rosa frowned, hoping that he would be nicer to her half-sisters in the future. If he showed affection more equally towards them, then it would be less likely for them to get jealous of Rosa and try to murder her.

CHAPTER 15

(RE)INTRODUCTION TO ART

"Time to get back to your lessons," Lady Asdeus said sternly to Deziara, who groaned loudly in response.

"Do we have to?" The girl shook her pigtails from side to side.

"Yes, now let's get back to it," the demoness grumbled and looked awkwardly down at Rosa, then glared at Faenor. "You, slave! Go get her nanny and send her to Study Room 13. I am not changing any diapers."

"Princess Morrigan doesn't wear diapers anymore, but I'll fetch the nanny anyway," Faenor replied and then disappeared into the winding corridors before Lady Asdeus could object. The demoness looked at Rosa again, this time with a bit less disgust.

"No diapers? That's good, at least. Now then, let's go, Princess Deziara. We've already lost a lot of time today."

With the constant grumbling and mumbling of Deziara in the background, Lady Asdeus weaved through the corridors until they arrived at a place that was a short distance from the library. At least according to Rosa's sense of direction, which wasn't the most trustworthy thing.

As they entered the classroom, Rosa's eyes lit up. Beyond the few desks, the large writing board, and shelves lined with books and stationery, she saw something she had hoped to find ever since the first day she came to this world. An easel and canvas propped against a wall with a box next to it, lined to the brim with paints of every color imaginable.

"Now, take the easel, set the canvas on it, and let's begin," Lady Asdeus instructed, and Deziara complied with a groan. Rosa began fidgeting as she saw her prepare the workspace.

"Can't we do something fun for a change?" The demon girl tried to bargain, but Lady Asdeus shook her head firmly.

"Art is a crucial part of your education. As a Princess, you need to understand how it's made, how to differentiate good art from bad, and also how to do at least a simplistic art piece yourself."

Rosa wanted to nod in agreement. She believed more people should try to understand art instead of just dismissing it as a mere hobby that was good for nothing but filling up spare time.

"But you make it sound so *boring...*" the girl groaned. The demoness glowered at her, making the child flinch and pick up the first brush that she came across.

Lady Asdeus then set Rosa down on the floor away from Deziara and began setting up another easel and canvas for herself, preparing to demonstrate her skill. She was about to open her mouth and begin the lesson but then remembered that Rosa was still there and noticed her staring longingly at the paints.

"I guess it couldn't hurt to give you something to do as well..." the demoness muttered, pulling out a piece of paper from one of the shelves along with a little container of colored sticks. They didn't look quite like either crayons or pencils.

Rosa snatched them eagerly, looking over them with unhidden enthusiasm.

"At least someone looks interested," the demoness said, turning her attention back to Deziara.

Finally having art supplies at her disposal, Rosa couldn't care less about what was going on around her. She took the orange stick out of the container and carefully examined it. It was neither a crayon, pencil, nor marker, but something completely new. Pressing it against the paper, the color lay down easily, not leaving any white streaks underneath. It wasn't very vibrant with the first stroke, so Rosa tried to layer it.

With each layer she added, the color became more vibrant even without her pushing hard. And the color was uniform. It was almost as if she was drawing on a tablet.

Finally, I get to draw again. It's been far too long.

Rosa flipped the page over and then began putting down one color after another.

First, a bit of light green. Just draw it haphazardly on the bottom of the page. Then take some red and color the top of the page gently, just enough to make it light pink. Then use dark blue to separate the two and create vague mountains in the background.

Draw a line that gets increasingly larger coming down from the mountains. And next to the riverbank, make gray rocks in the form of gray circles. Finally, use white to add some clouds.

When she was done, Rosa took a moment to stop and admire her handiwork. It was messy, streaky, and certainly looked like something a baby would draw. Her hands couldn't move the coloring stick as she wanted, so her lines were uneven and jittery. The supposed white clouds looked like nothing more than a smudged mess as the stick seemed to serve more as a color blender rather than an actual white color.

But even so, Rosa was delighted. Even if her hands couldn't draw the way they used to, she could do art again. Even if her lines had lost their precision and sharpness, even if she had no idea how to properly use these coloring sticks, it was all a matter of time before she'd be able to create exactly what she wanted.

"Look, Lady Asdeus! Morrigan is more interested in art than I am. Maybe you should teach her instead?" The demon girl ran over to Rosa and pointed excitedly at her drawing.

"I am sure that in due time, I'll be teaching her as well, but for now..." the demoness began, but then she saw Rosa's work and paused. She bent down and picked the page up, examining it carefully. "This is actually pretty impressive for a baby."

"See? You should totally teach her instead of me!" Deziara gave the woman a toothy grin.

"But she is still a baby," Lady Asdeus said, turning to the little girl's canvas. "Better show me what you've done."

Curious, Rosa shifted just enough to get a peek at her sister's work. The moment Lady Asdeus saw it, she gasped in shock. Rosa barely managed to contain a snort by instead pretending to cough.

There was a long stick figure drawn onto the canvas. She—as Rosa decided—had a vaguely curly mop for hair with black horns sticking out, overly large glasses on her round face, red lips that went outside of the face borders, and a squiggly line for the tail. However, the main focus of this piece was, no doubt, the two giant circles for breasts that filled no less than half of the canvas.

"Princess Deziara!" the demoness nearly shouted in outrage. "That is not what a princess should be drawing."

"I think it's pretty accurate," the girl mumbled quietly, and Rosa resisted the urge to nod along.

"We shall begin anew, and you won't be able to leave until you finish today's assignment."

"Aww..."

Lady Asdeus opened her mouth, no doubt to chastise the girl some more, when a barely audible knock resounded on the door.

"Enter," the demoness commanded, and the trembling frame of Gunna appeared.

"I was told that Lady Morrigan needs me here."

"Ah, yes. You must be her nanny. I just need you to make sure she doesn't cause a fuss or make a mess around here."

"Of course. I'll make sure your lesson continues uninterrupted." Gunna bowed her head low and then scurried over to Rosa while keeping a good distance away from Lady Asdeus. The dwarf woman looked even more nervous than she did around Alphegor, although the reaction was not as bad as around Azrael.

Maybe I should make some demon craziness chart based on Gunna's reaction. It's odd Gunna's reaction to Alphegor is much milder than towards other demons. Is he really more mild-mannered, or is she just used to him?

"What have you drawn here, Lady Morrigan?" Gunna asked in a barely audible whisper as she admired Rosa's handiwork. The nanny then smiled and gently patted her head. "That is very well done. I never thought you'd like drawing so much. Perhaps we should ask the king for your own drawing supplies."

Rosa was about to nod enthusiastically at the suggestion but paused.

How would Alphegor react if he knew that I like art? He's the Demon King, and he wants me to be his successor. He would no doubt be even more disappointed than my mother if he found out. No, worse than disappointed… perhaps he could decide that he has no use for me.

"No," Rosa replied simply as she fiddled with the colorful sticks.

"Are you sure?" The nanny looked dejected, but Rosa reaffirmed her decision with a nod.

I'll just draw here. Lady Asdeus probably has no idea what to do with me anyway, so it'll be a win-win for everybody involved.

"Well, if you're sure. I suppose you can just draw here," Gunna confirmed, then put another blank page in front of Rosa. "How about I draw some things for you?"

Rosa nodded again, and they spent the next two hours drawing with the colorful sticks. It was enjoyable, even with Deziara's constant complaints and Lady Asdeus' merciless lectures resounding in the background. It seemed like the rest of the day would be peaceful until a loud, incessant knock sounded on the door. Before anybody had time to react, it flung open, revealing Azrael.

"I am looking for my pupil," he announced and then squinted as he saw Lady Asdeus. "It's you. One princess isn't enough for you? Trying to butter up to His Majesty using his favorite daughter as well?"

The silver-haired demon sneered, and Lady Asdeus just waved her hand dismissively in response.

"You're one to talk. I've heard what you did. Swearing an oath to a baby." The demoness scoffed and threw one of her curls over her shoulder. "Really, Azrael, that has to be a new low even for you."

"I'm just thinking about the future. The current king won't remain on his throne forever," Azrael said, walking over to Rosa and then picking her up and lifting her high. "But what I have right here is the future queen of the whole Underworld—the demoness who will rule over everything."

Don't involve me in your schemes!

"That's a baby. She can't do anything right now. It'll be at least two millennia before the king even thinks of passing the throne to anybody, and in the meanwhile, you're bound to the whims of that snotty child."

How rude! I don't have snot.

"But... Morrigan doesn't have any snot." Deziara carefully looked at Rosa and then cocked her head in confusion.

At least somebody is on my side.

"Ah... That's not quite what I meant, Princess Deziara. I meant that she is still small and not capable of doing much," the demoness pacified the little girl and waved for her to continue her work. Deziara groaned loudly yet again and, with deliberate slowness, began dragging the brush across the canvas.

"We'll see about that. In either case, I'll be taking her with me now. Ta-Ta!" Azrael waved his hand and, before anybody could object, zoomed out of the study room.

"Wait..." Rosa wanted to protest, but Azrael shook his head, not slowing down in the slightest. The poor dwarf nanny ran after them as fast as her stocky legs would allow her, huffing and puffing.

"No, you owe me one. You barfed on me during our first lesson, then ditched the second lesson completely. I think it's about time we began working for real."

"Play?" Rosa tried to play dumb, but the demon laughed and mercilessly messed up the two small twin-tails Gunna managed to make out of the meager amount of hair she had.

"Nice try, kiddo, but I know that you're smarter than you're letting on. Besides, we have some other business to take care of as well."

"Other?" Rosa asked, this time actually confused about what he was talking about.

"Yeah, we still haven't dealt with your birthday present from the king, have we?" Azrael pursed his lips, and his eyebrows creased in a deep furrow. The color drained from Rosa's cheeks as she remembered the giant, red dragon egg.

"Eep!" A tiny hiccup escaped Rosa as her heart jumped.

"It's alright. I'm sure we'll manage… somehow." Azrael exhaled, then suddenly stopped and turned to walk in a completely different direction. "How about we swing by the kitchens first and see if they have some raw meat?"

"Eep!" Rosa hiccupped again and took a firm hold of Azrael's shirt.

CHAPTER 16

BIRTH OF A DRAGON

Armed with a large chunk of meat, Azrael strode purposefully towards the training room while holding Rosa with his other arm.

Oh, God, Jesus, Buddha, Zeus, Odin, and any other gods who might be listening—please help me survive this in one piece.

Rosa had no doubt that once the little beast hatched, she would be its first choice for a snack. If the egg was any indication of size, then the newborn dragon should be at least twice as big as Rosa. The meat they procured in the kitchen did little to calm Rosa's nerves. It wouldn't satisfy a dragon for long. Not if it was at least a little bit like dragons were described in stories.

"It'll be alright. Worst case scenario, I kill the little beast." Azrael forced a smile.

No, no, no! You can't do that. If you kill the "gift" from Alphegor, then he will no doubt level the whole castle to the ground. Along with everyone in it.

"Father angry," Rosa objected.

"I think he'll be angrier if I let the thing eat you," the demon retorted.

There's no winning here. Better get this over with.

They entered the empty training grounds where the dragon egg sat menacingly in the corner, waiting to cause mayhem. Rosa glared at the thing, hoping that the egg simply wouldn't hatch.

But how would it even hatch? We don't have to sit on it like hens, right?

"Hatch how?" Rosa asked as she tugged on Azrael's shirt. The demon seemed to be glaring at the egg with the same intensity as Rosa.

"Hatching a dragon isn't easy, little Princess. I imagine only a handful of demons would be able to do it. Unfortunately, I just happen to be one of the few who can..."

Suffering from success?

Azrael was about to put Rosa down, but she held on to his shirt with an iron grip.

Don't you dare to put me down! I don't want to be eaten.

"Don't worry. I swore an oath, remember? I have to protect you no matter what. And you still have my talisman to protect you from physical harm," he said. Thinking back to his oath, she realized she couldn't remember it clearly—it had happened so fast—but there certainly was something about him protecting her. She wondered if the dragon eating her whole could be some weird loophole.

"It'll be alright. As I said, if worst comes to worst, I'll kill it."

Rosa released her grip, and Azrael put her on the ground. Then he stepped in front of her and took a deep breath.

"Here goes nothing..." he muttered, extending his hand forward. Angry, blue flames burst from his palm and engulfed the egg from all sides. Heat surged through the room, and Rosa felt sweat bead on her skin.

Azrael continued roasting the egg for a while, sweat rolling down his face, his eyebrows furrowing in concentration.

"Hatch already, you little beast..." he muttered as his flames began to waver a little bit. A small cracking noise came from the egg, and Azrael instantly cut off the fire.

Rosa latched on to his leg, peering at the red egg. It looked like the flames hadn't done anything to it, while the ground and even the nearby walls had started to melt. Even with the flames gone, the room still felt blazing hot.

"C'mon! Hatch, you infernal thing," the demon muttered, not even blinking as he observed the egg.

Then another, louder crack echoed through the room. Rosa and Azrael both leaned closer, searching for any visible marks on the egg.

Crack, crack, crack. There was a tiny, barely noticeable shake. *Crack, crack, crack,* came from the egg, while Rosa's heart pounded anxiously. Finally, a little hole appeared on the top, and some movement could be seen within it.

Can it not get out?

As soon as she thought that, the egg burst open with eggshells and the inner fluid flying everywhere. Rosa clung to Azrael's leg as if her life depended on it, trying to understand where the eggshells ended and where the newborn dragon began.

"That's anticlimactic," Azrael exhaled, unimpressed by the little creature. "It's a runt."

The little red dragon lay on the floor, each leg going in a different direction. It had large, green eyes, two little nubs for horns, and small appendages on its back that probably should have been wings. Not to mention that it was small—in fact, it was smaller than Rosa.

What a waste of real estate. Tiny dragon in a huge package.

Azrael stepped forward and grabbed the hatchling by its tail, lifting it effortlessly. The little creature thrashed and let out a pitiful mewl, utterly helpless in his grasp.

"This is not a dragon. It's just an oversized rat." Azrael poked its soft belly, causing it to yelp. It looked so sad and weak that Rosa felt sorry for it.

"Food?" Rosa pulled on the Demon's pants and pointed towards the bowl full of meat sitting nearby.

"Yeah, I guess we should feed it," Azrael agreed with a sigh and threw the dragon to the ground without a second thought. It let out another yelp and then whimpered, curling up in a small shivering ball.

There's no need to be so mean towards it.

Rosa approached the trembling creature, debating whether she was brave enough to attempt to comfort it. Runt or not, it was still a dragon, and she had no doubt that it could bite off her hand if it decided to do so. But as it continued to whimper and tremble on the hard floor, Rosa made up her mind and went to pat it. It moved away when it saw her getting too close.

"Shhhh," she soothed it and outstretched her hand. She didn't move her hand any closer, waiting for the baby dragon to at least sniff it first. She saw this in a movie once so maybe the logic could be applied to a fantasy world. For a moment, they both just stared at each other, then the hatchling inched closer and sniffed her hand.

"Hey, Princess! Don't approach it so carelessly," Azrael reprimanded, but Rosa shook her head.

"Stop," she instructed him, but her voice was quiet and calm so as not to scare the dragon. It flinched when it saw Azrael looking at them but relaxed as the demon made no further move.

The hatchling crept closer and closer to Rosa, sniffing the air cautiously. Finally, its tiny snout gently nudged against her palm. She shivered from the sensation of its scales. They were still wet from the egg fluid, but at the same time warm and tough like stone.

"Good dragon," Rosa praised the little creature and reached out to pat its head. The dragon allowed her to do so, and began purring with delight under her touch. She even saw its little tail swish from side to side.

It really is like a dog.

Azrael nodded approvingly at the sight, then slid the bowl of meat closer to Rosa. The meat was neatly chopped into pieces, ready to be eaten.

"Hungry?" Rosa asked, presenting the bowl to the little dragon. It sniffed the bowl cautiously at first, then instinct took over, and it began chomping down the meat hungrily.

"It has a good appetite, at least," Azrael noted. "And he seems obedient, so that's good. But way more docile than other dragons I've seen."

Not going to complain about that. I'd take a docile runt dragon over a regular dragon any day.

"Even so... Where are we supposed to put it?" Azrael thought aloud, tapping his foot as he tried to come up with a solution. "Why don't you call your daddy over so he can decide?"

Rosa shook her head at that. She'd already called him once that day and had no intention of making it a regular thing. The novelty of this activity would surely wear off quickly for the king.

"Really? Now when he's actually needed, you won't call him? I can't just keep a dragon in my bedroom," Azrael grumbled.

I'm not keeping him in my bedroom either.

Rosa just pretended not to have understood him and turned her attention back to the little dragon. It was still scarfing down the meat energetically, its tail swishing from side to side.

"Name?" Rosa pointed at the dragon.

"It does need a name... Wait, is it a girl or a boy?" the demon mused, walking over to the little beast and then lifting up its tail. The dragon yelped, but Azrael just grinned and released it. It looked offended, but realizing there was still meat to be eaten, it returned to munching.

"It's a boy."

A male dragon. What would be a good name?

"Oh, I know. Let's call him Blaze," Azrael exclaimed, a spark of childish excitement in his eyes.

Really? You're a two-hundred-year-old Demon, and you want to name a dragon Blaze? Are we sure there's not a twelve-year-old boy sitting inside that body?

Rosa didn't bother to hide the disappointment she felt.

"Hey, don't look at me like that. It's a good name for a dragon. He is red and can breathe fire."

She shook her head vigorously and crossed her arms over her chest.

"Fine, fine, Your Highness," he mocked, sticking his tongue out. "Why don't you come up with a name then?"

A name for a dragon... What would be a good name for a dragon?

Her mind wandered back to all the stories and movies she'd seen with dragons. One animated movie instantly popped into her mind, and despite the dragon within it being completely different from the one in front of her, she couldn't help but want to put a little bit of her home into this new world.

"Haku," she said resolutely.

"What? Haku? What kind of a name is that? I've never heard a stupider name in my whole life." The demon pouted. "Blaze is a better name."

"No, Haku," she insisted, locking eyes with Azrael. He met her gaze, and for a moment, they were locked in a staring contest—his purple eyes fighting against her silver ones. Her eyes began to water, but she did not dare to blink. Azrael's eyebrow began twitching until he finally blinked and turned around dramatically, throwing his hands up in the air.

"Fine! Have it your way," the demon grumbled. "Just don't come crying to me if daddy doesn't like it."

Rosa smiled victoriously and went to pat Haku's head. The hatchling had finished its meal and was cautiously observing Rosa and Azrael. It mewled happily at her touch and coiled around her.

"Good Haku."

"Yes, yes, good Haku. Now where do we put him?" Azrael grumbled.

The door to the training grounds swung open, and an angry-looking Lucius entered, followed by a few bulky demon guards.

"Azrael, what the hell are you doing? I could feel the heat from your flames all the way from His Majesty's office…" The older demon trailed off as he saw the dragon coiled around Rosa. His expression turned to one of panic, and he waved at the guards. "Get that thing off of the princess at once!"

"No!" Rosa and Azrael yelled at the same time, stopping them in their tracks. The sudden noise startled Haku, who curled up into a ball by Rosa's feet and began trembling.

"For Darkness' sake, at least let me explain the situation first." Azrael sighed and then hurried to explain to Lucius the whole ordeal with the dragon.

"I apologize for my rash behavior. I had completely forgotten about His Majesty's… present." Lucius eyed the trembling dragon from behind his glasses, then cleared his throat. "Nonetheless, you should have informed His Majesty about your actions. He was quite furious that the temperature suddenly rose."

Azrael paled a little bit, then straightened up and leaned closer to the older Demon. "What do I do about the dragon, though?"

"I'm not sure. His Majesty charged you to deal with it, didn't he? So, deal with it," Lucius said dismissively, then turned to Rosa. "Do you like your present, Princess?"

Rosa thought for a moment as she patted the sleeping dragon. While initially she was terrified of the idea of having a dragon, now that the creature was sleeping peacefully curled up next to her, she was happy. It was like getting a puppy—she never had the pleasure of owning a pet before.

"Yes!" Rosa replied, and Lucius nodded with a smile.

"Wonderful. I shall go tell the king the good news then." Lucius bowed to her politely, then turned on his heel and began striding towards the exit.

"Wait... Where do I put the dragon?" Azrael shouted behind him.

"Figure it out!"

CHAPTER 17

THE ANNOUNCEMENT

"Haku, I know you can do it. I believe in you," Rosa urged the dragon as they stood in a secluded corner of the castle yard, away from prying eyes.

Before she had even realized it, three years had passed. Her days were always filled with endless lessons and constant supervision from her caretakers, leaving her little time for herself.

In a way, it was pleasant, as Rosa didn't have to worry about assassins catching her while she was unprotected. There certainly were a few attempts to take her life, but none of them ever got as close to their goal as the first one. Most never even made it past her regular guards.

But having lived in the demon castle for four years, it dawned on her that she was trapped here. She couldn't go past the castle walls, since Alphegor would go absolutely insane if someone even dared to mention the idea. And in a way, she couldn't blame him. She was merely four years old, and the outside world was nothing like Earth.

She couldn't walk outside to stroll through a park or nearby forest without worrying about the repercussions. Even if she were to discount the assassins who jumped at the first opportunity to end her, there were plenty of other dangers. Giant monsters and power-hungry demons ready to suck her dry of her magical power, according to Gunna and the gossipy maids.

But even if all these things seemed rational, Rosa felt like she was suffocating inside the castle. The gray walls looked like they were about to swallow her whole whenever she walked through them. The people inside always tried to butter up to her in one way or another, asking, *"How can I help you, Princess?"* or *"Do you need anything, Princess?"* But worst of all was her fear that Alphegor might discover her human soul.

She was afraid to see how his expression would twist in disgust and how disappointed he would be. She was afraid that he would denounce her just like Mother had. For that reason, she kept her passion for art a secret and only dared to do it during Lady Asdeus' lessons when the demoness gave the supplies to her.

The dragon, now the size of a large dog, flapped his tiny wings and jumped into the air, trying to take flight. But no matter how hard he tried, Haku just couldn't stay in the air. While his wings had certainly grown from the sad, little stumps he had been born with, they were still underdeveloped for his age.

"I guess your wings still need to grow a little bit." Rosa gently patted the dragon's muzzle, and he let out a soft whine. "It's alright. I'm sure you'll be able to do it one day."

"Princess Morrigan! Where are you? Please answer me, Princess!" Rosa heard one of her guards shouting somewhere in the distance, and she ducked behind the hedge, pulling Haku down with her.

"Shh, not a peep," she warned the dragon, who immediately went still.

"Princess Morrigan!" the guard shouted again, this time closer. The sound of boots thudded somewhere nearby. "Princess Morrigan!"

Rosa held her breath, listening. Then, the next shout came from farther away, and she exhaled in relief.

I do not want to go back to the castle right now.

"Found you!" Deziara's face suddenly popped out from behind the bush, startling Rosa so badly she fell onto her rump. Haku also jumped up, letting out a small puff of smoke from the fright, and Deziara burst into laughter. "Hahaha!"

"Quiet," Rosa reprimanded her sister and motioned her to hide as well. The guard must have heard the commotion as he turned around and started coming in their direction.

Chuckling, Deziara slipped around the hedge to join Rosa in her hiding spot. Now nine years old, the demon girl had become much more confident, although no less of a grumbler and troublemaker. She was the only one of her twenty-three sisters that Rosa got along with or whom she even saw on a somewhat regular basis.

"Why are you hiding?" Deziara asked, pulling Rosa up to her feet and brushing off the dust and dirt from her skirt.

"I don't want to go back to the castle," Rosa explained as she peeked around the bush to check for the guard. He had once again gone past them; the thought that she could have gone to the far side of the garden probably didn't occur to him.

"Why not? We don't have any lessons with Lady Asdeus today." Deziara scrunched her nose when mentioning her teacher's name. Rosa didn't hold any grudges against the woman, but that was mostly because she ignored Rosa most of the time and allowed her to play with the coloring supplies.

"I just want to..." Rosa contemplated whether she should get into the philosophical topic of craving a world beyond the same gray castle walls with a nine-year-old—especially considering she was trapped in the body of a four-year-old herself. The conclusion was a resolute no. Sighing, she said, "I want to play with Haku."

Deziara smiled and nodded, patting the dragon who effortlessly sank into her touch. "Yeah, it's fun playing with Haku. I still can't believe that Father gifted you a dragon."

Rosa still vividly remembered how Deziara had completely lost her ability to speak once she found out about Haku. It was fair to say that it was due to the dragon that the two sisters had gotten so close, for Deziara would always seek Rosa out just to play with him.

"Princess Morrigan!" the guard shouted from somewhere afar, completely off his mark.

"I don't think he'll find us," Deziara snickered, and Rosa nodded mischievously in reply.

"You two having fun?" Azrael's voice came from behind, and both girls whirled around. The white-haired demon loomed over them with a menacing glare. But despite the intimidating first impression, Rosa noticed a hint of a subtle curve at the corners of his lips.

"Run!" Rosa called and attached herself to Haku. The dragon swiftly threw her onto his back and leaped over the hedge. Deziara also scampered away, running as fast as her legs could carry her, disappearing somewhere amid the bushes.

"Nice try, you little rats," Azrael called out with a loud laugh, and before Rosa could realize what was going on, the mage had teleported next to them. He yanked Morrigan off Haku and grabbed Deziara by the scruff of her clothes, holding them up like a couple of trophy fish.

"Unhand me! I order you as a Princess of the Demon Kingdom!" Deziara flailed, trying to break free of his grasp.

"Nice try, Your Laziness, but you two are needed in the Main Hall. The King is about to make an announcement," he said and began walking towards the castle with the two girls dangling in his grasp.

"Father is?" Deziara asked, and Azrael put her on the ground while keeping a firm hold on Rosa.

I wonder what is so important that Alphegor has decided to announce it in the main hall. He's never done so before.

Rosa wriggled against Azrael's hold, hoping he'd take the hint and let her down on the ground.

"Nuh-uh. I know you. You'll slip into the shadows the moment I put you down. I'm not in the mood to chase after your shadow form," the demon huffed, then pointed at the dragon. "Haku, go home."

Haku drooped his head low and trudged to the far side of the yard where there was a small enclosure for him. Azrael had constructed him a sort of doghouse but for a dragon, where the poor beast had to spend most of his time since he was not allowed inside the castle anymore.

"I'll come by later, Haku," Rosa promised, and the little dragon perked up, his tail wagging ever so slightly.

* * *

Much to Rosa's surprise, the main hall was filled to the brim with demons—concubines, her sisters, servants, and even some more dignified-looking demons who she assumed worked directly under Alphegor. There was a quiet murmur going through the hall, as everyone seemed to wonder what exactly the big announcement would be.

Azrael boldly strode right through the middle of the crowd with Rosa in his arms and Deziara trailing behind him. Some gave him an annoyed glare, while others scoffed. He didn't have the best reputation. In fact, Rosa had never actually seen anybody be friendly with him.

As he finally reached the end of the hall, Rosa saw Alphegor standing there, tall and proud, the perfect picture of a demon king. She felt a bit smug about how good he looked; after all, he *was* her father. Nobody else in this room could even stand close to him. And yet, when he laid his eyes on Rosa, his expression softened.

"Had some trouble finding them?" Alphegor asked as he reached out to take Rosa. Deziara quickly ran over to stand by his side. Ever since the two girls had gotten closer, Alphegor also had become more affectionate towards Deziara, who always melted into a joyous puddle under his praise.

"They were in the far corner of the garden," Azrael said with a shrug, then bowed as he excused himself to stand beside Lucius.

"You've been getting out a lot lately," the king noted. Rosa fiddled with the golden button of his suit, not daring to meet his gaze, so he turned to Deziara. "Any idea why Morrigan is doing that?"

"She said she wanted to play with Haku," the girl responded with a bright smile. Alphegor nodded, accepting her answer, but he, without a doubt, knew that it wasn't the real reason why Rosa was hiding. He always had a knack for picking up whenever something was bothering her.

The three of them stood there, waiting for the rest of the crowd to gather. At some point, Deziara's mother appeared in the front row, and she gave her daughter a small, satisfied nod.

Lily had been ecstatic that Alphegor had finally been paying proper attention to their daughter, so her angry glares towards Rosa had grown into those of tolerance, almost gratitude at times. Rosa thought that she probably wouldn't try to poison her food—or at least that she was the least likely of all concubines to do so.

After a few minutes, Alphegor spoke up in that booming, kingly voice of his. "Thank you all for coming on such short notice. I have an important announcement."

All the chatter instantly died down, and everyone focused their attention on the king. Rosa felt just as uncomfortable being in front of such a large crowd as she did during her first-birthday party, but thankfully, she wasn't the center of attention this time.

"I'll be leaving the castle tomorrow."

Rosa felt like she'd been hit on the head with a hammer. Others seemed equally surprised by this announcement, murmurs instantly erupting through the dimly lit hall.

"Quiet!" Alphegor ordered, and silence returned. "The Fallen Ones have become far too bold lately, and it is necessary that I show them their place."

The demons nodded in agreement, and some even cheered at this proclamation while Rosa was left to wonder.

Who are the Fallen Ones? I've never heard this term before.

"I don't know how long it'll take. If things go well, I'll return in a month or two. However, you need to be prepared in case it takes longer."

Another wave of quiet murmurs went through the room while Rosa's heart beat faster and faster in her chest.

A month or two or maybe even longer? But what will happen to me while Alphegor's gone? The only reason why I've been able to live without fear was because I knew he would come the moment I called for him.

"While I am gone, Prime Minister Lucius will be the one to overlook the matters of the kingdom as well as the demon castle itself. I expect you to listen to his words as if they were my own. Is that clear?" These words were not a request but rather an order, his voice low and commanding, and everybody bowed their heads as one.

"Excellent. Dismissed." The king waved his hand, and without any further objections or questions, the demons streamed out of the hall. Some of the concubines looked longingly at Alphegor, but none dared to approach him. Even Deziara left, urged by her mother. Only Rosa, Lucius, and Azrael remained.

"Now, this is what I wanted to hear! It's been a while since I've been in a good fight. I'll get ready right away!" Azrael rolled his shoulder, clearly itching to go. But before he could get anywhere, Alphegor spoke up.

"You're not going anywhere," the king said in a firm voice and then looked down at Rosa.

"No... No. NO! I am NOT a babysitter," Azrael whined.

"You will protect Morrigan," Alphegor said with such ferocity that a shiver ran through Rosa's spine, and Azrael instantly straightened. "You are the only one strong enough to protect her, and your oath will compel you to do so."

"Why don't you just stay here, and I'll go and clean up the mess the Fallen have made?" Azrael suggested.

"You'll only create a bigger mess," Lucius countered. "Babysitting is a fitting job for you."

Azrael opened his mouth to object, but Alphegor's steely glare shut him up. Rosa's head was spinning as she tried to process the fact that, for the first time in four years, she'd be left alone without her strongest protector.

CHAPTER 18

GOODBYE

"Morrigan, don't be like that," Alphegor whined as Rosa sat in the corner of their room, refusing to look at him.

"Morrigan, come here." He tried to lure Rosa to the bed by waving her favorite chocolate candy—it was a blessing in itself that there was chocolate in the Underworld—but she still stubbornly sat in the corner, her cheeks puffed out.

Alphegor sighed and crouched down next to her, trying to look into her eyes.

"I have to do this. It is my duty as king," he said, and Rosa began to feel guilty about her little tantrum.

I know that you're the king, but that doesn't mean I'm okay with you just leaving all of a sudden.

She stubbornly refused to voice her thoughts, instead peering at the corner of the room. Alphegor sighed and scooped Rosa up into his arms, forcing her to look at him.

"I will be back before you even notice that I'm gone."

"I'll notice that you're gone after a few hours," she retorted, not daring to look him straight in the eyes. Instead, she chose to focus on his horns. Large and curved—probably some of the most majestic horns she'd seen on a demon. Her own horns resembled his, albeit they were much smaller.

Alphegor laughed at her remark and pinched her cheek. "And here I thought that you were more mature than Azrael. I see that you're still just a child."

Rosa gasped indignantly and swatted his hand away.

I may be in the body of a child, but I am still an adult on the inside. And I'm certainly more mature than Azrael, even if he is two hundred years older than me.

"Don't worry. Everything will be alright. Azrael will keep you safe, and you'll have Deziara, Gunna, and Faenor as your company." He reassured Rosa by gently patting her back.

Rosa opened her mouth to ask him to stay but hesitated, realizing she couldn't. He was a king—king of the whole Demon Kingdom which had many duchies within it. Although Rosa had no idea whether he was a benign king who ruled justly or a tyrannical king who forced everyone to obey—although she was willing to bet on the latter—he still had duties to attend to. He could not abandon them just because she wanted him here as her impenetrable shield.

"You have to come back soon..." she muttered instead, and Alphegor smiled.

"Of course. I'll come back as soon as I can," he assured her, then a wide grin spread across his face. "And I'll bring back souvenirs from the Fallen Kingdom."

"What is the Fallen Kingdom?" Rosa asked, voicing the question that had been on her mind since his announcement. There was still so much she didn't know. Her worldview was severely limited to the demon castle and the books contained within its walls. She couldn't even access the books she really wanted to read, as the librarians would always gently push her back into the children's section whenever she tried.

Alphegor's face hardened, and she almost regretted asking.

"It's not a simple thing to explain. The Fallen Kingdom is different from every other kingdom or country in the Underworld," he began slowly. Rosa knew that the Underworld consisted of many different countries, each usually representing a whole race. For example, from Faenor, she learned that there was a kingdom of Drow, and from Gunna, she found out about the Duergar Country. Both of these races were basically underground counterparts to their surface-dwelling kin and—according to both caretakers—had nasty tempers.

"The Fallen Kingdom doesn't have a single dominant race like ours, where demons thrive. Instead, it could be called a country of exiles."

"Exiles?"

"Yes. It lies in the very depths of the Underworld, in a place where even the fiercest of demons do not wish to dwell. Over time, all sorts of riffraff began gathering there and building settlements because nobody ever bothered them there. However, over the millennia, it has grown large enough to become its own country, and now they are eager to conquer their neighbors for resources," Alphegor explained, then ruffled Rosa's hair. "Sorry, that must have been too difficult for you to understand."

"Do they want to steal from the Demon Kingdom?" she dared to ask. The king seemed a bit surprised by her question but then nodded.

"That's right. So, your daddy will go and kick their butt." Alphegor grinned, and Rosa turned away, her cheeks tinting red.

Really? Daddy? I am embarrassed for you.

Rosa only ever addressed Alphegor as *Father,* even if he regularly pleaded with her to call him *Daddy, Dad,* or even *Papa.* She refused to use these sweet nicknames on a demon. They just didn't suit him. Not to mention that all of Alphegor's other daughters only referred to him as *Father.* There was no need for her to stick out like a sore thumb and make them more jealous of her.

"Come on, little one. It's getting late, and both of us need to rest."

He got up from the bed and carried Rosa over to her little bed, which was right next to his. She called it *little*, but on Earth, it would easily qualify as a queen-sized bed. It just looked little when compared to Alphegor's large bed.

He helped her dress into her silky, black nighty, and then gently tucked her under the covers.

"Good night, little one," he said, and with a clap of his hands, he turned off the light. She could hear the rustle of fabric as he undressed and then slipped into his own bed. For a while, she listened to the silence of the never-ending Underworld night. It was unnerving, and her heart wouldn't calm down enough for her to sleep. So, she silently slid out of her bed and crawled in next to Alphegor.

"Feeling lonely? I thought you were a big girl who would only sleep in her own bed." The demon chuckled but pulled her closer to his comforting warmth. Cuddling up to his side, Rosa listened to Alphegor's steady heartbeat.

"Today is different," she muttered and laid her head on his chest. "You'll be gone for a long time."

"It'll be just fine, little one. Soon you'll learn that a few months is nothing when compared to our long lifetime. We'll still have a lot of time to spend together." Alphegor stroked her hair, and slowly, she drifted off to sleep.

* * *

In the morning, a huge crowd of demons had gathered outside the demon castle walls to bid farewell to their king and brave demon warriors who were to stand by his side in battle. Those closest to him were gathered in the inner yard, standing in neat rows along the main exit road.

All of the concubines wept dramatically, although Rosa could tell how obviously fake their tears were. She even saw Vivian and a few of the others pull flasks out of their sleeves, probably full of water, and quickly drip them into their eyes. Rosa didn't suspect that anyone really believed that their tears were real.

Deziara was also standing among the concubines, right next to her weeping mother. In Lily's defense, she wasn't as dramatic or loud as the others. Deziara was completely silent next to her, with a steady stream running down her cheeks. She was one of the few demons whose tears were genuine.

"This has got to be the most obnoxious tradition ever," Azrael grumbled as he held Rosa in his arms. Gunna and Faenor stood close behind him.

"It shows their loyalty to the king," Lucius explained, standing right beside them. The older demon seemed pleased by the display, listening with closed eyes as if it were some pleasant melody.

"How loyal can they be if their tears are fake?" Azrael spat, looking even more annoyed. Rosa had to agree with him. It would have been better to see Alphegor off silently rather than listening to this chorus of fake wails.

The king slowly descended the castle staircase. He wore black battle armor, and his dark red cape flowed like a river of blood behind him.

He truly does look like the villainous Demon King. The people from Studio Goblin would be frothing at their mouths if they saw this.

As he strode through the inner yard, the concubines cried even more intensely, so much so that Azrael clicked his tongue in distaste. Some began waving handkerchiefs, probably hoping that he'd take one of them. But he went past them and instead stopped in front of Rosa.

"I'll be back soon, little one," he said quietly and patted her head with his large, gloved hand. Then he gave Azrael an icy glare, his voice turning cold and threatening. "If I see even a hair out of place on her head, then you'll be losing yours."

"Oh, she'll be fine. Stop being so dramatic," Azrael replied nonchalantly, but Rosa could feel a little tremor go through his body.

"Stay safe," Rosa whispered and silently prayed for him. Alphegor gave her a last appraising look, then turned his back to her and strode out beyond the castle gates. The demons outside cheered at the sight of him, yelling praises and ushering their king to annihilate the Fallen scum.

"Let's go inside," Rosa said, tugging on Azrael's sleeve.

"Don't have to ask me twice," he replied, and they quickly peeled away from the crowd, closely followed by Gunna and Faenor. Rosa glanced back one last time before Azrael slammed the castle door shut, separating them from the noisy crowd. "Finally, some silence."

But as the silence stretched around them, Rosa felt her heart grow heavy.

Alphegor will not return for a while...

A lone tear rolled down her cheek and fell onto her hand. She was never happy about Alphegor leaving, of course, for he was her main protector in this Demon-infested world. But she never expected that she would feel so *sad* seeing him leave.

"Oh, please, don't start the waterworks now," Azrael grumbled, noticing her tears.

"I am not!" Rosa quickly objected and hurriedly rubbed her eyes. "Something got in my eye."

"Sure." The demon rolled his eyes. Annoyed by his attitude, Rosa wriggled free of his hold. "Hey, where are you going?"

"To do whatever I want," she retorted, then turned towards

Gunna. "Could I have some art supplies brought to my room?"

"Art supplies? Of course, Lady Morrigan. I'd be happy to." The dwarf woman smiled from behind her beard and then hurried away.

"Why art supplies?" Faenor asked, appearing both perplexed and intrigued at the same time.

"I need to keep myself busy in the evenings somehow, now that Father is gone."

This is a chance to draw and paint without fear of Alphegor discovering my hobby. I always was so careful to only draw during Lady Asdeus' lessons, and I deliberately held myself back to appear less skilled than I actually am.

But until he returns, I can just use our room as an art studio. Only Gunna, Faenor, and some cleaning maids are allowed inside, so nobody else will discover what I'm doing.

"Why do I get a feeling that you're up to no good?" Azrael asked with a raised eyebrow.

"You're the one who is always up to no good," she retorted.

"Exactly. That is why I can sense when somebody else is doing something they shouldn't."

"I don't see how trying to keep myself busy is bad. You're just sad that Father left and don't want to admit it," Rosa taunted, attempting to divert his attention.

"Why would I be sad about that? With him gone, I am the strongest demon in this whole castle. Nobody can oppose me!" he gloated, lifting his hands high in the air.

"Alright, strongest Demon. Don't you have to go feed Haku?"

Azrael instantly slumped, annoyance clear on his face.

"You do know how to ruin a moment."

Rosa grinned and ran to her room upstairs, eager to try her hand at drawing and see just how much her skills had dulled over the years.

CHAPTER 19

SUNSHINE, LOLLIPOPS, AND DEZIARA

It was late evening. Alphegor had been gone for two days, giving Rosa some time alone each evening. Gunna initially offered to remain by Rosa's side until she fell asleep, but she managed to convince the nanny that there was no need. She couldn't leave without guards noticing anyway. Gunna, being kind and a bit gullible, agreed, and so Rosa's evenings were completely free and unsupervised.

The moment the dwarf woman was gone, Rosa melded with the shadows and slipped under the door. The two demon guards stationed outside her room were none the wiser to her ghosting past them. As Rosa learned over the years, shadow forms could only be seen by those who were actively looking for them. But the guards wouldn't have expected Rosa to make an escape.

So, after creeping her way to the study room, she pilfered some of the art supplies and made her way back. While Gunna had brought some to her, they were child supplies: charcoal, erasers, and coloring sticks. Rosa wanted to do something with actual paints, so she also needed brushes, a palette, and a container for water.

Another neat trick Rosa learned in her magic lessons with Azrael was the ability to turn physical things into shadows as well. It wasn't really a difficult skill to master since even the first time she blended into the shadows, she had pulled her clothes along with her without even thinking about it. As long as she held the object in her hands when she became a shadow, she could take it along.

And so, after a few sneaky trips to the study room and back, she had everything she needed to make her first masterpiece. Rosa propped the large canvas against Alphegor's desk. Well, it was the smallest canvas she could find, but it still felt large compared to her. Then she set out all the supplies and admired her workstation as her heart beat with excitement.

"What should I paint first?" she muttered quietly as her eyes shot from one bright color to the next.

"A waterfall hidden in a deep, lush jungle? Or perhaps the moon illuminating a calm countryside? Or perhaps a whale swimming near the surface of the ocean?" Rosa was brimming with inspiration, her smile growing wider and wider.

"Wait, I know!" She grabbed the yellow and white paint and began mixing them together. She could already see in her mind what she wanted to create. Her brush strokes probably wouldn't be as pre-cise as they were before, but Rosa was confident she could create her vision.

She was about to touch her brush to the canvas, then faltered and put it down, picking up charcoal instead.

"There's no need to rush. I have plenty of time, so I can take it slow," she muttered in English. The language almost felt foreign on her tongue; however, now was the best time to remember her roots. She hadn't had any chance to speak it with Alphegor around.

"Baby steps," she said and began drawing up a sketch on her canvas while quietly talking herself through it in English. The process was difficult as her hands had trouble reaching the top, and she wasn't used to moving around so much in her drawing process.

Two hours later, Rosa finished. She laid down her base, and the poor eraser was half its original size.

"That should be enough for today. I better put these away," she decided and began stashing all the supplies in the deep recesses of Alphegor's wardrobe. Nobody would dare to open it with the king gone, and the maids had no reason to clean already spotless clothes.

* * *

Each evening over the next week, Rosa continued to secretly work on her painting. She didn't pay much attention to what was going on during the day, instead constantly thinking of ways to improve her work.

If she had her way, she'd be painting all day long, but there was no good excuse to get away from her usual lessons. Not to mention that she did want to spend some time with Haku and Deziara. It helped her mind to unwind and relax.

"Are you alright, Morri?" Deziara asked after Rosa tripped over Haku's tail for the fifth time that day. While the dragon's body wasn't too large, he had an amazingly long tail that swayed behind him like an uncontrollable whip.

"Yes, I'm alright." Rosa wiped the dirt off her skirt absentmindedly as she pondered the best way to finish the painting.

"You seem... weird lately," her sister remarked as she helped to clear off the remaining dust.

"Do I?" Rosa snapped out of her thoughts.

If Deziara thinks I'm acting strange, then somebody else may have noticed something, too. Have I been careless because Alphegor is not around?

"Yeah. You seem to be bumping into a lot of things."

"Oh... I... I'm just thinking about a lot of... stuff..." Rosa stammered, her mind not gracing her with an eloquent answer. Deziara arched her eyebrow.

"What does a squirt like you have to think about?" She placed her hands on her hips and looked down on Rosa in a snobbish, rich-kid kind of way. Then suddenly, her bravado dropped, and a wide grin spread on her face. "Oh, I get it. You just really miss Father, don't you?"

"What? I... Yeah." Rosa nodded.

It's not really true, but it's not a complete lie either. A safe answer.

"I knew it! Well, it's completely normal. I miss him a little bit too." Deziara smiled and ruffled Rosa's hair, completely messing up Gunna's neat braid. Rosa pushed her hand away, trying to salvage whatever she could of her hair. "How about you come and eat dinner with me and Mother?"

"You and Lady Lily?" Rosa asked, making sure that she heard Deziara correctly.

A child from another woman eating together with a consort is com-pletely unheard of. The logical conclusion would be that they're trying to poison me.

"Yes, come on! It'll be fun." Deziara began pulling Rosa towards the castle entrance.

"Wait, wait, what about Haku?" She pointed towards the dragon, who looked at them with sad puppy eyes.

"Ah... Right... He's not allowed in the castle anymore." The girl slumped.

"It's alright. You can go eat. I'll stay with Haku." Rosa tried to wriggle herself out of the situation, but Deziara stubbornly shook her head. Once she had decided on something, it was nearly impossible to talk her out of it.

"There's still time until dinner, so we can play with Haku a little more and then go." The dragon instantly perked up at these words and began circling around them.

I need to find an excuse not to go. Even if Lady Lily is the least threatening of all four consorts, I'd still rather not give her such a golden opportunity. But what could I do to change Deziara's mind?

An idea struck Rosa, but she would have to execute it subtly, otherwise Deziara might feel slighted. It felt a bit silly, trying to be merciful to her older sister's feelings, but Rosa had grown quite attached to the little firecracker.

Rosa waited for her sister's attention to drift, and when Haku provided a distraction with his tiny wing flaps grabbing Deziara's attention, Rosa softly whispered, "Azrael."

Nothing happened.

Damn, he usually comes right away when I call him, but maybe he can't hear me unless my voice is loud enough.

"Azrael," she tried again when Haku was being especially rowdy, sniffing Deziara's armpits and making the little demon girl giggle and squirm.

This time, a dark shadow appeared in front of Rosa, and an annoyed-looking Azrael rose out of it. Deziara and Haku both froze the moment they saw the demon.

"What are you doing here?" The girl pointed an accusatory finger at the demon. He arched his eyebrow and looked at Rosa as if trying to understand why exactly she had summoned him.

"To check what you two troublemakers up to, obviously," he replied and bent down to peer at Deziara with a suspicious glance.

"We're not doing anything. Just playing with Haku, which should be what you're doing."

"My job is not to play with the dragon; it's to make sure it doesn't cause another fire in the castle." Azrael glared at the little, scaly creature, who lowered its head guiltily.

"Hey, that was an accident! Wasn't it, Haku?" Deziara protectively patted the dragon's head, who melted into her embrace and wagged his tail.

"Whatever. If you aren't planning on sneaking the dragon into the castle, I don't care what you do." Azrael waved his hand and was about to disappear into the shadows before Rosa grabbed his pant leg desperately.

The demon looked a bit surprised, while Deziara made a face like Rosa had just completely betrayed her.

"Morri, let him go! We don't need him to join our dinner," the girl protested.

Oh, thank God she's still a child who knows nothing about being subtle. If I'm lucky, Azrael will forbid me from going.

"What dinner?" he asked suspiciously, narrowing his eyes.

"That doesn't concern you. You're not invited."

"Morrigan." Azrael turned to her for an explanation.

"Don't tell him anything, Morri!"

Caught between a rock and a hard place. How can I warn Azrael about the doomsday dinner without making Deziara angry with me?

"We're just going to eat together," Rosa replied, hoping that the demon would catch on.

"Eat together?" Azrael asked, and Rosa could see how his mind slowly pieced together the puzzle she had laid out. "I'll join too."

"No! It'll be just me, Morri, and Mommy," Deziara objected and stomped her foot angrily on the ground.

"Princess, I think you're forgetting that Morrigan cannot attend dinner with you and your *mommy* alone. If she's to go, then she needs a caretaker with her," Azrael explained in a surprisingly calm and patient manner.

There's this sneaky grin on his face. Is he plotting something?

"She has two guards following her at all times!" Deziara objected and pointed towards the two demon men standing some ways away, trying to blend in with the dark garden hedges. Unfortunately, they were so bulky that they stood out like a sore thumb.

"Guards are a completely different matter. She needs an actual supervisor to go with her." Azrael smirked and pointed at himself with his thumb.

"No!" Rosa and Deziara objected at the same time.

I'm not sure what he is trying to accomplish, but there must be something in it for him if he's going willingly. Perhaps he wants something from Lady Lily? In either case, it smells like trouble.

"Sorry, but if you want to have dinner together, then I have to come along as well."

For a moment, Rosa considered asking Gunna or Faenor to be her escort. But if something were to happen, neither of them could really do anything.

"Then I'll just eat on my own like always," Rosa said.

"No! I don't want to leave you alone when Father is gone. It must be lonely to always be on your own. Besides..." Deziara's voice grew quieter, and she fidgeted awkwardly, her cheeks growing red. "I've always wanted to eat together with my sisters... But nobody ever wanted to eat with me."

Rosa could feel her heart clench.

This child only ever wanted to get along with her sisters. To spend some time together with them. But all the concubines are so busy trying to appeal themselves and their daughters to Alphegor that they can only ever see each other as enemies.

"Okay, I'll go to dinner with you then!" Rosa choked out.

What's the worst that could happen? Well, Lady Lily could try poisoning me, but Azrael would stop that from happening, right? He's bound by the oath.

"Splendid. Let's hurry up then." Azrael smiled pleasantly and, with a shrill whistle, ordered Haku to retreat to his house. The dragon huffed a smoky sigh of displeasure and then lumbered away.

"I don't want YOU to come," Deziara protested and made shooing motions at Azrael.

"Sorry, but if you wish to dine with your sister, then I'm coming along," he said with an ominous smile.

He is definitely plotting something.

Chapter 20

Dinner With Lady Lily

"This is an... interesting set of guests you've brought, Deziara," Lady Lily said when Deziara, Rosa, Azrael, and Rosa's two bulky guards arrived in one of the many dining halls. The huge castle had enough of those for each concubine to host her own party simultaneously and a dozen more for good measure.

The demoness was dressed more modestly than Rosa was used to seeing her. Her hair was tied in a simple bun behind her back, while her dark purple dress covered her ample chest. This was the first time Rosa had seen a concubine or a consort with her chest covered.

I guess without Alphegor around, there's no need to show off.

"I only wanted to bring Morri, but Azrael came along." Deziara glared at the white-haired Demon, who flashed a brilliant smile at the concubine.

"As Princess Morrigan's guardian in His Majesty's absence, I have to make sure nothing bad happens to her."

"Then, as her guardian, you won't mind standing along with the guards and not interfering with our dinner," Lady Lily replied with an equally sweet smile. Azrael faltered momentarily but managed to maintain his nonchalant expression.

"Surely you must understand that I have to taste everything the Princess eats."

"Then go ahead and taste it, and we'll prepare a fresh—*not poisoned*—dish for the Princess afterward."

The sparks between the two were almost visible. Deziara and Rosa stood aside, neither of them daring to say a word.

"My, my. I was sure that His Majesty's third consort would be more gracious towards her daughter's guests."

"Princess Morrigan is a guest, not you."

"But you must be aware that where the Princess goes, I follow. It was an order from the king himself. You wouldn't question His Majesty's orders now, would you?" This seemed to strike a nerve, causing Lady Lily's eye to twitch.

"Alright, so be it." The demoness snapped her fingers, summoning a demon maid who hurried to her side. "Prepare two more seats at the dinner table. One for Princess Morrigan and one for her... dog."

Azrael's smile remained intact despite the insult. In fact, he looked very pleased with himself.

"So, how was your day, dear?" Lady Lily turned towards her daughter, lowering herself to eye level with Deziara.

"It was great! Morri and I played with Haku a lot. He's making good progress with his flying practice. I can see his wings growing larger by the day."

"That's wonderful. How were your lessons?"

Deziara's smile fell, and she looked to the side. "It was... alright."

"Did something happen?"

"Nothing, really. It's just so boring. Who cares about the Seven Legendary demon lords? It's nothing more than a myth anyway," the girl protested with a huff. "It's not really fair that I have to listen to it while Rosa just gets to do what she wants."

Don't pull me into this. I'm technically not old enough to understand these things. Although, I have to agree that the way Lady Asdeus spoke about the demon lords was more boring than the prattle of my elderly college professor lecturing about art history.

"Even if it's boring, you have to pay attention. It is important for a princess to know these things," Lady Lily said, then nudged her daughter towards the table. "Let's go sit at the table."

Two sets of tableware had already been arranged on the long table across from each other. Lady Lily sat Deziara in front of one set before taking the empty seat next to her. Azrael, in the meantime, placed Rosa in front of the other set and took the seat directly across from the demoness. The two glared at each other with unhidden hatred.

"Finally, I get to eat with Morri. I only wish Father was here too," Deziara chimed, happily swaying from side to side.

"I'm sure we could convince him to eat with us once he returns. Wouldn't you like that too, Morrigan?" Lady Lily lit up at Rosa, who tried her best to return the smile, but it came out somewhat forced and awkward.

"Y-Yes. It would be nice."

"I personally like our setup right now," Azrael commented as he tapped his finger on the table.

"On what merit?" the demoness' gaze turned icy the moment he spoke up.

"I am the strongest demon right after His Majesty and the Princess' trusted guardian."

"Trusted guardian? Without that oath of yours, the king wouldn't even let you get close to the Princess."

"Oh, on the contrary—he was the one who sought me out to teach magic to the Princess."

Lady Lily arched her eyebrow, watching over Azrael's features skeptically.

"Why would he want *you* to teach Princess Morrigan? There are many great magic teachers with far more experience. You're barely out of your own mother's womb."

"Because His Majesty clearly understands my worth."

At that moment, the maids arrived, carrying another set of tableware for Lady Lily and Azrael, as well as some appetizers consisting of something akin to garlic bread and fish canapes.

"Try the volcano bread, it's good," Deziara urged Rosa, who saw no reason to deny her. She took the dark-looking bread and found that it was still warm. The crust was crunchy and crumbly, while the inside was soft with a generous dollop of garlic butter inside. The bread had a stronger flavor than regular white bread, while the butter with garlic also had pleasant cheesy notes.

"This is delicious," Rosa praised after swallowing the tasty morsel.

"Freshly baked," Lady Lily answered with a satisfied smile, nodding approvingly as she gestured for Rosa to have more.

"Princess, you should let me taste everything first before you eat it," Azrael reprimanded and pulled the bread out of her hand.

The more logical part of Rosa said that he was right and that she could have already eaten something poisonous. But the glutton in her reached out and grabbed the bread back, stuffing it into her face without any remorse.

"Deziara is eating it too," Rosa objected, pointing at her sister, who was likewise devouring the fresh bread.

"Oh, stop it with the poisoning nonsense already. I wouldn't poison my best friend's daughter." Lady Lily glared at Azrael as she broke a fresh loaf in half and gave one piece to Rosa and the other to Deziara.

Best friend's daughter? She's not talking about Alphegor—she always refers to him by his title. So does she mean...

"You were friends with my m-mom?" Rosa couldn't say *mother* as it instantly made her remember that last, fateful phone call. Nobody had ever talked about her demon mother, so she knew essentially nothing about her. She once tried asking Alphegor, but he quickly diverted the topic.

"Oh, yes. My dearest Eirwen was a demon like no other. How I wish she could join us at this dinner table at least one more time." There was melancholy in Lady Lily's eyes that Rosa had not expected to see.

Shouldn't a king's consort be more hostile towards the late queen?

"Can you tell me more about her?" Rosa ventured to ask. A pained smile spread on the demoness' lips, and she nodded.

"Somebody should tell you and it's not like this whelp would do her memory justice." Lady Lily shot Azrael another icy glare, then turned her attention back to Rosa. "I imagine the king hasn't really talked about her, has he?"

"No."

"I thought as much. The topic is no doubt too painful for him. There were never two demons better suited for each other than them," she began, and Rosa couldn't help but narrow her eyes in doubt.

Alphegor? Meant for only one woman? Then why does he have a whole damn harem full of women and twenty-four daughters to boot?

"I understand your doubt, Morrigan, but remember that your father is also the king of the Underworld. He has duties to uphold, treaties to forge, and some conflicts are better solved peacefully by way of marriage," she explained, which earned a confused look from Deziara, who had her mouth full of bread.

"You two will understand it better once you're older. Just trust me when I say that the king was—no, probably still is—mad for Eirwen. That is why he cherishes you so much, Morrigan. You are her precious daughter, somebody she gave her life for."

Wait... Gave her life for me? What does that mean? Is that just a nice way of saying she died at childbirth?

One of the maids suddenly spoke up with a calm, measured tone. "Lady Lily, I believe such topics are still too heavy for the Princesses." This was the first time Rosa witnessed any maid chime in during a conversation. Usually, they remained silent, only muttering among themselves.

"Oh, yes, I think you might be right. How about I tell you something else about her?" Lady Lily repositioned her glasses and gave Rosa a somewhat awkward smile.

Damn, it would have been nice to understand what she meant by Eirwen giving her life for mine, but I guess I can't push it now.

Rosa blurted out the first simple question that came to her mind. "What did she look like?"

"Eirwen was a real beauty. Her silky white hair cascaded nearly to the ground, and her silver eyes blazed with strength and passion. Despite her not being as large as any of the concubines, she had such charm that we just couldn't compare to her."

Not as large? I don't think any of the concubines are large... Wait... Is she talking about her breasts? I could have lived without knowing that bit of information.

"Did she know magic?" Deziara suddenly asked.

"Oh, yes. In fact, when it came to magic, there was nobody stronger than her."

"Not even Father?"

"Not even him. Poor doggy here was perpetually beaten by her." Lady Lily snickered and glanced at the disgruntled Azrael.

"Hey, she was my teacher, and we were training, so it doesn't count," Azrael grumbled.

"Yes, I imagine that's the only reason why His Majesty tolerates you. You were her only pupil."

"And she would have never found a better one." Azrael flashed a smile, regaining his confidence.

"Oh, don't be so full of yourself. Your magical prowess is a testament to *her* skills, not your own."

"We'll see once I've properly trained Princess Morrigan." Azrael placed a heavy hand on Rosa's shoulder.

Don't use me as a ploy to put yourself on a pedestal!

Rosa shook off his hand and was about to berate him when the maids came in with trolleys filled with plates. They placed the dishes in front of everyone, and once everything was prepared, they lifted the lids in unison.

Beneath the covers lay an elegant array of succulent meats and roasted vegetables that shone with a translucent glaze. It smelled so divine that Rosa instantly began salivating.

"It is time to eat. Dig in, everyone!" Lady Lily clapped her hands, and Rosa went for the food right away. Deziara likewise didn't hold back and began stuffing her face with gusto.

The meat was so soft and juicy that it instantly melted onto Rosa's tongue. The vegetables were cooked to perfection, and the sweet glaze made them taste more like a dessert than an actual meal. Even Deziara, who Rosa expected to be the kind of child who hated vegetables, ate them with pleasure.

"Lady Lily, would you be willing to bend my ear a little while we eat?" Azrael asked softly.

There it is! I knew he wanted something from her.

"You'd bend it even if I wasn't willing," Lady Lily retorted, not lifting her gaze from the plate in front of her.

"Perhaps, but I believe my request will be beneficial for us both.

"Oh, really? I highly doubt it, but go ahead and say your piece. I am curious as to what kind of nonsense you've come up with this time."

"It's not nonsense. In fact, I believe this topic is quite important for our whole kingdom. No, the whole Underworld." Lady Lily arched her brow at this while delicately chewing on a piece of carrot. Azrael took her silence as an indication to continue. "Don't you think it's time we start thinking about the next demon queen?"

Lady Lily stopped chewing while Rosa did her best to appear as interested in her meal as Deziara was.

"It's been only four years. I don't think such a decision needs to be rushed," she finally replied after swallowing her food.

"Yes, we do have our powerful king to watch over us, however, don't you think the burden is too heavy for him alone? The late queen helped him quite often with state affairs. Or so I've heard." Azrael smiled pleasantly.

What is he scheming? I highly doubt he cares about Alphegor's workload.

"I am certain King Alphegor is capable enough to understand whether he needs help or not. Besides, he could ask any of us consorts or even concubines for help if he so wished," Lady Lily countered coolly and dabbed the already-clean corner of her mouth with a napkin.

"Can he, though?" Azrael asked, and Rosa felt his gaze linger on her.

He can't ask for help because of me? Is it because Alphegor fears what concubines might do to me?

"But I believe we have a solution right here at this dinner table. After all, you seem to hold the Crown Princess in high regard."

Lady Lily frowned, and her gaze drifted towards Rosa as well.

Feeling the sudden weight of their scrutiny, she chewed at the meat enthusiastically, although it had lost all of its previous appeal.

"Why don't you just think about it? I'd be willing to help you out if you'd need support," Azrael finished, and put a large piece of meat in his mouth, chewing it with a self-satisfied smirk.

Chapter 21

Window to the Past

Once the dinner with Lady Lily and Deziara was over, Rosa secluded herself in her room, convincing her nanny that she was tired and would go to sleep right away. Gunna wanted to help her dress, but Rosa gently rejected her offer, instead urging her to enjoy the free evening.

Azrael wants Lady Lily to become the next demon queen? Previously, when speaking to Lady Asdeus, he claimed that he was going to profit if I were to become the queen. What the hell is he plotting?

Rosa paced around the room, as she tried to unravel Azrael's reasoning, but no matter how much she thought and pondered, she couldn't come to grips with what his true goal might be.

I don't know enough about demons to draw any conclusions. Their actions seem so contradictory at times.

With a sigh, she decided to put the matter aside for today, and instead return to things that really mattered. She pulled her art supplies out of Alphegor's closet and set everything up.

"Today, I am going to finish this," Rosa told herself, and began mixing paints on her palette and then laying them down on the canvas. This time she worked with the smallest brush, refining the details and fixing any mistakes that might have crept in.

For two hours, her focus was only on her painting. Her little hand began to tremble by the end of it, making detailed work even more difficult, but she persisted.

"There..." she said and took a few steps back. "It is finished."

Gentle orange and yellow tones dominated the painting. It was a cityscape, or to be exact, it was the view from her apartment window. She had lived on the seventh floor in a large building that had a wonderful view of the whole city. It was taller than most of the other nearby structures; in fact, the surrounding area was mostly made up of private homes. Due to that, from her window she had a clear view all the way to the sea.

Lush trees were planted along the streets, littering the small city with life and greenery, while the sparkling sea in the distance with its setting sun gave a sense of tranquility and peace. Rosa purposely avoided overly bright colors in the painting, instead keeping to gentle pastels.

A tear ran down Rosa's cheek as she looked at the painting. She never thought her small apartment was anything special. In fact, she had hoped to move out of it as soon as she got more comfortable at her new job. But now, after living in the Underworld for four years, she wished nothing more but to be back in that tiny space she called home, sipping peppermint tea and looking over the city as the sun set over the sea.

After a while, Rosa wiped away her tears and clapped her hands over her cheeks to bring some vigor back into her body.

Nothing would happen just because she cried—she had to keep moving forward. Rosa hid her painting and all the supplies in the wardrobe. After cleaning herself up and dressing into her nightie, she crawled into her bed and fell asleep.

* * *

The next day started like any other. She dressed and ate in Gunna's bubbly company—although the nanny herself wasn't allowed to eat together with her—while being watched by the demon maids. Normally Morrigan didn't pay much attention to the maids since they never bothered to engage in a conversation with her. But they seemed more tense than usual. As she ate, she heard some maids whispering among themselves.

"How horrible. I bet they've become more bold because His Majesty is away."

"They'll regret it once he returns. Stealing away children of all things."

Stealing children? What is that about?

But Morrigan couldn't catch any more of their chatter and had to resign herself to going to Azrael's lesson without finding out anything more.

Once she reached the training grounds, he greeted her with a mischievously sweet smile right from the get-go.

"Good morning, Princess! Had a good night's rest?"

Rosa squinted her eyes at him suspiciously.

He's plotting something again.

"Yes." Rosa dragged out the word slowly while carefully observing his features.

"Have lots of energy?" He smiled broadly. A picture of innocence, if not for his black horns and the tail that kept flicking from side to side like a cat preparing to pounce on its prey.

"Yes?" she answered with uncertainty.

"Wonderful! Then I believe it is time that you learned something new. Your shadow form is very good; you don't get queasy anymore and you're way ahead of your sisters when it comes to speed."

"Something new?" She cocked her head.

Is he talking about what else I could do in shadow form? But what else could there be? Shadow spears? Restraining people with shadows? Snuffing out lights?

"Yes. I was seven when I learned my second ability, but since you have a slightly superior magical potential, I believe you're ready for yours right now," Azrael explained and then pulled a familiar box from his pocket. It was the gift she had received from Lucius—the alexandrite gem.

He actually admitted that? Never thought this prideful demon would admit to anyone being better than him.

But this isn't so bad. I thought I'd have to stay in my shadow form until the point of complete exhaustion and keep pushing myself past my limits to unlock some new ability... Or something like that.

"Alright. How... How do I learn it?" She took the gem from its box and turned it around in her hands. It shone red and purple, and an occasional glint of emerald appeared as she lifted it closer to the light.

"You absorb it," Azrael said nonchalantly with a wide grin on his face.

"A-Absorb it?" Rosa stared down at the alexandrite, dumbfounded. She poked it with her finger and it felt exactly as she expected—rock solid. "How?"

"Just accept it into your body."

"Huh?" Rosa stared at Azrael as if he were a lunatic.

You cannot accept gems into your body. What is this nonsense? Is he just messing with me?

Azrael smirked in a victorious fashion. "You don't understand it? With your talents I expected you to do it naturally. I succeeded with my first try."

So, you're just gloating. Pompous prick.

Rosa had the urge to throw the gem in Azrael's face, but he'd probably stop it with some magic.

"Your explanation sucks," she announced, and this seemed to strike a nerve.

"There is no explanation, Princess. You just absorb the gem."

"How do I absorb it? I am not a slime, I cannot absorb things."

"No, you are a demon and you can absorb magic," Azrael retorted as Rosa glared at him. They stared at each other for a tense moment, then the demon clicked his tongue in annoyance.

He finally relented and crouched down next to her. "Alright, alright. I'll try to explain it as your mother explained it to me. You see this gem, right? What does it feel like?"

"Like a rock," Rosa answered in annoyance.

"Yeah, that might be the problem. Do not think of it as a rock. Think of it as a very hard, dense piece of magic."

How am I supposed to think of something as magic? Isn't magic just energy? Like electricity.

Rosa tried to imagine the gem being a little battery charged to the brim.

"Did you imagine it?" he asked, his voice quiet and calm.

"I think so?"

"Well, now imagine that you're taking all that energy into your body. Imagine it flowing from your hands to your limbs and then spreading out through your whole body," Azrael instructed. Rosa nodded and then imagined the electricity within her gem battery beginning to enter her body. She felt a small pulse in her hand and recoiled, throwing away the gem. It clattered across the floor until it came to a stop.

"Hey, why'd you do that?"

"My fingers got zapped," Rosa exclaimed, cradling her hands close to her body.

Maybe imagining it as electricity wasn't a good idea. A normal person wouldn't want electricity in their body.

"Zapped? Is that some made-up word of yours?" Azrael reached for the gem, then placed it back into her hands. "Try again, and don't be afraid when you feel the magic flow into you. Close your eyes— that might help you imagine it."

Rosa nodded and closed her eyes. This time she imagined the gem being a piece of ice. She imagined it melting and the water from it flowing into her body. This time, the feeling was much gentler, and she could feel how it flowed smoothly, settling down in her every cell. Once she reopened her eyes, the gem in her hands was gone.

"I... I absorbed it?" she asked, unsure.

"You did, Princess. Good job." He rustled her hair with an un-characteristically warm smile on his face. However, it didn't last as it soon became distorted by a nasty grin. "I, however, was better."

"If you were better at explaining, I would have gotten it right on the first try," she objected.

"Nobody likes a sore loser, Princess."

Rosa puffed out her cheeks and wondered if there was something nearby that she could throw in his stupid face.

"Alright, alright. Let's get to our first shapeshifting lesson then. Hopefully, it'll go better than the gem absorption. But it will require you to use your imagination," Azrael teased, and then suddenly his shape warped. A few seconds later, Alphegor was standing in his place.

"Whaa?" Rosa exclaimed in surprise. For a second, she believed that it was actually Alphegor standing there in front of her, but then

Azrael's signature grin marred his face, and Rosa winced. "Turn back. You're ruining Father's image."

"Aww, here I thought you'd be happy to see your daddy again."

"Not when I know that it's actually you," Rosa grumbled.

Azrael laughed, and the fact he still looked like Alphegor made for a rather distressing sight, as the Demon King never showed such goofy expressions.

Alphegor's features shifted, slowly morphing and moving. A few moments later, a large, white deer stood in his place. Its horns seemed to emit an ethereal glow, while its pristine white fur looked to be made of pure snow.

"You can shapeshift into animals too?" Rosa asked as she admired the majestic deer. Suddenly Azrael's grin appeared on the deer as well, and Rosa jumped back in surprise. "Do you have to ruin everything?"

"I just wanted to demonstrate that you can turn into just about anything you can imagine," the white deer Azrael said solemnly.

"Can you turn into inanimate objects?"

The deer shifted its stance, deep in thought. Then he shook his head and turned back into his familiar Azrael shape.

"You can, of course. But it's not very pleasant, and I don't recommend it.

"Why not?"

"Because as living creatures, it is natural for us to be moving. Even if our bodies aren't moving, hearts, our blood, and other organs are constantly working." Azrael was prepared to say more, but noticing Rosa's intent gaze, he snickered. "It's too difficult for a kid like you to understand. Just be content with turning into other beings. If you can, that is."

Rosa shifted uncomfortably and looked down at her hands. Changing shape sounded a bit scary.

I wonder how it actually works? Am I changing my actual body along with all of the molecular structure? Or is it just that I appear different to others and my actual body is the same? But such a question is clearly too advanced for a four-year-old to ask.

"So I just... imagine being somebody else?"

"Yes, just like you imagined absorbing the stone into yourself. Don't think too much about it the first time—just turn into whatever is the first thing that comes to your mind," Azrael said and crossed his arms over his chest, observing Rosa with interest.

"Okay... First thing that comes to my mind..." she mumbled and closed her eyes. For some reason the painting she finished yesterday popped into her mind, and she thought of her tiny apartment. Rosa remembered how she looked in her full-body mirror—how she looked as a human.

Before she could shake the visage away and imagine something else, she heard a whistle from Azrael and opened her eyes. He wasn't as tall anymore, even if still a bit taller than her, and looked less intimidating than before. As she looked down at her hands, she saw her familiar slender fingers. Pale but most definitely with more color than her demon skin.

"I certainly wasn't expecting that..." Azrael drawled, looking surprised.

"What? What do I look like?" she asked, despite knowing perfectly well how she looked.

Dammit, this is not what I wanted, but my old body was the first thing that came into my mind.

"How is this even possible?" Azrael squinted his eyes at her and scratched his chin thoughtfully.

This is bad! As Morrigan, I shouldn't have seen any humans before now and yet I shapeshifted into one. This is really, really bad!

CHAPTER 22

THE EXPOSED SECRET

Rosa wondered whether she could quickly shift back to her demon self, but it wasn't like doing so would undo the damage she had done.

"Would you like to see what you've turned into?" Azrael asked, his lips pursed together, and his eyebrows furrowed.

"Y-Yes," Rosa said shakily, praying that Azrael wouldn't get suspicious of her. He disappeared into the shadows for a few minutes and then reappeared, holding a full-body mirror in hand.

"Come take a look." Rosa walked up to the mirror slowly. Her heart beat like crazy while Azrael observed her every step.

What is he thinking right now? Does he suspect that there's actually a human in this body? I need to look surprised. If I play it well, he might think it was just a child's imagination running wild.

Finally reaching the mirror, Rosa looked at her reflection and did her best to feign surprise. Of course, what stared back at her from the mirror was her very familiar human self. Same platinum blonde hair, same pale skin, same blue eyes. It was a stark contrast to the dark-skinned, white-haired demon holding the mirror. In fact, they probably couldn't have been more different.

"W-What a strange shape..." Rosa said with a forced chuckle. "Did I fail?"

"You look different, so no—you shapeshifted correctly," he replied, his signature smile returning to his lips. "I just didn't expect you to try mimicking your mother."

"I..." Rosa gaped at him for a moment, then recalled the conversation she had with Lady Lily.

My demon mother had white hair, and the platinum blonde hair I had as a human is pretty close.

"You must have been snooping around the king's stuff. Little rascal. Not that I blame you—I'd be curious about my mother too. You did get some things wrong, but it's to be expected on the first try." Azrael laughed, and Rosa exhaled in relief.

"Yes, I only saw her portrait once." She smiled as she lied through her teeth.

"That is not enough information to shift, Princess." Azrael pointed his finger up, and smirked. "You need to have a clear image when you transform, not just some vague idea. It's easier to transform into people you have seen from all angles."

"Really?" Rosa chuckled awkwardly.

"Yes, really. Now change back into your normal shape and let's try to transform into something else this time," he commanded, then propped the mirror against a nearby wall.

Rosa did not need any more encouragement. She closed her eyes and imagined her demon child self, instantly feeling herself becoming smaller. But before she could fully open her eyes, she heard the door to the training ground open.

"Excuse me, but Lady Asdeus sent me to retrieve Princess Morrigan for her lesson," came the shaky voice of Faenor.

Morrigan changed back into her demon form, but she had no doubt that the elf had seen her transformation.

"Really? Tell her to wait. It's not like she's actually teaching the Princess anything useful." Azrael tried to wave Faenor off.

The elf shifted uncomfortably. "L-Lady Asdeus has decided that it is time for her to begin her studies in earnest. She believes the Princess is ready," he said in a trembling voice, not daring to meet Azrael's eye.

Caught between a rock and a hard place. Poor Faenor. If he goes back to Lady Asdeus without me, then he'll get punished. But how is he supposed to convince Azrael, who doesn't have even a sliver of compassion for slaves? I suppose it's best if I intervene.

"I'll go with Faenor. I'll practice shapeshifting by myself later," Rosa assured Azrael. The white-haired demon sighed.

"Fine. I suppose I'll just go rest instead," he relented, although she had a feeling that the demon was not averse to having some extra free time. Faenor's shoulders visibly relaxed as he walked up to Rosa, reaching out his hand for her.

"Let's go. Your sister is already with Lady Asdeus."

Rosa nodded, wondering what exactly the demoness wanted to teach her.

It's likely she'll start with reading and writing, but thanks to Faenor I already recognize letters. I've never had a chance to practice them, but I imagine it shouldn't be too difficult.

* * *

It urned out that Rosa had been right about her prediction. Lady Asdeus was set on teaching her how to read and write. So she had a giant letter—one of the Demon alphabet letters—written on the blackboard in front of her.

How quickly do children begin understanding letters? They probably don't get it right on the first try.

Rosa glared at it and wondered how she could mess up in a way that would appear natural for a child. Hopefully, she looked at

Deziara, but Lady Asdeus was drilling some math equations into her, causing the girl to grip painfully at her ponytail in sheer desperation.

Alright, let's just go full-on stupid.

She drew random squiggly lines, not bothering to make them neat or in any way resemble what was in front of her.

"Done," she announced with a smile. Lady Asdeus checked over Deziara's work one more time, then walked over to Rosa's desk. Her face instantly scrunched up, and the corners of her mouth dropped.

"Princess Morrigan, I believe you didn't understand the task I gave you. It was to draw this exact letter. I've seen you draw very nice pictures before," the teacher said and pushed a stray lock from her face.

Drat... I guess I overdid it. Let's try to make it at least somewhat legible this time.

"Oh, I understand it now." Rosa plastered on a smile and turned the notebook to a fresh page. This time, Lady Asdeus remained by her side, watching her every movement.

I'll go slow and press hard. Lines always look ugly that way.

She dutifully copied the letter, but it looked unsteady, as if it wasn't sure of its own existence.

"Wonderful! That's a great start. Now you need to repeat it fifty more times," Lady Asdeus said with a smile.

Fifty? Are you crazy? Who forces a four-year-old to write a single letter fifty times? I may not be a preschool teacher, but I'm pretty sure that is not a good education method.

Nonetheless, the task was set for her, so she had to obey. Rosa had witnessed plenty of times how Lady Asdeus dealt with Deziara when she tried to cut corners. It would always result in needing to do more.

"Okay..." Rosa mumbled and began slowly drawing crooked-looking letters. It was actually tiring, trying to do each of them wrong but in a different way. After all, no two mistakes were alike so she had to make sure that hers weren't either. Sometimes, she'd make some lines deliberately longer; other times, shorter. Occasionally she wouldn't connect the letters right or draw way beyond where a line should end.

"Please, be more careful. Try to copy the letter exactly as shown." The demoness came up to Rosa and crossed out half of the letters with a bright red ink pen. "Do those again."

You want me to redo ten whole letters? You monster! No wonder Deziara is always complaining about your lessons.

"Okay..." Rosa barely managed to contain her displeasure and slowly began tracing the letter again. Her little hand was getting tired because she had been pushing the ink pen rather hard.

I still have like fifteen left... I wish I could just go at normal speed. I'd be done already.

"Deziara, very well, you can go for today," Lady Asdeus suddenly announced, and the demon girl threw her hands in the air joyfully.

"Yay! Finally!" She was about to run out of the study room but then paused and looked at Rosa with a piteous gaze. "What about Morri?"

"She'll finish her letters and then will be free to go as well," the demoness declared with the sweetest smile.

"Isn't she too small to write so many letters?" Deziara asked with an arched eyebrow and inched closer to Rosa.

My true ally. Tell her, sister!

"She is the king's heir, so she is expected to exceed other children in this kingdom. Don't worry, I'll never make her do anything she isn't capable of," Lady Asdeus explained, then smiled wickedly as she added, "Or perhaps you wanted to review the equations one more time?"

"Nope!" Deziara replied resolutely and was out the door in seconds.

No... Don't abandon me here!

"Come on. The sooner you finish, the sooner you can go." The demoness tapped Rosa's desk with one of her sharp nails. She had no choice but to continue painstakingly writing letters.

After what seemed like forever, Rosa finally drew the last lines and slumped down in her chair.

"I'm done..." she announced and looked at her tiny ink-stained hands. They were trembling from exertion.

"Let me see." Lady Asdeus took the notebook and carefully assessed her hard work. A wicked grin twisted her features, and Rosa felt an unpleasant chill pass through her. "Most wonderful. Most wonderful indeed..."

Her expression grew wider, almost manic at that point, and she bent down to show the notebook to Rosa.

"Tell me, how can a four-year-old child count to fifty so perfectly?"

What? Can't four-year-olds count that much? Why did you ask me to do exactly fifty, then?

Rosa gaped at Lady Asdeus like a fish, her heartbeat growing steadily faster.

"I... Faenor taught me how to count," she finally managed to say, hiding her trembling hands in her skirt.

"Oh, yes, he's taught you many things, hasn't he?" Lady Asdeus circled Rosa like a lioness closing in on her prey. "He's told me lots of things about you. How clever you are for a child so young. How curious you are about everything within this world."

Why is she looking at me like that? Something isn't right.

"He also told me that you've recently learned how to shapeshift. This morning, in fact," she added in a sickeningly sweet voice.

Rosa's heart hammered in her chest, and she felt herself becoming light-headed.

Faenor saw my transformation into a human. I had a feeling he already suspected the truth, but I always believed that even if he figured it out, he wouldn't tell anyone. Did he tell Lady Asdeus? Does she know what I really am?

"Oh, Princess, please do not look so alarmed." The demoness chuckled softly and placed a hand on Rosa's shoulder. Rosa shivered under the touch—her grip was firm.

If she knows I'm human, I need to run.

But before Rosa could move, Asdeus crouched beside her, smiling.

"I understand that you must be feeling very frightened right now, but I assure you, I mean you absolutely no harm." The demoness gently caressed her shoulder while looking her straight in the eye.

"I don't understand what you're talking about," Rosa said, trying to play dumb.

"There is no need to pretend anymore. I know that you're actually a human." The serene curve of her lips never faltered, and Rosa felt her blood run cold.

She knows. A demon knows that I'm a human. What is going to happen to me now?

"Faenor, would you please come in?" Lady Asdeus walked over to her table and rang one of those servant bells she had sitting there. After about half a minute, Faenor came into the room. The elf appeared confused at first, but then realization hit him, and his ears drooped.

"You two look as if someone has died." Lady Asdeus chuckled, then turned back to Rosa, crouching before her once more. "I understand that this situation must be very scary for you. You were a human one moment, and then the next, you were surrounded by demons who hate humans more than anything else. However, there is nothing to fear. I will help you."

"You will?" Rosa asked warily. "Why?"

"Because I've watched you grow since you were just a little babe. Even if you are human, I've grown to care for you. I do not wish for anyone to do you harm," Lady Asdeus said and put her hand on Rosa's shoulder. The gesture was supposed to be reassuring, but her hand was cold and made Rosa shiver.

"So you won't tell anyone?" she asked.

"Of course not! If the king were to find out... No, I do not even wish to think of such a horrid scenario. But do not worry. Me and Faenor here will protect you. Won't we, Faenor?" the demoness said sweetly.

"Of course," Faenor confirmed and bowed his head.

So Alphegor really would kill me if he found out. He always seemed so caring towards me, but perhaps it was only because I'm his perfect prodigal heir. If he knew the truth...

"It'll be alright, Princess Morrigan." Lady Asdeus' voice was smooth and soothing. "We'll make sure that nobody *ever* finds out."

Chapter 23

Suspicion

When Rosa left Lady Asdeus' study room, her mind was in a haze.

She had long suspected that Faenor knew of her human past with the way he'd been teaching her. The elf often spoke about humans and the Overworld, and he even mentioned that elves knew of people who were reborn. But to think that he would reveal it to Lady Asdeus—she had no idea the two were so close.

It'll be fine, right? She said that she won't tell anyone. But can I really trust her? I never interacted much with her outside of those lessons. It always felt like she viewed me more like a pest.

As she stood there, contemplating her best course of action, she noticed her demon guards looking at her. It wouldn't be anything unusual; after all, it was their job to keep their eyes on her. But Rosa didn't feel safe anymore. She felt that if their gazes lingered for too long, they'd realize what she really was.

I... I need to get away.

She ran as fast as her little legs could carry her through the winding corridors of the castle. Glancing over the shoulder, she saw that the guards, as always, were following her at a brisk pace. Intimidated by their presence Rosa slipped into the closest wall shadow.

She felt much safer and calmer in her shadow form since she couldn't hear her thundering heart or feel her trembling hands. Not to mention that she could zip through the corridor at a speed the bulky guards couldn't hope to match on their feet. Within a few minutes, she was already inside Alphegor's room.

Just an hour ago, it was her safe haven—the one place where nobody could intrude or hurt her. But now, the familiar room looked dark, vast, and threatening. She breathed heavily through her mouth as her heart thudded in her chest. As the silence stretched on, she began feeling dizzy. Slowly, with careful steps, she staggered over to her bed and slid down to the floor beside it.

What do I do? I never expected anyone to find out that I'm a human. The demons here hate humans so much that they've disposed of everything made by humans. Lady Asdeus says that she'll keep my secret. But I'm not sure I can trust her, and if somebody else finds out some other way... And Alphegor—what would he do?

An image of Alphegor's welcoming expression mixed with her mother's disapproving one flashed through Rosa's mind. She covered her mouth in horror.

No, no, no. Anything but that. He can't find out. He can't!

Suddenly, Rosa noticed that her familiar bed felt smaller than it should have. She looked down at her hands and saw pearly white skin. She gasped and ran to the mirror that stood by Alphegor's ornate wardrobe. She saw her horrified, human self gazing at her from the mirror.

"I shifted without even trying?" she muttered, reaching out to touch her face in the mirror. When her fingers connected with the cold glass, she recoiled and shook her head vigorously. "No, I cannot take this form in the demon castle! I must turn back."

She took a shaky breath, closed her eyes, and imagined herself regaining her demon form. Once her eyes opened, a little demon girl looked back at her in the mirror. But something wasn't quite... right. It was like her form lacked some definition.

Did I shift into my demon form instead of just returning to it? Can that even happen? Does it even make sense?

Rosa carefully examined her horns and saw they were smaller than they should be. The tail, which was missing its pointed tip, looked more like a rat's tail.

Relax. Breathe in and exhale out. Slowly.

Rosa closed her eyes again and repeated the exercise. Bit by bit, her tense muscles began to relax, and her heartbeat calmed. When she opened her eyes again and looked in the mirror, she saw that this time her form was indeed the real her instead of a shifted apparition.

Why did Faenor have to tell Lady Asdeus! Couldn't he have talked to me about it first? He should have checked if I was alright with him telling her—because I am definitely NOT! Even if she seems sympathetic to my situation, I just can't trust her.

Rosa paced around the room, her little tail flicking behind her like a whip. Occasionally, it would strike a bedpost or a wall, making her grumble at the *misplaced* furniture.

I have to make sure that nobody else finds out about my human past. Perhaps I can talk it out with Lady Asdeus, and she could teach some more things about demons as a whole. She could tell what things not to do and how to act properly.

But that didn't feel right to Rosa. She didn't want to talk about her human past with anyone in this world. It felt like somebody had forcibly exposed a secret she had been keeping safely hidden.

And what if I accidentally anger Lady Asdeus? Would she just expose my secret to everyone then? And where's the guarantee that Faenor won't tell somebody else? This is such a mess. I need to confront him and make him promise. But... would he even listen? He could just tell Azrael, and then my head would fly...

Mentally exhausted, Rosa slipped out of her clothes and crawled into her bed. Instead of feeling safe and comforting, it felt far too large. She felt exposed and unprotected. It took her a long time until she finally fell into uneasy sleep.

* * *

Rosa woke up from a gentle knock on the door.

"Lady Morrigan, are you awake?" Gunna's familiar and sweet voice resounded. Rosa jolted up and nervously looked around the room. The lights were still on from yesterday; apparently, she had forgotten to turn them off.

"Lady Morrigan?"

"I'm awake now. Come in," Rosa said and slipped out of the bed. The morning air felt surprisingly chilly, and she realized that she only had her undergarments on.

"Good morning, Lady Morrigan!" Gunna chimed happily, but her smile disappeared as soon as she saw Rosa. "High Miners, did you sleep without properly dressing yourself?"

"I... I was very tired yesterday," Rosa mumbled, looking away.

Does Gunna also know that I'm a human? Did Faenor tell her? They are rather close, after all.

"You should have called me for help. You know I would have come running," Gunna huffed, pointing at the golden bell standing by Rosa's bedpost. It was specifically made for high-standing demons to be able to call their slaves at any time. They weren't needed to summon the demon staff since demons could hear their name being called no matter how far it was. Just as Alphegor and Azrael would come to Rosa when she called them.

"I will next time," Rosa said awkwardly, and Gunna exhaled.

"Alright, I'll hold you to that promise. Now, let's get you dressed." The nanny went up to Rosa's smaller dresser, and after a minute of rummaging around it, she pulled out a black-and-white dress with a very puffy underskirt. She was humming the whole time, as she usually did, but her every movement was suspicious to Rosa.

She seems to be acting the same as usual. Perhaps she is not involved in this after all.

"Lift your hands up, Lady Morrigan," the dwarf woman asked and gently pulled the dress over Rosa's head. Her movements were measured and gentle, moving Rosa's hair out of the way before it could get snatched against the many buttons on the back.

Once the dress was all buttoned up, Rosa sat down on the little chair by her small table, and Gunna began to slowly and methodically untangle her hair.

"Did you have a difficult time sleeping last night? Your hair is messier than usual." The nanny gently patted Rosa's head as she combed her hair.

"I had a hard time falling asleep..." Rosa admitted.

I really hope Gunna is not involved, but I better not show or tell her anything unnecessary, just in case she is.

Her thoughts wandered to her painting, which was still hidden deep in Alphegor's wardrobe.

Maybe I should destroy it before anybody finds it... It would be foolish to leave any more ammunition lying around that could be used against me.

The thought was painful—she had worked so hard on that painting, and she really liked it. It was a peaceful slice of home. Something that always made her feel happy and calm.

"Lady Morrigan!" Gunna waved a hand in front of Rosa's face.

"Huh?"

"I said that it's time to eat breakfast. You really must have slept badly. Poor child. I'll see if perhaps I can find some calming tea in the kitchen to help you fall asleep this evening," Gunna said and then took Rosa's hand. Her callused palm was large and warm, and Rosa held on to it tightly.

Please, Gunna. Do not be like Faenor.

They exited the bedroom and then headed across the hall to Alphegor's dining room. It was where she and Alphegor would eat breakfast every morning before the king had to go and do whatever it was that he did throughout the day.

A few maids were already dutifully standing in the dining hall, waiting for Rosa to arrive. Their expressions were unreadable, like always, but she couldn't help but wonder if any of them suspected her of being a human.

Gunna helped Rosa get into her chair where she usually sat across from Alphegor, and then retreated. Gunna was not allowed to eat at the king's table, so she stood some way apart from the other maids, who never failed to show their disdain towards the dwarf woman.

"This morning, we have a fire lizard egg omelet with dread herbs and black tomatoes," announced the maid who brought breakfast every morning, then placed the plate in front of Rosa. This omelet was nothing like those on Earth.

Instead of a beautiful sunny color, these eggs were sort of purplish, while the herbs were black. The flavor wasn't too different, but the fact that even food in the Underworld was in dark colors spoiled Rosa's mood even further. She poked at one of the perfectly cut pieces of tomato, wondering if it was safe to eat.

Carefully, she nibbled on the tomato. It tasted the same as always, so she dared to put all of it in her mouth. She continued eating slowly, making sure that nothing tasted any different from normal. In fact, it took her twice as long to finish.

"Is everything alright, Your Highness?" one of the maids asked once Rosa had pushed away the plate, indicating that she was done eating.

"Y-Yes. Everything is fine," Rosa replied nervously.

Did I do something suspicious? Something a demon wouldn't do?

"If the food was not to your liking, you can always request the chef to make something else," the maid clarified, and Rosa relaxed.

Oh, she was talking about the food.

"No, it was tasty," Rosa assured her, and the maid bowed before taking the dirty plates.

"Shall we go find Faenor and read some stories now?" Gunna helped Rosa down from the chair. She almost tripped over her feet when the nanny mentioned Faenor. "Careful now, Lady Morrigan. We wouldn't want you to get hurt."

I do not want to meet with Faenor. I do not wish to see him, speak with him, or be anywhere near him.

"Could we do something else today?" Rosa asked, not daring to meet her nanny's gaze.

"Of course, we can. But I thought you loved listening to his stories?" Gunna cocked her head in confusion. "Did you perhaps argue with him? We can talk it all out and make amends."

"No, we didn't argue... I just want to do something else today," Rosa said, trying to avoid the unpleasant subject.

"Well, that's alright. What would you like to do?" Gunna asked with a smile.

"Can I go play with Haku?" Rosa asked, and the nanny's smile faltered. For some reason, Gunna never went together with her to visit Haku. She had a feeling that the dwarf woman was afraid of him.

"O-Of course. Perhaps, you should ask Lord Azrael to take you there," she suggested. Rosa nodded in agreement.

"Azrael," she called out, summoning her teacher. After a few minutes, a very annoyed-looking Azrael emerged from a shadow in front of her.

"Princess, is this something important? There's been an incident I need to attend to," the white-haired demon said, scratching his head in annoyance.

"Incident?" Rosa asked.

"One of the slaves has disappeared. The elf that was assigned to read for you. You haven't happened to see him today, have you?" he asked, peering behind them as if Faenor could have hidden behind their backs.

"No," Rosa replied, shocked that Faenor had suddenly disappeared.

Did something happen? I have a really bad feeling about this. Could Lady Asdeus know where Faenor could have disappeared to? Or perhaps he just ran away. Too ashamed to face me after what he had done. But even if that were true—where would he go?

"His slave roommates haven't seen him since yesterday." Azrael rubbed his temples in annoyance. "Really... All this ruckus for a slave."

Azrael turned to leave, then as if remembering something, he stopped and addressed Rosa. "Oh, there will be no magic lessons today. I have to solve this issue first. You can go straight to Lady Asdeus."

And then he was gone, muttering angrily.

"So, can I go play with Haku?" Rosa asked, and the nanny nodded as she fidgeted uncomfortably. She could tell that the dwarf wanted to join the search for Faenor. "I can go on my own."

"A-Are you sure, Lady Morrigan?"

"I won't be alone. I still have my guards with me," Rosa assured, although she wished she could be alone.

"Well, alright," the nanny conceded and, with a last nervous glance in Rosa's direction, left the girl alone. Without a second thought, Rosa slipped into the shadows and ran outside of the castle before the guards even had a chance to notice her.

CHAPTER 24

BECOMING AZRAEL

The next week was an absolute mess in the demon castle. Faenor's disappearance put even the high-standing demons on edge. Rumors were circling that somebody had killed him, and the whole situation was just blown out of proportion. Others believed that he had managed to escape and were worried that other slaves might follow. Rosa used the confusion to hide and avoid her lessons.

"Princess Morrigan!" one of the guards yelled from somewhere in the distance. She was so used to it by now that it became like a background noise at this point. Hidden inside Haku's dragon house, Rosa was confident that the guards wouldn't dare to search for her there. Nobody ever wanted to deal with the finicky dragon.

Haku let out a low whine and nudged Rosa's hand gently with his snout.

"It's alright. We can stay here and play," she said, scratching the scales behind his ear.

It is certainly nicer here than in the castle.

The dragon house had recently been upgraded in size and now resembled a small stable. Except that everything was made from stone instead of wood. One corner had a large, flat boulder where Haku would usually sleep, while an assortment of dragon toys lay in the opposite corner. These changed often and could consist of anything beginning from old furniture and ending with giant balls of frozen blood.

Haku whined again, tilting his head towards the entrance, his giant, adorable dragon eyes pleading.

"No… I don't want those guards to find us…" Rosa muttered and grabbed a broken leg of a chair, waving it in the air. Haku jumped from side to side, eager to catch it. Rosa threw it slightly in front of her, and the dragon grabbed it, chewing on the wood viciously. Less than five seconds later, it was completely reduced to splinters.

"Runt or no runt, you're still a mighty beast, Haku." Rosa giggled and threw another piece of wood, which was likewise annihilated in seconds.

"Hiding here again, Princess," Azrael's voice resounded from the entrance, and Rosa whirled around to see him leaning against the doorframe. "It's not really fun searching for you if you're always going to hide here."

Rosa leaned close to Haku, warily observing the white-haired Demon. He sighed and strode closer to her.

"What's up with you lately, little Princess? You've been hiding constantly and even skipping Asdeus' lessons."

Rosa flinched when he mentioned the demoness' name, and Haku nuzzled against her gently, feeling her distress.

"I just miss Father," Rosa said, using the same excuse she had given to everyone who asked her that question.

"Aha, sure. Do you really think I'll keep buying that every time? That is not the face of a child who misses her father," Azrael grumbled and poked Rosa's forehead. She swatted his hand away, not hiding her annoyance.

"Yes, it is," she persisted. It wasn't a complete lie. Part of her wished for nothing more than for Alphegor to return and for things to go back to normal. Another part of her feared his return more than anything else.

"Fine, fine. Keep being stubborn. But you cannot stay here. Come now, we're going to learn some shapeshifting."

"I don't wanna." She buried her face in Haku's neck, and the dragon coiled around her like a protective wall.

Haku is my only ally. He probably doesn't care if I'm a human, elf, or demon as long as I give him scratches.

Azrael groaned and tried to pry the dragon away from her. "Come on! It is important for you to learn the basics so you don't accidentally exhaust yourself from shifting."

This caught Rosa's attention. All magic in this world had limits and dangerous drawbacks if used improperly. For example, she knew that her shadow form only worked in shadows, obviously, which made it a really powerful skill to have in the Underworld. But one could get stuck in their shadow form if they didn't know how to exit from it safely.

I should learn more about shapeshifting. Maybe I'll figure out why I accidentally transformed into a human and find a way to prevent it.

"Alright. I'll go." Rosa gently ran her hand over Haku's back, and the dragon uncoiled.

"If you don't go—Wait, you will?" Azrael stared at her in shock. "I expected you to put up more of a fight."

"Should I argue some more?"

"No, no! Let's go." Azrael grinned, and before she could protest, he scooped her up in his arms.

"Hey, I can walk on my own!"

"Enjoy it while you're still small. I won't be carrying you around when you're older," he said with a grin. "Besides, you're slow."

Rosa puffed out her cheeks and crossed her arms.

Do not be fooled by his smile. Just because he's being friendly doesn't mean he is trustworthy. Who knows what Azrael really thinks of humans.

* * *

"Now then, let's continue our shapeshifting lesson. We really should have done this a week ago, but the whole missing elf fiasco ruined all my plans," Azrael grumbled. They were both at the training grounds again. Both of Rosa's guards were standing by the entrance, following her every movement.

Rosa's expression slumped at the mention of Faenor. After a whole week of searching and investigating, nobody managed to uncover what had happened to him. She was a little worried. There were talks among the maids that people had been going missing lately in the capital, and that Faenor just might have been one of the victims of these mysterious disappearances.

"Hey, don't be so depressed. We'll get you a new slave."

"No!" Rosa objected with such ferocity that the demon flinched. She lowered her gaze and spoke in a much quieter voice. "I don't want any more slaves."

Having one betray me was quite enough.

"Alright, I got you—no more slaves. Let's just focus on the lesson for now." Azrael scratched the back of his head awkwardly, then took a deep breath. "Tell me what you know about shapeshifting."

Rosa pondered the question for a moment. "It allows me to change into anything I can imagine."

"Yeah, that's the very short version of it. But tell what is actually changing? Your body or just your perception of it?" he challenged with a smile.

Why are you asking this from a four-year-old? A child that small wouldn't understand the difference between the two.

So, she blinked her eyes at him while cocking her head to the side. Azrael's face fell and it was like he finally remembered that she was, in fact, four.

"Right... Wrong question..." The demon scratched his chin, then tried again. "Do you think I really turned into that deer, or was it just an illusion?"

Alright, now this is something a four-year-old might understand.

Rosa began thinking about the question in earnest, remembering the moment she turned into her human self. It felt completely effortless, and while it definitely required some energy from her, it wasn't a large amount.

"Is it an illusion?" she guessed.

"Wrong! It is very much real." Azrael grinned and then took the form of the same white, ethereal deer. "Come, touch me."

She scrunched her nose at his wording but obeyed anyway. Touching the snowy-looking fur, she felt its softness as well as the strong muscles in his legs. He bowed his head, and she touched his white, glowing horns. Those, too, felt very much real—firm with peach fuzz around it.

"It feels real," Rosa conceded.

"And it is. At least the type of shapeshifting the two of us use." Azrael turned back to his normal self. "There's also an illusionary type of shifting, which is far more common, but Lord Lucius was kind enough to give you the superior kind."

Rosa opened her mouth to ask why it was so easy for her to change shape, but stopped herself.

It is too advanced of a thing for me to ask. I'll have to be content with what knowledge Azrael shares on his own.

"Was there something you wanted to ask?" Azrael suddenly

crouched down, peering straight into Rosa's eyes. She held his gaze firmly.

"How do I turn into a deer?" she asked. A perfectly reasonable question from a curious kid.

"Very good question, actually. I imagine it would be very hard for you to turn into one, and honestly, it's better that you don't do it. At least not yet."

"Why not?"

"Because it requires a lot of energy to change into something that is very different from you. The more different it is, the more energy it requires."

So, the reason I changed into my human self so easily was because it is similar to my demon self. But there is a significant difference between a child and an adult, isn't there?

"I imagine it must have taken you some energy to transform last time, but not too much since the shape was still humanoid. Why don't you try turning into me today? That should be a little bit harder," Azrael urged.

"Turn into you?" Rosa winced.

"Hey, what's with the grimace? I would think it is a pleasant task to turn into a handsome demon like myself." Azrael tried to put on his most charismatic smile, but it looked so strained and awkward that Rosa started laughing. He glared at her.

"Okay, okay, I'll do it," she said, collecting herself.

Good thing he's nowhere near as charismatic as Alphegor. Otherwise, I might have taken him seriously.

Rosa took a deep breath to calm herself, then closed her eyes. She imagined herself becoming Azrael. She tried to think of every single detail of his body—the clothes, the height, the shade of his skin. Once she thought she had accounted for every detail, she opened her eyes.

As she did, Rosa felt like she had lost a little bit of her energy—as if she had gone on a rather long walk.

Azrael stared at her intently, assessing every detail. "Not bad for a first time, but I think anybody who knew me would instantly be able to tell that you're not actually me."

He gestured to the same full-body mirror, still propped up against the wall where he had left it last week. Rosa walked up to it and was surprised to see that it was indeed Azrael staring back at her. Or something similar to him, at least.

I shouldn't be surprised, but seeing somebody else in the mirror is still odd.

Rosa leaned in closer and noticed that a few things were definitely not right.

"So, what did you do wrong?" Azrael asked, peering into the mirror over her, um, *his* shoulder. Seeing two Azraels right next to each other was beyond confusing.

"The hair is too short," she pointed out, comparing herself to the real Azrael. "And the horns are too straight. I think the jaw is too small? Like a girl's."

"Yeah, what else?"

Rosa peered at the mirror, trying to find anything different, but everything else seemed to align.

"That's it?"

"Are you sure?" He narrowed his eyes, and she stared at both images carefully.

If he's asking like that, there must be something, but I can't find anything else. The eyes are right in shape and color, as are the lips and other facial features. His height and clothes are also right.

"Yes?" Rosa answered, confidence waning.

"What about this?" Azrael poked Rosa's cheek with his tail, and she realized her version of Azrael had no tail.

"Oh."

"Oh. It's a pretty big deal to forget about a demon's tail. But I'll give it a pass. From afar, you perhaps wouldn't be able to tell the difference." Azrael reached out to ruffle her hair, but she stepped back.

"Morri, are you here?!" Deziara suddenly burst into the training room, two of her guards following closely behind her. Her face turned into that of disgust once she saw two Azraels. "Why are there two of you now?"

"Obviously, because this is my long-lost brother." Azrael threw his arm around Rosa, grinning from ear to ear. Rosa, however, had no intention of indulging him and relaxed herself to shift back into her normal form.

"Morri!" Deziara smiled and ran up to Rosa, burying her in a hug. "That really scared me! I wouldn't know what to do with two of those idiots."

"Sorry. I was learning shapeshifting," Rosa replied, enjoying the warm hug.

"Oh, right, you did receive that stone from Lord Lucius. Look at what I can do!" Deziara backed away a few steps and then produced a little ball of fire in her palm.

"Wow!" Rosa clapped, genuinely impressed. She hadn't expected Deziara to actually be able to do any magic, even if she was the older sister.

"I bet you're here on behalf of your teacher," Azrael huffed in annoyance, and Rosa flinched. Deziara's fireball vanished, and her lips pressed together in a thin line.

"She did ask me to find Morri..." the girl admitted.

No, I don't want to meet with Lady Asdeus again. I know she said she'll keep my secret, but the thought that I'll be left alone with her makes me nervous. What if I say something that could make her change her mind?

"Oh, don't make those giant piteous eyes," Azrael groaned and ruffled his hair.

"Huh? Me?" Rosa touched her face and noticed that it was indeed suspended in a semi-scowl.

"You can't blame her. Lady Asdeus' lessons are so boring."

"But you have to attend her lessons," Azrael said strictly.

Deziara raised her eyebrow. "Since when are you so prim and proper? You don't even listen to Father," the girl accused.

"That's different. I'm the strongest demon in the Underworld. Besides, I can't cancel your lessons." He shrugged, and Rosa could feel her heartbeat slowly increase.

Would it be alright if I just slipped away into the shadows? But if I keep hiding, Lady Asdeus might start thinking that I am avoiding her on purpose.

"No, you can't do that, Princess," Azrael groaned, and Rosa stared at him in confusion. "Looking all sad, like you're about to cry. I can't stand it when children or women cry."

"Then do something about it!" Deziara proclaimed as she wrapped her arms around Rosa. "Morri is sad!"

Dammit! I need to get better at controlling my expressions. They can read me like an open book.

"Alright, alright, but only this time!" Azrael conceded and threw a glance towards the vigilant guards.

"Yay!" Deziara cheered. "What are we going to do?"

"You two haven't been outside the castle yet, right?" he asked in a barely audible whisper.

CHAPTER 25

IN A DEMON CITY

Rosa couldn't believe what was happening. Four demon guards lay on the floor unconscious. After hearing Azrael's suggestion to take the girls on a "field trip," both sets of guards had objected and insisted they remain in the castle. The white-haired demon responded in kind, with a wave of his hand that left the four men slumped to the floor.

"Did you kill them?" Deziara shrieked.

"Of course not. I just put them to sleep. Tomorrow morning, they'll wake well rested and completely unaware of our plans." Azrael snickered, then ushered Rosa and Deziara forward. "But let's hurry before anybody decides to check up on us."

That was a good enough reason for Rosa to grab Deziara by her hand and drag the older girl along.

"You want to go, Morri?" she asked somewhat nervously.

"Yes!"

I've wanted to see the world outside the castle walls ever since I first arrived in this world. I will not let this chance slip by.

"Well... I guess if you want to."

"What? Are you scared?" Azrael teased as he led them through the corridors. He appeared to be taking them towards the part of the castle meant for servants. The maids stared at him in surprise, their expressions shifting to full-blown shock once they noticed the two princesses with him. They quickly scattered out of his way, not daring to object despite their clear desire to do so.

Is it alright if so many servants see us here? None of them would suspect us of trying to leave the castle, would they? I don't even know where Azrael is taking us.

Finally, he led them into a room that seemed to be used for storage. It was small and rather cramped, with dusty shelves that were filled with various cleaning supplies—clothes, rags, random tools. Azrael snapped his fingers, and three dark, shabby-looking cloaks floated towards them from one of the shelves.

"Put these on," he commanded, throwing the largest cloak around his shoulders.

"What? This dirty thing? No way." Deziara poked the floating cloak and stuck out her tongue in disgust.

It's not that bad. A little worn, but some of my clothes in the human world saw use after ten years, despite the odd stains.

Rosa took the smallest cloak and put it on. It was still a bit large for her, but at least it hid her frilly Gothic dress underneath.

"Well, if you'd rather go and learn…"

"No!" Deziara snatched the cloak and begrudgingly put it on, wincing all the while.

"Good. Now then, Princess, your red hair stands out a bit too much. You have to change to a different color now."

Rosa nodded in agreement, then closed her eyes as she imagined her hair changing to a different color—something dark and inconspicuous.

She imagined how it felt to dye her hair, how the color seeped into it, changing it all the way to its roots. Once she opened her eyes and checked, she saw that it was the same black color as Deziara's.

"Wow! You actually did it, Morri. That's amazing. Now we match!" Deziara cheered.

"Great choice. Nobody would ever dare to conclude that you're anything but sisters."

"We ARE sisters," the older girl protested.

"And now you LOOK like sisters. Come! We can't dally for long." Azrael pushed one of the shelves aside, revealing a dark passage behind it.

Deziara's eyes sparkled. "A secret tunnel! I knew that there had to be one in the castle."

Azrael chuckled. "One? Sure, let's say there's only one."

So, there's definitely more. It would be useful to find more of them. This one is so far from Alphegor's room that it wouldn't be very useful in an emergency.

They stepped inside the tunnel, and Azrael pulled a lever on the side of the wall. The shelf then slowly moved back to its original position. The inside of it was pitch black, and smelled of musty old clothes. Even with Rosa's superior night vision, she had trouble seeing where she was going.

"I can't see anything!" Deziara complained.

"Wait a bit," Azrael said, and then a small flame appeared in his palm. Although it was no larger than a candle flame, it was more than enough for Rosa to see everything around her. Not like there was much to see—just dark, dingy walls and never-ending darkness ahead. "This might take a while, so be patient. I don't want to hear any 'are-we-there-yets.'"

"You didn't say we'd have to walk," Deziara grumbled.

"You can still go back to the lessons."

Deziara muttered something under her breath and began walking. Rosa followed behind her, but then Azrael bent down and picked her up with his free hand.

"Since you're still small, you get a free ride."

"Hey! Why can't you carry me too?" Deziara protested.

"Because you're too big. Now less grumbling and more walking."

* * *

After approximately half an hour of walking and listening to Deziara's constant complaints about her hurting feet, they finally reached the exit. Azrael pulled a lever, and the entrance wall moved to the side, revealing a small room filled with brooms, buckets, and other cleaning supplies.

"Where are we?" Deziara covered her nose with the corner of her cloak and sidestepped a giant cobweb in one of the corners.

"I'll tell you when you're older." Azrael smirked as he maneuvered around the many buckets, then opened a door that led out into a dark corridor. However, it was nothing like the castle hallways. The walls were made out of a completely different material, something resembling plaster, albeit more gritty and dark brown in color.

There were no fancy chandeliers with little lava bulbs; instead, dim lanterns lined the walls. The floors had the occasional hole, and overall, the entire space felt anything but comfortable.

"Where have you taken us? Do you intend to sell us as slaves?" Deziara muttered, but latched onto Azrael's leg despite her protests, glancing warily around.

"No, this is just a passage we need to get through. Did you really think that we would exit in a place where everything would be as pristine as within the castle?" Azrael quipped as he led both girls into what appeared to be a medieval pub of some sort. Except that it was completely empty. Nobody was even watching over the space.

"Where is everyone?" Rosa asked, and Azrael just shrugged.

"The owner is probably sleeping in the back, drunk," he explained nonchalantly.

They soon left the dingy place behind, coming out into a dark side alley.

"Is this the city?" Deziara asked. The look on her face signaled that this was the last place where she wanted to be.

"It's part of the city but not our main destination. I bet you two would love to see the market." Azrael smiled, and Rosa felt a bit of excitement rise in her chest. She had always loved going to the market in the human world. You never knew what you'd find there, and quite often, the vendors were willing to give a discount to good customers.

"Is it that place where everybody gathers to buy cheap things? I don't want to go there," Deziara objected, stomping her foot down.

No, don't do this to me. Let's just go to the market before Azrael brings us to a brothel or casino or some demon equivalent of that.

"I suppose you could just wait for us in the pub," the demon replied.

"You'd leave me inside that horrid place?" Deziara chastised him. "What if someone kidnaps me?"

"Nobody would care about some random kid in a pub. As long as you don't go yapping around that you're a Princess." Azrael glared, and Deziara covered her mouth.

"I'll come along," she conceded, and Azrael began walking through the narrow street. It was dirty and completely devoid of any life.

As Azrael continued to lead them forward, the street grew wider, and Rosa saw some small demons huddling against the walls. They wore tattered and dirty rags. Their hands—or perhaps it was better to call them limbs—were long and thin like spider legs, while their skin looked a sickly shade of purple. Their faces also weren't completely humanoid, instead being more elongated with long sharp noses.

Seeing them, Deziara clutched Azrael's leg so tightly that he could barely move forward.

"Don't worry, they're just imps. They can't do anything to you," he explained and ushered the demon girl to move forward.

So these are lesser demons? I've heard of them before, but never expected they'd look so different.

Rosa observed one of them, but they appeared completely disinterested in them, instead chewing on what appeared to be some old, hard pieces of bread.

I expected them to be scarier than this. But they just look pitiful.

As they continued through the streets, the faint hum of chatter grew louder from up ahead. Peering past the narrow side alley, Rosa caught glimpses of demons moving through the shadows. When they finally stepped onto the main street, Rosa's breath hitched in her throat. Before her stood the scene of an underground city.

Gothic-style houses made from dark stone stood tightly together, bright lights coming from their windows. Sharp, metallic fences separated them from the streets, while neat lanterns illuminated the cobblestone roads.

Looking further ahead, Rosa noted how the street was never perfectly straight but rather went up and down like a rollercoaster ride. The most impressive sight was undoubtedly the demon castle, which stretched high up into the darkness, acting almost like a lighthouse in the eternal black of the underground.

demons of every size, age, and shape imaginable filled the street, their voices merging into a cacophony of chatter. Some looked more humanlike than the demons in the castle, while others resembled the side alley imps, except livelier. Rosa spotted demons with leathery wings, or extra sets of limbs, and even some with animallike features.

"Wow!" Deziara's gaze darted from one demon to the next, unable to settle on one particular person.

"They're so... different," Rosa noted, trying to take in as many of the varying features as she could. Yet, no matter how much she looked, she just kept seeing new things—animal tails of every size, varying skin colors, and even scales. Cat eyes, fin ears, bug wings—it just went on and on. The variety was dizzying.

"Oh, yeah, you two haven't really seen lesser demons much," Azrael acknowledged with a smirk and swiftly inserted himself and both girls into the stream of people. He held Deziara's hand as well now, keeping them close and out of the way of burlier demons.

"What makes them lesser?" Rosa asked, still scanning the crowd.

"Lesser demons have ancestry that isn't fully demonic. The more their blood is mixed with other species, the more their appearance diverges. That is doubly so if they have a monster ancestor."

"Monster ancestor? How is that possible? Is their mom a monster or something?" Deziara laughed as if the idea itself was ludicrous. Rosa, on the other hand, paled from the horrible image that formed in her mind.

No, don't think about that! That is not something I need to think about.

Rosa shook her head and pointed towards a larger open area that she saw forming further ahead. "Is that the market?"

"Yes, the Grand Linberor Market, the largest market in the whole Demon Kingdom," Azrael announced, and both girls peered forward, trying to see past the growing crowd of demons. After a while, they finally reached a huge square lined with various stalls. The people went this way and that, trying not to bump into each other as they sought out various stalls.

The feeling was very similar to the market in the capital. Vendors were shouting at the customers, who were going from stall to stall in search of better deals. Aside from the people themselves and the darkness of the underground, it was basically the same thing.

"So, what would you like to look at? Pretty clothes? Jewelry? Food?" Azrael asked, looking over the stalls, before picking a concrete direction where to go.

"I doubt there's anything good here anyway," Deziara grumbled, peering from behind Azrael.

"Sweets?" Rosa suggested. She hadn't had those nice chocolate treats Alphegor always got her in a while. Apparently, the maids didn't know where the king got them from, as the castle's kitchen didn't even have any chocolate. A horrible mistake in Rosa's mind.

"You do seem to have a bit of a sweet tooth." Azrael smirked, then turned towards the far side of the market, where the smell of sweet pastries and bread wafted through the air. Rosa inhaled the air and hummed. It smelled absolutely delightful, even if most of the scents were unfamiliar to her.

Azrael walked past most stalls, not sparing them a second glance despite the intricate delicacies on display. Rosa stared at them longingly, wondering if she'd have to force the demon to stop. But he finally stopped in front of a simple-looking stall.

The vendor attending it didn't shout for attention like others, and the treats displayed seemed rather plain compared to their neighbors. What did make it stand out was the crowd gathered in front—it was far larger than anywhere else.

Azrael coughed, and the demons in the line who were bickering as to who was there first looked at him in annoyance. But as soon as they took in his appearance, the lesser demons parted, letting him straight to the front of the line.

"Hello!" he greeted the vendor with a smile.

"Back for some more already?" The vendor, a round woman with horns smaller than even Rosa's and catlike eyes and ears, returned the smile. "Oh, I didn't know you had children already at your tender age."

"They're my sisters," Azrael replied without missing a beat, and Rosa nodded, playing along with his lie. Deziara scrunched up her nose and looked at Azrael as if he were insane.

The woman chuckled. "What a pair of cuties. What would you like to have, dearies?"

"What are those?" Rosa asked, pointing towards the array of differently colored rolls. She had no idea what to call them as they didn't look like anything she'd seen on Earth. Their colors varied from white to black, with every other color in between. If they weren't in the market's food section, she'd be convinced they were modeling clay of some sort.

"This is magic delight," the woman replied, and Rosa cocked her head in confusion.

That explains nothing. It sounds like Turkish delight.

"Oh, I've heard of these! They're supposed to taste like magic." Deziara perked up and excitedly began looking over the treats.

Magic has...flavor?

Rosa looked at the rather dull-looking treats, trying to discern what each could taste like, but she knew too little about magic to make any guesses.

"Would you like to taste some samples first?" the woman asked, and both girls nodded eagerly. She pulled out a little tray with cubes of various colors set out on it and offered it to them.

Rosa picked out a translucent orange cube and popped it in her mouth, while Deziara picked a dark purple one. The flavor that exploded onto her tongue was like nothing she had experienced before. It was like a hot flame had erupted into her mouth, but not in the sense that it burned. It tingled her tongue and swirled around, warming her whole body. It was sweet, yet spicy, while the texture was chewy like jelly.

"Wow! Mine tastes like shadow magic. It's sweet, yet a little bit bitter. And I'm pretty sure I can see a little better now." Deziara looked high up into the never-ending darkness above as if trying to find something within it.

"Oh, yes, my treat will give your body a little temporary boost. Want to try some more?" The vendor generously handed the plate of samples to Deziara. "Take your time tasting them, and then come back to buy the one you liked the most."

"You heard her, squirts. Enjoy!" Azrael smirked and lowered Rosa next to Deziara, who was already enjoying her next sample. Both girls continued munching on the odd treats while Azrael returned his attention to the vendor, picking out some for himself.

Rosa couldn't stop eating one magic cube after another. It was almost like an addicting gacha game—she never knew what she would get next. Whenever a new flavor exploded in her mouth, she felt the very essence of magic hit her tongue.

As she was about to take her fifth sample, a strong pair of arms grabbed her from behind, instantly muffling her voice and pulling her away from her unsuspecting sister and distracted guardian.

CHAPTER 26

DEMON IN DISTRESS

Rosa opened her eyes to find herself in a small, dirty, empty room. Or perhaps, it was supposed to be a storage shack. It was hard to tell in the complete dark. Her hands were tied with a heavy rope, and her mind was muddled as if she were drunk.

What happened?

Her vision blurred as she forced herself upright.

I feel like I'm going to barf.

She inhaled deeply, waiting for the nausea to subside, then took another look around. The only way out she could see was a metal door that looked so heavy that she suspected she wouldn't be able to budge it even if she somehow found a key. Rosa then noticed that the pendant she always kept hanging around her neck was missing.

Azrael will be so mad about his gift being stolen. But I can't worry about him now. I need to get out of here. Wherever "here" might be.

Rosa tried to turn into one with the darkness, but then realized that she was unable to do so. She wriggled in her bonds and tried again. Nothing. She was still in her fleshy form.

Why can't I turn into a shadow? Did they feed me something that stops me from using magic? Or is it because of these weird bonds?

At that moment, the heavy metal door swung open with a loud creak, and two cloaked figures walked inside. One was a tall demon man with an ugly, almost piglike face. He had no hair, and his ears also looked like that of a pig. The other was a slender woman with long, thin arms and legs. Her face was somewhat elongated, and she had two sets of eyes. Both were lesser demons, no doubt.

"She's already awake? You didn't give her enough serum!" The woman smacked the man on his arm but he seemed completely unbothered by the gesture.

"I gave her the whole bottle. The stuff is meant for lesser demons—this one's a pureblood," he grumbled in response.

"But she's a child!"

"Pureblood is pureblood. Not like it changes anything now that she's awake." The man shrugged and lumbered closer to Rosa.

"Stay back!" she hissed at him. The man laughed in response.

"Oh, look! This one is feisty. Most children just cry for their mommy. Then again, you don't have a mommy to cry after, do you?" The demon nearly doubled over from laughter, and an occasional piglike snort escaped his nose.

"And your daddy is far, far away and can't help you either." The woman cackled like a hyena.

They think they're so clever. It's seriously pathetic. I should just call Azrael and get this thing over with.

Rosa took a breath and was about to call out when the pig demon closed the distance between them in one stiff stride and clamped his large hand over her mouth. She nearly gagged from the nasty smell that came from him.

"Don't you even think about shouting for your guardian. One wrong move and I'll snap your head clean off your shoulders," he hissed, and then put a dirty gag in Rosa's mouth. She tried desperately to spit the nasty thing out, but it was too large.

Gross, gross, gross. I'll get a stomachache from this vile thing.

"Let's just get her to the designated point before we're found," the spindly woman hissed. The man unceremoniously threw Rosa over his shoulder and lumbered out of the shack.

Good gods, would it kill you to take a bath? You smell like you rolled in a cow patty.

They exited into a dark and narrow alleyway, similar to the one Azrael guided them through earlier. The two thugs made sure to avoid any lights and scurried from one street to the next with surprising agility.

But despite the seemingly horrid situation, Rosa did not feel scared. Alright, that wasn't fully true. She was scared of the pigman's horrid scent and feared it might permanently ruin her sense of smell.

I have to get away from these two somehow. If only I could remove the gag and call for Azrael, then the problem would be solved within seconds. But it's just too large. I'd need my hands to pull it out. But the rope seems to be made from metal. There's no way I can get it off.

Rosa tried to turn into a shadow again, but it still didn't work, despite the nasty smell having completely sobered her up.

There must be something I can do... Wait...

She couldn't turn into a shadow, but perhaps she could turn into something or somebody else. Maybe the thugs only countered her shadow ability, not her ability to shapeshift. Rosa closed her eyes and imagined herself turning into Alphegor. When she opened them, she found that nothing had changed.

Alright, so all of my magic is blocked... Great. I need to figure out a way to call for Azrael then.

The demons stopped in the middle of a dingy street and then began knocking on the wall of a building in an odd pattern. It was dead silent for a moment, and then a small opening appeared in the wall and grew larger and larger until it formed into a sizable entryway.

The piglike demon slipped inside, nearly knocking Rosa's head against the entrance, and the spindly woman followed close behind.

"Hey, be careful with the merchandise, you oaf! He won't pay us nearly as much if she's damaged."

"Calm down. She's fine, isn't she?"

"Just make sure she stays fine. Now put on your mask," the woman commanded and secured a white fox mask to her face. The pig demon struggled to remove his red wolf mask from his pocket with one hand and then fumbled several times before managing to secure it to his face. It completely mismatched his piglike physique.

Taking a last glance at each other to make sure that their masks were secure, the two demons opened the door at the end of a dark corridor and entered what could only be described as a palace. A burgundy-and-gold carpet lined the floor, the walls had an exquisite purple-and-gold wallpaper, and the chandeliers had jewels hanging down and clattering gently against each other.

A stately demon with a gold mask gently inclined his head towards the two kidnappers.

"Welcome. You've come to sell today?" he asked, throwing a short glance towards Rosa.

"Yes. We're here to meet Phantom," the woman answered.

"Follow me," the gold-masked demon answered and began walking along the ornate corridor.

Despite being slung over a smelly Demon's shoulder, Rosa couldn't help but be amazed at how rich everything was. There were even paintings on the wall, displayed with utmost care as if in a museum. But something about these paintings struck Rosa the wrong way.

Most of them depicted a person of some sort, usually a child. They were drawn and dressed in beautiful clothes that perfectly matched this extravagant place. However, their faces looked tormented, piti-ful, and often on the verge of tears. Their hair was also disheveled most of the time, and there were bruises and dirt all over their bodies.

Are these demons slaves?

"Please, wait for a moment." The demon with the golden mask stopped in front of a large silver-and-gold door that had a dragon carved on each side. As he slipped inside, Rosa tried to catch a glimpse of the room beyond, but he moved too swiftly—whatever lay within remained a mystery.

The pig demon shifted his weight from one leg to another while the woman tapped her foot nervously.

"He better not go back on the deal..." the man loudly stated.

"He might if you keep shouting like that!" The woman elbowed him, then glanced at Rosa. "Can't you remove that nasty thing from her mouth? It ruins the image."

Yes, please, do remove it!

"Do you want Azrael to come and burn this whole place down?"

"I doubt he could enter here. But I suppose it's better to be safe than sorry. I just wish you could have picked out something a little better. It might lower her price."

"It's the girl he cares about, not the damn rag."

The stately demon returned from the room, holding the door wide open for the kidnappers.

"Phantom will see you now."

The demons hesitated, shifting nervously before finally stepping inside. Rosa's eyes widened in shock. The walls were carved from al-abaster and shaped into a depiction of a luscious garden. But instead of paint, jewels were used in a variety of colors and patterns. The floors were lined with a carpet that shone just like gold.

And the treasures within the room... Rosa wasn't even sure how to describe them all. There were display cabinets lined at the end wall that had ornate jewelry, vases, and what could only be described as mystical artifacts. There were delicately carved statues and even a giant, jewel-encrusted harp.

In the very center of this treasure trove, on a giant gold chair—no, rather, it would be better to describe it as a throne—sat a demon of formidable stature who wore a black mask that covered his face completely. His black hair was combed back, and his large horns curved to the sides, making him appear even more intimidating.

How can he see anything if his eyes are covered by the mask? Or are the eye slits hidden somehow?

"H-Hello! It is a great honor to meet you, Phantom, sir," the spindly demon mumbled and bowed her head low.

"A very big honor," the piglike demon added as he followed. Rosa, still slung over his shoulder, had no choice but to stare at the gold carpet before the demon rose again.

"Have you brought her?" Phantom asked in an ice-cold voice, his tail flicking once as he tapped the armrest of his throne.

"Yes! We followed your instructions and brought you the Crown Princess," the pig demon replied and lowered Rosa to the ground, depositing her in front of the black-masked man like an offering.

The moment his hands had let go of her, he shrieked, and Rosa looked back to see that one of his ears had a hole in it, blood pouring out of the wound and down to the Demon's face.

"She's worth more than this whole city, and you treat her like some common slave? What is that disgusting thing in her mouth?" Phantom's voice reverberated through the whole room, and some of the treasures began to tremble and rattle from its intensity. Both demons fell to the floor, groveling at his feet.

"I am so sorry, Phantom, sir! She was about to call for her

guardian. We just grabbed the first thing we had to shut her up." The woman had her head pressed to the floor as she explained. The piglike demon was clutching his ear, also bowing, but not quite as low as her.

Phantom stood silent for a moment, and Rosa had a feeling he was assessing her condition. But it was hard to tell with the mask covering his face.

"Very well. I'll forgive you this time." Phantom slowly stood from his chair and approached Rosa. He crouched down in front of her, pulled the dirty rag out of her mouth, and then incinerated it.

Rosa knew that she should have screamed for Azrael right then and there, but the man's presence was so overwhelming that she barely had the mind to even breathe.

"Pretty little Princess. The rarest, most valuable treasure in all of the Demon Kingdom," his voice purred, and a shiver ran through her spine. She took a deep breath to scream, but her mouth was forced shut, and she was unable to open it. "Bad girl! We wouldn't want to cause a scene by calling your guardian, would we now?"

"Um... how about... our payment?" The spindly demon woman dared to bring her head up from the carpet, looking at Phantom with eyes filled with greed. He clicked his tongue in annoyance and then snapped his fingers. The stately demon pulled a bag filled with what sounded like coins and threw it in front of two thieves.

They both lunged towards it, grabbing and trying to push each other out of the way. When the woman finally managed to open the bag, her face fell, and she glared at Phantom. "This is less than what we agreed on."

"The state you brought her in, you should be happy that you're getting paid at all. I'm sure that the necklace you stole from her will more than make up for what's missing," Phantom said in a cold voice and then waved his hand at them. "Now begone!"

"Hey, now! You have no idea what we went through to get her! We had to wait for months and months until she finally got taken outside the castle. Not to mention the informant asked for double the price and that this little brat was together with Azrael. If he had seen us, we'd be dead already. You will pay us the full price!" The pig demon lumbered towards Phantom.

Rosa watched in horror as he threw a blue fireball at the kidnapper. A bloodcurdling scream echoed through the chamber—but it was brief. Within seconds, the fire had engulfed the demon from head to toe, burning him so quickly that after the blink of an eye, there was nothing more than a smoldering pile of ash left. The acrid scent of burnt flesh lingered in the air, making Rosa's stomach churn.

"This is plenty, Your Graciousness! The fool just never understood the true value of money... OH, please spare me!" The woman fell to the floor, hitting her head against it as she begged for her life.

"Begone!" Phantom repeated, and before he could even finish the word, the woman grabbed the bag of coins and scurried out like a cockroach.

"Of course! Thank you!"

"Useless drivel," Phantom spat, then snapped his fingers again. "Clean this up, Bas."

"At once, My Lord." The golden-masked demon bowed before extending his hand, summoning water from his fingertips. The liquid swirled around the ash and bloodstains that were etched into the carpet, and moments later, it was completely spotless. The last traces of the pig demon were gone, just like that.

"Now then, what shall I do with you, my dearest?" Phantom drawled out in a sweet voice as he removed the mask from his face.

CHAPTER 27

PHANTOM AND LIGHTNING

Rosa watched as Phantom removed the mask, revealing an eerily familiar face. Rugged yet handsome features with piercing black eyes. He looked so much like Alphegor, Rosa would have claimed them to be twins.

She wanted to ask who he was, but her mouth was still forced shut with magic. Seeing her struggle to speak, Phantom smiled pleasantly and caressed her cheek with a gloved hand.

"It's amazing. I wouldn't have believed it unless I'd seen it. A face so similar to Eirwen's. Truly, you are her daughter," he said, then passed his hand through Rosa's hair which was back to its natural red. "It's just a shame you have your father's hair. White hair would have suited you far better."

A cold shiver ran through Rosa's spine as his eyes seemed to pierce straight into her soul.

What does he want from me?

Suddenly she felt her mouth open, freed of its bonds. This time, she did not hesitate and screamed at the top of her lungs, "Azrael!"

Phantom laughed at her as if it was exactly what he expected to happen.

"Good. This time you didn't hesitate. Let's see if that pup is worthy of being your guardian."

A breath later, the door was violently smashed open, sending bits and pieces scattering across the room. Azrael stood there, breathing heavily, sweat dripping down his forehead. Phantom nodded in satisfaction and clapped his hands twice.

"Very good reaction time."

"I'll be taking her back now," Azrael hissed and strode towards Rosa, electric discharge crackling at his fingertips, and his purple eyes glowing.

"Go ahead and try, pup," Phantom cackled. Icy spears materialized behind him and launched themselves at Azrael with blinding speed. Azrael swatted them away as if they were mere flies, and the other demon increased the speed of the barrage.

"Is that the best you have, old man?" Azrael laughed and launched a crackling orb of lightning towards Phantom. He caught it in his arm as if it were a regular ball and then squeezed it until it disintegrated into nothing.

Phantom smiled menacingly. "Now, now. We have only just begun."

The floor suddenly cracked open, and massive, gnarled vines shot up, coiling around Azrael's limbs. But before they could take proper hold of him, they all burst into hot flames and burned to ash. He grinned victoriously but then kneeled over and spat up blood onto the golden carpet.

Phantom waved his finger in the air, shaking his head in disapproval.

"The first rule of magical combat is not to get caught by any attack. I thought Eirwen would have taught you better."

"W-What did you do?" Azrael gasped, clutching at his chest.

"Just a little poisonous trick. Now, don't just sit there on the floor. Weren't you going to retrieve the Princess?" Phantom reached forward and, with a single touch, disintegrated the ropes around her hands. He then grabbed her by the wrist, his hand cold and rough.

"Let go!" she snarled and tried to pull free, despite knowing that it was futile.

"See? She needs her guardian. Why aren't you saving her?" Phantom let out a wicked laugh, watching as Azrael struggled to get to his feet.

"I just needed to take a moment to think." Azrael grinned, despite the trail of blood on his chin.

I need to do something. Azrael clearly is no match for this guy. Second-strongest Demon, my ass!

Rosa frantically looked around, trying to figure out what she could do. Turning into a shadow was out of the question while Phantom had a firm grip on her. But there must be something.

An idea popped into Rosa's mind, but she needed to time it well. She hoped that Azrael would be able to distract Phantom at least a little bit.

"Take this, you old fossil," Azrael roared and launched a blue lightning bolt at Phantom. The demon deflected it, sending electric sparks through the room, and retaliated with a blue orb of hot fire. Azrael dodged and then began hurling one lightning bolt after another at Phantom, hitting some of the treasures in the room and instantly melting them into puddles.

"Be careful now. You wouldn't want to hurt your princess now, would you?"

"I can't hurt her even if I tried!" Azrael shot back, then continued pelting Phantom with his magic.

"You've sworn an oath!?" The demon seemed caught off guard, and Azrael did not let the opportunity go to waste. With a swift hand gesture, he materialized a golden spike out of the carpet. It came dangerously close to Phantom's ear, causing him to flinch back, and Rosa used the chance to imagine herself becoming Alphegor, growing to his size and gaining his strong features.

"Boo!" Rosa punched Phantom straight in his face, causing him to gape at her in surprise. It didn't do any damage, of course, but in that moment of shock, he lost his grip on her hand. She instantly turned into her shadow form and sped straight towards Azrael.

"Bye!" Azrael exclaimed, and as Rosa materialized by his leg, he snatched her off the ground and pulled her into the shadows.

When Rosa opened her eyes again, she was back in the familiar castle training grounds.

"W-We're safe?" Rosa asked tentatively and looked around the room, expecting Phantom to crawl out of the ground or wall.

"Yes. He can't follow us here," Azrael assured her with a heavy groan, then collapsed to the floor, blood dripping from his mouth.

"W-We need a healer!" Rosa panicked and was about to rush out of the room when Azrael grabbed her with his bloody hand.

"It's fine. It'll be too troublesome to explain... this... to... Lucius." Azrael fainted, and Rosa ran out of the training grounds, calling out for help.

* * *

"Out of all irresponsible things you could have done." Lucius waved his finger angrily at Azrael, who was lying in bed, not daring to meet the older Demon's gaze. Rosa sat on a little chair at his bedside with Deziara stuck to her side like a barnacle.

"In my defense, I never expected anybody would have the nerve to kidnap the Princess from right under my nose." Azrael shrugged and took a sip from his medicine bottle. His hand shot to his mouth as he gagged from the foul-smelling concoction.

Lucius' voice rose higher. "The king had forbidden princesses from leaving the castle! Is that not reason enough?" Rosa had never seen him so angry. Lucius always seemed so calm and collected.

"He can't keep them locked up forever," Azrael muttered and tried to pour the medicine into the bedside drawer. Rosa slammed the drawer shut and glared at him. Apparently, the poison Phantom had injected into Azrael was really dangerous and, if not treated properly, could leave permanent damage.

"Their bodies haven't even fully matured yet! No sane person would take children under thirty years of age out of their home." Lucius was basically yelling at this point, but Azrael didn't seem to care in the slightest, instead looking piteously at Rosa, who motioned for him to drink the medicine.

"You're treating them like prisoners by keeping them locked up in the castle."

"Azrael!" Lucius hit the bedside table, and it instantly disintegrated into a small pile of dust. Both girls stared at Lucius with wide eyes, while Azrael still didn't seem to care in the slightest.

"What's done is done. I can't reverse time and the Princess is safe. That's all that matters," Azrael mumbled and, after pressing his nose shut, downed the medicine in one swift swig. His complexion turned a bit green as soon as he swallowed. "This medicine is already punishment enough."

"Don't be so mad, Lucius," Rosa asked softly, wanting to move past the unpleasant incident. "Azrael did save me."

"Because it is his obligation to do so, Princess! He is bound by his oath." Lucius huffed and then slumped down into a chair, rubbing his temples.

It's his obligation to save me...

The thought that Azrael saved her because of the oath, and not from his free will was not pleasant. Rosa still felt grateful towards him—that's why she was sitting by his side. But it would have been nicer if he had saved her just because he didn't want anything bad to happen to her.

Deziara's hand trembled, and Rosa looked at her sister. The girl seemed to have been affected by the incident even more than Rosa herself. Deziara had not let go of her since she returned to the castle. Day or night, it didn't matter—Deziara refused to leave Rosa's side even for a moment.

"What's wrong?" Rosa asked as she saw large tears welling up in Deziara's eyes.

"It was my fault..." Deziara mumbled as her hands trembled. "I was right next to Morri. I should have noticed. As the big sister, I should have protected her."

Why is this child feeling guilty? There clearly was nothing she could have done. Except for getting kidnapped alongside me.

"No, it's not your fault. It's the kidnappers' fault." Rosa tried to console her, but Deziara shook her head stubbornly.

"The Crown Princess is right. You are just a child. There was nothing you could have done." Lucius put his hand on Deziara's shoulder as tears began streaming down her cheeks.

"B-But... Morri could have been killed..."

No, Phantom had absolutely no intention of killing me—that is certain. But I can't exactly admit that I understood that. What did he even want in the end? And why does he look so much like Alphegor?

"Nah! It was a slave trader's hub. They wouldn't kill her." Azrael waved his hand dismissively, but there was a sort of hardness in his eyes Rosa couldn't quite understand.

"How can you be so nonchalant? The Crown Princess almost got sold as a slave!" Lucius snarled and grasped his head as if in pain.

"We'd just have to track her down then. It's not like she was in mortal danger. As soon as she could call for me, I'd go and get her. It's as simple as that." Azrael slumped back in his bed, wincing in pain as he did.

"L-Let's never leave the castle again," Deziara sniffled, and Rosa nodded just to calm the girl down. In reality, she'd like to see more of the capital, but clearly, that would have to wait until she was able to protect herself.

"No, not unless the king allows it. Now excuse me. I have to go and write a detailed report on this whole mess." Lucius stood up and turned to leave when Azrael perked up in the bed.

"Y-You're not sending the report straight to His Majesty? Are you, Lucius?" the white-haired demon asked nervously.

"Oh, I would love to do nothing more than tell the king of this mess right now," Lucius growled, but then his shoulders slumped. "But I cannot disturb His Majesty while he's on the battlefield. He'd be so worried he'd rush straight back to the castle, and that could have dire consequences."

Azrael relaxed back into the bed, and Rosa felt her own tension ease. She was not ready for Alphegor to return just yet.

"Don't you dare to look so relaxed," Lucius warned. "The moment he returns, it is the first thing I'll be reporting to him." With that, he stomped angrily out of the room.

Rosa looked at Azrael, who closed his eyes and laid his head back wearily.

"You two should go. I need some rest after all that yelling."

"Alright. We'll come back later," Rosa said, getting out of her chair and pulling Deziara along.

"You don't have to."

"You won't drink your medicine otherwise," Rosa retorted and left the demon alone in the healing room. Deziara huffed as soon as they were out the door.

"Why do you even care what happens to him? If it wasn't for his stupid idea to go out, then none of this would have happened." Deziara glared at the door, as if sheer hatred alone could pierce through it and reach Azrael on the other side.

"But I did want to go out..." Rosa admitted, and Deziara relented, wrapping her hand around Rosa's shoulders.

"Let's just wait until we're older, okay?" the girl suggested, and Rosa nodded. She had no real intention of staying cooped up in the castle until adulthood, but she certainly would have to find a way to protect herself before venturing outside again.

I'll get stronger anyway. In case I have to flee the castle.

Rosa shivered from the unpleasant scenario. Would Phantom try to capture her again if she left? Or would some other demon do her in before that? She'd rather avoid either of those scenarios if possible.

"Let's go do something fun, okay? We haven't visited Haku since we returned from the city," Deziara suggested.

"I'm afraid that will have to wait," Asdeus' sweet voice echoed from behind them, and both girls turned to face her with amazing speed, their eyes wide.

"Lady Asdeus," Deziara uttered, scrunching her nose in displeasure. Rosa wasn't sure how to react to the demoness' sudden appearance. But Lady Asdeus ran up to both girls and pulled them into a hug.

"I was so, so worried about you two! I don't know what I would have done if something happened to you," she said while hugging them, but Rosa felt that she sounded a little insincere.

CHAPTER 28

WRITING LESSONS

To Rosa's surprise, the lessons with Asdeus went by without any issues. She had forced her to write another letter fifty times, but since Rosa didn't have to try so hard to appear stupid, it was much easier.

The demoness had attempted to send Deziara away, no doubt to talk properly with Rosa one-on-one. But the girl outright refused to leave Rosa's side, saying she wouldn't leave her no matter what. Rosa made no attempts to shake her sister away, since she appeared rather shaken by the whole kidnapping incident. In all honesty, she felt assured by Deziara's presence.

"Deziara, you did very well today. You can leave now." Asdeus smiled sweetly at the demon girl.

She's trying to remain alone with me again. I wonder if there's something she wants to say that she doesn't want Deziara to hear.

But Deziara still had no intention of letting Rosa go again. She grabbed her chair and pushed it right next to Rosa's.

"I'll wait for Morri to finish again!" she said stubbornly and crossed her arms over her chest. Rosa noticed that Lady Asdeus let a frown slip for just a fraction of a second, but quickly changed it to a pleasant smile.

"Alright then. But it might take a while. She's still *slow* since she is learning." The demoness accentuated the word *slow* and looked Rosa straight in the eyes. The eye contact made Rosa flinch as a cold shiver ran through her spine.

Is she annoyed? Or is that just my imagination?

"It's okay. I can help her," Deziara chimed and then went to grab another ink pen for herself. "Let me show you how to draw this letter."

Deziara proceeded to slowly explain in which order to draw lines and repeated her demonstration several times.

Bless this child. Despite being bratty at times, Deziara is truly kind.

Rosa nodded enthusiastically at Deziara's explanation and proceeded to follow her instructions. She drew the letters crooked, but her sister still praised her every time and encouraged her to keep going.

Oh, how I wish I could show her my paintings. I bet she would love those.

But Rosa quickly dismissed the thought. It was far too dangerous. What would Deziara say about her having a human soul? Although Rosa was sure that her sister had not encountered humans before, the adult demons must have surely taught her to be wary of them. Perhaps even hate them.

"Alright. That will be enough for today." Lady Asdeus dismissed both girls once Rosa had done her writing exercises to her satisfaction. Her little hands were really tired again, and she wondered why she insisted that Rosa had to write so much. Her progress was already far beyond what a normal child could do.

"Now we can go play!" Deziara cheered and began dragging Rosa outside, no doubt intending to visit the little dragon again.

"Yes," Rosa agreed, and soon both girls were bending over backwards from laughter as Haku chased his own tail, alarmed by the bell they attached to it. The noise confused the creature, as whenever he tried to locate the source of the sound, his tail moved with him, making the bell chime in a completely different place.

Later in the evening, both girls sat on the bathroom floor, waiting as Gunna filled the bath with water. Deziara always scrunched her nose at the nanny but had begun acting far more respectfully towards her than the first time they met.

"Pour in lots of water so we can play in the bath!" Deziara commanded, observing the dwarven woman with a keen eye. Gunna shifted uncomfortably and then threw a nervous glance at Rosa.

"I'm afraid that won't be possible," Gunna began.

Deziara jumped up to her feet and pointed a finger at her. "Why not? I am the Princess. If I ask for something, it must be fulfilled."

Gunna shifted uncomfortably again, then stopped pouring the water and put the orb to the side of the bath.

"You see, Lady Morrigan is afraid to take a bath in water that is too deep," the nanny explained with a somber expression. Rosa recalled the first time she took a bath in this world, how she had gone underwater, and Alphegor had to pull her out. The experience reminded her of how she died, so since then, she only washed in baths where water was never above her knees.

"You're afraid?" Deziara looked at Rosa sympathetically, all of her previous bravado completely gone. Rosa nodded, ashamed to admit that even something as simple as an overfilled bath scared her.

What would happen if I saw the sea again? Would I have enough courage to swim in it? Probably not.

"Well, that's alright then. Make lots of bubbles." Deziara smiled cheekily.

"Of course," Gunna replied with a smile and began foaming up the bubbles from the soap.

After the warm bath, both girls snuggled close to each other in bed. Deziara kept giggling from time to time as she brushed away one of Rosa's stray locks.

"Your hair is tickling me," she squealed.

"Yours is tickling me too," Rosa objected and began giggling as well. Deziara wrapped her arms around her, huddling closer. In fact, they were so close that Rosa could hear Deziara's steady heartbeat.

"This is really nice," the older girl hummed, but then her smile faded, and a sigh escaped her lips.

"Why are you sad then?"

"I—I just wish I could have done this with our other sisters too."

"Oh... Have you ever tried?"

"I have. But whenever I tried talking to them, they would either brush me off or their mothers would do it for them. Despite being sisters, we could never really do anything sisterly." Deziara sighed again, then looked down at Rosa and smiled. "But now I can. I am so glad you were born, Morri!"

Deziara brushed Rosa's hair gently. Slowly, her eyes fell shut, and steady breaths escaped from the girl.

It is wonderful to have a nice sister.

* * *

Rosa walked towards the study room, dragging her feet. It was time for another lesson with Lady Asdeus. But this time, Deziara was not by her side.

After spending every waking and sleeping moment together for more than a week, the novelty of having sister time all the time was wearing off. Deziara wanted to return to her mother's side, while Rosa craved some time alone.

It wasn't like she disliked time together with Deziara, but the girl was quite the chatterbox. Rosa barely had any time to organize her thoughts when Deziara would spring three new suggestions or questions at her. It was tiring, to say the least.

That morning the girls agreed to return to their old schedules, with only occasional sleepovers to spend some quality sister time together. So, Rosa walked to Asdeus' lesson without her cheerful sister to lighten her heavy mood.

I don't know why I feel nervous whenever I'm around Asdeus. Well, it's because she knows my secret, but there's something more to it than that. I have this unpleasant feeling in my stomach whenever she's around.

Gunna's warm hand gave Rosa some courage, but she knew that the nanny would not stay during the lesson. Slaves in the castle were not given much leisure so if there was a chance to give them work, the head maid was sure to occupy them. Especially since Rosa didn't require the extra supervision anymore.

"Good luck in your lesson, Lady Morrigan," Gunna said with a smile and opened the door to the study room.

"S-See you later, Gunna." Rosa forced a strained grin, trying to hide her anxiety. She took tentative steps inside the study room and saw Lady Asdeus sitting behind her desk with a notebook in hand. Once she noticed Rosa, she snapped it shut and rose.

"Princess Morrigan. You're late," she announced as the door shut behind Rosa. Deziara was nowhere to be seen.

"W-Where is Deziara?"

"I'm afraid her schedule will be slightly different from now. She has shown a good aptitude for magic, so currently, she'll be focusing on improving that. In the meantime, I'll focus on tutoring you, Princess Morrigan." Lady Asdeus purred as she walked up to Rosa, staring down at her.

"Did you arrange that?"

"Perhaps. But it is true that Deziara requires more lessons in magic. While I am more than capable of tutoring her myself, this is hardly the right place for it."

"So, what is going to happen now?" Rosa asked nervously, the unpleasantness of the situation growing stronger with each passing second.

"Exactly what I promised I would. Tutor you. I'm not sure what else we would be doing," she replied, motioning for Rosa to sit. Without taking her eyes off the demoness, Rosa went to her tiny table and sat down behind it. Asdeus went up to the shelf that contained all the stationery and pulled out a note and ink pen.

"You're just going to continue tutoring me?" Rosa asked, staring at the ink pen in disbelief. It made sense that their lessons would continue as usual, but for some reason, Rosa expected something... more.

"Yes. I don't know what else you would expect me to do? I understand you might feel a bit anxious because I know you are a human. But as I said before, I mean you no harm. I will not treat you any differently than my other students." She yawned, then propped a chart with the demon alphabet in front of Rosa. "Write this letter fifty times."

Again with the fifty times? Oh well, I guess it's not that bad. Just a bit tiring.

Begrudgingly, Rosa took the ink pen and began the task. Unlike the first time, she didn't bother making the letters look bad. Of course, she didn't write in her neatest handwriting either, instead opting for a quick and messy approach, just to get the task out of the way.

"Done," Rosa announced after approximately ten minutes. Lady Asdeus raised an eyebrow, then came over to her desk. She glanced over the letters, then pulled out her red ink pen seemingly out of nowhere and crossed out three of them.

"I'm afraid these won't do. These won't do at all." Her lips curled into an eerie smile. Rosa looked up at her, and suddenly, Lady Asdeus seized her hand, wrapping it in a tight grip and pinning it to the table. "I'm afraid I'll have to punish you for your mistakes."

Before Rosa could protest, the demoness pressed her sharp nail against Rosa's palm. She stared at it for a moment as if nothing happened, and then pain began to swell in her palm. It was barely noticeable at first, but quickly grew in intensity. Rosa tried to scream, but Asdeus pressed her other hand over her mouth to keep her quiet.

"Shhh. It's alright. We all make mistakes. But in order to learn, there needs to be punishment," she whispered sweetly in Rosa's ear and then removed her nail. The pain receded almost instantly. Then Asdeus pressed her nail again, and Rosa screamed into her hand—the pain was excruciating.

"I'm sure that next time, you'll try harder." Asdeus pressed her nail the third time, smiling in satisfaction all the while. Rosa whimpered, tears rolling down her cheeks. It hurt far worse than any knife cut she had the misfortune of experiencing before. The demoness released both of her hands and looked at her with great satisfaction.

"H-How dare you?" Rosa growled, cradling her hand although there were no visible injuries. "I-I'm going to—"

"You're going to…?" Asdeus let the question hang, giving Rosa a knowing look. Sweat began rolling down her temples as she realized that she couldn't do anything about it. She couldn't tell anyone because then Asdeus would no doubt reveal her secret.

"Y-You can't do this!" she protested weakly.

"This is how all demon children learn. As a human, I am sure you are not aware of this method, but demons do not let their children get lazy," Asdeus explained with a stern expression and then smiled. "Good thing that I am your first teacher. As a human, you might have made some horrible mistake if it was somebody else."

But that can't be right. Would demons really treat their children this harshly? I've never seen Deziara get punished like this, and she is quite the slacker.

"Now, now. Enough gawking. Get back to your task. There are still many letters to write. And do try not to make any more mistakes."

Rosa paled and took the ink pen into her trembling hands.

Suddenly the letters that looked so simple and easy before, looked much larger and more menacing. She trembled as she remembered the pain Lady Asdeus had caused her. Praying to all the gods she knew for help, Rosa carefully began writing down letters, making sure they were as perfect as she could manage.

It's alright. As long as you don't make any more mistakes, it'll be alright.

CHAPTER 29

LIBRARY RAID

Rosa sat in the corner of Alphegor's room, silent tears rolling down her face. She clutched her right hand as phantom pain still lingered despite the wound being completely untouched. She had lost count of how many times Asdeus had pressed her nail against Rosa's skin, but the number was so large that five times in either direction made no more difference.

I need to find a way home as soon as possible... I don't know how long I can endure this.

Rubbing her hand absentmindedly, Rosa wondered if and how she could find a way back to Earth. She needed to find magic that could either send her back in time or allow her to travel through worlds. Both seemed so far-fetched, even in a world where she could turn into a shadow.

I can't take these lessons with Asdeus anymore. I need to find a way to get away from this world. Not just because of her but also in case Alphegor finds out about me being a human and is... less than happy about it. There is a slight chance that he might accept it, but I can't take such a gamble.

Rosa wiped away her tears, then with a determined nod, slipped into her shadow form. She was about to slip under the door like she usually did when sneaking out of her room for art supplies. But

Asdeus had warned her that she'd have more guards watching her. So, she turned to the window instead.

Carefully, she hovered over to the windowsill and peered down. A dizzying drop stretched below her—Alphegor's bedroom was located near the very top of the castle.

It shouldn't matter, right? I'm a shadow right now. Shadows can't fall. Can they?

Her human instincts were screaming at her—urging her to go back. But she knew that her fears were irrational. She couldn't fall as a shadow. Slowly she glided across the windowsill, going closer to the edge. A few centimeters at a time, she went past the ledge, willing herself to stick close to the wall.

I can't fall. I can't fall, she repeated in her mind and slowly began gliding down the castle wall.

Most of the windows were completely dark, with only a few rare exceptions still having the lights on. As Rosa descended further, her speed increased, the natural fear of heights slowly lessening. At last, she reached the castle grounds.

That wasn't so bad. Now I have to find the library window, sneak inside, find the book that could have information about traveling to other worlds, and then sneak back into my room. Easy.

Rosa knew the inner layout of the castle pretty well by now, but finding which specific windows belonged to the library was more difficult than anticipated. They all looked the same, after all.

The library is on the third floor and spans three floors up. It is also located on the opposite side of the castle, not too far from the Main Hall.

Rosa, still in her shadowy form, dove under the bushes, and circled from behind the castle while avoiding all the prominent routes. Even with her superior speed in the shadow form, it still took her fifteen minutes to get all the way around the massive building.

But thankfully, any further troubles of locating the library were quickly resolved as she saw nine dimly lit windows spanning across three floors in a neat 3 by 3 pattern.

That must be it. But why are the lights still on? Do they not turn them off during the night?

Rosa crawled up the castle wall again, going straight for the closest open window. Looking inside the library, she saw that the light inside was much dimmer than during the day and wouldn't be enough to read comfortably, even with a demon's improved vision.

Two demon guards, one sitting on the first floor of the library by the entrance and the other on the third floor near the staircase, were looking over the stacks of shelves with heavy eyelids. Their gazes were unfocused, and one of them was steadily drooping his head lower and lower.

Okay, shouldn't be too difficult.

Rosa slipped behind the nearest bookshelf and then watched for the guards' reaction. Nothing. Neither of them seemed any wiser about her presence. She slipped a few rows deeper into the library and then searched the shelves.

Time magic or teleportation magic is probably what I should be searching for. Or perhaps some book that generalizes in rarer and more powerful types of magic.

She went from shelf to shelf until she found a section named *Forbidden Magic*. It was small and hidden in the deepest corner of the library, but it still seemed rather accessible for something that was supposed to be forbidden. Perhaps, what was forbidden for others was just regular literature for demons.

Let's see what we have here...

She scanned several titles—*Monster Fusing Manual, Necromancy for Beginners, Conniving Chaos Conundrums*, and *How Not to Get Summoned by a Human...*

What's with these titles?

Rosa kept searching until she finally stumbled upon a couple she thought could be useful—*Unusual Magic Through the Ages* and *Magic from Other Worlds*. She would have liked to flip through them a little more before grabbing them but was afraid of attracting the attention of the guards.

She emerged from the shadow, expecting to grab the book right away, but realized that she was too short and couldn't reach.

Stupid tiny legs.

Rosa closed her eyes and then imagined herself taking on Azrael's shape. It was a double precaution—if she got caught, nobody would dare to do much against him, even if he was breaking some "don't enter the library after ten" rule. He was one of the strongest demons around, after all.

Opening her eyes, she snatched the two books, but in her haste, she pulled another book with her that fell to the ground with a gentle thump. She grabbed that one too, and then quickly blended into the shadows underneath the shelf.

"Who's there?" a gruff voice called out, and Rosa heard footsteps approaching.

Time to scram.

Slithering from underneath the shelves, Rosa hurried to the open window and then rushed outside, down the castle wall, and then made the trip back to the castle backyard.

I think I'm good. Just need to climb back... to my room. Has it always been so high up?

Rosa mentally prepared herself and then started moving up the wall. It was a very odd feeling—with no body for gravity to push down on, she effortlessly moved higher and higher. It didn't matter if the surface was completely smooth, she didn't need any footholds. In a few minutes, she was back in Alphegor's room with three large books clutched in her tiny hands.

"These felt much lighter when I was in Azrael's skin," Rosa huffed and heaved the books into her bed. She slid under the covers and pulled the first book into her lap.

"*Unusual Magic Through the Ages,*" Rosa murmured as she read the title, then began flipping through the weathered pages. The book appeared old as the paper had already yellowed with age, however it appeared to be well cared for. Unfortunately, the contents of it were not very useful to Rosa.

It described odd magics that could be useful only in very specific scenarios and were rarely beneficial to anybody. For example, one chapter described how, by manipulating the inner structure of a fruit, one could turn it from sweet to sour but not the other way around. Rosa read that particular chapter twice to make sure it didn't work both ways.

There were more sinister magics as well, but Rosa didn't bother to read them. In the end, the book had no mention of any time magic or magic that could transport a person to another world.

"Onto the next one." She sighed and then dragged the second book in front of her. It was titled *Magic from Another World*. She was feeling quite hopeful about that one, eagerly flipping it open.

Unlike the first book, this one seemed rather new, some pages refusing to separate from each other and instead huddling together in a cluster Rosa had to hold down to read.

After reading just a few pages, Rosa knew that this book wouldn't help her. It described, or rather, *attempted* to describe how technology from Earth worked. It spoke about smartphones as if they were some magical tablets with unlimited power. Cars were described as loud beasts used for carrying people and things around.

Computers apparently were far too difficult for them to comprehend, and they called them *oracle machines* that would grant the user any knowledge they wished for and could even materialize things after a certain amount of time. Rosa wondered whether they were talking about online shopping.

But it is a good sign that they know about the existence of Earth. That means that somebody had gone there and came back to tell others of it.

Rosa pushed the book aside and then eyed the third book that she had grabbed in a hurry. It was smaller in size, and there was a tear on the front cover. When she took it in her hands, it felt like the poor thing would just fall apart.

"Let's see—*Rarest Magic*," she read the simple title aloud, and her heart skipped a beat. "This is it! This might be the book that I needed."

Rosa carefully opened it, making sure not to pull the fragile pages too hard, and began reading through the contents. Her stomach began to churn after just a few pages. It spoke of vile rituals where one could sacrifice part of other beings to enhance themselves, or even outright kill them for magical power.

Rosa was tempted to slam the thing shut but persevered and read until the end. And she was rewarded for her effort. On the very last page there was a short paragraph that spoke about magic that could transport a person to another world.

"Extremely rare and difficult to wield. The only person known to wield this magic is Queen Eirwen. The stone which she obtained the magic from is kept a secret and it is strictly forbidden to be used by anyone but the queen," Rosa read, and then slowly shut the book.

"So, my demon mother could wield it. Perhaps she used it to pull me from the other world into this one…" Rosa mused but then shook her head. "No! How ridiculous. What use would a demon queen have for a human girl?"

She laughed to herself, but her laughter died down as she began to ponder—how exactly *was* she brought into this world? It was such a burning question when she had just gotten here, but as years went by, the matter lost its urgency.

But how could I find that out? It's not like I can go and ask Alphegor.

Rosa sighed, and after hiding the books in Alphegor's desk, she went back to sleep. She didn't know how late or, rather, how early it was, but she decided to get what little sleep she could.

The next morning, Rosa barely managed to get out of bed. Gunna had a hard time waking her up, and most of the morning went by in a sleepy haze. She only truly realized what was going on once she was back in the study room, alone with Asdeus.

"Shall we continue our lesson from yesterday, Princess?" The demoness smiled. Rosa gritted her teeth as the demoness put a fresh notebook and ink pen in front of her.

"What shall I write?" Rosa growled, not bothering to hide her distaste for the woman. She tapped her sharp nail against Rosa's desk, and she flinched remembering how it felt pressed against her skin.

"It seems like you have forgotten good manners today. How about you write these two letters fifty times each," the demoness cackled. Rosa had no choice but to grit her teeth and begin writing.

I still know so little about this world. If I understood its magic and structure a bit better, perhaps I'd at least know where to search.

Rosa almost jumped out of her seat as a realization hit her. Asdeus gave her an odd glance, and she pretended to be engrossed in her writing.

Faenor's gift! It was supposed to be a comprehensive encyclopedia of magical gems. It should help me understand exactly what I'm searching for.

CHAPTER 30

ELF'S APOLOGY

Appearing as calm and collected as possible after a long afternoon with Asdeus', Rosa hurried to find her nanny. She found the dwarf woman cleaning the floors in the hallway in front of Alphegor's room.

"Gunna!" Rosa called out and hurried to her side.

"Lady Morrigan. What's the matter?" The nanny put the dirty washcloth into the bucket and wiped her hands on her apron.

"Do you remember the gift Faenor gave me on my first birthday?" Rosa asked through ragged breaths. Gunna stroked her beard as she thought it over, then clapped her hands together. "Oh, yes! I remember now. Would you like me to bring it to you?"

"Yes, please. To my room," Rosa replied, and the nanny nodded and hurried away. Meanwhile, Rosa went to wait in her room, away from the guards' prying eyes. She tapped her foot impatiently as she waited for Gunna to come.

After a few minutes, the nanny arrived with Faenor's book in her hands. It looked far larger in the dwarf woman's hands than it had in the elf's. Rosa was also relieved to see that the front cover had no writing on it, so the guards or anybody else who happened to see Gunna would have no idea what was inside it.

"Here it is. Would you like me to read it for you?" Gunna suggested as she placed it on Rosa's table.

"N-No. I just remembered that it had pretty pictures," she hastily replied and then added, "I just wanted to take a look at it again. Now that Faenor has disappeared."

The nanny nodded solemnly. "I understand. You must miss him. I'll leave you to it then, Lady Morrigan. Call me with the bell in case you change your mind."

Rosa nodded and watched the dwarf woman leave. She waited for a few minutes until she was completely certain that the nanny was gone and then opened the book.

I hope this can shed some light on what I need to be searching for.

Rosa was about to turn to the table of contents when a small, folded paper fell out from seemingly nowhere and slid underneath her hand.

"What's this?" Rosa picked it up and began unfolding it. Once it was fully open, she realized it was a letter. The handwriting was elegant and easy to read, and also somewhat familiar. It was Faenor's.

For a moment, she considered just throwing it out the window. She didn't want to read any fake well-wishes for her first birthday from a man who betrayed her secret. But in the end, her curiosity won over, and she began reading it.

Dear Princess,

If you are reading this letter, then you have opened my first birthday gift to you without me around to read it to you. You may have grown up into a magnificent woman now, but more likely than not—I am no longer in the demon castle.

In fact, I have most likely betrayed the trust you've shown me and returned to my homeland. While I do not have any right to beg for forgiveness, I am going to ask for it anyway—forgive me, Princess Morrigan. I have done the most heinous crime against you, and so I shall try to make it up to you, even if just a little.

If you have sought out this book, then you have no doubt been searching for a way back to your world. It must have shocked you that I knew that you were actually with a human soul, but know that people from other worlds do occasionally come to Doppelta. In fact, most know of their existence, rare as it may be, and it is an especially well-known fact among us elves who strive to learn as much as possible from the otherworldly visitors.

You, however, have been put in a position more difficult than most travelers, and so I hope to offer you an escape back to your home, which no doubt is a more peaceful place. The magic you seek is called "Dimensional Travel," and it can be learned from one of the rarest gems in our world— a purple diamond.

These gemstones are so rare that only two cases are known to exist, one in the Overworld and one in the Underworld. While the odds seem to be stacked against you, you actually have the best chance of obtaining the Underworld's purple diamond.

The previous owner of it was your birth mother, the late Demon Queen Eirwen, and after her death, many thought that the ability was lost with her. However, it is known among elves that magical gems of such high quality do not disappear with the death of their owner.

It is very likely that the purple diamond was hidden in the demon castle's royal treasury, awaiting the day it would be needed. Unfortunately, I do not know where the treasury is or the dangers that await those who seek it out; however, you, as the Crown Princess, are one of the rare people allowed to access it.

I pray that you manage to find a safe passage home.
Your friend,
Faenor

As soon as Rosa finished reading the last word, the letter flew out of her hands and then burst into flames, leaving not even a single trace of its existence behind. She blinked a few times, barely able to process the information Faenor left for her.

The purple diamond that has dimensional travel ability is in the Royal Treasury. And I am allowed inside it?

Rosa stared up at the dark ceiling, putting her hand on her forehead and exhaling heavily. Faenor had handed her the answer she desired on a silver platter. No more sneaking around at night, rifling through obscure library books in secret.

"But if you're my ally, then why did you tell Asdeus the truth?" Rosa whispered and then covered her eyes with her palm. She couldn't fully understand the elf. Was the freedom so precious to him that he'd risk her life for his? He clearly knew that demons finding out about her human soul would bring her horrible repercussions, and yet he had done it anyway. It was a pure stroke of luck that Asdeus hadn't exposed the fact that Rosa had a human soul.

"Why Faenor?" She wished the elf was here to answer this question, but he was not. According to the letter, he was now free. That made Rosa feel a little better. Only a little bit.

I hope that the knowledge you left will help.

* * *

Rosa stared in the mirror in annoyance, looking at her own version of Azrael as the real Azrael pointed out all the flaws in the transformation.

"You're lacking a bit of hair volume in the front. I almost look like I'm balding. Also, you made the buttons on my suit gray when they are clearly silver," he prattled while Rosa listened with her hands crossed over her chest, wishing for the whole lesson to be over soon.

For two weeks straight, Rosa had to transform into Azrael day after day, trying to get his features right down to the last strand of hair. The worst part was that the vain fool kept changing his clothes each and every day and expected her to get those right too. He claimed it was a good exercise for adaptability.

If you haven't noticed, I am still a four-year-old girl. You should be celebrating that I am willing to transform into you at all.

"Don't use my face to glare at me. It doesn't suit me at all. Better channel that energy to fix my hair." Azrael poked her forehead, and she swatted it away. She closed her eyes and then tried to fix the hair, although at this point, she had stared at Azrael's hair so much that she couldn't even make any sense of it anymore. Kind of like when you repeat one word so many times that it starts losing all its meaning.

"There! Is that better?" She opened her eyes and once again glared at the white-haired Demon.

"No."

"What now?" Rosa groaned and threw her arms in the air in defeat.

"You're still scowling." He wiggled his finger in front of her face, and she was tempted to bite it.

I am supposed to be looking for the Royal Treasury, but this guy has been holding me in these stupid shapeshifting lessons for weeks.

It was a blessing in an odd sort of way—Azrael completely denied Asdeus whenever she tried to drag Rosa off to her "lessons." He claimed that it was crucial for Rosa to master shapeshifting as soon as possible to avoid any accidents that could seriously impact her health.

Rosa believed that Azrael just loved looking at himself too much. The idiot could probably spend the whole day staring at his reflection. And if that reflection happened to be three-dimensional—all the better. Rosa, on the other hand, had seen Azrael enough times to never want to see his face again.

"Can we do something else for a change?" Rosa complained and shifted back into her demon self. She could now shift back without the need to close her eyes—that was how much she wanted to be out of Azrael's skin.

"Like what?" Azrael asked with a mischievous grin on his face.

Like go to the Royal Treasury and get the purple diamond so I could get the hell out of this world before everybody finds out that I am actually human.

But she couldn't say that, of course. Her focus shifted to her guards who stood by the entrance. She didn't have to worry about them overhearing anything since Azrael had made a soundproof barrier around the training ground after the whole kidnapping incident. So perhaps, Rosa could ask a series of innocent questions that may lure the desired answer out of him.

"How about... you tell me more about the castle?" she tried lamely, not able to come up with a good question on the spot.

"I thought you hated the castle. Judging by how eager you were to get out of it." Azrael winced, no doubt remembering the nasty run-in with Phantom. He still had to drink the nasty medicine once a day to get rid of the last remnants of the poison.

"Yes, and it was horrible. So, I'm trying to find fun places within the castle. Do you know any?"

"Fun places?" Azrael scratched his chin in contemplation. "There is a lot of hidden stuff that could be considered fun."

"Like what?" Rosa asked eagerly, hoping that the Royal Treasury might be included in the list.

"Well..." Azrael drawled, then shook his head. "No, I can't tell that to a little squirt like you. You need to do some growing up first."

He reached out and ruffled Rosa's hair, making it stand up in every direction. She grumbled and tried to even it out again.

"I thought you were the fun guy," she persisted, trying to entice the demon. Azrael was prone to causing mischief, so surely a bit of teasing could get the desired result.

"I *am* the fun guy!" he announced and proudly put his hands on his hips and raised his nose high. "Tell me what you want to do, we'll do it."

That was easy. He really is a kid on the inside.

"How about finding some treasure?" Rosa smirked, but Azrael instantly shook his head.

"Oh, no, no, no! I do not want to get another long lecture from Lucius, just because I snuck into the Royal Treasury or something."

"The Royal Treasury!" Rosa didn't even have to fake her excitement, allowing her natural glee to give her voice a higher pitch. Just like a child who had just heard of the most awesome thing in the world.

"No! It is forbidden!" He wagged his finger at her, but the gesture lacked the will behind it.

One more push and Azrael will surely cave in.

"But aren't I the Princess? Can't I go anywhere within the castle? Father said that I can." Rosa whimpered, making her best sad puppy-dog eyes.

"No means no. And those large, cute eyes will not make me change my mind." Azrael crossed his arms over his chest and stared down at her. She continued staring back at him, widening her eyes even more and turning her lower lip out to make it quiver as if she were about to cry.

Azrael looked away, then glanced back at her. His expression slowly softened until, finally, he threw up his arms in defeat. "Fine, fine! Let's go see the Royal Treasury. But we are only *looking!* We, namely you, are not going to take anything from it. Do you understand?"

"Yes! Thank you, thank you!" Rosa cheered earnestly. If she had known that convincing Azrael to do her bidding would be so easy, she would have done it right away.

CHAPTER 31

TO THE ROYAL TREASURY

Azrael threw a careful glance at the guards who were standing by the entrance, none the wiser about their nefarious plans. The sound barrier that Azrael created worked perfectly. Rosa did feel a little bit bad for them, since if they got caught, they would most likely lose their jobs.

But it was just their jobs that were at risk. For Rosa, this could be a question of life and death. She wasn't worried about Azrael, though. The demon had a way of slithering out of any real punishment, only having to deal with some minor inconveniences for his transgressions.

"Now, listen carefully. If we want this to succeed, we cannot get caught. Do you get it?" Azrael warned, and Rosa nodded her head. That would be the ideal scenario, although she had a feeling that it was quite unlikely.

"Good. Now, to execute it, we're going to have to be very, very stealthy and go at night, when there's the least amount of guards and spying eyes."

"Are we going to sneak in as shadows?" she asked, although it was unlikely that there would be no countermeasures against demons in their shadow form. Then anyone who had a shadow form could just do what they wanted in the castle.

"No, that won't work. We're going to do it the old-fashioned way." Azrael grinned and rubbed his hands together like some movie villain.

"Old-fashioned way?" Rosa cocked her head.

"You'll see when the time comes. We're going to do it at night. I'll come to your room once everything is ready. You—"

The training room door swung open, and the clatter of Asdeus' heels resounded through the empty space. Rosa could recognize it anywhere, and she did her best not to let her fears show. Azrael's face also grew cold.

"I see you've completed your lesson for the day. I shall be taking the Princess with me now. We're already falling behind schedule," Asdeus said with a sweet smile. Rosa was tempted to turn into a shadow and run away, but managed to restrain herself.

"Who cares about your stupid schedule? She's four, she doesn't need to learn how to write yet. Normal children learn that at seven."

"One could argue that she has no reason to study magic at her age either. Normally, four-year-olds haven't even awakened their ability at this age," Asdeus retorted and then looked at Rosa. "But our Princess here is very special. Besides, you've held her up for long enough."

Azrael pressed his lips together in a thin line but had nothing to say against that.

"Come now, Princess. We have a lot to learn."

With trembling footsteps, she followed Asdeus, mentally preparing herself for yet another one of her torturous lessons. Her fingers twitched in anticipation.

I have to endure it for just a little while longer. Soon I'll be able to get out of here.

As she exited the training grounds, she threw a last glance back at teeth. But before she could properly decipher his reaction, Asdeus tapped on her shoulder, forcing her to move forward.

* * *

Rosa leaned against Alphegor's wardrobe, staring at her trembling hands. Asdeus made her "corrections" thirteen times that day. The skin on her arm was clean and unblemished without any signs of injuries. But she could still imagine the horrid pain Asdeus' nail brought.

"I have to end this soon. I don't think I can take it for much longer," she mumbled to herself in English, hoping to find solace in her own language. She would have to endure just a little while longer. And then, she'd go back to her tiny apartment.

She'd draw seascapes and landscapes of forests and plains filled with life and greenery. She'd start her job at Studio Goblin and help them create animated movies greater than anybody had ever seen before. And best of all—Asdeus would not be there.

But neither would Deziara. Nor Gunna. Nor Azrael. And definitely not Alphegor.

The thought was surprisingly painful.

"What are you doing?" Azrael's familiar voice broke Rosa out of her contemplation and she jumped in surprise. The white-haired demon stood by the window, his expression sunken with concern. It was not a face she'd seen on him before.

"You scared me!" Rosa jumped to her feet and glared at him.

"I've been here for a while, and you've just been sitting there daydreaming." He strode towards her and looked over her body as if inspecting it. "Are you alright?"

What an odd question.

"Yes?"

Azrael opened his mouth to say something, then closed it and adopted his usual casual grin. "You're ready to see some treasure?"

"Yes!" Rosa nodded.

"Excellent. This will be a great test for your shapeshifting skills." Azrael nodded, then extended his hand towards Rosa.

"Shapeshifting?" she asked and tentatively took his hand. For a moment, they disappeared into darkness, and Rosa soon found herself down in the castle's backyard.

"Yes. You see, the Treasury is protected from most magic, so the only way to get in is to do so by physical means."

"You don't want me to shift into a dragon and break in, do you?"

"No, of course not. Brute force won't help anyway. We must be delicate. And dare I say—this method is only possible because of you, Princess." Azrael's eyes sparkled with mischief, a sly smile curling on his lips.

He's like a little kid who is about to break into a candy store. God, I hope this actually works. It's probably the only chance I'm going to have at finding that gem.

"Why me?" Rosa asked as Azrael crouched down in the bushes. She followed suit and saw one of the patrol guards making his way through the backyard.

"Because you're the king's heir, obviously. I'll explain more once we get there. Now sit quietly and observe the guard as he passes by. Take in every detail you can," he whispered and then disappeared into the shadows. Rosa also adopted her shadow form and waited.

A few minutes passed before the demon guard finally strode by the exact bush they were hiding in. Rosa did her best to memorize everything she could about the demon. She'd seen him before in passing, so she was able to focus on more unfamiliar parts of him.

Once the guard's patrol led him a good distance away, Azrael slipped out of his shadow form. Rosa followed suit.

"Did you memorize everything you could?"

She nodded.

"Good. Now we're going to the first floor of the castle, right before the servant wing starts. Do you know the place I'm talking about?" Azrael kept his voice low, occasionally throwing a glance over the yard.

Rosa nodded again. She remembered that particular part of the castle from their excursion to the city. The contrast between the main castle and the servants' quarters was so stark, she couldn't forget it.

"We're going to go there as shadows. You'll have to move very fast. And once you're there, you have to emerge from the shadow disguised as a guard."

"Why can't I transform into the guard here, and then you teleport us back into the castle?" Rosa objected, wondering what about the limits of his ability. She also doubted whether she could do a transformation right after exiting from the shadows.

"Because all teleportation magic is monitored within the castle."

"And shadow forms are not? Besides, didn't you just teleport us downstairs?"

"They're impossible to track. And nobody cares if somebody teleports outside. Now prepare to go on three." Azrael lifted three of his fingers and began a silent countdown. Rosa wanted to object, but before she could, the countdown was complete, and he was gone.

Damn, Azrael! Give me a moment to respond at least.

Rosa slipped into her shadow form and then sped into the castle, heading through the empty corridors straight towards the servants' wing. She saw an occasional guard or maid doing their daily duties, but overall, the place was rather empty.

As they neared the designated spot, Rosa did her best to concentrate on the guard persona, trying to recall every detail. She imagined herself taller, with muscled arms, and wearing the classic dark uniform all the guards wore. But then she lost control of her shadow form and fell to the floor with a loud crash.

"That wasn't very graceful." A guard with Azrael's voice looked down at her, grinning from ear to ear.

"You went too quickly." Rosa rushed to her feet and almost fell over again. The guard's body felt far too large and heavy. It was difficult to move—like she was wearing a full-body suit.

"You imagined yourself shifting too soon. But it's alright; I don't think anybody noticed." Guard Azrael looked around, and after a few moments of silence, he nodded to confirm his words.

"What if somebody had been here?" Rosa grumbled.

"It's fine. I would have put them to sleep."

Of course, you would have...

"Come, we're going down now." Azrael motioned towards a narrow, dimly lit corridor and Rosa followed. The place was almost too narrow for the bulky guard, and Rosa had to walk carefully so as to not accidentally bump into the occasional bucket or mop propped against the wall.

Slowly, the corridor began to veer left and down on an increasingly steep slope. Rosa began to fear she might slip when the corridor abruptly ended. There was no door, no lever, no nothing—just a dead end.

"What's this?" Rosa asked Azrael, who was grinning from ear to ear.

"Just watch," he said, then began stomping his feet.

Rosa was about to roll her eyes at him—the gesture looked like one of Deziara's temper tantrums—but she realized his stomping wasn't random; it had in a deliberate pattern.

After a minute, a low rumble came from the wall, and it began to part like a slow sliding door. It opened into a tunnel with a staircase that led further downwards.

"After you, milady." Azrael bowed in a mocking sort of way.

"You go first," Rosa retorted. She had no intention of going into that dark, suspicious place first. If some weird guardian monster would jump at them, then Azrael could take the brunt of it.

"As you wish." Azrael cackled and then proceeded downstairs. Rosa followed shortly after, struggling to fit the guard's giant feet on the narrow staircase.

"Can't we turn back now?" she asked.

"No. It is important that we remain in this form until we pass a certain threshold. Once we are downstairs, do not talk. If somebody asks you something, either nod or shake your head. Or better yet, say nothing at all."

Rosa was curious to know what exactly awaited them further ahead but decided to remain silent. She didn't want anyone to overhear them talking. Azrael was unlikely to give a straight answer either way.

Soon, Rosa saw a brighter light up ahead as they descended into a chamber of sorts. Three exits branched out from the space, and in its center sat a massive demon guard with a completely unreadable expression. If a mountain were to be made into demon form, this was what it would look like.

"What's up, Chad?" Azrael greeted him with a friendly smile and a wave of his hand. Rosa cringed inwardly as Chad merely blinked, showing not the slightest interest in having a conversation.

"Your pass?"

"Of course. Here you go, buddy." Azrael pulled something out of his guard uniform and presented it to Chad. Rosa glanced at it, and it appeared to be a piece of paper with a signature on it. Chad looked down at it and then just grunted. Rosa couldn't tell if it was approval or not, but Azrael maintained his cheerful demeanor and proceeded towards one of the corridors.

"Thank you, Chad. Always a pleasure talking with you."

Rosa was about to follow Azrael, when Chad suddenly spoke up. "Your pass?"

She froze mid-step and turned to look at Chad, unsure of what to do. Azrael quickly rushed back and threw one hand around her shoulder.

"Oh, we're going together. Partners and all that." Azrael chuckled.

Oh, no! There's no way he's going to buy that cheap lie. This is as far as we get.

"Okay," Chad replied and then his gaze wandered away from her, looking at the entrance door again as if they didn't exist anymore.

"You heard the man. Let's go, partner." Azrael pulled her along into the corridor, a victorious grin spreading on his face. Rosa was about to object to his half-assed methods when she noticed a change in the air. It felt heavy, like before a thunderstorm, and then there were lots of odd slashes and burn marks along the floor and walls.

"W-What is this place?" she whispered, not realizing she had clutched Azrael's sleeve.

"Welcome to the Dungeon, Princess!"

CHAPTER 32

DEMON CASTLE DUNGEON

"Dungeon?" Rosa exclaimed, her voice echoing into the long chamber in front of her.

Sinister chandeliers, that shone with unnatural purple light, hung from the ceiling, casting an eerie glow on the floors below. The walls were covered in slashes, scratches, and weird dents, while the corridors split into multiple pathways.

The floor bore clear signs of combat—scorch marks, giant footprints, cracks, and oddly embedded stones, that Rosa was convinced would activate a deadly trap the moment she stepped on them. Not to mention the occasional dark smear which no doubt was dried blood.

"You didn't think it would be easy getting to treasure? One must always overcome some obstacle to get there." Azrael grinned victoriously, still disguised as a demon guard.

I knew he agreed too easily. He's trying to scare me off, isn't he? A normal four-year-old would no doubt turn their tail and go back to bed. But I must get that purple diamond. It's my ticket home.

So she thought, but thinking and doing were two different things. Rosa would have liked nothing more than to return to her bed and forget about this ominous place and its various marks of past victims.

"Let's go then," she said with as much bravado as she could muster and took a step forward. Azrael instantly yanked her back just in time for a flurry of arrows to rush past her nose, causing her to let out a small yelp.

"Be careful. These dungeons are filled with traps." The demon tried to appear scared, but she could see how the corners of his mouth twitched upwards, and his eyes gleamed with joy.

Damned Demon! Fine, if you want to play dirty—let's play dirty.

"But I'm sure you know how to get through here, right? You're so strong and agile and amazing, Azrael. I've never seen anyone do magic as well as you do, Azrael." She laid it on thick, trying to appeal to his ego. In reality, she hadn't really seen anyone besides Azrael and Phantom do magic beyond the simple levitation maids used to reach faraway corners. But there was no need to tell him that.

"Of course, I can! This is a piece of cake for me." He lifted his head high, a proud smile creeping across his lips.

"I bet you could even do it while dragging someone as weak as me around. You're so amazing, Azrael!" She continued her barrage of compliments, and Azrael scratched his cheek.

Is he getting embarrassed? That's kind of cute.

"I—I mean, I could, but it's quite dangerous, Princess. Perhaps we should—"

"Really? Show me! I want to see you do it. You always look so powerful when you do magic, Azrael!"

The demon couldn't take it anymore. Shifting back into his true form, Azrael grinned widely from ear to ear and waved his hand with a flourish.

"Don't you worry, Princess! You just leave the difficult part to me and enjoy the show. I'll show you *exactly* how amazing I am!"

Rosa returned to her childlike self, doing her best to suppress a grin.

I can't believe he actually fell for that. Vanity will be your downfall, Azrael.

"Yay!" Rosa cheered in a childlike manner and allowed Azrael to pick her up. He settled her in his left arm while making sure his right hand remained free.

"Now, hold on tightly, Princess. While I am all-powerful, I do still need my hand to fight in case we encounter something unruly," he warned, and Rosa grabbed his shoulders, gripping him tightly.

"Are you sure you can do this?" Rosa asked, glancing further into the dungeon. Surely it must be the most difficult dungeon in the whole Underworld if the Royal Treasury lies at the end of it.

"Yes. Besides, we're going to take a shortcut."

"Shortcut?"

"Yeah. It's still dangerous, but it's made in a way that people who need to access the Treasury can do so."

Good to know. So, we're not going to face the worst of it. He should have started with that.

"Show me. I'll need to be able to do this one day, too," Rosa urged, and Azrael nodded.

"Alright, alright. Let's go then," he replied and then sped straight into the dungeon. Rosa watched in horror as arrows, spikes, fire, lightning, glass, and every other possible projectile shot behind them, missing them by less than a few centimeters. It was like he activated every possible trap on purpose.

Before Rosa could find her voice to complain about it, the ground beneath them vanished, sending them plummeting into a deep chasm. She screamed while Azrael laughed as if he were on some rollercoaster ride.

"This is my favorite part!" Azrael exclaimed while she clung to him for dear life. After what seemed like an eternity, they fell into a giant empty chamber. Rosa feared they might just fall to their death, but at the last moment, Azrael waved his hand and slowed their descent, allowing them to land as softly as a feather.

A deep, rumbling growl echoed through the chamber. Rosa's breath hitched as she spotted a giant serpentlike creature slumbering in one of the openings in the wall. It was easily the size of a house, with six snakelike heads and short, webbed legs. There was saliva trickling down from its six mouths, and as its eyes flicked open, it hissed furiously at them. If Rosa had to name it, only one word came to mind—Hydra.

"Hey there, Levi. How are you doing?" Azrael waved at the monster, whose demeanor instantly changed. It produced a sort of whining noise and lowered its six heads to Azrael's level.

"W-What is that?" Rosa squealed and tried to scramble as far away from it as possible. Unfortunately, Azrael held her tight, and she had no choice but to watch the horrible creature slither closer and closer with its giant heads.

"How rude. This is Levi. He guards the secret passage to the Royal Treasury in case somebody wanders in here," Azrael explained and patted one of the giant heads. Rosa stared at how the six heads fought over attention, each pushing the other out of the way to get some pats. "Would you like to pet him?"

"HUH?" Rosa screeched, and much to her dismay, Azrael lowered her to the ground, right next to one of the hydra's heads. It moved left and right, eyeing her from all sides.

Don't eat me, don't eat me, don't eat me!

"This is the Crown Princess Morrigan, Levi. She is your master's daughter, so be nice." Azrael's lips curled as he watched all of the heads turn their attention towards her. The creature got excited at the word "master" and began flicking its forked tongues at her, one head after the other.

Rosa stood as stiff as a rock, trying her best not to scream each time she felt the monster's cold scales touch her skin and clothes. Her limbs were as tense as a bowstring, as she refused to relax in fear of accidentally touching the monster. After each head seemed to have sniffed her to their satisfaction, they began nudging her hand the same way Haku would when he wanted pats.

"He likes you, Princess. Give each head a pat. Just be sure to pat them an equal number of times. They get jealous easily." Azrael snickered, observing the scene from the sidelines.

I swear you will pay for this!

Mechanically, Rosa reached her head up and somehow forced herself to pat one of the heads. It leaned into her touch, cold and moist scales sending a shiver through her whole body. Looking at the head so close, she wondered whether it would even notice if it accidentally swallowed her. She was so small in comparison.

One after the other, she patted the horrid creature's heads until Azrael finally deemed it necessary to end her torture and shooed the heads away.

"That's enough for first greetings. Here, have a snack." Azrael pulled a pouch that hung by his belt and then fished something from inside it. The hydra perked up and rushed towards him at once. The demon threw some round objects, each head snapping one out of the air, and then the hydra lay down on the floor, chewing in satisfaction.

How can something so small satisfy such a large monster? Can it even feel it among those giant teeth?

"What did you give him?" she inquired as Azrael strode to pick her up again.

"I'll tell you once you're older."

I don't think I want to know anymore...

With Rosa secure in his grip again, Azrael left the hydra and the chamber behind, going towards a door she completely failed to notice before. It was the same texture and color as the cragged walls, the only thing that betrayed its true purpose being the door handle.

He opened the door, and the scene changed completely. The gloomy dungeon was replaced by a pleasant room with neatly polished marble floors, clean walls, and quaint couches for sitting. It was like one of those waiting rooms in the bank. Only with fewer people.

At the end of it stood a giant, round door that protruded outwards at least half a meter. It appeared to be made out of steel and had intricate carvings that spiraled inwards. But despite it being a door, Rosa saw no handle, no keyhole or turning mechanism of any sort.

"Is that the Royal Treasury?" Rosa asked, raising her eyebrows. "Why is nobody guarding it?"

"There's no need to guard it. There's no way of opening it." Azrael shrugged and strode towards it.

"No way to open it? But how do we get inside?" Rosa asked quizzically.

"Only those who are *supposed* to get inside can get inside."

Rosa glared at him for continuing to talk in riddles. "Then why did we come this far if we can't even get inside?"

"We can get inside."

"But you just said—"

"Just trust me on this, Princess. We're going to get inside, no problem." Azrael smiled, and she noticed a dark shadow pass through his eyes. She wondered what that was, but decided not to dwell on it. The demon always had a scheme or two hatching.

"How exactly?"

"Using these tiny, pretty hands of yours. Granted, I'm not 100%

sure it will work, but knowing the king, he no doubt has already given you access to all his treasures," he explained as he approached the giant round not-door. "All you have to do is just touch it."

Does it have a biometric reader or something?

Rosa was a bit angry at how nonchalant Azrael was about the whole situation, but then again, this was supposed to be just a fun excursion to kill some time. She'd have to accept the outcome and search for a different way to enter if it didn't work out.

Let's hope it does work.

Rosa reached out her hand and touched the round metallic slab. It felt cold and smooth to her touch, and she felt a small tingle coming from it.

"Did it work?" she asked, glancing around for any signs of change. Azrael was searching too, pacing from one side of the door to the next.

"I don't know. It doesn't look like it did." He clicked his tongue, but then the door began to rotate slowly. He took a few steps back, and they watched as it began spinning faster and faster. After a moment, it was spinning so fast that the patterns on it blurred completely. And then the door began shrinking, each of the outer rings disappearing until finally, it all seemed to roll into a tiny ball. The ball fell to the floor with a heavy thud, rolled to the top of the opening, and began glowing with a bright light.

"Wow," they both exclaimed, and Azrael lowered Rosa to the floor. They walked towards the entrance and saw gold glitter in response to the light at the door. When they entered, Rosa felt like her jaw might drop off.

The Treasury was filled to the brim with gold coins, gold bars, jewelry, gems, weapons, armor, and everything else that could be considered valuable. And the place itself was huge, about the size of a football field.

But how am I supposed to find anything here?

Rosa scanned the overflowing treasures, trying to figure out if there was any sort of organization to it. However, everything appeared to be thrown in without any rhyme or reason. There was armor standing on top of a pile of gold coins, swords stocked among gold bars, and gems lying everywhere. It was as if this was all some inconvenient trash pile that was getting in everybody's way.

"What a mess." Azrael whistled and stepped deeper into the Treasury, carefully avoiding a pile of jewelry.

"How is anyone supposed to find anything in here?" she exclaimed, barely managing to hide her frustration.

"Locator spells, probably. I don't see any other way," Azrael explained. "Since we're already here, want to look around? But remember, we cannot take anything!"

"Yes," Rosa replied, still gripping his hand as she leaned against him, wary of slipping into the unstable piles of gold.

I have to find that gem somehow. And take it without Azrael noticing.

CHAPTER 33

FIRST FLIGHT

Rosa looked from one pile of treasure to the next, hoping to recognize a purple glint somewhere among them. Occasionally she would notice a purplish gem that would make her heart jump. However, none quite looked like diamonds. At least, she didn't *think* they were diamonds.

I don't even know what a purple diamond is supposed to look like. That book on gems didn't have a drawing of it. Could it be mistaken for a different purple gem like amethyst? Aren't there other gems that could be purple?

The realization made Rosa sick to her stomach. She was so close to her ticket home. It was somewhere within this room, and yet she had no idea what it even looked like.

She kept scanning the room frantically, her eyes darting from pile to pile, from one gem to the next. But they were all so similar that she couldn't tell whether she was looking at a diamond or a piece of quartz.

"What's wrong, Princess? Is this a bit much for you?" Azrael bent down to look at her, and she snapped out of her panic.

"Oh... I... Yes. I just never expected there would be so much treasure." She forced a childish smile onto her face.

Stay composed. Otherwise, Azrael will start suspecting you too.

"It is the Royal Treasury. There is no other place in the world that contains so much gold and jewels," Azrael noted and then nonchalantly grabbed a pile of coins, letting them slip through his fingers and fall back down with a loud clatter. "Currently, we're the richest people in this whole world."

"This is not ours! Didn't you say not to take anything?" She glared at him, and the demon chuckled in response.

"I have no intention of taking anything. I just wanted the bragging rights of having broken into the Royal Treasury."

Aren't you supposed to be in a high government position? How is this guy even allowed to make any even remotely important decisions?

"Of course," she deadpanned and resumed her search for the diamond.

"Is there anything in particular you want to see?" Azrael asked, and she froze for a moment.

I can't just ask him to show me the diamond. That would be way too obvious.

"Are there any magical gems in here?" she asked, trying to appear innocent.

"They are everywhere. There's four by your feet, another eight in this pile that I can see, and another five over there." He pointed from one pile to the next.

Why couldn't they have organized the Treasury? Laid down all gems in one place, arranged by their rarity preferably.

"But they all look the same. How would one know if a gem has a strong ability or not?" She tried to steer the conversation towards the rarer kinds of gems, hoping to get a clue from Azrael.

"One has to study to recognize them, I'm afraid. No quick way of telling gems apart," Azrael said and scooped a few gems into his hand.

"For example, among these gems, two have particularly rare and strong abilities, two are mediocre and four are quite common."

Rosa stared at the gems intensely, but none of them appeared purple. Or like diamonds.

Who knew that telling some fancy rocks apart would be so hard?

"What about this one?" Rosa grabbed the closest purple gem and showed it to Azrael.

"That's a common one. It lets you speed up the growth of surface plants. Mostly useless in the Underworld."

"And this one?"

"That one allows you to manipulate metal."

"This?"

"With that one, you could find a person using an object they've touched before."

Rosa kept asking again and again, making sure to grab the most promising purple gems that she could find, but none of them had an ability even remotely related to dimensional travel.

"I think that's enough, Princess. We need to get back before your nanny notices your disappearance." Azrael yawned and stretched out his arms. Rosa was surprised that he was willing to indulge her this long, but she still didn't want to leave.

If only there was a way to find that gem.

Rosa looked deeper into the Treasury but seeing the many gems flickering in the light, she knew that it could take her several weeks of digging through all the treasures before finding the gem—if she could even find it at all. Maybe she had already dismissed it or walked past it.

"Okay, let's go back," she said with a resigned smile and made her way towards the exit. Azrael followed closely after her, occasionally supporting her when she slipped on a rogue coin or two.

As they exited the Treasury, the ball that emanated light into the chamber shut off and rolled to the ground. It began spinning faster and faster and started expanding outwards, adding one layer of metal on top of another. After a few mesmerizing minutes of observing the oddly satisfying process, the door was sealed once more.

"Ready to go?" Azrael asked and crouched down to pick Rosa up.

"Yes," she said solemnly and glanced at the Treasury door one last time.

I couldn't find it... What am I going to do now?

* * *

At some point during their journey back, Rosa had fallen asleep in Azrael's arms. She only woke when he was already putting her underneath the sheets.

"Huh?" she mumbled, half-asleep and not fully understanding what was going on around her.

"Sleep, Princess. We're back in your room," Azrael said sweetly, and she allowed herself to be lulled back to dreamland.

The next time Rosa woke, she did so with a sharp jolt, almost instantly jumping up to her feet.

"Wow, you scared me there, Lady Morrigan! Good morning," Gunna said in her usual cheery voice and fixed a few strands on Rosa's face. "You were sleeping so softly this morning that I decided not to bother you. Are you feeling rested now?"

"I... Yes, Gunna. I feel good," Rosa said.

"I am happy to hear that. Did you have a hard time falling asleep yesterday?" the nanny asked and began preparing Rosa for the day.

"A little bit," Rosa replied, avoiding direct eye contact.

I went through all that trouble but still couldn't find the purple diamond. What am I supposed to do now? Should I try getting into the Treasury again? But there's no way I could convince Azrael to do it a second time without arousing suspicion. And I don't think I could get past those traps on my own, especially if I can't use my shadow form.

"Then I could prepare some calming tea for you in the evening," Gunna offered, and Rosa nodded absentmindedly. Tea certainly wouldn't be enough to solve this.

After forcing herself to eat some sandwich with fluffy bread and mild-tasting fish, Rosa was intercepted by Deziara.

"Morri, let's go play," the girl cheered, her ponytail bouncing from side to side as she ran towards Rosa. While she wasn't in the mood for any playing, Rosa didn't have the heart to deny Deziara and allowed the girl to drag her along.

As she predicted, Deziara took her straight to Haku's enclosure, where the dragon greeted them with great enthusiasm.

It's actually been a while since I properly played with Haku. I've been so occupied with thoughts of getting home that I've completely neglected him.

Haku, however, the ever-cheerful dragon, jumped up and down in joy and puffed out smoke, his tail slapping into walls and toys with incredible strength, sending them flying in every direction.

"You've grown quite a bit, Haku," Rosa said and patted the dragon on his red, scaly snout. The dragon was growing at an amazing rate—he was already at almost the same height as Deziara, and his previously stunted wings had grown to an almost normal size.

"Yes, maybe he'll be able to fly soon." Deziara affectionately patted Haku's wings, and the dragon shivered, the touch tickling his sensitive membranes.

"Why don't we go out for some practice?" Rosa suggested, hoping that by concentrating on Haku, she'd be able to forget her woes, if only for a short while.

Haku jumped up and down impatiently, occasionally scratching at the stone floor beneath him. Rosa was surprised to see that his nails left visible scratch marks.

He's becoming stronger by the day. I wonder if it'll even be safe for me to come to Haku if he keeps growing at this rate. I know he wouldn't hurt me on purpose, but he's still young and gets excited easily.

"I think he'd like that," Deziara agreed and opened the stable doors, allowing the dragon passage outside. He zoomed out like an arrow, forcing Rosa and Deziara to run after him.

Once outside, Haku instantly spread out his wings and began flapping them, creating strong gusts that nearly knocked Rosa off her feet.

"Oh, maybe today is finally the day. I feel it in my gut," Deziara declared and began waving her hands up and down, imitating the motion of wings in flight. "Do it with me, Haku!"

Rosa began waving her hands along with Deziara, and Haku redoubled his efforts. The residual wind was so strong that both girls were forced to back away or risk being knocked over.

"One last push, Haku! Take a big leap and then flap your wings with all your might," she instructed, and the dragon focused his green eyes on her. Rosa was surprised to see understanding in them.

The dragon stopped the intensive flapping, lowered his body, and then leapt high into the air. He spread his wings and methodically pushed them down with enough force to propel him upwards. Failing to maintain flight, he tried again and again until he succeeded in steadily rising above the backyard.

"He did it!" Deziara squealed in a high-pitched voice, and Rosa cheered alongside her. Haku produced a low growl and spewed out a ball of fire high above the castle. It went up like a firework and then slowly dissipated into the darkness.

The dragon then made a clumsy turn and began descending towards the girls. They scrambled aside as he landed clumsily and rolled straight into a hedge. The guards watching the girls nervously ran forward when the dragon descended but relaxed once they saw that they were safely out of his way.

"I can't believe you did it, Haku! You can fly!" Deziara ran up to the dragon, who was now covered in residual bush, and gave him a hearty scratch under his chin. Rosa followed right after Deziara and began pulling the loose branches off the dragon while inspecting him for injuries.

It would be a shame if he injured his wing right after his first flight.

She lifted up his wings, inspecting the membranes for tears, but everything looked intact.

"Well done," Rosa praised and patted the scales on his back.

"Do you know what this means, Morri?" Deziara asked with a starry-eyed expression. Her enthusiasm was so strong that Rosa had to take a step back.

"No?"

"It means we can fly on his back!" the girl announced. Rosa blinked and looked at Haku. While Rosa had read plenty of stories about dragon riders or dragon tamers that conquered their enemies through the bond with their dragon, she never expected to ride on Haku one day.

How would I even stay seated on him? I would no doubt fall off and slip to the ground at the first turn. No, thank you!

"S-Sure." Rosa chuckled nervously.

She didn't want to sour Deziara's mood with reality at that moment, so she decided to save that conversation for when the time came.

"But I think I might be too heavy for Haku to carry in flight. He needs to grow a bit more."

"Yes."

"Hmm..." Deziara suddenly came close to Rosa and looked her over with a scrutinizing eye.

I have a bad feeling about this...

"But you might be just the right size," Deziara announced with a wide grin on her face.

"W-What? Me?" Rosa fumbled and took several steps away from the dragon.

"Yes! Don't you want to fly?"

"No!" Rosa shook her head vigorously. She had always been fearful of heights and thought of those who jumped out of airplanes and climbed mountains to be absolute madmen.

There is no way in hell that I am flying on a juvenile dragon who cannot even land properly yet. Or any dragon, for that matter.

"Why not? I bet it'll be fun," Deziara whined, and Haku's tail and wings dropped to the ground, his eyes large and pleading.

"Why are you sad, Haku? Don't tell me you wanted me to fly on your back?"

The dragon perked up instantly, wagging his tail and scuttling close to her.

"No, no, no! I am going to fall."

Rosa backed away, but Deziara grabbed her hand.

"It's alright. I'll catch you if you do. Besides, Haku can't fly very high yet. Even if you did fall, I doubt you'd get hurt," the girl said nonchalantly and began pulling Rosa towards the dragon.

Haku positioned himself low to the ground, and Deziara pulled Rosa onto his back.

"No, I am pretty sure it would hurt a lot!" Rosa squeaked and put her hands around Haku's neck in an iron grip. Of course, he was unbothered by it and instead stood up on his feet and unfurled his wings.

"Haku, please! This could end really badly."

"Do it, Haku!"

Ignoring Rosa's pleas, the dragon jumped into the air and began flapping his wings. She screamed as the ground grew further and further away from her. It was nothing like that time she had to get down the castle wall in her shadow form. Being a shadow gave a sense of safety and weightlessness.

But this was completely different. Her hands felt clammy and slippery as she held on to Haku's neck. Her short legs clutched tight onto his back as she held her body as close to the dragon as possible. Gravity was definitely eager to pull her down to the ground.

"You're flying! It's amazing, Morri!" Deziara cheered from the ground, and Rosa dared to glance her way. It was actually funny looking down at her sister as Haku glided sideways in a gentle arc, making sure to keep his body upright.

"This... isn't so bad..." Rosa admitted as the dragon circled around the yard a few more times. The soft breeze felt pleasant as it brushed through her hair. It was the closest approximation of wind in the underground. "But how about we end this for today?"

The dragon obliged her and this time, circled down slowly, making sure to loop around the yard several times before finally landing like an airplane that slowly descended on the runway.

"That looked fun!" Deziara cheered.

"It was scary."

After she got off the dragon, her legs wobbled as she walked.

"Princesses! Princesses!" A guard ran towards them at full speed, huffing and puffing. "The king has returned!"

Chapter 34

Return of the King

"Father is back?" Deziara and Rosa exclaimed in unison. The older girl nearly jumped from excitement, barely able to contain it. Rosa, however, felt a mixture of emotions wash over her. At first, she felt excited about Alphegor's return, but she quickly tempered this emotion as caution took over.

I'll have to be very careful with Alphegor around. He's really sharp and might pick up on something from Asdeus.

"Yes, Princess! He kept the victory over the Fallen a secret in order to return to the demon castle as soon as possible. But soon, the whole Demon Kingdom will celebrate his glorious victory," the guard announced, giddy from excitement.

"That is wonderful! Where is he now? We must greet him right away. Isn't that right, Morri?" Deziara grabbed Rosa's hand, and she nodded, caught up in her sister's enthusiasm.

"His Majesty went to his room to wash up first. He has spent more than a month on the battlefield, after all. But I am sure that you can meet him as soon as he is dressed," the guard replied, and Rosa's heart stopped at that moment.

Alphegor went to wash up and change clothes? But I... I never removed my painting from his wardrobe.

Rosa staggered back, feeling bile rise up from her stomach.

"What's wrong, Morri? You suddenly look very pale." Deziara turned to her, reaching her hand out to touch Rosa's face. Rosa stepped back, shaking her head in horror.

"He'll see… He'll know…" she muttered. Her head was spinning, and her hands shook.

He'll know I'm a human. Maybe he's already seen the painting. The painting of another world. Nobody else is allowed inside his room. He'll find out I am human. Maybe he already knows and is on his way here. What will he do to me?

"Know what? What's wrong, Morri?" Deziara's eyes were filled with concern as she took a step closer to Rosa. But before her sister could take hold of her, Rosa slipped into the shadows and ran.

She headed straight towards the castle gate and slipped through without pausing for a second. The four guards never even noticed her, so she continued rushing forward.

Faster! Faster! Before he realizes that I am gone. He might decide to just kill me. I can't take that chance.

Rosa couldn't cry any tears in her shadow form, but she felt like she was breaking apart. The cityscape around her blurred as she rushed through as quickly as she could. A small, lone shadow that nobody would notice.

But it felt like everybody knew where she was going. She felt as if a thousand eyes were observing her and telling Alphegor where to find her.

I have to be far away from here. Somewhere where Alphegor cannot find me. Somewhere away from the Demon Kingdom.

She kept rushing from street to street, from building to building, until slowly, they became sparser. Large buildings were replaced with smaller houses and streets until those too dwindled.

Darkness overtook the scenery as the lights from houses grew increasingly sparse. Eventually, all artificial lights were gone, and Rosa could only see the occasional bioluminescent mushroom or plant. They seemed to be lined some distance from each other as if to indicate a pathway through the unrelenting underground.

But Rosa had no time to ponder their arrangement. Her only goal was to run away as far as possible. Away into the never-ending dark—where nobody could ever find her.

* * *

"Finally, I got all the blood off my hands," Alphegor grumbled, stepping outside of the bathroom. He had wanted to see Morrigan straight away, but he didn't want to scare her with blood and dirt that soiled his whole body after the relentless battle.

I should have razed the whole Fallen Kingdom off the map for making me spend so much time away from Morrigan.

At first, Alphegor hadn't thought much about leaving Morrigan alone. After all, he left his other daughters alone all the time. Their mothers and nannies were more than sufficient to take care of them.

But it had always been different for Morrigan. Right from the start, she didn't have a mother to rely on, so Alphegor had to step up and fill the role that should have belonged to Eirwen. Even discounting that, there was something special about that child.

Alphegor wasn't thinking about her magical potential, although when the elf slave had confirmed her astounding magic while she was still a babe, he had been ecstatic. But no, it was about her personality. She had him firmly in her grasp, making him dance to her little whims. In that way, she was very much like her mother.

But even with all that charisma, he had not expected to miss her so dearly while away on the battlefield. He constantly worried whether the concubines were planning to poison her or send assassins. He worried whether she enjoyed the food she ate or if she could sleep comfortably at night with him gone. The little girl spent three years sleeping next to him before she was comfortable enough in her own bed.

He worried whether Azrael would find a way to circumvent his oath and cause Morrigan any harm. Even if he knew it was impossible to do, he was still worried. And Alphegor also wondered whether she missed him at all. Or if she could continue on with her days as if his presence never mattered in the first place.

How foolish! I am a king. I should not be worried about something so trivial.

And yet he was.

Alphegor sighed at his foolishness and approached his wardrobe to find himself some fresh clothes to wear. He opened the door and picked out the first outfit that he saw, putting it on in a hurry. As he swung the wardrobe door shut, a loud clatter came from inside it—as if something had fallen.

"What was that?"

Alphegor opened the wardrobe again, checking inside for anything out of place. To his surprise, there were a bunch of art supplies scattered on the wardrobe floor. He leaned down to take a closer look and saw that a small canvas had fallen amongst the paints and brushes.

"How did that get here?" he asked aloud, although he already knew the answer. Nobody could enter his chambers besides Morrigan, her nanny, and the cleaning maids. The dwarf woman had no business rummaging through his wardrobe, and neither did the maids since his clothes didn't need to be washed while he was away. So, it was no doubt Morrigan who had put these inside his wardrobe.

"Little rascal, what has she been up to?" Alphegor chuckled and picked up the canvas, wondering what kind of a "masterpiece" the little demon could produce.

As the gentle pastel colors of an unknown world with rectangular buildings filled his vision, Alphegor nearly dropped the painting. His breath hitched as he took in every single detail of the foreign world. Of Morrigan's old world.

"She remembers... How is that possible?"

He traced his finger over the painting when a loud, panicked knock resounded on his door. Alphegor waved his fingers, and the painting disappeared—safely hidden in a pocket dimension.

"What is it?" he growled, irritated at the disturbance.

"Your Majesty! You must come," said the panicked voice of one of Morrigan's guards. He had specifically picked out this demon as her guard, as he was one of the strongest and most trustworthy warriors at his disposal.

Alphegor went to the door and opened it, giving the guard a merciless glare. But he barely seemed to register the king's fury as his features were already filled with panic, his face deathly pale.

"This better be important for you to dare to bother me," he warned, but there was an unexplainable heaviness growing in the pit of his stomach—like he had swallowed something poisoned.

"Your Majesty, Princess Morrigan ran away!" the guard blurted out.

"Ran away? What do you mean, *ran away?*" Alphegor smashed his hand into the door frame, destroying it and leaving a giant hole in the nearby wall. The guard flinched back, his face turning even paler.

"M-My colleague told both Princess Deziara and Princess Morrigan about your return, and then Princess Morrigan turned into a shadow and disappeared," the guard stammered, fumbling over his words.

"Then why are you still standing here? Go after her!" Alphegor roared.

The guard jolted into motion, stumbling over his own feet as he scrambled away.

Alphegor smashed the door frame a second time, completely destroying the adjacent wall.

Why would you suddenly run, Morrigan? Is it because I returned? Because of the memories you regained? Or did you have them from the very beginning?

Alphegor wanted to understand her reasoning, but he knew he had no time to waste. The little girl was incredibly fast in her shadow form. If he were to linger, she could even find herself in one of the neighboring kingdoms.

Alphegor took a breath and then allowed his senses to expand outwards, hoping to feel his link to Morrigan. But instead of her, he was bombarded by Deziara's loud wails.

That's right, Deziara was with her. She could give me a clue as to why Morrigan suddenly ran off.

The king let the darkness envelop him as he willed himself to reappear in the castle yard. Deziara stopped her crying for a moment, shocked by his appearance. But her eyes quickly filled with tears again, and she threw herself at Alphegor.

"F-Father! M-Morri suddenly disappeared," the girl cried and hiccupped, barely able to form a coherent word. He crouched down on one knee and patted her head in a soothing motion.

"Tell me exactly what happened. Down to every last detail," he said, trying to make his voice as calm as possible. Showing his own distress would only upset Deziara more.

"We were just playing with Haku when a guard came and told us that you have returned." Deziara hiccupped again but did her best to explain.

"And then she ran?" Alphegor asked impatiently.

"No." Deziara shook her head. "Morri looked very happy that you were back. I asked where you were, and the guard replied that you went to take a bath and change your clothes."

"And then?" Alphegor urged her on, doing his best to keep his hand steady as he stroked his daughter's hair.

"Then she suddenly looked very pale, and she said something weird."

"What did she say?"

"She said, 'He'll see. He'll know,' and then just disappeared," Deziara finished, and a whole new set of giant tears began rolling down her cheeks.

"Thank you, dear! This is very helpful. I'll find Morrigan and bring her back. Don't you worry." He gave her a last stroke on the head and then got up.

So Morrigan most likely got scared when she realized that I would see her painting. Is it because she fears my reaction if I were to find out about her human past? If I had known that she remembered her past, I would have reassured her a long time ago.

"Really?" Deziara looked at him with large eyes as she wiped her tears on the sleeve of her dress.

"Yes, without a doubt," he confirmed as he looked at the castle gate.

I'll find her no matter what.

"Azrael!" he called, and a few seconds later, the white-haired demon emerged from a shadow in front of him.

"You're back already? That was fast." Azrael smirked, casually raising his hands behind his head.

"Morrigan has run away. Find her at once," Alphegor commanded, and Azrael's face instantly hardened to a more serious expression.

"Ran away? Why would she do that?" he asked.

"It doesn't matter why. Your only concern is to get her back safe and sound."

"Tracking her shadow form isn't easy."

"But it's not impossible. Alert me as soon as you find her." Alphegor glared, and Azrael gave a curt bow.

"At once, Your Majesty," he replied and then slipped into the shadows. But just before he disappeared, Alphegor noticed the slightest hint of a smirk on his lips.

Is he somehow involved in this? It would be better if I found Morrigan first, but I can't take any chances.

"Your king is speaking!" Alphegor suddenly boomed, his voice increased in volume by magic. It reverberated through the whole castle, causing everyone to stop in their tracks and listen.

"Princess Morrigan is somewhere outside the castle in her shadow form. Spare no resources and find her! Inform me as soon as you have any clue as to her whereabouts," he ordered, and demons began pouring out of the castle, dispersing to search for the little princess.

Please stay safe, Morrigan. The outside world is too dangerous for a little demon like you.

And with that thought, Alphegor slipped into the shadows and sped through Linberor, grasping for any sign of his precious daughter's whereabouts.

CHAPTER 35

THROUGH THE DARK OF THE UNDERWORLD

Rosa lost all sense of time as she ran through the seemingly never-ending dark of the Underworld. She believed it'd been at least several hours since she escaped from the demon castle, and she was beginning to tire.

I can take a short break now, can't I?

She slipped out of her shadow form, cautiously looking around her. The darkness felt all the stronger in her physical form, encroaching on Rosa from all sides. As a demon her vision was far better than a human's in the dark. But here, where only odd bioluminescent mushrooms and plants gave some light, even this improved vision was not enough for her to reliably see further than a few meters ahead.

Where do I go now?

Rosa felt so small and helpless in the dark. But there was no going back anymore. Her time as Alphegor's daughter was over. The thought pierced her heart like a shard of glass, and a hot tear rolled down her cheek.

"I wanted to stay with him..." she muttered as more and more tears rolled down, dripping onto her dress and hands.

"It felt... like he could accept me as I am," she whispered into the darkness, telling it her silent hopes as it was the only entity left that would listen.

"I wanted to be accepted as I am. But I am not even the same race," she cried and looked down at her hands. They were human hands—pale and pink, not the ashen pale hands of a demon. She had once again shifted into her human form without even noticing.

I don't belong here. I have to find a way back home.

Rosa hastily wiped her tears—there was no time to wallow in sorrow. She had to keep moving forward and get away from the Demon Kingdom. It didn't matter where she went as long as she couldn't be found.

She exhaled slowly in an attempt to calm herself and then looked around to observe her surroundings. The scenery was still just as quiet and dark as before, with an occasional quiet rustle from a bug or bat.

Where am I? Is this still the Demon Kingdom? Must be. I can't be fast enough to leave its border within a few hours. Then again, I know nothing about the topography of the Underworld. Nobody has ever bothered to show me any maps.

Rosa kept walking through the dark on foot as she felt too tired to switch to her shadow form. She hoped to find some place to rest, but realistically where would she even be able to do that? The Underworld was still so foreign to her.

What would be considered a good shelter in the dark? On the surface, a cave would be a good choice—but what if you're already underground? A cave within a cave? How would I know that it wouldn't collapse on top of my head while I slept?

Rosa suddenly stopped gasping as a realization hit her.

What am I going to eat and drink?

She eyed one of the glowing mushrooms suspiciously and bent down to observe it closer. Its little cap shone with a bright blue hue, while the stalk appeared more subdued.

I don't know anything about Underworld mushrooms, but if biology taught me anything, eating unfamiliar plants and fungi is not a great idea. It could make me hallucinate or give me a stomachache. Or maybe even worse...

She shook her head and then stepped away from the mushrooms. She didn't dare to risk eating it and so decided to instead search for some settlement. While it could be risky, as Alphegor would no doubt order the whole Demon Kingdom to search for her, she could remain safely hidden in her shadow form.

"Yes, it'll be alright." Rosa tried to calm herself by speaking aloud. For a moment, everything was silent, but after a few seconds, a low, rumbling cry resounded somewhere from the darkness as if to answer her.

That did not sound friendly.

She strained her eyes, searching for any movement, but everything was completely dark and still. Perhaps it was just seismic activity that made the noise. Unwilling to think about the horrid monsters that might be hiding, Rosa decided to ignore the noise and keep going.

She managed to take exactly three steps, when the low cry resounded again, this time closer. Rosa stopped, and her eyes darted around in the darkness, trying to make out anything within it. Nothing. She could see nothing, but there definitely was something out there.

Perhaps it would be safer if I continued on as a shadow.

As Rosa was about to slip into her shadow form, she saw a giant maw lunging straight at her. Out of pure instinct, she jumped back, avoiding the sharp teeth by less than a centimeter. She could feel the heat that emanated from the creature, and a few droplets of its spit landed on her hands and face.

The creature retreated into the darkness before she could register its appearance, but Rosa had no intention of sticking around. She slipped into her shadow form and rushed away, vaguely following the mushroom-illuminated trail. She heard a bellow from behind her, and it echoed through the darkness, bouncing off from unseen walls.

Sorry, I have no intention of becoming anybody's dinner.

Rosa pushed on, leaving the hungry beast raging in the darkness over his lost meal. She heard its cries for a long while until they finally died down completely. Whether it was because of the distance she covered or because it had simply calmed down, she didn't know.

She decided to take no chances and kept moving forward. The further away she was from the castle, the better. But her strength was starting to wane, and she knew she had to find a place to rest soon. Much to her relief, she noticed a few lights flickering somewhere in the distance.

A settlement, perhaps? I could take what I need from the shadows and then run. But then I wouldn't get to rest. Maybe it's better to change my appearance?

As Rosa got closer to the lights, she saw that there were crude clay and stone buildings erected in what appeared to be a little underground village. There were lamps hung on the side of the houses and occasional posts with larger lamps on top. Compared to the rich demon capital, the place looked very desolate and decrepit. But even here, there was life.

Better shift some distance away from the village so nobody notices me.

Rosa hid behind some large stalagmites growing upwards like odd, sharp stone trees and materialized out of her shadow form. There wasn't much energy left in her, so she decided to keep her shifted form familiar and simple. She took her adult human shape but applied some Demonic features—gray skin, small horns, pointed ears, and a tail.

Ideally, she would have liked to take the shape of a lesser Demon, as it would certainly draw less attention, but she was afraid to use too much of her energy. Azrael had warned her that difficult transformations could make her faint or even fall into a coma. To create a more ignoble appearance, she imagined herself wearing ragged clothes with a gaunt face, sunken eyes, and bony limbs.

After inspecting as much of her new appearance as she could in the dim light, Rosa took a deep breath and then hobbled towards the village. She didn't know exactly how merciful these Demon villagers would be towards strangers, but she hoped that her pathetic appearance would at least earn her a scrap of food and a roof over her head for the night.

Approaching the village, Rosa saw some demons chatting on the side of the street. As she had predicted, they were lesser demons—both of them rather short and stocky. Not quite as short as dwarfs but much shorter than an average pure-blooded Demon. They had broad shoulders, short but beefy arms, large hands, and long nails.

When they noticed Rosa approaching, both demons stopped their conversation and turned towards her. Their faces were most peculiar—very small, beady eyes and large, black noses. In a way, they reminded her of moles, the only giveaway of their Demonic blood being the tiny horns on their foreheads.

"H-Hello," she dared to address them in a shaky voice.

"Hello, stranger. What brings you to our tiny village?" one of the mole demons asked apprehensively, taking half a step in front of their companion. It was the stockier and larger one of the two. Whether this one was male or female, Rosa couldn't tell, but the other mole demon took a step behind the bulkier one.

"I mean no harm. I am but a weary traveler." Rosa lifted up her arms to deliberately show how thin she was and her pale complexion. The mole demons relaxed a little, although the scowl from the larger Demon's face never disappeared.

"A traveler? At this nook of the Underworld? Whatever are you searching for in this hellhole?" the larger demon sneered, crossing muscular arms over a broad chest, displaying the impressive, large claws in their full glory.

If I knew something more about these demons, perhaps I could appeal to them. Why is it that nobody ever taught me anything about the Demon Kingdom? Oh right... because I am four.

"I suddenly got attacked by a large beast with a giant maw. It attacked so quickly I barely managed to avoid it and get away." She figured telling a partial truth would give her words some credibility. The smaller mole Demon's eyes widened in shock, and it shifted uncomfortably from foot to foot.

"What did the beast look like?" the stockier demon asked with narrowed eyes, but his posture relaxed a little bit.

"I—I didn't see anything besides its gaping mouth. It disappeared into the dark so fast."

The mole demon opened his mouth to say something , but his smaller companion spoke up instead. "Dear, other demons don't have such good night vision as us. They wouldn't be able to spot the Talpidot in the dark."

The larger mole nodded at his companion, his scowl finally relaxing in a more neutral expression.

"Talpidot? Is that what it was?" Rosa asked, the name completely unfamiliar to her.

"Most likely. They are large, nasty creatures that usually hide in the darkest recesses of the Underworld. It's not rare to encounter one around here. Unfortunately, it is rare to survive a meeting with one, however. How'd you get away?" the mole demon asked, leaning closer.

"I just ran. Ran as fast as I could," Rosa replied, determined not to reveal that she could take a shadow form.

"You must be a mighty fine runner then. Or really lucky. What about your stuff?"

"I—I had to abandon it. It was weighing me down," Rosa lied. Both of the mole demons nodded at her explanation.

"Smart. Better to lose your stuff, than your life. I suppose you're looking for a place to rest now," the stockier mole demon said, and Rosa nodded.

"Yes. And some food and water, if it's not too much to ask. I can work to repay it," she offered, hoping that it might entice the demons to help her out.

"Nonsense. You're already all skin and bones. You're welcome to rest in our home and eat at our table," the smaller demon said and pointed at one of the nearby houses with her long claw. "I am Kurmina, and this is my husband Henris."

"It is nice to meet you. I am..." Rosa paused for a second, realizing that she couldn't introduce herself as Morrigan. Her human name was as good of a substitute as any. "I am Rosa."

"Let's head inside, Rosa, and you tell us every last detail of your encounter with the Talpidot. We've been trying to figure out how to get rid of them for ages," Henris grumbled and began waddling towards his house with Kurmina following behind him.

At least I can relax for one day. Hopefully.

CHAPTER 36

CHASING A PRINCESS

Rosa opened her eyes to find herself in a cramped space no larger than a broom closet. The bed had been far too small for her half-human-half-demon transformation, so after making sure that the door could be locked, Rosa took her natural child demon form.

Her sleep was restless as the bed was barely any better than solid ground, not to mention that she kept having nightmares. Specifically, she kept seeing Alphegor's face as it had looked like when he killed the assassin that had attacked her when she was just a baby. Except in her nightmares, his blade was embedded in *her* chest.

She'd stare at him in horror, and then he would pull out the blade and say, "You're no daughter of mine" in her mother's cold voice. The nightmare woke her up every time, and it kept repeating itself throughout the night. After the third time, Rosa completely gave up on sleeping and instead waited for the mole demon couple to wake.

The food they had offered to her last night was just as horrifying as the monster that almost ate her. It was some dark brown sludge that reminded her of mud with bugs and worms swimming in it. Rosa barely managed to hold back a disgusted grimace when it was presented to her.

Initially she thought her hosts were making fun of her, but after they dug into their own meals with much enthusiasm and vigor, Rosa had no other choice but to force the gruel down her throat. It tasted exactly as it looked, and she prayed that it would not make her lose her already meager stomach contents.

"Are you awake yet?" She heard a gentle tap on her door and Kurmina's voice behind it.

"Yes, I am," she confirmed. After checking her transformation for any mistakes, she unlocked the door and stepped out of the little room.

"I am sorry we couldn't offer you someplace better to sleep. It must have been difficult with your long limbs." Kurmina sighed, looking over Rosa with a gaze that suggested long arms and legs were a hindrance of some sort.

"It's quite enough. Don't worry," Rosa assured her.

I think I wouldn't have been able to sleep well last night, even in the most comfortable bed in the universe.

"Still, I feel bad. We finally have a guest after such a long time, and that's the best I can offer? To make up for it, I made a special breakfast this morning." The mole demoness appeared somewhat giddy, clattering her claws together.

"Thank you. I appreciate that." Rosa perked up, hoping to have something more food-like for a meal. The two of them went to the tiny kitchen, Rosa with her head bent down as the ceiling was too low to accommodate the full height of this form. Henris was already sitting at the table, sipping a hot drink with what appeared to be a newspaper in hand.

"The world has gone completely mad," he mumbled as he read the paper.

"What's wrong, dear?" Kurmina asked, as she went to the small stone stove and retrieved a pot from it. She placed it onto the stone table and then grabbed three clay plates and forks.

"The news, the news, Mina. They made a special edition and delivered it to this forsaken place within a day. But when it comes to sending help to deal with Talpidots, then nobody is available for months." Henris clattered his large claws against the table, creating a shrill noise that made Rosa wince. Kurmina didn't appear bothered, instead busily scooping... something onto the plates.

Rosa had no idea what it was. It was dark gray and had bluish grains within it. It reminded her vaguely of something children would make from the soil in the playground, but they happened to find pieces of a shredded plastic toy and used that as an ingredient.

"Well, it must be awfully important if they delivered it all the way here," Kurmina said solemnly and offered the dish to Rosa. She accepted it with a forced smile, looking cautiously at the unappetizing pile of supposed food.

"Important? Bah! One of the royal brats decided to play hide-and-seek and ran away from the castle. Why should we care about it? It's not like the little pipsqueak could have made it all the way here." Henris crumpled up the newspaper into a ball and threw it on the floor near the stove.

Rosa's fork fell out of her hand and clattered to the floor.

"Oh, I-I'm sorry. How clumsy of me," she said in a shaky voice and hurriedly picked it up and set it on the table.

He's searching for me even here. I can't stay in the Demon Kingdom for long. I must leave right away.

"Are you alright, dear? You look awfully pale all of a sudden." Kurmina looked at Rosa, who got up from the table and slowly inched towards the exit.

"I-I'm alright," she muttered, but she felt paralyzed with fear.

Alphegor must be enraged. What if he has some magic to track me? I need to get out of here as soon as possible.

Kurmina and Henris suddenly gasped, and the stockier demon jumped on his feet and snarled at Rosa. "Shapeshifter!"

Rosa realized how the previously cramped shack had grown larger, her head no longer pressed down by the ceiling. Her bright red locks flowed over her shoulders, indicating that she had reverted back to her original form.

"I... I'm sorry!" she muttered and then slipped into her shadow form, rushing out of the house before Henris or Kurmina could even realize what had happened. Soon she was alone in the dark of the Underworld, running as fast as her shadow form allowed her.

* * *

Rosa ran through the darkness for as long as she could take the strain of her shadow form. She didn't know for how long she ran or how far she had even gone. She saw glimpses of city lights and made sure to stay away from those. She continued through the dark, guided only by her sense of urgency and fear.

But she could not maintain this pace forever. Eventually, she grew tired and emerged from her shadow form. She hobbled along a river of lava, finding the light it emanated to be safe and comforting—unlike the heat it radiated, which was anything but soothing. Still, Rosa did not want to retreat back into the darkness of the Underworld.

How far have I even gone? Am I beyond the Demon Kingdom now?

She looked around, large bags underneath her eyes, as if she could find the answer lying somewhere in the dark. But all she saw was the slow, steady flow of lava and the volcanic ash along its deadly riverbank.

Rosa felt utterly exhausted; her stomach rumbled incessantly, her mouth felt so dry that her tongue was beginning to crack, and her eyelids were constantly trying to force themselves shut. This horrid feeling was only made worse by the sweltering heat coming from the lava, which forced her already dehydrated body to expel even more precious fluids in the form of sweat.

I can't keep going like this for long. The only way to truly be safe is to be well beyond the Demon Kingdom's borders. But how do I even know whether I am out of the Demon Kingdom or not? It's not like there's signposts in this damned hellhole.

Rosa tried to come up with an answer, but her mind was so exhausted that even pushing her feet to move forward was becoming an overbearing task. Each step was more difficult than the last, and Rosa wondered whether she would collapse.

As she shook her head and pushed herself forward, she noticed a slight change in the flow of the lava. Instead of a slow, smooth flow like Rosa was used to seeing while walking alongside it, there were odd bumps and ripples.

"What's that?" Rosa said and stopped to look at the weird formation in the lava. For a while, it bubbled and rippled, and then the lava began to expand upwards. She took a few steps back but was too curious to run away outright.

It's bound to be dangerous, but I don't really have the strength in me to run.

The lava formation grew larger and larger, giant globs of it falling onto the ashen soil, creating a plume of smoke as the lava slowly rolled back into the river. As it continued pouring down, the creature underneath was finally revealed. Dark glistening scales covered a giant monster that vaguely resembled a salamander.

It rose out of the lava river with a giant, flat head pointed towards Rosa. She looked at it both in awe and fear. The tough scales repelled the lava as if it were water and not molten pieces of rock and fire. In fact, the creature appeared almost cozy in the hot pool.

That's amazing. A creature that can live inside lava. It would make for such a wonderful and powerful painting.

Unfortunately, the *lava salamander*—she decided to call it for the time being—had no interest in posing for any paintings. It locked its large, bright-red eyes on to Rosa and began making its way onto the shore.

Oh, shit!

Rosa turned and ran. The creature didn't appear very fast, but she was already exhausted beyond the point of being able to take her shadow form. Outrunning even a slow creature would not be easy.

She heard it scrambling onto the volcanic shore, its claws digging into the rocks below. Rosa threw a quick glance back and saw that the salamander actually had very long and slender legs. As a whole, it looked rather mismatched—a giant head and a tail that looked like a salamander's shape with long and muscular legs.

The beast didn't hesitate to use those legs as it began running towards Rosa with astounding speed, narrowing the distance between them in mere seconds. Horrified, she tried to push herself to turn into a shadow but found herself too drained of energy.

Is this how I die? Eaten by a giant monster? I suppose it is better than being tortured by my father.

Rosa continued to run with all the strength her little body could muster. Even if she knew it to be futile, she would not just await her death. The loud footsteps of the beast got closer and closer, and she could feel the heat radiating from its body. She put every last ounce of her strength in her legs, but they were barely able to hold her weight, buckling under the strain.

Rosa fell and expected to collide with the hard ground, but instead felt firm strong hands catch her. She looked up and saw none other than the familiar white-haired Demon.

"Sorry for being late, Princess," Azrael said with a slight smile and lifted Rosa up into his arms. The salamander, shocked by his sudden appearance, stopped and snarled.

"Shut up, you overgrown lizard, and go back to your lava," Azrael shouted and then snapped his finger, producing a loud, thundering sound. The salamander yelped and ran straight back into the lava, disappearing as if it had never even been there to begin with.

"How—"

"These guys are easily spooked by loud noises. If you had screamed loud enough, I imagine it would have given up eventually," he explained. He wore his signature grin as he ruffled Rosa's hair. "But you sure do look awful, Princess."

Rosa suddenly realized that Azrael must have been sent by Alphegor to capture her and tried to break free of his grasp.

"Let me go!" she snarled and thrashed around.

It would have been better for that salamander to eat me rather than get dragged back to the possibility of being tortured by Alphegor.

"Wow, calm down, Princess!" Azrael tried to keep his hold on her but in the end, set her down. "I am not here to hurt you."

"Alphegor sent you, didn't he?" she accused, pointing a finger at him. "I'm not going back."

"I never had any intention of taking you back," Azrael replied, crouching down to her eye level.

"What? But—"

"Doesn't he know that you're a human? Probably does."

"Probably? Didn't he tell you to capture me because I am a human?"

"Do you really think the king would announce to the whole kingdom that the daughter he declared as his heir is actually a human?" Azrael grinned, and Rosa paused to think.

No, even if he were to rip me to shreds afterwards, that would cer-

tainly leave a bad impression on his subjects to have been fooled by a human for so long. The question is...

"Why are you here then?"

"Oh, that is quite simple. I have come to send you back to the human world," Azrael said and produced a small, translucent gem from his pocket. Looking at it closely, Rosa saw how its unblemished and perfect appearance shone with a light purple hue.

CHAPTER 37

BACK HOME

Rosa gaped at the purple diamond nestled snugly in Azrael's palm.

"You snatched it from the Treasury?" she asked accusingly.

"Sure did. I saw you looking for it, but I'm sorry to say that you walked straight past it. I guess you expected it to be more... purple." Azrael snickered.

"It is called the purple diamond," Rosa retorted as she examined the gem from every angle, then stared at Azrael when the realization hit her exhausted mind. "You knew that I was a human even back then?"

"Oh, I knew way before that."

"Since when?" Rosa gaped at him in shock.

"Hmm..." Azrael straightened to his full height and rubbed his chin in contemplation. "I can't pinpoint it exactly, but it was sometime between your first and second birthday. You were just too advanced to be a normal baby."

"I... I wasn't that advanced..." she mumbled, although she knew he was right.

"You're a horrible liar, you know. But it doesn't matter now. The king has figured out your secret, no doubt due to some terrible blunder on your part." Azrael shrugged and paused, looking at Rosa. She sighed.

"I left a painting of my world in his wardrobe..." she admitted, too tired to come up with a snarky retort.

"You what?" Azrael gaped, then rubbed the bridge of his nose and finally sighed. "Well, what's done is done. The good thing is that I have Dimensional Travel right here. Ideally, I would have liked to have some time to practice with it, but we don't have much of a choice now."

"You're going to send me back to Earth?"

"I'll certainly try. Never done dimensional magic before, so I can't guarantee anything."

"Why?" Rosa narrowed her eyes on him, expecting him to say that it was all a joke and that he would send her straight back to the castle. "Don't all demons hate humans?"

"Oh, we do—without a doubt. Always summoning us to do their bidding and then making us out to be the bad guys. When I realized that I had sworn an oath to one, I felt my lifespan shorten by like five hundred years." He gasped in mock horror, holding one of his hands to his forehead.

"So why are you helping me?"

"For the same reason. I can't hurt you or harm you in any way, and to be honest, I would feel bad for hurting somebody so helpless. It's no fun, really." Azrael sighed, and Rosa glared at him.

"So, you just want to get rid of me?" she snarled.

"Pretty much. You have to admit that being tied to another person, demon or not, is pretty dreadful. And now, with all the perks of said bond gone, I am quite eager to annul it." Azrael shrugged and shook his head.

"So, your intention was always to just use me," Rosa asked as she glared icy daggers at him.

"Yeah. Ideally, you would have grown to like me over the years, realizing my awesomeness, and then when you were old enough, I'd propose and become the next Demon King." He grinned at his own plan, but his expression quickly fell, and he sighed. "So much for that."

"You were trying to groom me! Gross!"

"Groom you?" Azrael cocked his head, unfamiliar with the term.

"It means that you're basically a pedophile."

"I am not!" He gasped and shook his head fervently. "Do not make a mistake. I never had any attraction towards you. All I ever wanted was to use you to become king myself."

"Jerk." Rosa sighed, disappointed and tired from it all. She never wanted to see another demon again. "If you're here to send me home, then just do it."

"With pleasure." He smirked and closed his palm around the gem. After a moment, he opened it again, and the diamond was gone. He flexed his fingers tentatively as if measuring his newfound power.

"So? Can you do it?" she asked, her voice filled with annoyance.

"I think so? I'm not completely certain. Could you give me your hand?" Azrael outstretched his arm towards Rosa, and she took a step back, regarding it like a poisoned blade.

"Why?"

"If you think of your world while I am trying to open the portal, it will be easier for me to pinpoint the right location. Or do you want to end up on the other side of the planet?" he asked, raising an eyebrow at her.

She sighed and gave him her hand. Then she closed her eyes and thought of her home. Of the small apartment from which she could gaze upon the whole city. The place where she could paint as much as she wanted without anybody ever judging her for it. Hope began to return to her as she thought of returning there.

"Good. We're almost there. Imagine the city in more detail. Think of the streets, the buildings, and the landmarks," Azrael instructed.

She thought about the small shop which stood on the nearby street corner. About her favorite trail which stretched through the forest, which cast a cool shadow even in the middle of summer. About the quaint street with its small houses that led to the vast, open sea.

"Yes! I got it!" Azrael cheered, and Rosa opened her eyes. She saw a portal with the same sandy beach and the sea she had imagined on the other side. She recognized the wooden trails with a large billboard by their side, which described proper behavior on the beach along with numbers to call in case of an emergency.

A smile crossed Rosa's lips, and she took a step towards the portal when a loud voice boomed through the whole area. No—the whole Underworld.

"STOP!"

Rosa turned around towards the source of the voice, and across the lava river, she saw Alphegor. He was gasping for breath and had large bags under his eyes.

"Morrigan, don't!" he called in a desperate plea. Rosa shook her head and jumped into the portal.

For a moment, everything seemed to disappear. She couldn't see, she couldn't hear, she couldn't even feel. But after a moment, she regained her senses and found herself on the familiar beach, gentle moonlight illuminating the world.

Rosa looked around in awe. Despite it being the middle of the night, she could see everything in crisp detail. She saw grains of sand shimmering around her feet. Her small, gray feet. She reached up to her head and felt the firm texture of her horns.

"I am... still a demon," she said in horror.

Of course, I'm still a demon. The spell transported me to Earth, but I went in Morrigan's body.

But even so, a soft curve formed on her lips. She could easily take her human shape once she regained her strength. The most important thing was that she had returned.

Rosa began to laugh and fell into the soft dunes, letting the sand slip through her fingers. It felt cool and refreshing after the blistering heat Rosa felt from the lava river. But there was no lava here. No demons. No Azrael. No Alphegor.

The trace of happiness waned from her face as she remembered Alphegor's desperate cry right before she jumped into the portal.

Why did he sound so sad?

Rosa shook her head and decided not to dwell on the matter. She was back on Earth, far away from Doppelta and could resume having a normal life again.

* * *

Thanks to the dark of the night, Rosa was able to safely journey back to her apartment without anybody noticing. The inside of the building had also been empty, so after taking the elevator, she headed straight to her apartment on the seventh floor.

Part of her feared that after four years, the landlord would have long since found a new tenant for the place. But her spare key was still masterfully hidden behind the post box, and she could slip inside without any trouble.

As she closed the door of the apartment, she was surprised to see that everything was exactly as she had left it. Even the canvas of a failed painting stood against the wall, propped up by a pair of shoes. She smiled fondly at it and headed deeper inside.

Everything was quiet, but it wasn't the same type of quiet as the Underworld. Instead of utter silence, Rosa could hear the occasional noise of a car as it passed by. There were also gentle footsteps of her upstairs neighbor and running water from somewhere within the building. It was peaceful, but not truly quiet.

Rosa's stomach grumbled, adding yet another noise to the quiet of the night, and she went to the kitchen to check the food in her fridge.

Everything must be rotten by now. Maybe I have some pasta in the pantry. That can stay good for years, right?

Much to her surprise, the food in the fridge wasn't covered in mold. In fact, it looked fresh. She grabbed the carton of milk and smelled it. Her nostrils were instantly assaulted by the putrid smell, and Rosa nearly gagged.

"Okay, that has definitely gone bad." She set the milk aside and opened the vegetable drawer. The cucumbers were oddly squishy, and so were the tomatoes, but the carrots and the cabbage still looked good.

That's odd. Some time has definitely passed since I left, but it doesn't seem to be too long.

Peeved by this oddity, Rosa went back to the main room and grabbed her tablet. She tried to unlock it with her finger at first, but the device didn't recognize the foreign fingerprint. She clicked her tongue and then typed in the code instead.

Good thing I used my birthday as the code. Otherwise, I would have long since forgotten it.

She checked the date and saw that it was July 23rd.

Odd. Wasn't it July when I got pulled into Doppelta? I don't remember for sure.

Rosa opened her email to check the date when she received the message from Studio Goblin. Much to her surprise, the date was July 7th.

Only two weeks have passed? How is that possible?

But her stomach rumbled incessantly again, forcing her to return to the kitchen, where she decided to take care of more urgent matters. After scarfing down two portions of instant ramen noodles, Rosa, driven by exhaustion, fell into her bed and fell asleep.

She was woken up by a loud notification coming from her tablet. Bleary-eyed, she got up and almost fell out of the bed in shock.

"I am really back. I am home," she muttered and laid back down. It wasn't nearly as large or as comfortable as the one in the demon world, but it was certainly better than the one the mole demons offered her.

Thinking about the Underworld, she realized that things would never be the same as before. She'd seen things she had never thought were possible. She had done things no human would ever be able to do. And she wasn't even a human anymore. Her small form, horns, and tail were a strong reminder of that.

That doesn't matter. I can transform into my human self whenever I need to. It won't be a problem.

Rosa rolled off the bed and went up to the mirror. The disheveled form of Morrigan greeted her—hair sticking in every direction, dress torn and dirty. She discarded her clothes and then took on her human form just as she remembered it.

Perfect! Nobody will be able to tell the difference.

Nodding at her own reflection, Rosa headed into the shower, eager to wash away all the dirt and grime that had piled on to her body over the last few days. It felt absolutely divine. After a long and steamy wash, she came out feeling squeaky clean.

She picked out a long, blue summer dress with bright colors from her wardrobe and put it on, admiring it. It had been so long since she could wear bright colors. The Demon Kingdom had a very Gothic sense of fashion so a bright, cheerful dress like this had been impossible to find.

As Rosa admired the dress, her tablet began playing the tune of birds chirping, which she had set up as her ringtone for the chatting app. Curious, she went over to check it. Her heart nearly stopped when she saw the name on the screen. Mother.

CHAPTER 38

SECOND CHANCE

Rosa stared at the screen in disbelief. The woman who had declared that Rosa was not her daughter was calling of her own volition—on the chatting app, no less. She must have tried calling her phone first, but considering that it was currently at the bottom of the sea, she probably didn't have much luck.

But why? Did she have a change of heart? Doesn't seem very likely.

Rosa reached for her tablet with a trembling hand and, after exhaling a breath, answered the call.

"Hello?"

"What took you so long to answer? I've been trying to reach you for several days now!" resounded the familiar and yet somehow foreign voice of her mother. She sounded angry, just like she usually did when speaking with Rosa.

She tried to contact me before? Am I dreaming? Is this some sick joke on Azrael's part? Will I wake up and find myself in Alphegor's torture chamber?

Rosa pinched her leg to make sure it was real, and the pain indicated that it was.

"Well?" Mother pressed, her tone thick with annoyance.

"I... I lost my phone," she lied. She didn't want to talk to Mother after everything she had said to her. For a moment, she considered just ending the call, but Rosa was curious to know what the woman actu-ally wanted.

Mother cleared her throat and said, "I suppose I can't blame you too much. Your new job must be keeping you busy. How is it going, by the way?"

The question caught her completely unprepared. Her mother never bothered to ask about anything related to art, yet now she was inquiring about her new job at an animation studio. Rosa still clearly remembered how Mother had said that a respectable business would never call themselves "Studio Goblin."

Really? Judging a whole company solely based on its name. How petty can one be?

"It's... busy. There are lots of new things to learn," Rosa replied awkwardly, hoping that Mother would get to the heart of the matter.

"I imagine so, dear. Do tell me more about that company. Your sister told me that it is one of the biggest animation studios in the country," she said with a rare hint of excitement in her voice. The word *sister* pulled Rosa's thoughts to Deziara. She couldn't even properly recall the features of her human sister. They seemed vague and dis-torted from the passage of time.

So that's what this is really about. She learned that Studio Goblin is actually one of the big guys, so now she is inclined to talk to me again.

"Well..." Rosa began, unsure of what to say. She never really had gone to Studio Goblin. No doubt her internship was terminated by now.

"Actually, don't tell me over a call. There is probably too much for you to say. We'll come visit you over the weekend," Mother said, her voice almost unrecognizable in its excitement. Such emotions were never directed at Rosa, only towards her younger sister.

"I don't know if it's a good idea... I still have much work to do," she said, trying to talk her way out of the unpleasant visit. It was the last thing she needed right now—to host her family and entertain them before she'd even gotten her bearings back after returning from Doppelta.

"Are you too good to meet your family now?" Mother's voice instantly turned cold and ruthless.

"No, that's not what I meant—"

"Then we are coming! I'll be expecting you to be a gracious host. See you then," she said and then ended the call before Rosa could object. She stared at her tablet for a few seconds, then sighed and slumped down into her bed.

Great. Now, I'll have to listen to another lengthy lecture on why I am a failure because I have lost my job. Just what I needed right now.

She lifted her tablet above her head, and went to her email, expecting to find an angrily worded message from Studio Goblin. On the very top of her received email list, there stood an unopened message from them. She braced herself mentally, and opened it, ready to accept the rejection. Much to her surprise, the letter contained an address, date, and time for when she should come to their headquarters. July 25th, 8:00 am.

Rosa gaped. That was tomorrow. She still hadn't missed her chance—she could still work in Studio Goblin and fulfill her dream! She practically jumped off the bed and headed straight to her wardrobe. An appropriate outfit was necessary for such an occasion.

* * *

With the GPS app open on her tablet, Rosa went through the busy street, checking the nearby buildings for the Studio Goblin sign. She wore a tight pencil skirt and a white blouse, trying to adhere to the business-casual style. The clothes felt oddly coarse against her skin, and they restricted her movements so much she was almost tempted to head back home to find something more comfortable.

I never found my demon clothes uncomfortable, even if some of them looked like a Goth's fever dream. The fabrics they use for princesses are probably much higher quality than anything I've snagged from the clearance rack at the local store.

Rosa paused as she finally spotted a tall building with the Studio Goblin sign in large green letters above the front entrance. She smiled and headed straight for it, her low heels clattering against the paved road. The shoes felt even more uncomfortable than the clothes, not to mention that the constant *click-clack* that came from them reminded her of Asdeus.

Rosa shook her head, dismissing the unpleasant thought, and entered the building through its glass door. The foyer was neat and lined with posters of their previous animated features. Behind a modern, sand-colored desk sat a young woman dressed similarly to Rosa. She had dark brown hair tied neatly into a bun, giving her a polished, professional appearance.

"Hello," Rosa greeted her somewhat nervously.

"Hello. How may I help you?" she asked with a polite, professional smile.

"I am here for my internship," Rosa replied.

The woman nodded, opening a notebook that sat at the corner of her desk.

"Name?"

"M—Rosa Smith," she stuttered, nearly calling out her demon name.

Get a grip, Rosa. You're back on Earth now. You are a human.

So she tried to convince herself, although she knew full well that underneath her human face hid a little demon girl. But there was no time to think about that—she had to focus on the task in front of her.

"Take the elevator to the sixth floor, and go to cabinet number 665," the woman said and pointed towards the elevator. Rosa nodded in thanks and headed towards it.

The whole situation felt so odd to her. Just a few days ago, she was racing through the Underworld, running for her life, and yet now she was riding in an elevator at Studio Goblin. She should have felt happy and relieved, but there was a strange heaviness weighing down on her.

It'll pass, Rosa. Focus. You need to make a good first impression.

As the elevator reached the sixth floor, Rosa was greeted by a long, monotone hallway with many doors lining the walls, each with its own number. She searched for room 665 and found it at the very end of the hall. After taking a moment to gather her nerves, she exhaled and knocked.

"Come in," a feminine voice replied from behind the door.

Rosa opened it and peered inside. The room was rather small and stuffed to the brim with shelves overflowing with papers. In the middle of the room was a desk behind which sat a tired-looking woman in her thirties. She was rubbing her temples as she stared at the drawing tablet in front of her.

"Hello. I am here for my internship," Rosa said awkwardly, feeling as though she had just interrupted something.

"Internship..." the woman muttered as she dragged her stylus across the surface of the tablet. Then, as the information finally registered in her brain, her eyes snapped up to meet Rosa's. "You're the new intern?"

"Yes," Rosa confirmed and was shocked when the woman groaned loudly and slammed her stylus onto her desk.

"Ugh! I can't believe he actually pushed the intern onto me when

I was already falling behind schedule. I am going to demand a bonus for this bullshit," she mumbled and began searching for something among the sea of papers on her desk. "What was your name?"

"Rosa Smith," she replied meekly, wondering whether it would be better to just leave.

"I'm Penny. Give me a moment," she grumbled, digging through the papers. As the search dragged on, and she was unable to find the desired thing, she threw up her arms in frustration and slumped back into her chair.

"Is everything alright?"

"Okay, I am going to be brutally honest with you, newbie. I currently don't have the time to deal with you. There's a deadline coming up for the concept art I need to submit for the new movie, so that is currently my priority," Penny explained as she rubbed the bridge of her nose.

"So what am I supposed to do?"

"I don't know, to be honest. I've never dealt with interns before. Why don't you just grab that chair over there and come watch me work?" she said in a resigned voice and then straightened, taking the stylus in her hand again.

"Alright." Rosa took the chair and positioned it behind Penny so she could see the tablet. It appeared that she was working on some sort of dark landscape, but the piece was still in its early stages, so Rosa couldn't tell what exactly it was supposed to be.

Penny got right back to work, furiously laying down one color after another, drawing as if it were a speed challenge of some sort. Rosa watched the woman with keen interest, admiring how she added one layer of color over the other. First black, then dark blue, then dark brown. Rosa couldn't understand what exactly she was trying to create.

The scene is certainly dark. Perhaps it takes place at night, in a forest, a cave, or a dark mansion.

Penny switched the color to dark grayish and began laying down large squares in the middle of the picture. They looked rather awkward and blocky at first, but then she began adding darker shadows, giving the building more definition. Then using dark blue, she drew in arched windows and afterwards began defining a brick texture.

It's a Gothic castle similar to the demon castle back home. Wait... Why did I just think of demon castle as my home? How foolish. I am back home now. This is where I belong.

Rosa shifted in her seat as she continued to observe Penny's work. She watched how the woman used various features within her drawing program to multiply the patterns she had created and laid them over the whole castle. She made cracks in the walls, copied them, and spread them around, giving the castle a more decrepit look.

The demon castle never had a single crack in the walls. Everything was always new and clean.

The stylus glided towards the windows next, making the glass shattered in places, drawing broken shards on the windowsill. Penny even went as far as to draw blood dripping down from one of the windows. Rosa shifted uncomfortably, feeling her hold on the transformation slip for a bit.

Is sitting still for long periods of time somehow harder to maintain the transformation than while walking? Or perhaps it is just more difficult on Earth? Less magic here or something akin to that? I wish I could have found out more about how magic truly worked.

Penny nodded to herself, seemingly satisfied with the castle, and then began work on its surroundings. She drew black dead trees with broken branches, scattered around where the castle yard should be. Instead of the dark greenery Rosa had grown accustomed to, dark thorny bushes took their place, clearly intending to turn away anyone who dared to come close.

That's just too much. No one in their right mind would plant so many thorny bushes in their yard. What purpose could they possibly serve other than annoying the poor gardener?

As the woman continued adding menacing details throughout the piece, Rosa grew increasingly uncomfortable in her seat. It felt very hard against her flesh, and her body began feeling heavy.

I wish I could take my smaller form. It is always more comfortable in it.

"What do you think?" Penny asked suddenly, breaking Rosa out of her thoughts. She looked at her piece from various angles, as if trying to find something in it.

"Me?" Rosa asked, surprised by the sudden question. They had sat in complete silence for more than an hour.

"Is there somebody else here?"

"I suppose not..." Rosa muttered and then took a careful look at the drawing again. While it certainly looked dark and menacing, it also appeared somewhat dull and lifeless. It had the base of the demon castle, but none of its magnificence. No grand lanterns to illuminate the outside or the intricate statues of grand dragons or beasts.

"I think it could use a bit more... life," Rosa said, and Penny whirled around in her chair, looking her straight in the eyes.

"Okay, I didn't explain the concept I was going for, my bad. It is supposed to be a demon castle," she said in a condescending voice.

"I understand that. But there are people living there as well, are there not? Shouldn't there be some lights in the windows? Everything appears very uniform, but I think a real castle would have more variation. Some taller towers, and some shorter ones. And it wouldn't be so worn out and broken. This castle just looks abandoned."

Penny looked at Rosa as if she were insane, her eyebrows furrowing into an angry grimace. "Ah, why did I even ask? What would a newbie who barely knows how to hold a stylus know about drawing concept art?"

"Let me educate you, intern. The castle of a villain always has to look as decrepit, lifeless, and uninviting as possible. People would not live there, in fact, they wouldn't even go near it. They need to be afraid of the monsters that are living there."

"They are not monsters!" Rosa jumped up from her seat, glaring down at Penny. The woman looked at her incredulously, one eyebrow raised. Rosa felt hot tears welling up in her eyes and touched her face, shocked by her own emotional outburst.

What is wrong with me? It is just a drawing, not the real demon castle.

"I... I'm sorry. I'll be leaving now," Rosa mumbled and rushed out of the tiny office.

"Good. I'll be sure to report this to the higher-ups. You have no business working at Studio Goblin if you're going to be so unnecessarily emotional! Perhaps you should have checked yourself into a mental ward instead!" Penny shouted behind her.

By the time she was out the door, tears were flowing down her cheeks, but it wasn't due to the rejection. It was the aching realization that she missed the demon castle and could never return to it.

CHAPTER 39

MEETING MOTHER

Rosa felt absolutely horrible. Her head hurt from the lack of sleep, and her nerves were a complete wreck due to the impending visit from Mother.

Rosa spent the whole morning running herself ragged as she tried to prepare a satisfactory meal to present to her family. She cooked a pork loin in the oven, hoping to end up with tender meat and some crispy skin on top. Unfortunately, something went wrong with the temperature setting, and she ended up with tough meat and chewy skin.

She also tried to cook up some vegetables in the oven—potato wedges, carrot slices, and cauliflower. Those also turned out all wrong. The potatoes turned out a bit burned because she had placed them too high on the oven rack. Meanwhile, the carrots and cauliflower turned out too hard since they were placed too low.

"This is just horrid... I am out of practice," Rosa muttered and began cutting up some fruit and putting it on the plates. That would have to be her saving grace for the time being.

"This is bound to be a disaster anyway." Rosa sighed and tried to come up with a way to nicely tell her mother that she had been fired from Studio Goblin on her first day. Perhaps it would have been better if she had missed her internship date altogether. At least then, she would have avoided the embarrassment of what happened with Penny.

In the end, she would receive a lengthy lecture from Mother about what kind of failure she was and no doubt would be disowned for the second time. Rosa certainly wasn't looking forward to it, but she also didn't fear it as much as she thought she should. After being away from Earth for so long, her mother's opinion had become irrelevant. It simply could not compare to what she had experienced in Doppelta.

Dinnertime with Alphegor had always been pleasant and fun for her. He'd always eagerly ask for her opinion on the food they ate, paying special attention to the desserts she enjoyed the most. The desserts a princess could receive in the Underworld were truly sublime, and she would have eaten them in spades had the king been a bit more lenient towards her.

But Alphegor cared for her health, thus making sure that she ate a well-rounded diet. It was this attention to detail that made her respect him even more. He also always asked how her day had gone and what she had studied, carefully listening and assessing her answers. Unlike Mother, who never wanted to hear a word that she said and only insisted on her own opinion.

The doorbell rang, startling Rosa out of her thoughts and making her accidentally cut her finger. She hastily washed the blood off and went to open the door. Behind it stood Mother and Rosa's little sister, Violet. The pair looked like older and younger versions of each other, respectively. Dark brown hair, tied into a neat bun for Mother and into a ponytail for Violet. Short, petite physique and dark chocolate eyes, which observed everything with unreserved scrutiny.

"Hello. Mother, Violet," Rosa greeted them with a forced smile.

Violet looked wholly uninterested in what was going on, instead typing something on her phone.

"Hello, Rosa! It is so good to see you," Mother said cheerfully, but it sounded so fake and over-the-top, that Rosa nearly cringed.

"It is good to see you too. Come in." Rosa kept her fake smile to the best of her abilities and stepped aside to let them in. The two women stomped inside without bothering to take off their shoes, tracking dirt onto the clean apartment floor.

If I had done that in your home, you would have thrown me out instantly.

But Rosa didn't voice her thoughts aloud. There would be enough conflict later.

"What a quaint apartment you have. Quite interesting decor," Mother said, trying to sound flattering but Rosa could see the tremor at the corner of her mouth. She didn't like it.

"Why don't you take a seat at the table, and I'll bring out the food. We can talk while we eat," Rosa offered as she hurried to the kitchen without waiting for their reply. It had only been a few minutes, but she already wanted them gone.

She was barely over the threshold when both of them already began nitpicking and judging her every step.

Violet gave a dismissive, "This place sucks," from the living room.

Her mother responded with a hushed, "Not so loud, Violet. She might hear you. I am sure Rosa will get a better apartment after she receives her first paycheck."

I can hear you both perfectly fine.

Rosa looked down at the failed feast she had prepared. It looked sad and unappetizing, only solidifying the unpleasant feeling growing in her chest.

Perhaps I should just outright say that I lost the job. No doubt they would leave right away then.

Rosa picked up the plates and, one by one, carried them to the living room table where Mother and Violet waited. Mother smiled at her pleasantly, but it faded as soon as she saw the failed vegetables in Rosa's hands.

"What is that?" she asked, pointing at the plate.

"Potatoes, carrots, and cauliflower," Rosa replied dryly and set the plate on the table, retreating back to the kitchen before Mother could say anything more. She returned with the visibly tough piece of meat, and Mother pointed at that too.

"What is that?" The furrow in Mother's eyebrows deepened, as did Rosa's irritation.

"Pork," she replied and hurried to retrieve the fruit. When she returned, she saw Violet poking the piece of meat with a fork and sneering at it as if it were some dead animal she found on the side of the road. Rosa gritted her teeth and put the fruits on the table with a little more force than necessary.

"Rosa! There's no need to hit the table just because you've failed to cook up a proper meal. It is most disappointing that you couldn't host us properly, but I didn't expect you to fix your ways right away," Mother said as she pushed the plate of vegetables away from herself.

"Should have just ordered a pizza. In fact, can't we just order some now?" Violet chimed, and Mother's hard gaze softened.

"Of course, dear. What an excellent idea! Why don't you find something? Rosa will pay since she is treating us." Mother's expression remained pleasantly serene as she looked at Rosa, who balled her fists at her sides.

It's okay, they will leave soon enough. Just endure it.

"Of course, Mother," she replied, plastering on a fake smile.

"Excellent. While we wait, let me tell you everything you've missed," Mother said and then went on a lengthy rant bragging about Violet's studies, Father's achievements at work—he was too busy to visit, apparently—various gossip regarding relatives Rosa barely knew, and every other topic imaginable that didn't involve Rosa.

She listened to her mother's rant, counting down the seconds until the doorbell finally rang, signaling the delivery guy's arrival. Rosa instantly ran to the door to answer it, relieved that Mother's ranting would be over. Unfortunately, she didn't account for the amount of pizza Violet would order—six large pizzas, each with exuberant toppings, which cost over a hundred euros.

Why the hell did she order so many? We could barely finish one of these.

Grumbling, Rosa paid the delivery guy and brought the giant stack into the living room.

"I see you ordered a wide variety for us to choose from. Most thoughtful of you, Violet," Mother praised.

"Yeah, I figured I could take the leftovers to Kyle's party afterward."

Why you little! You just used me to buy pizzas for your friends.

Nonetheless, Rosa swallowed her complaints and instead offered the pizzas to them with a smile.

Just a bit longer.

"So Rosa... Tell us about your new workplace," Mother said, and Violet finally seemed to perk up from her phone.

"Yeah, I heard it's like the biggest animation studio in the country."

"It is pretty big," Rosa replied awkwardly, hoping they would leave it at that, but obviously, they both stared at her, expecting more.

"So, tell us more," Violet urged impatiently. "How much do you earn?"

Is that all you care about? Money?

"Well, I…"

"Violet, she is still an intern. They don't make much. Tell us about your growth potential. How long until you can take on a serious management position?" Mother leaned closer, and Rosa could practically feel the heaviness of her expectations weighing her down.

"Management position?" Rosa asked.

"Yes! That's why you joined, isn't it? Initially, you do the small jobs of an artist, but after some time, surely you would be able to climb up the ranks and become a manager."

"Why would a management position be better than an artist's position?" Rosa asked, her voice low as she was trying not to show the anger growing within her.

"Isn't it obvious? Artists never get paid well. It is really nice that this Studio G-Go—oh whatever its name was—takes on such sad souls like you and gives them a chance to learn a proper job."

"Proper job? You still think that being an artist is not a proper job?" Rosa growled, her knuckles turning white from how hard she was clenching her fists.

"Rosa, we've been through this many times already. Being an artist is nothing more than a childish fantasy. Real people do not earn money that way." Mother waved her hand dismissively as if the thought itself was offensive.

"But these people clearly make money by creating art," Rosa argued.

"They don't really make art, though. They make animated movies," Violet interjected, her eyes focusing back on her phone.

"And how do you make animated movies without drawing it first?"

"Computer graphics, duh." Violet stuck out her tongue, and Rosa could feel herself nearing her boiling point.

"There's no need to get angry, Rosa. I am sure you are just frustrated that you cannot get the good positions right away. But if you follow the examples of your betters, then surely you will be able to reach a management position in no time at all."

"I do not *want* a management position," Rosa objected, and Mother looked at her incredulously.

"W-What do you mean? Of course, you do."

"No! I do not. And in fact…" Rosa paused to think whether she really wanted to make a scene. But looking at Mother's cynical expression, Rosa decided that there was no need to hide anything. "I don't even work there anymore."

"What?" Mother shot up to her feet, slamming her hands on the table.

"I went there and got fired on my first day. Happy?" Rosa stood to meet her mother's gaze while Violet observed the situation with unhidden glee.

"Fired on the first day?" Mother gaped in shock, her mouth opening and closing like a fish out of water.

"Yes. I went to their office and watched an artist prepare concept art. She asked for my opinion, and I gave it. Turns out it was the wrong opinion, so I am now left without an internship."

"Then go back and ask for forgiveness! You finally landed a normal job and messed it up on the first day. If only you could listen to what the betters tell you!" Mother put her hands on her hips, glaring at Rosa. This is how Rosa was used to seeing her.

"I will not beg or grovel before anybody," Rosa announced, remembering Alphegor's words. The king had always taught her to remain strong and proud—that was how a demon princess should behave. But she never thought his lessons would linger within her so strongly.

"The audacity! I knew this whole thing was too good to be true. You never listen to a word I say, instead insisting on childish fantasies. I hoped that maybe my words would have finally sunk in when I heard you got a job in a large company. But now I see that there was no way of fixing something that was born broken."

"And what have you accomplished?" Rosa snarled, looking at her mother with a defiant glare.

"What?" Mother asked, taken aback by the question.

"What have you done in your life that's so amazing? Before you met Father, you worked as a waitress, and after marrying him, you quit your job entirely, leeching off his money," Rosa sneered. Something seemed to snap within her mother. She stomped around the table and then slapped Rosa with all her might. It didn't hurt as much as she expected. In fact, she barely registered the pain—it was nothing compared to what Asdeus had done.

"Feel better now?" Rosa smirked. Mother's face turned red from anger when she realized that her slap didn't bring the desired results.

"Violet! We are leaving!" she announced and stomped out of the apartment.

"I knew it'd be like this," Violet mocked, and, after grabbing all of the pizzas, followed after Mother, slamming the door behind herself.

Rosa watched them leave, and after she was sure they were gone, she fell into her bed, drained from the confrontation. She had expected this ending, of course, but that didn't make it any less awful. Much to her surprise, she didn't feel sad about it. A little angry and certainly disappointed, but Mother's words didn't hurt her the way they had before.

"At least they won't bother me anymore," Rosa muttered and looked over at the dinner table where the vegetables and meat she worked so hard to make lay untouched.

Seems like I'll be eating meat and vegetables for quite a while.

She got up from the bed, ready to clean away the table and the remnants of the unpleasant encounter, when she heard some kind of shouting coming from the hallway. At first, she paid no mind to it. Her neighbors weren't exactly quiet, and it wasn't rare to hear a whole family argument unfold. But the voices grew louder and more... familiar.

There was a woman's voice, which definitely was her mother's. Rosa pondered whether a poor neighbor had bumped into her and was now getting the vocal beating of a lifetime. Curious, she went closer to the door and pressed her ear against it, trying to make out what she was shouting about.

"This is an outrage! I shall call the police this instant," Mother bellowed at the top of her lungs.

"Calm down, crazy human. I was merely curious about the device," responded a cheeky, familiar voice speaking in the Demon language. Rosa threw open the door and rushed into the hallway to make sure her mind wasn't playing tricks on her. Rosa froze on the spot as she saw Azrael and Alphegor standing in the hallway.

CHAPTER 40

BIRTH OF MORRIGAN

Rosa stared in disbelief at the scene in front of her. Azrael stood with Violet's phone in hand, poking and prodding it. Violet stood trembling behind Mother, her eyes filled with fear, while Mother pointed a finger at Azrael, yelling at him to return the phone. But the most shocking part was Alphegor, who stood a few meters away from the scene, tapping his foot impatiently.

Azrael and Alphegor both had no Demonic features, but their clothes still stood out like a sore thumb when compared to Mother and Violet. Azrael wore some odd skintight leather clothes, while Alphegor had one of his fancy suits on. One looked like he was ready to go to a punk rock concert, while the other was about to go to a cosplay convention. Both of them looked like they didn't belong.

How are they here? Why are they here? How is this possible?

Rosa stumbled back a step, and Mother took notice of her.

"Rosa! Don't you just stand there! Call the police immediately," she commanded as Violet trembled behind her. Azrael's and Alphegor's attention went to her, and Rosa froze. Azrael clearly recognized her—he had seen her human form before, but the demon made no attempts to point it out.

"Azrael, I tire of this. We must find Morrigan, not squabble with humans. Return the toy to the child," Alphegor commanded, speaking in the Demon language. With a pout, Azrael threw the phone back at Violet. The girl lunged forward and caught it as if her life depended on it.

"Alright, alright. Let's search for her," Azrael said and gave Rosa a knowing smirk.

Alphegor doesn't recognize me in this form. If I just stay quiet, then he will leave and never find me.

But seeing Alphegor made her heart ache. While his demeanor was still majestic and strong, she noticed signs indicating he was actually in distress, like the occasional nervous twitch of his finger or how his eyes went from one place to another, never staying anywhere for long—searching.

"You cannot assault people like this! Rosa, for God's sake, stop standing there like a mute and call the police," Mother yelled, taking a step towards her.

"I don't think that's necessary," Rosa said quietly, but the moment her mouth opened, Alphegor's eyes snapped to her.

"Morrigan?" he exclaimed and took two steps forward, his eyes wide with disbelief. "Is that you?"

"I... I..." she stuttered, not sure what to do. A surge of panic gripped her, and she wondered whether running would do her any good. And then a tear rolled down Alphegor's cheek.

"My daughter. I've found you," he uttered and rushed towards her. Before she realized what was happening, Alphegor pulled her into a hug, holding her close to his body. His familiar warmth engulfed her like a safe blanket.

"F-Father?" she uttered in the demon tongue. Her body trembled, and her mind reeled as she was unable to process the situation.

It feels like he is relieved, no, even happy to have found me. Shouldn't he be mad? Shouldn't he drag me back and throw me into the castle dun-

geons? And yet he is hugging me, holding me just as gently as when I was a baby.

"Rosa, what is going on? Why are you hugging this stranger?" Mother yelled, but Rosa barely registered her words. Her attention was wholly on Alphegor.

"I am so sorry, my child. I am sorry for not noticing that you had memories of your past life. If I had known, I would have explained everything to you straight away," he said, pulling back from the hug, his gaze taking her in. "So this is what you looked like as a human? A bit similar to your mother now when I take a look at you properly."

"You knew?" Rosa asked, her voice barely above a whisper and her hands trembling as Alphegor held them.

"Of course, I knew. I am your father," he said in a gentle voice and patted her head so carefully and tenderly—it was as if he thought she could break if he pressed any harder. The dam inside Rosa broke, and tears began streaming down her face like a waterfall. Alphegor pulled her back into a hug, gently rubbing her back.

"Outrageous. Associating with men like these. Are there no lows to which you won't fall?" Mother said, daring to take a few steps closer to Rosa and Alphegor. But the king turned his head and glared at the woman, stopping her dead in her tracks.

"Get out of here before I lose my patience, human," he commanded in the Demon language, and Mother shrank back. She did not know the meaning of his words, but the ferocity behind them could be understood without question. She looked to Violet to say something, but the girl was already running down the stairs.

"Violet? Violet, wait for me," she called and hurried after her.

"Why don't we take this someplace cozier?" Azrael suggested, snickering at Mother's swift retreat.

"Come inside, Father." Rosa pointed towards her small apartment, wiping the tears from her eyes with her other hand. Alphegor nodded with a small smile and, with his hand on her shoulder, went inside. His large hand felt warm and comforting, and it gave her a sense of peace she hadn't felt since he left for the battle.

Azrael followed right after them, closing the door behind himself. Before she could properly tell them to relax, he threw off his shoes and sprawled out on her bed as if he owned the place.

"Finally, I can relax." The demon sank deep into the pillows without a single shred of shame. Alphegor pulled out one of the chairs by the table and urged Rosa to sit in it. She followed his instructions absentmindedly, unable to process the ongoing events.

Once she was seated, Alphegor pulled out another chair for himself and sat down. His Demonic features appeared again, as did Azrael's. It was a surreal sight—two of the most powerful demons in the Underworld were crammed into her tiny apartment. She would have laughed if she could. But there was a heavy knot in her stomach, and she couldn't bring herself to look at Alphegor.

"Don't use Morrigan's bed as you please." Alphegor waved his hand, and Azrael levitated up into the air. The demon appeared surprised but didn't resist, instead resigning himself to Alphegor's will. The king levitated Azrael to the kitchen, slammed the door shut, and then drew a square in the air in front of the room. His fingers shimmered with a faint, magical glow.

"I want to have a private talk with my daughter," Alphegor said and looked at Rosa, his tail flicking nervously from side to side. "Would you be willing to hear me out?"

Rosa nodded demurely, still not daring to meet his gaze. She twiddled her thumbs nervously as she tried to come up with something to say.

I ran away assuming that he would kill me because I am a human. But turns out he knew all along. I've made such a mess for nothing. What can I even say? Sorry? How could that ever be enough?

Alphegor sighed, looking tired and unsure. Perhaps he too was contemplating how to begin. His eyes landed on the food on the table.

"Do you mind if we eat while we're at it? I've just realized it's been a while since I've had a proper meal," Alphegor asked in a soft voice.

"I don't mind, but perhaps I can order some food for you. These dishes that I've made didn't turn out quite like I wanted them to," Rosa muttered and was about to clear the plates away. Much to her surprise, Alphegor grabbed them before she could and piled the empty plate in front of him with a mountain of vegetables and meat.

"There is no way I am missing out on my daughter's cooking!" he announced, and without a second thought began shoveling everything down his throat. Rosa watched in horror at how, in a matter of minutes, most of the plate was cleared.

"Father, surely, I can offer you something better," she said helplessly. But Alphegor's face lit up with a wide grin.

"What are you talking about? A meal cooked by my daughter is the most delicious meal in this world," he exclaimed and then reached out to pat her head. Rosa could feel her heart swell with joy, and tears of happiness streamed down her face. Alphegor seemed surprised for a moment before his expression softened.

"Thank you," she muttered and then noticed how the world had grown larger around her. She'd turned back into her demon child form without even thinking about it.

"There's no need to thank me," he said, then let out a sigh as he slowed his eating. "In reality, this whole mess is my fault. If should have been more attentive and noticed that you had retained your memories.”

“Father, could you please explain? How exactly do you know that I am a human?”

“You are not a human anymore, Morrigan. You are a demon through and through. But you were a human in your past life. I think it’s better if I explain exactly how you were born.” Alphegor took a deep breath while Rosa listened intently.

“You see, Morrigan, demons are born differently than other living beings. Normally, when a female becomes pregnant, a soul attaches itself to the child while still in its mother’s womb.”

Rosa nodded at this. She had read and heard many arguments where people tried to determine at what point a child still within the confines of their mother’s body became a person. Some claimed it was only after the child was born. Rosa believed that if the child could move, then surely, it was already alive and sentient.

“It is different for demons,” Alphegor continued. “demon mothers grow an empty vessel within themselves, and they give birth to that empty vessel.” He stared at his fork as if recalling some memory in its reflection.

“An empty vessel?”

“Yes. Their heart beats, but there is no soul. The parents must attach a soul to the vessel for the child to be truly born.”

“So you attached my soul to this body?” Rosa asked, flicking her demon tail.

“Not quite. I tried to—I performed the ritual I always had for when my daughters were born. It always worked flawlessly, but with you—I couldn’t. Something went wrong.” Alphegor’s eyes were dark and downcast; the memory was clearly painful to him. “I couldn’t find a soul suitable for your body. The heartbeat within the vessel was beginning to weaken, it couldn't keep working without a soul.

"So your mother, Eirwen, took matters into her own hands. Despite her exhaustion from giving birth, she used all of the magic she had to find a soul. And she found you—a human soul from a different world. I was shocked at first, but Eirwen said that you called for her," Alphegor explained and his hands began to tremble.

I called for her? Was it when I was struggling in the sea? I don't remember much from that moment. It's such an unpleasant memory...

"So she pulled my soul into this body when I died at sea," Rosa said somberly.

"Yes. She used the last bit of her strength to do it—gave her life for yours. Eirwen could hold you only once before her life slipped away," Alphegor said as he hid his face behind his large palm. "The last words she said to me were 'Protect Morrigan.'"

Rosa's chest grew tight, and her eyes welled with tears. Her demon mother, despite knowing her for but a brief moment, gave her life for hers. She sacrificed herself for a human when Rosa's human mother would denounce her simply for the things that she liked.

Rosa—no, *Morrigan*—got up from the chair, walked up to her father, and put her small hand on his shoulder.

"I am sorry for doubting you, Father. I am so sorry for running away," she said softly, and Alphegor looked at her with a mix of relief and sorrow.

"I never blamed you for it, Morrigan. There is nothing to apologize for," he said with a bittersweet smile as he put his large hand over Morrigan's. Then the warm expression vanished, and Morrigan could see fear flash in his eyes. "If you wish to remain in the human world, I will not stop you. But I wish for you to return home."

She paused to think.

Do I want to go back to Doppelta? I came back to Earth in order to lead a peaceful life. But what would I do next if I remained here? My dream job in Studio Goblin is lost. But even if it weren't, I don't think I would enjoy working in such a setting—crammed into a tiny room in front of a computer and forced to hit deadlines without any care for quality.

My mother, father, and sister don't even care for me. They never had and never will. Even if I were to get a "normal" job like Mother wishes, she would still find some fault in me. She would never be happy with what I do.

Morrigan looked at Alphegor and thought of her time together with him. How he always attended to her needs, listened to her, and cared for her. He named her his heir, but at the same time, his teachings were always patient, and he never outright demanded things from her.

Even if this role seemed like a burden too heavy for her to bear, Morrigan was sure that Alphegor would guide her and support her through it. He would make sure that she was ready for it, instead of forcing it upon her prematurely.

"I wish to go home with you, Father," she replied with a smile. Alphegor's expression beamed with happiness and he scooped her up into a smothering hug.

"That's my girl! I knew you'd come through," he said as he wrapped his arms around Morrigan. She smiled as her whole being filled with warmth and peace. To think that she would find happiness in the arms of her demon father.

EPILOGUE

"Why does this always happen to me?" Morrigan grumbled as she noticed the dark storm clouds approaching from across the sea. She, her father, and Azrael were standing on the sandy beach, and streams of people hurried past them, eager to avoid the storm. But even if the weather was turning dark and gloomy, Morrigan's heart was beating with excitement.

To think that I would be getting excited about returning back to the Underworld, where the sun doesn't even shine. But I want to see everyone again—Deziara, Gunna, and Haku. I want to go back to my and Father's room and enjoy a peaceful evening talking to him.

"Why does what happen?" Alphegor asked, looking at her. She remained in her human form to avoid scaring any passersby. The king looked unbothered by the approaching storm. In fact, his strong stature made it look demure in comparison. Morrigan's chest swelled with pride.

This is my father. He truly is my father.

"The thunderstorms. There was one right before I went to Doppelta, and there is one here now," she explained, pointing at the thunderclouds looming from across the horizon. "I hoped to see the sun after so long without it."

"Silly Princess." Azrael shook his head and snickered, crossing his arms over his chest as if challenging the storm head-on. "We are demons. We don't need the sun."

The king stood tall and proud. "I never thought the day would come that I would agree with Azrael, but he is right. We do not need the sun like the surface dwellers. We are creatures of darkness, we thrive in it, grow with it, embody it."

"I do miss it a little bit," she admitted, and Alphegor's features softened.

"We can go to the surface of Doppelta and look at it there," he said.

"Really? demons are not forbidden from going to the surface?" Morrigan cocked her head curiously.

"Oh, the surface dwellers certainly won't be happy about seeing us, but what can they do? They don't even know proper magic." Azrael smirked, and kicked a stray rock lying in the sand, sending it flying across the vast beach until it fell into the sea with a loud splash.

"It is not outright forbidden," Alphegor added. "Besides, you can shapeshift, so it shouldn't be a problem if you change your appearance just like you have now."

She nodded, relieved that she would not have to spend her whole life underground like a mole. Or those mole demons. Even if they did seem like nice enough people.

Suddenly, the tablet in her bag vibrated, notifying her of a new message. Curious, she opened it and saw an email from Studio Goblin titled *"Regarding Internship."*

What's this about?

Morrigan tapped on the message and checked its contents. It turned out to be a lengthy apology letter where one of the heads of the Human Resources Department explained how there was a mistake with her internship. Oddly enough, the letter was worded in such a roundabout fashion that, in the end, the whole incident turned out to be her fault entirely. But since they were *generous and understanding towards newcomers,* they would look past it and allow her to return.

Morrigan scoffed at the message and was about to put the tablet back into her bag when she realized that it would be utterly useless in the Underworld.

"What's the matter?" Alphegor asked, looking at her intently.

"It's not important, Father. I just realized that this won't work in the Underworld." With a wry smile, she tossed the tablet as far as she could into the sand. It didn't go very far, but Azrael, picking up on Morrigan's thoughts, snapped his fingers, and the device burst into flames, leaving a pile of molten goop behind.

The waves in the sea grew larger by the minute, and Morrigan observed how the waves churned the water, creating white foam. The strength of it scared her as this grand element had taken her life once. Fear coiled tight in her chest, but she couldn't bring herself to truly hate it.

She twirled around, looking at Alphegor who regarded her quizzically, sensing her unease.

"Before we go back to Doppelta. Can I ask you something, Father?" she said as a low rumble of a faraway thunderstrike resounded across the beach.

"Of course, little one. Ask anything," Alphegor replied, taking a step closer to her. The dark clouds steadily covered the sky, slowly turning the already murky day into something akin to late evening.

"I am not sure I can be called little." She chuckled awkwardly, rustling her foot in and out of the sand. "After all, I was twenty-four years old as a human."

Much to her surprise, Alphegor laughed at this. "Do you know how old I am?"

Morrigan paused and tried to recall any mentions of Alphegor's age. But no matter how much she racked through her memory, she couldn't recall it. In fact, she didn't even remember him celebrating his birthday once, although she herself got a grand party every year.

"No. You never told me."

"If you're as old as me, you stop caring about age. I only celebrate my birthday once every ten years, mostly out of obligation to my subjects," he said. "Would you like to guess how old I am?"

I know Azrael is over two hundred years old, and that is considered very young for a demon. So Alphegor is definitely older than that. He also once mentioned that dwarves live up to eight hundred years, which also isn't a lot for a demon.

"Two thousand three hundred?" Morrigan guessed, and Alphegor chuckled while Azrael roared with laughter. She looked back and forth between them, blush creeping into her cheeks.

"I am 8,737 years old," the king said.

Morrigan stumbled over her own foot, nearly falling into the sand. Alphegor caught her at the last moment. She shot him an apologetic glance, but he just steadied her on her feet with a calm smile.

"I never expected you to be that old," she exclaimed and began inspecting her father's face for any signs of aging. The wind began picking up its pace, making both Alphegor's and Morrigan's hair sway along with it. She saw how his red hair was still bright in its color, not a single gray hair in sight. He did not look a day over thirty.

"I am not even the oldest demon out there. Lucius is already over ten thousand years old. So you see, Morrigan, even if I were to add your human years to your age, you would still be just a child in my eyes," he explained with a warm expression.

Morrigan opened her mouth to object but then closed it. Would she also live to be that old one day? The thought seemed completely ludicrous. Even people who lived to eighty years seemed old, and yet right now, she was standing in front of a man who had lived that long a hundred times over.

It's scary. How much will I have to live through in the thousands of years ahead of me?

"Isn't it hard to live that long?" Morrigan asked.

"Sometimes, little one. Times change, people change, and sometimes it is hard to change with it. Sometimes you wish that things would freeze at one point in time and remain there," he said as another thunderstrike rumbled, this time closer.

Morrigan wondered whether she would be able to take on the challenges the future held for her. It scared her. She was the daughter of the Demon King now. His heir. Somebody who was bound to become the next demon queen.

Can I really undertake such a huge responsibility? The only thing I've ever been good at is art. I've never wanted the power to rule over others.

Alphegor stepped closer and set his hand on her shoulder. "Don't worry. No matter what happens in the future, I'll be there to protect you, help you, and guide you."

She smiled at him and then remembered the question that had been burning within her for a while. She looked down into the sand.

"Father, did you see the painting in the wardrobe?" she asked, staring at the sand by her feet, despite knowing the answer.

"Hmm..." Alphegor pondered, then waved his hand in the air, and like magic, her painting appeared out of nowhere. He held it in his arms, smiling from ear to ear.

"How did you do that?" she asked, staring at the painting. It looked exactly as she remembered—a perfect copy of the sunset view from her apartment windows. She thought back to how she had spent many evenings working on the details to get it just right. There was also a somber feeling to the painting as it was done while Alphegor was away and she had to spend her evenings alone.

"A little pocket dimension trick I'm sure you will learn in time. I figured it's better if I don't leave it behind," he said and gave the painting an appraising look.

"Do you like it?" Morrigan dared to ask, twiddling her thumbs. She was afraid to know the answer, but at the same time, she needed to know in order to move on properly.

"Of course. My daughter is an artist at age four. I couldn't be more proud! It looks exactly like the view from your apartment window," Alphegor exclaimed and held the painting up like a trophy. "It is a true masterpiece!"

A hesitant smile quirked her lips. "So you don't mind if I continue painting?" she asked tentatively as a gust of wind caressed her cheek, signaling the approaching storm.

"No. In fact, I'd love to request a portrait of myself. Could you do that?"

Morrigan couldn't believe the words she heard. All her life, she had been seeking recognition and acknowledgment from her parents, but instead, all she received was hatred and disapproval. When she was reborn as a demon, she believed that her dream of being an artist would become unobtainable—nothing more than a memory that would grow dimmer and dimmer with each passing year. But she couldn't have been more wrong.

This strong, menacing, and unyielding demon king accepted her the way she was. He appreciated her company, enjoyed the silly little things she did for him, scolded her when she did something wrong, and praised her when she did things right.

"Thank you, Father. I will get straight to it as soon as we get back home," she replied and turned back to her smaller demon self. The humans had long since vacated the beach, the three of them being the last ones left there.

"You heard her, Azrael. Time to go home," Alphegor announced and reached down to take Morrigan's hand. She took it without hesitation and smiled.

I can't wait to see everyone again! I'll be able to show Deziara my true painting skills—I'm sure she'd like that. And Gunna would too. She'd probably cry from happiness if she saw me painting. Gunna has always encouraged art by offering me painting supplies, after all.

"Well about that..." Azrael cleared his throat.

Morrigan felt the first drops of rain begin to fall from the sky.

Alphegor glared at the white-haired Demon. "Hurry up, Azrael. I do not wish to get soaked by this horrid surface weather."

Azrael cringed and took a step back. "Well, you see... I kind of, sort of, might not have enough energy to do that..." He drew out every word as slowly as possible, and loud thunder filled the area once he was done. Rain began to fall heavily, soaking them all in a matter of seconds.

"What?" Morrigan and Alphegor both shouted, while Azrael just chuckled sheepishly as the rain continued soaking them all the way through their clothes.

Need another story to keep you satiated until book two of *Demon Queen Wants to Paint* is released?

Check out *Heir of the Haloed Sun*!

Two worlds. One Destiny. And a love that will change everything.

Seventeen-year-old Temperance Maher never believed her grandmother's fairy tales about Emeriz—a world of magic, royal bloodlines, and lost heroes. But when a cherished family heirloom whisks her into that very realm, she finds herself at the heart of a prophecy she's fated to fulfill.

Hunted for powers she doesn't understand, Temperance's only chance at survival lies with King Frederick—a young, devoted king who will stop at nothing to overthrow the tyrannical High Queen.

With war on the horizon and a heart-wrenching choice before her, Temperance must decide: fight for a world she has come to love, or return to the one she's always known. Because in Emeriz, destiny may light the way, but only she can claim the journey.

Don't miss the start of this spellbinding Romantasy Adventure about a reluctant heroine thrust into a magical world, a charming monarch with a tragic past, and an enchanting romance that could ignite an empire.

Thank you for reading a MoonQuill original novel. More exciting stories can be found on at www.moonquill.com.

We would greatly appreciate it if you could take a moment to leave a review. Each one helps the author and supports their ability to continue writing fantastic books for everyone to enjoy!

Scan the QR code below to subscribe to our mailing list and be notified of new releases. You'll receive 4 e-books for free!